COLD HEART, CRUEL HAND

A novel of Hereward the Wake
and the fen rebellion of 1070-1071

Laurence J. Brown,
author of *Housecarl*

First published in 2004

PUBLISHED BY
PAUL MOULD PUBLISHING

ISBN 1-904959-04-0

Printed in Great Britain by
CLE Print Limited

For Kaye, with love,
as always.

Cold heart and cruel hand
Now rule across the land

Anglo-Saxon Chronicles

"I appoint no one my heir to the Throne of England as I did not attain that High Honour by hereditary right but wrestled it from the perjured King Harold in a desperate battle with much effusion of human blood. I have persecuted its native inhabitants beyond all reason; whether gentle or simple I cruelly oppressed them. Many I unjustly disinherited, innumerable multitudes, especially in the county of York, perished through me by famine or the Sword. Having therefore made my way to the Throne of that Kingdom by so many Crimes I dare not leave it to anyone but God alone, lest after my death worse should happen by my means..."

Attributed to William, King of England, on his deathbed. Rouen, September 1087.

Orderic Vitalis, a Norman Monk.

Prologue

York

1070

They left York by the Jubber Gate, what remained of it, like thieves in the night. Behind them smoke from the blackened timbers of the burning City billowed skywards, choking the night air, obscuring the moon, covering their escape.

Every so often the man would cast an anxious glance over his shoulder to ensure they were not being followed. His wife, her face pale and drawn, clung tightly to him, her eyes flitting from the darkness ahead to the small child clutched to her husband's chest, cocooned in his muscular arms. She prayed they would soon reach safety, some undergrowth or undulation in the land to cover their retreat, to bring their suffering to an end.

York was doomed. Five days ago, after a stubborn fight the Norman army had forced the City walls, and then the gates, ending the insurgents' resistance. Those that could not escape were butchered where they stood: men, women, children, babies. There was no discrimination between young and old, innocent and guilty; no mercy either. Babies were put to the sword, mothers raped and then murdered, houses looted and burned. It followed a familiar pattern: kill, loot and burn until all was gone. This was the Conquerors' way with the Saxons, those that did not bend to his will. It had been so for four years and now the north was a blackened wasteland from the Humber to the Tyne, from the Severn to the Mersey.

Ranulf looked back again; a quarter of a mile and still no pursuit. If they escaped it would be a miracle. By all laws of reason they should be dead, lying butchered and broken with the rest of their comrades in the City or dangling from the City walls like some of their leaders, captured and tortured, then left to rot as an example to the others.

For five days, since the Normans had stormed the City, Ranulf and his family had evaded capture, eventually finding refuge amongst the corpses of their comrades, their bodies thrown into a burial pit as the purging of the City proceeded. For the last two days they had feigned death, man, woman and child, burying themselves ever deeper beneath the pile of insensate bodies to avoid detection until they thought they would go mad.

And then the opportunity that they had been praying for had arisen. The gate momentarily unguarded, the moon obscured by cloud and smoke, they had seized their chance. Hearts in their mouths they had crept forward, clinging to the shadows, Hal's tiny face tearful but blackened against detection, sworn to silence by his mother. He had manfully nodded his understanding, a boy of three, not really understanding but sensing his mother's distress, the importance of doing as asked. God alone knew what effect it was having on his tender mind.

And then they were up to the gate, their hearts pounding like hammers in their breasts as they paused, expecting a challenge at any moment before making the final bid for freedom beyond the walls that had held them prisoner for five nightmare days and nights.

They headed south, searching all the while for some cover in which to hide, to rest. There was precious little of that, for the land had been stripped bare by the local populace and by the

Conqueror's army in their search for food and timber for their camp fires. The land was in the grip of a famine. Years of war had wasted both the people and the land and now the people were starving.

Ranulf knew that unless he could find food and shelter soon their chances of survival were slim. It was over two hundred miles to where they were heading and without food they had no chance. Alice's face was already thin and gaunt, her beauty marred by the ravages of hunger. Hal was surviving on what Ranulf could scavenge, depriving himself of much needed nourishment in order that his offspring should not suffer. But Hal was suffering, needed food and rest more than either he or Alice. He hugged the boy to him, protectively, compassionately. Somehow he would see that the boy lived, even if it meant sacrificing his own life.

And deep down he knew that he should already be dead; that his life was lived on borrowed time. He should have died with his comrades on Caldbec Hill four long years ago. It was his duty to have done so and the fact that he still lived was due only to the futile order given to him by the late King, Harold Godwineson, to abandon the field of battle to save his Queen. He had failed, and now both were dead. He blamed himself and sometimes, when the guilt became too great, he wondered why he had been allowed to live when so many good men, better men than him, had died. Perhaps God was punishing him by allowing him to live, to see for himself the legacy of defeat on Caldbec Hill.

That legacy was life, if one could call it that, under Norman rule. William the Bastard, called "the Conqueror" by his men, had no love, no time, for the Saxons. His conquest of England had been based upon the promise of land to his supporters; land that had once belonged to the Saxons. One by one, at an ever increasing pace, the Earldoms and Shires and Villages and Hundreds had been handed out to his Norman supporters, resistance by the Saxon nobility, those that had survived Caldbec Hill, being ruthlessly and efficiently crushed until virtually the whole of the country was in Norman hands.

After Caldbec Hill Ranulf had sworn an oath to fight the Normans until the last one had been driven from the shores of England. That Oath was now in tatters, the Saxon cause irredeemably lost, the Norman dynasty in supreme command. All over England the Conqueror had erected fortresses from which to govern, to control the people; timber fortresses perched high on moated hills, impregnable against all but the most determined attackers. And there were precious few of those. Without a King to lead them, without a figurehead to unite them, their revolts had been sporadic, doomed to failure.

It was hopeless, and even though Ranulf recognised the fact, he also knew that he would continue to wage war on the Conqueror for as long as he could. He owed it to his King and his comrades, dead four years now, to continue the fight; that they should not have died in vain.

And so he headed south with his wife and son to make an unlikely rendezvous, hastily arranged with his fellow rebels before the Norman army had flooded into York to end their resistance.

They had covered half a mile when he heard, in the distance, the sound of horses' hooves. They were iron shod, heavy. It was a single rider, a Norman. He would recognise the sound anywhere; only the Normans had horses that large. Only the Normans had anything. He handed Hal to Alice and ushered them away into the darkness. He hunkered down behind a small piece of scrub and waited for the rider to approach. He unhooked the sword that hung at his side and eased it from its scabbard. The sword was one of only two possessions that he had managed to retain during four years of fighting and running. The other was a slim stiletto, tucked into his belt, both weapons a reminder of the past, the memories etched deep into their steel like the scars that he bore on his body. The sword was *Requitur,* the Sword of Kings. It had once belonged to Alfred the Great and to every Saxon King since. He had picked it up by mistake in the gloom gathering over Caldbec Hill and had kept it safe ever since. It never left him, and since that day four years ago it had tasted Norman blood eleven times.

The rider was approaching quickly. His eyes now accustomed to the darkness, Ranulf could see that he was only lightly clad, no mail armour, no helmet. A courier or messenger perhaps. It did not matter. What mattered was the horse, a lifeline for them all. Heart pounding, his breath coming in short bursts, he waited for the rider to approach. Ten yards…five, and still he waited, crouched behind the scrub. The man was almost past him when he made his move, springing forward, swinging *Requitur* in a great arc that gave the man no time to react, no time to avoid the blow. The blade hit the rider in the chest, knocking him from the saddle. Moments later Ranulf was upon him, driving the point of *Requitur* down through his chest. The man hardly made a sound as he died.

The mare was a few yards away, having bolted in panic. The rider was dead but the mare was the prize and now Ranulf felt a different kind of tension as he slowly approached her. One false move and she would be gone. Whispering softly, arm outstretched to reach for the reins, he made it to within five yards before the mare shied and trotted away, eyeing him nervously. He cursed under his breath and tried again, this time, keeping his arms by his side. He got to within two feet of her, sensed that she was about to bolt and lunged for the reins. His hand grasped leather and he knew that he had her. He stroked her chestnut mane, nuzzled her cheek and whispered soft words into her ear. She was his.

He checked the rider's saddlebag and found some papers, sealed with wax. He could not read, English or Norman, and so discarded them. What he did find was a hunk of dried bread and some hard cheese. Manna from heaven. He called to Alice and Hal and they divided the food between them, saving a little for the journey.

They were safe at last. With food in their bellies and a solid mount beneath them they would head south, for the Fens, for a rendezvous with their comrades and with the most charismatic Saxon of them all.

And there, in the last Saxon stronghold in England they would challenge the Conqueror to fight them on their terms, on ground where his cavalry was of no use, where chain-mail was a hindrance rather than an advantage, and where the Conqueror's massed ranks of infantry would founder and sink beneath the treacherous miasma of the fens.

They were going to the Isle of Ely, to the camp of refuge, to fight for Hereward the Wake.

Chapter One
York
Spring, 1070

William Fitz Osbern sighed and rubbed tired eyes still sore from the acrid smoke hanging over the devastated City. He raised the note and considered it again; it bore the King's seal, immediately familiar to anyone who knew it: the King astride his charging destrier, shield held firmly in his left hand, his lance in his right, like some immortal God of war. His eyes moved from the seal to the signature just above it: *William Rex,* the signature of the Conqueror. He had no doubt that it was genuine. He lowered the note toward the candlelight illuminating his tent and read it again. It was addressed to himself, the Commander of the northern army:

"*...Congratulations old friend. Now that the City is at your disposal I trust you will not hesitate to bring the rebels to Justice. An example must be made of them to demonstrate the futility of rebellion. The King's peace must be maintained. You will ensure that no stone is left standing, no criminal unpunished. I know that I can count upon your support in this great endeavour.*

Once the viper's nest has been cleansed you will bring the northern army south, to make rendezvous with me at Cambridge. Rebellion has broken out in the Fens, Peterborough sacked, its treasures stolen, my people put to the sword. The rebel leader is one Hereward, a Saxon calling himself the Wake. The local populace flock to him and each day he grows stronger. But I will crush this rebellion before it catches fire. I shall enclose the fens in a ring of steel and strangle the life from it. You will join me at Cambridge in two weeks time. By then I anticipate that my orders will have been executed along with the remainder of the rebel contingent..."

Fitz Osbern rubbed his eyes and sighed once more. This was an awful land, he reflected, an awful land and an awful people. How many had he hanged in the last eight days? A thousand? Two thousand? And still he was rounding them up. In the morning there would be yet more hangings, more corpses dangling from the City walls for the crows to feed upon until all that was left was their bones bleaching in the chill spring wind as an example to others. He closed his mind to his thoughts and attempted to concentrate upon the note.

"When was this found?" he waved the note at the Captain standing motionless before him.

"Two hours ago Sir," the Captain said. His eyes were fixed on a point two feet above Fitz Osbern's head and they never wavered from it.

"The courier – he is dead?"

"Yes sir; stabbed through the chest."

"Do we know who did it?"

"No Sir."

Fitz Osbern hesitated for barely a moment.

"Find ten Saxons, question them and then hang them." His eyes slid down to the note and then back to the Captain. "And if you don't get an answer hang ten more."

"Yes Sir."

Fitz Osbern read the note again. *You will join me at Cambridge in two weeks time*. The date was partially obliterated.
"Do we know when the courier was slain?" he fired the question peremptorily but the Captain hesitated only briefly before venturing his response.
"Three days, Sir, we believe, from the condition of his corpse."
Three days. Three days lost. He regarded the Captain, a steady man who had been with him for two years now and noted the fresh cuts, barely healed, to his heavily muscled forearms. He had been one of the first men into the City, forcing the gate for others to follow…
"Tell the men we shall be marching south in four days. Tell them that I want every rebel rounded up and hanged before then. I want this business finished before I leave."
"Yes Sir." The Captain's eyes betrayed no emotion as he headed for the tent flap. He had had similar orders many times over the past two years. The capture and hanging of rebels was nothing new. His hand was on the flap before Fitz Osbern's voice pulled him up again.
"Captain!"
"Sir?"
"Those Saxons, the civilians, hang them anyway."
"Yes Sir."

The Captain left to go about his duties. Fitz Osbern placed the note onto his war chest, a temporary desk, and regarded it again. Another rebellion; this time in the Fens. The Saxons were a beaten people but did not know it. Or perhaps they did. Perhaps it was simply their way of finding some reason to live; some cause to fight for, no matter how hopeless. He sighed yet again. He had become rich beyond his wildest dreams since the Conquest, since the bloody victory on Senlac Hill and yet for all that he would give anything to be home again, in Normandy.

Instead he was going to the Fens, a stinking wilderness of sky and mud. It was rumoured that the fen dwellers had webbed feet, that nature had intervened to prevent them sinking into the endless marshland. He would soon see. This Hereward, whoever he was, would need winged feet if he were to escape the Conqueror's wrath. He thought again of the fens; bleak and cold and hostile and silently cursed his luck. He walked over to the tent flap and lifted it. His eyes, red and smarting from the smoke and lack of sleep, gazed southwards, beyond the smouldering City, beyond the fens, beyond the shores of England to Normandy. There, Summer was just around the corner: lush green fields, sparkling rivers, trees heavy with apples and a sun so warm and benign that the very thought of it calmed his sour mood.

He closed his eyes and dreamed of Normandy.

Chapter Two
The Isle Of Ely
Spring 1070

The giant Saxon stood apart from his comrades as he watched the dragon ship slide smoothly away from the jetty. His grey eyes, the right a little darker than the left, showed no sign of emotion as the oars protruding from either side of the vessel's sleek, curved timbers dipped and rose in unison, propelling the dragon ship away from the land, heading north under a lowering grey sky towards the German Sea.

Distant thunder rolled across the fens promising rain and the Saxon absently pulled his cloak a little tighter about his shoulders. On board the dragon ship orders were being shouted to those not engaged at the oars and now he could see its heavy trapezoidal sail being unfurled from the masthead, its crew panting with the effort as they heaved on the ropes whilst others fought and punched the flapping canvas into shape until, caught by the wind, it suddenly billowed and hardened like a shell, transformed instantly into a thing of beauty.

With its sail filled the dragon ship picked up speed, leaving a muddy froth in its wake and, the Saxon realised, more problems than he could ever have imagined.

On board the vessel, standing beneath its fiercely glaring prow, Sven Erithson, King of Denmark, waved a final farewell to the land, his feet firmly braced against the motion of the craft. The Saxon raised a reluctant hand in brief acknowledgment. Sven Erithson was smiling, his teeth showing white against the brown bush of his beard. The Danish King was clearly content with life, as well he might be. For on board the vessel that carried him up the Ouse towards the German Sea and then home to Denmark was a King's ransom in gold and jewels and silver. All of it from Peterborough Cathedral, stolen from the very same people that the Saxon had sworn to protect.

Hereward the Wake was not sorry to see Sven Erithson depart. The enterprise had been a disaster from beginning to end, his greatest mistake being to enlist the rapacious Danish King as an ally and now he had incurred the redoubtable wrath of William, Duke of Normandy, and, for the past three years King of England. William the Conqueror was well named and the Wake knew, even as he watched his so-called ally disappear up the muddied waters of the Ouse that he would now have to face the Conqueror alone. He sighed, and as the first drops of rain fell onto his weather-beaten face he turned towards the men standing on the jetty; men, who, like himself, had gathered there to watch the Danish King depart, anxious to be rid of their erstwhile ally.

These were good men, he thought, men whose qualities of loyalty and honesty had been so obviously lacking in the Danish King. They were hard fighters too, skilled with bow and sword and axe. And soon, he guessed, those qualities would be tested to the limit. He studied them subconsciously, unaware, almost, that he was doing so: Wynter and Lightfoot, his boyhood friends, each as strong as an ox, their arms and legs like massive oaks. Beside them, in stark contrast, stood a tall, ungainly man whose long limbs gave him the nickname that he bore. The Heron carried a long staff of hardened ash that never left him; a staff that he could use to leap streams and crack skulls to equal effect. He had once rescued four men from the Normans at Wroxham Bridge armed only with his staff and had earned both an instant reputation and a price on his head. This trio were his closest allies, but there were the others too: Osbernus, Alsinus, and Lefwinus, men from his own village of Bourne, and the two twins, remarkably alike, Hurchillus and Villicus, both from Drayton. All of them had come to join his rebellion. Yes, he thought, they were good men and like himself they carried a hatred of the Normans that consumed their souls, a hatred that had led them on the inevitable path to rebellion. A man could only take so much before he turns and these men had reached that point many months ago. In his case it had been the loss of his father's estates, his lands at Bourne, handed by the Conqueror to Ivo Taillebois, Sheriff of Lincolnshire, payment for his butchery on *Senlac Hill* as the Normans had chosen to call the great battle of 1066. *Bloody Lake* it meant; *Bloody Lake.* He should have been there, fighting alongside his King, instead of kicking his heels abroad, fighting petty wars for mercenary pay.

And whilst he had been absent his lands had been given to Taillebois, his brother murdered, his severed head displayed over the entrance to Bourne Castle. Such an outrage, such a calculated insult, could not go unavenged. Upon his return to England he had removed it in the dead of night and replaced it with the heads of three of Taillebois' own men, choked to death with his bare hands. He had heard the rumours that had been spread, that he had killed fourteen of Taillebois' men, but even he was not capable of that alone. He had been declared an outlaw, with a price on his head, and had made his way here along with his closest companions. He laughed at the thought, a cynical laugh touched with deep sarcasm. If he were an outlaw what did that make the Conqueror and his butchers? Whatever crimes he had committed they were as nothing compared to that of the Conqueror.

An outlaw. He had never seen himself as such until now, until the botched attempt to save the Saxon Church's fortune from the grasping clutches of Bishop Turold, another of the Conqueror's henchmen, had seen it stolen by the King of Denmark as payment for his support. That support had been the slaughter of innocent men and women; a few Saxons as well as Normans, a slaughter that he had been powerless to prevent.

And now the Danish King was going home, his dragon ship stuffed full with priceless works of art, gold crucifixes, silver chalices, and enough coin to feed a nation for ten years. And that was another problem. His followers were starving and yet day by day, hour by hour, volunteers were flooding into the camp offering their services and expecting to be fed. He was not a miracle worker, although he knew that many of the volunteers saw him as one. He was coping, just, by having the meres and rivers and reed beds surrounding the Isle methodically emptied of life: Fish, eel, waterfowl, crustaceans of every kind, but they could not last forever and when they ran out he was uncertain where the next mouthful would come from.

And summer was just around the corner. *Summer.* As a boy he had loved the summer months, a chance to escape the drab weariness, the monotony of winter and spring beneath huge grey skies hanging over an empty landscape. It was a lonely land, the vast emptiness reaching out to touch the soul with melancholy. He had always loved the summer but now the arrival of summer was a time to fear, to prepare against. For in the summer the waters surrounding the Isle would recede, the Isle would be an isle no longer, and the Conqueror would seize his opportunity.

Thunder rolled overhead and the rain suddenly lashed down, drenching the men on the jetty. The Wake, already soaked to the skin, shivered inside his cloak and looked to the heavens. Everywhere the sky was black and heavy with no sign of the sun.

He did not mind. It could rain all year for all he cared. Anything to keep the Isle of Ely just that: an island.

The Conqueror was already amassing his forces at Cambridge, ready for the first assault. Reports had been coming in for days of large numbers of heavily armed infantry assembling beneath the Lion Standard of the Norman King, a huge tented village that was there for one purpose only: the destruction of himself and his tiny rebel force.

He needed to buy time. Time to prepare, time to build the dams that would retain the precious water, his greatest asset, time to train his volunteer army, and time to plan the destruction of the enemy, an enemy equally determined to destroy him, the last bastion, the final outpost of Saxon England.

The dragon ship of Sven Erithson had almost disappeared now, hidden behind a sheet of torrential rain driving horizontally across the bleak wilderness. Soon, he knew, it would have to navigate the narrows near to the confluence with the Little Ouse and then it would be plain sailing to the open sea. He was glad. At least he would not have the Danish King to complicate matters. Now it was all up to him and his small guerrilla army. His grey eyes watched the dragon ship negotiate the final bend and then it was gone, the brightly coloured sail disappearing into rain-shrouded reeds as though it had never existed. But its King had left behind a legacy of hatred that he had not, could never have, anticipated. He cursed beneath his breath and rubbed his bearded chin, deep in thought. He should have known that Sven Erithson's offer of assistance would contain a hidden agenda, but the slaughter of innocent people and the theft of the Church's fortune? He had not foreseen that. And now the Conqueror was determined to exact revenge, to crush his little rebellion as ruthlessly as he had crushed every one before. He cursed himself for a fool and looked skywards, as though to seek divine inspiration. The rain lashed down, plastering his blonde hair to his head, streaming down his face, giving the appearance of tears. He needed to buy time, but how? A hand touched his shoulder and he turned to see Torfrida, his wife of twenty years.

"Come inside," she said. "You will be no use to any of us if you die of cold." There was a hint of criticism hidden behind the compassionate words but he smiled at her nevertheless, the same indulgent smile for twenty long years, the first since Sven Erithson had sailed away.

"You are right," he said, "as always." He saw that his comrades were still on the jetty, watching him, reluctant to find shelter from the driving rain until he made the first move himself. It was a strange kind of etiquette in this empty wilderness, a mark of the respect and affection that they felt for him.

"A sorry lot of water rats we are," he said to them as he examined his sopping wet cloak, ringing it out in his massive hands. "Let's get dry." It was one of the things they admired in him; his humility, his ability to speak to them as equals despite his unquestionable status as their leader. The men left the jetty, most nodding an informal salute as they passed, hurrying to escape the downpour, leaving the jetty deserted save for himself and Torfrida. He put an arm around her shoulder and pulled her to him. She was a small, shrew-like figure with a narrow face, a face that had grown hard since their ejection from Bourne Castle. Torfrida had borne the hardship, the depravation, with a thinly disguised stoicism that had sometimes tested his patience although he tried hard to ignore it. Together they hurried through the ankle-deep mud of the camp until they reached their hut, a simple thatched dwelling with one room only, a dwelling that had replaced Bourne Castle as their home.

Surrounding their hut were dozens of similar dwellings, most of them smaller than theirs but otherwise identical, their sole purpose being to provide shelter and warmth for his growing band of followers. Smoke billowed from the roofs of most of them and the smell of their cooking fires gave an edge to his hunger, reminding him again of his mounting problems.

Already they were surviving on rations and he knew that it would only get worse. He needed to find food. He needed it to rain, as much as he detested it, and he needed trained warriors to match the infantry of the Conqueror. Wynter, Lightfoot, The Heron, the rest of the men on the rain-swept jetty could all fight, could hold their own against any Normans, but they were just a handful. He needed more. He needed trained and skilful fighters, an army of them. Where such men would be found he did not know.

He had heard rumours that his nephews, the last of the Saxon Earls, Morcar and Edwin, were on their way with their men. Dispossessed of their Earldoms of Northumbria and Mercia they had chosen to throw in their lot with him; one final, desperate, stand in the fens, but they had not yet arrived. So too, the survivors of the massacre at York; none of them had yet been seen. And if they did come he would not know how to feed them. But first he must find them. Tomorrow he would lead a scouting party south. The only way onto, and out of, the Isle was by way of Aldreth. There was a narrow bridle way, under water for most of the year, but he knew how to cross it, a secret known only to himself and a very few others. One foot wrong and the traveller would find himself dragged beneath the swamp before he could blink.

He threw off his wet clothes and dried himself before a damp fire, ignoring the choking fumes, enjoying the warmth on his naked, heavily muscled body. Torfrida was busily engaged preparing a meal of salted eels for them, careless after so many years of his intimate nakedness. He stared vacantly into the fire and pondered his many problems, searching for solutions. And the longer he thought on them the greater his certainty became. For in

the final reckoning he knew precisely what would be needed to defeat the Conqueror:
He would need a miracle.

Chapter Three

The Fens

Ranulf was bone weary, the mare all but finished, and the food long gone. How they had kept going for mile upon mile he simply did not know. His mind had sometimes wandered on the journey south, recalling terrible events four years earlier when he had marched south with different comrades, all dead now, to fight for a King that had been his friend. This time things were different. There was no Saxon King on the Throne, no Guthrum, no Cnut, and, in reality, though he hesitated to admit it, no hope.

He looked at Alice, sitting astride the mare, her arms wrapped protectively around Hal to prevent him falling from the saddle. Hal was asleep, his body swaying to the motion of the mare. Alice too, was fighting sleep, the exhaustion etched deep into her sallow complexion as she fought to keep her eyes open.

They had slept, when they could, beneath the stars. Not that the stars had been visible behind the perpetual blanket of grey cloud that covered the land and soaked everything with a plangent rain that never seemed to abate. Ranulf, cold and miserable himself, was becoming fearful for the health of both Alice and Hal, neither of who had his own iron constitution. They needed food and rest, somewhere to shelter and clothes that were warm and dry. He imagined a log fire crackling and sparking in a huge fire grate, filling his world with warmth but the image did not last and soon the perpetual beat of the downpour brought him back to the misery of their present situation.

The only good news was that he was certain that they were nearing their final destination. The blackened wasteland of the north had slowly given way to green fields and trees, and as they headed still further south, and then turned east, the land had flattened into a vast wilderness with huge grey skies hanging over an empty landscape. And now there was water. So much water that he had to carefully choose their route east, to remain on the narrow paths, often nothing more than a mud track winding its way across the vast inland fens stretching to the horizon. Soon, he knew, he would have to find a boat or a vessel of some kind to carry them across the fens to the Isle of Ely. Where such a vessel would be found he did not know but he had not confided his fears to Alice.

He looked at her again. Like the son in her arms her head was now tilted forward, resting on her chest, her weariness having finally conquered her resolve to remain awake.

"Not far now, my love," he said, just loud enough to rouse her. For a reply she gave him a smile, showing her small white teeth, and as she did so he was struck by how beautiful she was. Even now, deprived of sleep and food, her beauty, faded and ragged like the clothes she wore, was both natural and enduring, shining like a beacon against the grey, rain-filled sky. She could never be anything but beautiful he realised, for he loved her and his love for her was everything.

He looked around at the watery landscape, at the meres and fens that seemed to stretch away forever. Where this journey would end he could not say. He knew only that Alice and Hal were the one reason for going on, for enduring what for many men, many Saxons, had become unendurable.

"I love you," he said on an impulse, reaching up and placing an arm around her tiny waist. She glanced down at him, at his upturned face with its rain-sodden beard, the red beginning to turn grey, the pain etched into every line and wrinkle as though the last four years had finally caught up with him and left a permanent impression there.

"I know," she said. "I love you too. I will always love you." She smiled at him then, a smile of reassurance, dispelling for a moment the melancholy that had come over him. He watched her study their son, still sleeping in her arms, oblivious to everything.

"Hal needs to rest," she said. "He's all done in." He knew she was right. They were all done in. He stared ahead, at the empty fenland stretching out before them. Somehow he had to cross it.

"Soon, my love," he said, with more conviction than he felt.

Ahead of him the mud track forked right and left. He decided to take the left fork; the path wound its way between rain-shrouded meres and reed beds, but could lead to something a little firmer. He set off again, careful how he placed his feet. The mare reluctantly followed, snickering nervously as though she could sense danger. Alice said nothing but clutched Hal ever tighter to her breast, causing him to murmur a protest in his sleep. They rounded a stand of reeds inhabited only by herons and cranes and Ranulf saw to his dismay that two hundred yards ahead the path disappeared beneath the murky waters of the fens. He looked around for an alternative route, a way forward through the mire, but all he could see was a world of water, of water and pain and misery. They would have to turn back. He edged past the mare - there was barely enough room to do so - and slowly retraced his steps. Eventually, by gentle coaxing, the mare was persuaded to follow him, her hooves slipping and sliding dangerously close to the edge of the path. He led her by the reins until they reached the fork and this time he turned right. Ahead of him he could see a small copse of trees on a slight rise in the ground, one of the few landmarks of any kind in this desolate wilderness. If nothing else the trees would provide some cover, somewhere for Alice and Hal to rest whilst he attempted to find some food and a way out of this endless morass.

Alain de Bernay watched the Saxon trio approach his carefully laid ambuscade and despite the rain and the cold that chilled to the bone a smile crossed his dark face. He would have been handsome but for the livid scar running from his forehead to his jawline, caressing the corner of his left eye on its journey across his face. It had been a moment of carelessness many years ago but had served him well in the years since, a permanent reminder never to relax his guard until the fight was finished.

Le Couteau, as he was universally known, had no equal with the knife and the corpses of five Saxons, renegades from York, were testimony to that fact. Their bodies had been carefully disposed of, weighted down beneath the fens to render them invisible. They had died like cattle, braying their fear as he had cut them to pieces. He considered himself an artist, but an artist must have the right material to work with and the five dead Saxons had been poor material. The first Saxon, handed the knife that he always offered his victims, had hurled it away as though it were on fire and then his bowels had opened as he had fallen to his knees, begging for mercy. But what mercy could there be for a traitor? He had taken just three cuts to die. The second one, slashing and hacking like a Breton butcher had taken six, and the third, the only one with any knowledge of how to use the weapon, just nine. Saxons four and five had been despatched in mere seconds, two cuts each. *Le Couteau* spat in disgust. Poor material indeed.

Le Couteau hated England. He hated the miserable weather, he hated the army food, what there was of it; he hated the people, whom he regarded as little better than dogs, and he hated the fact that since the Conquest he had barely had an opponent worthy of the name. Eighteen Saxons he had despatched with his foot-long knife, the blade honed from the finest Toledo steel, and not one of them had caused him to break sweat.

In Normandy, as a boy, he had been taught that the use of the blade was the finest skill a man could possess and so he had spent hours practising; day after day, week after week, year after year until he had grown into a man and there was not a move he did not know, a finesse that he had not acquired. But he had never killed a man, until he had quarrelled with his tutor one hot July day and pulled the blade from its sheath. His tutor had demanded satisfaction and so they had fought. It had been a stupid fight, an unnecessary fight over his lust for the tutor's fourteen year old daughter, and the tutor had died because of it. It was still his greatest triumph, the pupil vanquishing the master. Ninety-seven cuts the tutor had taken to die, his skin virtually flensed from his bones before *Le Couteau* had slipped the blade between his ribs, puncturing the heart and ending the contest. He could close his eyes and still recall in intimate detail every one of those ninety-seven cuts. He had been close to perfection that day. Close, but not close enough, for *Le Couteau* knew that his greatest triumph still lay ahead. *One hundred cuts.* The figure had eluded him for eight long years but one day he knew he would achieve it. And then he would gain the immortality he deserved.

But for now he had a job to do. He had been sent to the fens by his Commander, William Fitz Osbern, a man that readily appreciated his talents. Fitz Osbern was heading south with his army from York to join the King, but the army could only move as fast as the slowest unit. And so *Le Couteau* had been sent ahead with a dozen picked men and instructions to hunt down and execute the renegades from York. And a hundred yards away three more of them were walking straight into his arms. He signalled to his men, carefully hidden behind the trees and reeds to make ready to spring the trap, and one by one received their silent acknowledgement.

He returned his gaze to the Saxon trio and studied them. A man, big and strong but obviously tired, a woman, his wife perhaps, mounted on a mare, and in her arms, a small child, probably her son. He returned to the man, scrutinizing every aspect of him. There was no doubt that he was a warrior of some kind; the heavily muscled shoulders and arms and the way that he carried himself all spoke of a military background. The mail suit also, rusted and torn, was further confirmation of this. And then he saw the weapons carried at his belt. A sword, bejewelled and expensive no doubt, but of infinitely more interest to him was the much smaller weapon tucked into the Saxon's belt and which he immediately recognised as a stiletto. A *stiletto,* long and thin with a needle-like point and wickedly sharp edges, a weapon used by the Italian assassin. *Le Couteau's* face slowly creased into a grin at the possibilities this unexpected development presented to him. He motioned to his men, hidden from view, that these three were to be taken alive and through the parting reeds received again their nods of assent.

He lifted his eyes and looked to the heavens. The rain was cold on his face, continued to pour from heavy grey clouds that filled the sky but still the grin remained for unexpectedly a ray of sunshine had appeared to brighten the day.

Hal had finally awoken and from beneath the soaking rag that covered his head he stared sullenly at the endless world of marsh and water that slid away to the horizon. His eyes, blue like those of his father, had a piercing intensity about them and watching him, Ranulf wondered what thoughts lay hidden behind them. Hal was only three but despite his tender years he had seen so much, suffered so much, that at times he seemed much older, as though the sins of the world were carried upon his narrow shoulders. Yet for all that there was a quality of innocence, of other worldliness, about him that seemed to captivate those coming into his presence. Ranulf felt it himself sometimes, spending whole minutes staring into the clear blue eyes set in the pale face framed by the raven hair whilst Hal played with his mother, unaware of his father's silent observation. But innocence is eventually lost to the corruption of the world and Ranulf could not help thinking that the corruption was already present in the small child carried now in the weary arms of his mother, a corruption that was insidiously eating away at his innocence, planting seeds of hatred in his soul…

They were almost at the copse when he noted a movement from the corner of his eye. It was almost nothing: it could have been the rain beating against the reeds, but some primal instinct caused him to turn toward the movement, his hand to grasp *Requitur's* hilt.

"Ranulf!" He whirled around, toward the sound of Alice's voice and to his utter despair saw what Alice had seen just moments earlier. Six Normans on the path before them, still more emerging from behind the reeds and trees, their swords drawn, ready for use…

He ripped *Requitur* clear of its scabbard and hurried to place himself between the enemy and the mare, knowing, even as he did so that the odds were hopeless. The thought flashed through his mind that this finally was the end; here, in this God forsaken wilderness. Pray God the end would be swift.

"Ride hard my love!" he cried, a sob in his voice as he parried the first blow, turning instinctively to parry the second. Whether Alice had heard his words he could not say for all his attention was upon the threat to his front. He was about to parry again when a blow to the back of his head stunned him, causing him to stumble, to see stars. A second blow, heavier still, landed beside the first and as he sank to the ground a wall of blackness hit him and he knew no more.

Chapter Four

The nine Saxons waded through mud and water that reached up to their waists, each of them grimly silent in the cold grey dawn. For two hours the Wake had led his small band south, carefully picking his way through the reed beds and marshes until they had reached the uncertain path that ran from Ely to the tiny hamlet of Aldreth, the southernmost point of the isle. At Aldreth the path ended abruptly, disappearing beneath the treacherous fens, the basin of the Ouse. No man ventured into these fens without good cause, or a boat, for to do so was to invite death. Countless numbers had perished beneath the treacherous swamps of the Aldreth fens and the Wake, heading the small party that now followed him in single file was acutely conscious of the fact that one wrong move and he would be joining them. The Aldreth fens were impassable on foot, or so it was believed. But he knew differently. And now he was searching for the submerged pathway, a narrow spine of land that lay just inches beneath the surface of the water. Only he and his small band knew of its existence, a secret jealously guarded, for its worth to them in their present predicament was beyond any price: a way into the isle, and, just as importantly, a way out.

But as the small band of Saxons slowly worked their way south, ever deeper into the swamp, the Wake knew that they were in trouble. For try as he might he could not find it.

The path had been carefully, if discreetly marked: posts, disguised as reeds, had been driven deep into the swamp to mark the line of the path but the recent storms must have dislodged them and now he could not find it.

Behind him The Heron was probing right and left with his staff, searching for the pathway that lay somewhere beneath the morass threatening them on all sides. The Wake called him forward.

"Take the lead," he said. "Be our eyes, our way forward." He gave The Heron a smile, proof of his confidence. The Heron, a man of few words, returned the smile and carefully edged past him, probing forward with his staff, sweeping the dark waters with a slow rhythmical movement as he searched for the path that lay somewhere beneath the mud.

"Like stirring a pudding it is," Wynter muttered beneath his breath, the third man in the file, his long two handed sword strung in a scabbard down his spine, a great steel backbone that caused him to move awkwardly almost comically, erect until the sword was unsheathed. And then, with that dreadful weapon held easily in his two great fists he became a man transformed, a fearsome warrior with no thought other than to swing the great weapon again and again until the reason for drawing it lay dead at his feet.

"Yes," the Wake replied, overhearing Wynter's remark, "but we must find the path otherwise we shall have to retrace our steps. I dare not venture much further." The water was up to his waist and he was a tall man. He looked behind; some of the others, Lightfoot and the twins, Hurchillus and Villicus, none of them as tall as he, were now in water up to their chests. They would soon be out of their depths in more ways than one. It was madness to go on. He reluctantly made a decision.

"Fall back," he said, "but be careful. Single file again." His voice was touched with disappointment and some of the men echoed it under their breaths as they turned to go back but he knew that it

was not aimed at him. They would follow him anywhere, to the gates of hell if he asked them. The heavy rains had obviously swollen the waters to new heights and the spine of land now lay under feet, rather than inches of water. He felt their disappointment but there was nothing to be done. They could not go on.
"Here! Here it is!" He turned at the cry and saw to his surprise that The Heron had not followed him but was ten yards ahead, and over to the right.
"Here it is!" The Heron said again, animatedly jabbing at the water with his staff, demonstrating the resistance it was meeting two feet under.
"We were too far to the left. We can go forward – look!" He leant on his staff, and raised first one long leg and then the other as he climbed onto the spine that lay hidden beneath the murky waters of the fens. As if by magic he was suddenly four feet taller than the rest of his comrades. The Heron was a man of few words and even fewer emotions, being of a solitary nature like the bird whose name he bore but there was a look of triumph on his face as he walked proudly backwards and forwards along the spine, demonstrating the proof of his words.
"Good man!" the Wake cried. "You are well named my friend." He turned to the others.
"Our man of the fens has found the path! Mark it well for our return." He grinned, despite the cold and his soaking wet clothes and saw that they were all grinning too, and laughing and joking amongst themselves. Hurchillus and Villicus were virtually indistinguishable as their faces creased into identical mirrors of the other. At times like this their desperate plight seemed far away, as though they belonged to another world, another time… They were a fine body of men, he thought, if only he had more of them…

He allowed The Heron to help him onto the submerged spine then turned to give Wynter a hand. Soon all nine were strung out along the spine, heading south towards the ancient camp of Belsar's Hill, one of the few areas of high ground for miles around, now overgrown with brambles and trees. Perhaps, the Wake thought, Morcar and Edwin might have made their camp there, unable to progress further without boats or a guide. He could only hope so. Morcar and Edwin; or some of the survivors from York. He would need all the help he could get once the Conqueror made his move and his instincts told him that that day was fast approaching. The Norman King was not noted for his patience. He continued south, under eternal grey skies to search for his allies.

Chapter Five
Belsar's Hill

He came to a sense of awareness very slowly; shadows within shadows, eddies of light swirling within the blackness and then points of grey, punctuated by pain, drawing him from the blackness, bringing him back to the first level of consciousness. His mind crawled from its cocoon vulnerable and fragile, and with its emergence came a new layer of pain, the dim recall of awful events. His mind rebelled, unable to bear the thought of what it might mean and for a while the blackness descended once more. But he could not shelter within the darkness forever and after a period that could have been hours or mere minutes his awareness gradually returned. Whatever it was that must be faced he could not avoid it; it was as inevitable as death itself. Carefully, so as not to draw attention to himself, he opened his eyes and looked around.

He was not in heaven; that much was clear, and it was too cold for hell. It had, at least stopped raining for the air was strangely quiet save for the drip of rain from sodden leaves and the laughter of foreign voices around their cooking fires. His head pounded as though someone was beating it with a club and he realised that his vision was still blurred for he could not focus his eyes clearly. He closed them again, hoping that his captors had not noticed his return to consciousness. He tried to think. He could only recall the recent past, the last moments before the darkness descended, his cry of anguish, the pain, and with it the descent into a deep unconsciousness... *Alice; Hal;* What had become of them? Had they escaped or were they held prisoner? *Or worse?* He pushed the thought away and gingerly tried to move his hands, which felt strangely numb and awkward. The effort caused arrows of fire to lance through his wrists which, he realised, were held tightly behind him. His chest too, felt tight, as though some great weight were pressing upon it. He moved his hands again, fighting the pain, and this time felt the cold, sharp, bite of metal upon them. They had him in irons; he was manacled to a tree, the same tree against which he now rested, the chain having been passed around the trunk to prevent any chance of escape.

Why he still lived he could not yet fathom. The Normans usually showed no compassion toward their Saxon adversaries, still less those that had openly defied the Conqueror in the way that he had over the past four years. Perhaps they had some other use for him, a hostage of some sort, a bargaining counter, although why he should be so special he did not know. He did not hold his life to be especially valuable, save to himself and his family. He would simply have to wait, to abide events, to see how matters unfolded. If only he could obtain some news of Alice and Hal. He would willingly give his life for theirs if he had the choice, if they were not already dead... He coughed unintentionally as he tried to draw a breath; the tightness in his chest was making it difficult to breathe. Even as the sound emerged from his throat he cursed himself. Several of the Normans seated around the campfire glanced in his direction and two of them now rose from the fire and walked over to him.

One of the men was heavy and thickset, with several days' growth on his chin. He was wearing mail-fisted gloves and a long Norman sword swung at his side as he marched confidently towards him. He was a commanding figure, full of menace, but it was the smaller man that caught his attention and held it, for despite his slighter frame and lack of height Ranulf's instincts told him that this was the one to be wary of. He noted the scar running from the forehead down to the jawline; noted too the dark, almost obsidian eyes staring out of a cruel face, and the easy, casual way that he carried himself, as if he were stalking something, or someone. He was almost feline in his movements, Ranulf thought, like a cat, easy, graceful, but when he pounced, as deadly as hell. He would have to be careful, so careful…

The two Normans had reached him now, were standing over him so that he had to raise his face to see them clearly. The smaller man spoke first. His English was fluent but overlaid with the accents of France.

"My name is Alain de Bernay," he said softly. Mark it well for you shall come to hate it." He smiled a cold smile that welcomed no response. "And this," he said, motioning to his colleague, "is Captain Bonchamp." Bonchamp said nothing but continued to scowl down at him.

"You are a renegade, yes? from York?" De Bernay spoke softly again, but now there was an edge to his voice; measured, controlled, demanding.

"No."

De Bernay nodded and Bonchamp's mailed fist smashed into Ranulf's jaw, snapping his head back against the tree, causing him to see stars and his mouth to fill with blood. It was several moments before his head cleared and when he again looked into de Bernay's face he saw the unmistakable look of triumph hiding behind the scowl. Ranulf knew then that his instincts had been right, for this man was of a type he had met only rarely in the last four years of fighting. A sadist, whose only pleasure lay in the infliction of pain for his own gratification. Hugh de Bohar had been another, but he had been laying in the earth for four years now, his

heart torn apart by the point of Ranulf's sword. But now de Bernay was speaking again, repeating the question:
"You are a renegade from York; Yes?"
"Yes." There was little point lying.
"Better." De Bernay smiled a humourless smile.
"And you were joining the traitor that calls himself "The Wake?"
"You already know that." Again the nod, and this time Bonchamp's fist slammed into his solar plexus, driving the wind from his lungs and forcing him to double up in pain.
"You learn slowly, Saxon." De Bernay shook his head, as though regretting the need to give the order.
"I shall ask the question again, and this time you shall answer as directed. You were joining the traitor that calls himself "The Wake; Yes?"
"Yes."
De Bernay smiled again.
"Good," he said. "Good. So by your own admission you confess to waging war on the King and allying yourself with traitors."
"I do not recognise your King." Ranulf knew what was coming and braced himself for it. The blow this time was a little lower, to his stomach, and he retched with the pain but his empty gut refused to void any contents. Bonchamp, evidently enjoying his role, rubbed his mailed knuckles and grinned and Ranulf silently swore to settle with him if the opportunity ever arose.
"What you think is of no consequence," De Bernay said. "Still, I detect a spirit in you that is rare in your pathetic race." Ranulf shrugged.
"Your mail coat and sword," De Bernay continued, "are some of the finer examples that I have seen, although poor by our standards of course. You are a Knight of some kind?"
"A Knight? No."
"Ah, a warrior then?"

"A housecarl."
"Housecarl?" De Bernay could not immediately place the word and turned to Bonchamp for assistance.
"One of the Godwinesons' bodyguard," Bonchamp volunteered. "Swore an oath to die on the field of battle for the bastard. This one obviously forgot it."
"A coward then." De Bernay made the obvious deduction. He turned to Ranulf.
"You are you a coward, Saxon?" he sneered. "You fear death?"
"Death? No – do you?" He glared back at de Bernay with such intensity that just for a moment he could see that the Norman was genuinely surprised. De Bernay looked at Bonchamp and then turned again to speak to him. This time his voice was softer, altogether more conversational.
"Men call me "*Le Couteau,*" he said. "Do you know the word Saxon?"
"No."
"The knife," he said. It means "the knife," he repeated the word, almost whispering it, as though loving the sound of it on his lips.
"So?" Ranulf asked. De Bernay smiled.
"Do you know what happened to your so-called King?" he said.
"He died a hero on the field of battle."
"He died a foresworn, lying bastard and was disembowelled by me in front of the whole army! I made him eat his own cock!" The scar on de Bernay's face had turned a livid purple in his sudden excitement but he hardly seemed to notice. "...and afterwards I stuck his head on a lance." He sneered triumphantly into Ranulf's face, and at that precise moment Ranulf felt such hatred for the man that he wanted to burst his chains and throttle him with his own hands. Somehow, with a supreme effort, he fought down his anger and tried to sound calm, rational.
"My wife and son," he said, "they still live?"

De Bernay nodded. "They are safe enough for the moment." In truth de Bernay had considered killing the child and offering the woman to his men, but he had had cause to reconsider. The woman, though a Saxon, was undoubtedly beautiful beneath the filth and the squalor that presently covered her body and face and he wanted her for himself. He had always had a healthy appetite for women, and, occasionally, young boys, and looked forward to the time when he could sample her delights. Perhaps also the boy's... But there was another reason why he had not yet killed her. From long study of man's nature he knew that men fought better when they had something to fight for. And so he had decided that they should live...at least for a while. He drew a long knife from his belt, and fingered it lovingly.

"Toledo steel," he said. "The finest steel in the world. Hannibal smashed the legions of Rome with steel such as this. And afterwards they adopted it themselves. It made them the masters of the world." He ran a finger along the edge and drew a small trace of blood. He showed the finger to Ranulf. "The slightest kiss will draw blood," he said. "Imagine what would happen if I were to draw the blade across your throat." He mimicked the action, and smiled as Ranulf met his eyes, refusing to look away.

"But that would be too easy a death, I think." He withdrew the knife and turned now to Bonchamp, holding out his hand. Bonchamp placed another knife in his hand, a knife that Ranulf immediately recognised as his own; the stiletto that he had carried for four long years.

"This is yours?" De Bernay asked. Ranulf nodded.

"You can use it?"

"Well enough."

"*Well enough*!" De Bernay turned to Bonchamp and laughed. "We shall see, my friend," he said. "We shall see." He faced Ranulf again.

"The stiletto," he said. "Favoured weapon of the Italian assassin. Perhaps, Saxon, you are also an assassin, captured whilst attempting to assassinate our King. Was that your intention?"
Ranulf knew that de Bernay was simply playing with him now but he was beginning to tire of the game.
"No, but if I could, I would have."
"You piece of Saxon shit!" De Bernay nodded angrily and Bonchamp hit Ranulf on the jaw, jolting his head back to crack against the trunk.
"Again!" Once more the fist slammed into his jaw and this time he felt the sensation of warm blood spreading across the back of his head. Quite unexpectedly a wave of nausea washed over him as the world began to spin beneath a halo of stars. Before he knew it he was sliding into the welcome arms of unconsciousness once more, a temporary release from his torment.

Though Ranulf did not know it because his back was to the tree, Alice had been able to watch the interrogation by de Bernay from her position on the ground. She had seen Ranulf insolently answer de Bernay; had seen too, the sickening blows that he had taken from the great bull of a man at de Bernay's side. And now he had sunk into welcome oblivion. She suspected that whatever answers Ranulf had given de Bernay would still have found an excuse to beat him because, like Ranulf, she recognised the type all too well.

De Bernay frightened her. There was an aura of evil that he carried about him like a cloak. She saw that his own men were careful in his presence, speaking guardedly lest they incur his anger. He had interrogated her before questioning Ranulf, promising life for herself and Hal if she answered truthfully. She had willingly done so. She had nothing to gamble with, no cards to play, save, perhaps her womanhood. And she pushed to the back of her mind the hour when that particular favour might be called upon. She tried to concentrate upon Ranulf, to think of some way to extricate him from the clutches of de Bernay, but it was very difficult. It was a miracle they still lived and why that was so she simply did not know. By all laws of reason they should now be lying butchered in the swamp and why they weren't she could not understand; unless de Bernay had other plans for them. And in that small thought she took what comfort she could. She shivered with the cold.

She was tied to Hal, back to back, their hands individually tied behind them, a rope around them both, binding them together. Hal had been crying, for his father, for himself. She had tried to comfort him as best she could with soft words and hollow promises but they had made very little difference. How could one comfort a three year old in such circumstances? Eventually, mercifully, he had subsided into a deep sleep, a release from the racking sobs and the demons that haunted him. Now she could feel the rise and fall of his slight body as he breathed against her. She felt so sorry for the lad. Ever since he had been born they had been running and hiding. Must they run forever? Even as she thought it she knew that the time for running was finally over. They would meet their fate here, in these dismal fens. They had journeyed south in the hope that at last they would be free; at least for a while, but now those hopes were dashed. One way or the other it must end here for there was nowhere else to run. There was no possibility of escape and she was sure that de Bernay would not simply release them. He was not the man to do that. She shivered again, but this time with the thought of what he might have in store for them.

Behind her back she reached out and clutched Hal's hands, an instinctive, maternal reaction, and then another thought struck her: If she could reach his hands surely she could also reach the cords that bound his hands together? It was a slim chance, almost nothing, but it was something to cling to. She felt behind her, sliding her hands down to his slender wrists, running her fingers lightly over the cords that bound them together. The bindings were tight, but the cord was dry, and if she worked on them, she might, eventually, be able to loosen them enough for him to slide his hands through. And once his hands were free anything was possible. She felt for the cord, running her fingers backwards and forwards until she found what she was sure was the end. Heart pounding she quickly went to work…

Alain de Bernay speared a piece of duck from the fire and pushed the meat into his mouth. Hot grease ran down his chin and he fastidiously wiped it away as he regarded the Saxon again. He had still not recovered from the beating that Bonchamp had handed out and his bandaged head lay slumped against his chest. De Bernay had given orders for the head wound to be bound, to staunch the flow of blood, but it was not for compassionate reasons. De Bernay was not a compassionate man. He wanted the Saxon to live because the Saxon intrigued him, and because he recognised that in this Saxon he might finally have an opponent worthy of his attention.

Who the Saxon was he did not know, but there was a quality about him that de Bernay had rarely met before. It was as though he had been to hell and back and cared not a whit whether he journeyed there again. He recalled the Saxon's eyes; the way they had met his own when he had asked him whether he was afraid of death, and of his reply. The look too, when he had held the knife to the Saxon's throat…

He plucked another piece of meat from the fire and wandered over to where the Saxon was chained to the tree. His head remained on his chest; he was still in the deep sleep of the unconscious. But when he came round it would be time to begin. He had delayed long enough, longer than he had intended. He had not meant Bonchamp to beat the Saxon senseless for what triumph would there be in defeating a wounded animal? But the Saxon had roused his anger and he had overreacted. He dismissed the thought and concentrated instead upon the fight, the pleasure, to come. Stripped to the waist, and chained to each other with the length of chain that now bound the Saxon to the tree, they would perform a *pas de deux,* a dance of death, until the Saxon was stripped of his flesh. It would be *Le Couteau's* Toledo steel against the Saxon's stiletto. And there could only be one outcome.

He studied the Saxon, the eyes and cheeks puffed, the lips bloodied and swollen. Perhaps, if the Saxon lived long enough, he would be able to cut the lips from the mouth; at least he would die with a smile on his face…

He wandered back to the warmth of the fire and the laughter of his comrades. He was anxious to begin but knew that he must be patient. He filled his mouth with more of the duck and his black eyes danced with light, reflecting the flames from the fire as he anticipated the fight and another triumph for *Le Couteau.*

Chapter Six

Hal's bonds were definitely loosening but it was so slow, so painful. For how long Alice had been working on them she could not tell with any certainty save that it seemed like hours. At first she had worked with a feverish intensity, unmindful of the pain whilst she carefully worked the cord through one knot after another, but now her wrists were aching beyond endurance and she was having to take frequent rests to ease the chafing of her bonds, the recurring bouts of cramp that sent arrows of fire through her wrists.

She guessed that it was about mid afternoon for the light was beginning to fade but it would be several hours yet before nightfall and by then they could all be dead. She looked over towards Ranulf and saw to her relief that he was finally stirring from his unconsciousness, his limbs moving stiffly, painfully, like a much older man as he gently exercised them back to life. Her relief was tainted by fear however, for she guessed that de Bernay would see this and now resume where he had left off. And what that would mean she dared hardly speculate.

She was overcome by sudden emotion; felt tears prick her eyes. She had thought that she had no tears left but she was wrong, and now they rolled freely down her cheeks as despair overcame her. It was hopeless, for all three of them. Why the Normans could not have done with it and finish what they obviously intended without this protracted torture she did not know. It was more than she could endure. She lifted her head towards the heavens and closed her eyes. Sobs racked through her, constrained by her bonds. She prayed for their lives, but without hope, for what kind of God would allow them to endure what they had endured? She hated God, if he existed.

The tears ended, replaced by anger. They would all die here, and perhaps the sooner the better. Her only regret was for her son, who had never known life. She gazed across the fenland, wondering what it would have been like on Eel Island when she saw a face staring at her from between the parting reeds. She blinked quickly, wondering whether her mind was playing tricks and looked again. But it was still there; the face of a man, framed by blonde hair, with peculiar grey eyes that were smiling but at the same time concerned. A finger came to the lips and she realised that the man wanted her silence. She nodded imperceptibly, saw the reeds close, and the face was gone as though it had never existed. For thirty seconds she stared at the space where the face had been but could see nothing save for the reeds rustling in the breeze, the occasional passing bird. Perhaps, she thought, she had been dreaming; she was exhausted, physically, emotionally. But she *had* seen it; without any question.

In a fever of excitement she resumed work on Hal's bonds, ignoring the pain, the cramp in her wrists, all else forgotten whilst the words echoed around in her head: *Forgive me God, I'm sorry God, so sorry God, so sorry...*

Alain de Bernay had seen the Saxon's return to consciousness; had noted the way that he had worked his limbs within the confines of his shackles and decided it was time to begin. He had delayed enough already. It was dangerous to linger in one place for too long and he had already been here for two days. He felt ready to begin, having sat in contemplative silence for over an hour whilst he prepared body and mind for the contest, imagining the moves he would make, the wounds that he would inflict; wounds that would bring the Saxon to the point where he would beg to die. And after the Saxon's death he would take the woman as his prize. It would be a fitting culmination: *the coup de grace.*

He rose from the fire and motioned to his men that he was ready. He walked over to where the Saxon sat manacled to the tree. He saw that the Saxon's left eye had virtually closed and knew that this would make it easier for him. He regretted this; the Saxon had fight in him and he was looking forward to a contest. But with only one eye the Saxon would be unable to judge distance with any accuracy; his attacks would be clumsy and wild whilst his defence would be seriously compromised.

"You favour your right hand?" he said. The Saxon nodded, saying nothing. He knew this already but it pleased him to be proved right.

"Release the right hand," he said to Bonchamp who walked around the tree to unlock the manacle on the Saxon's right hand and then pulled the Saxon roughly to his feet. The chain dangled from his left wrist to the ground. The Saxon rubbed his right wrist gingerly and stamped his feet as though to bring some feeling back into them.

"Remove his chain-mail and jerkin." De Bernay gave the order and now another Norman, Legrun, stepped forward and began to unpick the buckles on Ranulf's chain mail. It was a time consuming task, a task that commanded the whole of Legrun's attention. He had been with de Bernay for over two years and knew precisely what was required of him. He feared de Bernay, as most men did, for his unpredictable nature and violent passions, but de Bernay had treated him well and had not hesitated to choose him as one of his twelve picked men. Legrun could be relied upon; and so, engrossed as he was in the task of removing Ranulf's mail shirt, he did not hear, was unaware of, the arrow that pierced his neck and killed him on the spot.

Moments later the air was full of arrows, followed by a dull thump as they found their targets. Four Normans died within the first five seconds, taken by surprise before they could react. And suddenly the air was full of noise, the cries of orders being barked, the scrape of swords being ripped from scabbards, the clash of steel and the cries of the dying. And above it all could be heard the distinctive cry of one man, a man that the Normans would come to hate and fear in equal measure:

"A Wake! A Wake!"

The Normans stood no chance. Surprised, and now outnumbered they fell back before the Saxon onslaught. Death had come to visit them from the cold grey fens and though they fought hard they died where they stood, hacked down by the swords of Hereward and Wynter, the short-handled axe of Lightfoot and the iron-tipped arrows of Hurchillus Villicus and Alsinus, spitting from their great hunting bows like rain. Only two men reacted without hesitation; de Bernay and Bonchamp; and de Bernay, with the instincts of a cat, raced toward the mare, tethered to a distant tree, his one chance of escape.

Bonchamp saw what de Bernay intended and on the instant made a decision. The mare could only carry one of them, but there was still one place where he might find safety. The fight was lost; all that mattered was his self-preservation.

Alice had seen it all as though in a dream; the release of Ranulf from his manacles; the arrow piercing the Norman's neck and then the mad rush of the Saxons as they assaulted the Norman encampment. So engrossed was she in watching the blonde figure of the Saxon as he hacked down one man after another that she almost forgot her efforts to free Hal. But now, seeing Bonchamp heading toward them her senses returned and with a frantic tug on the bonds she managed to release Hal's wrists from their grip. His tiny hands shot loose, he struggled out of the bonds that tied him to his mother and at last he was free.

"Run to your father!" she cried and Hal, tears streaming down his cheeks, started to run. He looked around for his father and through his tears saw him standing alone, a forgotten figure on the edge of the fight, the chain still hanging from his wrist.

"Father! Father!" he cried, his tiny legs propelling him over the ground. He saw his father turn towards him, saw the surprise, and then the look of horror cross his father's face. At first he did not understand but then he saw the reason for his father's distress, felt Bonchamp's arm sweep him from the ground and in the same fluid movement the cold steel of a blade at his throat. He screamed and started to sob.

Ranulf reacted before anyone. His hand instinctively went to his hilt but *Requitur* was not there; he had been stripped of his weapons. But he knew that he must do something and so he advanced toward Bonchamp, the chain held now in his left hand, a weapon of sorts, and Bonchamp retreated in the face of the Saxon's advance, the wicked blade still pressed against Hal's throat. A noise drummed in his ears and glancing over his shoulder Bonchamp saw that de Bernay had freed the mare; was making good his escape, his arms and legs pumping as he whipped every last ounce of speed from her. Arrows whistled past de Bernay but every yard carried him further clear. De Bernay had left him to his fate. He cursed the man under his breath before turning his attention to the Saxons, who now had him surrounded. Only the boy separated him from an instantaneous death.

"Stay back!" Bonchamp snarled. "Stay back or the boy dies!"

"Kill the boy and you shall certainly die." The blonde Saxon now spoke, his voice firm, cutting across the boy's sobs. Ranulf studied him, the bloodied sword held in his right hand, the sweat beading his brow; even so he could see that the Saxon was in total control of himself. And three archers stood beside him, their bows trained upon Bonchamp. A glance behind told him that the fight was over; Norman corpses littered the ground and were being searched by the some of the other Saxons.

"You!" Bonchamp snarled at the nearest Saxon whose sword, Ranulf saw, was also stained with blood. "Drop your weapon!" This man now looked towards the blonde Saxon, obviously the leader. He appeared not to have heard him; his grey eyes remained fixed upon Bonchamp.

"No one drops any weapons, Norman," he said, "until you release the boy."

"You think me mad!" Bonchamp barked, his eyes wild now, the desperation in his voice clearly evident. "The moment I release the pup I am a dead man."

"The boy will not save you," the blonde Saxon said, "but I offer you the chance of life. The question is are you man enough to take it?"

"You speak in riddles Saxon! Explain yourself!" The response was mocking but Ranulf could tell that Bonchamp's interest had been aroused.

"Release the boy," the blonde Saxon said. "Let him go and you shall fight his father, man to man, in a fair fight. If you win, you go free."

"And if I lose I will be dead any way. I take my chance with the boy."

"The boy will not save you," said the blonde Saxon quietly. "Hurchillus will take out your eye before you can blink. Villicus will pierce your throat and Alsinus your heart. The only question is which arrow will kill you first. Either way you will be dead before you hit the ground. The boy will not prevent this."

Bonchamp paused to consider. The boy's father was the housecarl. And like de Bernay he knew that the housecarl was in a poor way. The blows he had landed had been heavy, designed to weaken the Saxon. And his left eye was closed. It was hardly a fair fight but the blonde Saxon, for reasons best known to himself, had given him this chance. He dare not refuse it; he dare not, the Saxon's archers were lethal.

"What weapon?" he said eventually and the blonde Saxon now looked at the housecarl.

"Swords," Ranulf said.

"Very well." Bonchamp pushed the boy away from him and Hal ran to his mother who had been released from her bonds. The two hugged each other, mother and son together, tears flooding down their cheeks as the preparations for the fight were made.

"Why not kill the bastard now?" Wynter said to the blonde Saxon. "There's nothing to stop us."

"I gave my word," the blonde Saxon said, "and the father deserves his chance for revenge. I fancy we shall see some sport."

"The Norman's a big bastard, though...and strong. And your new friend is not exactly in the best condition."

"True enough," the blonde Saxon said. "But the housecarl has hatred in his heart, and we both know what that can do."

"Aye," Wynter said. "It can make a man reckless." The blonde Saxon smiled, genuinely amused by the remark.

"What's your name?" He spoke now to the housecarl.

"Ranulf; Ranulf Redbeard."

"Well, finish him quickly," he said. "I should hate to let him go." Ranulf glared at Bonchamp who was busy preparing himself for the fight, practising cuts with his heavy Norman sword.

"If he kills me I hope you gut the bastard," he said. "Where's my sword?"

Requitur was eventually found in de Bernay's bedroll and handed to him. Ranulf saw that it needed a new edge, but there was no time to worry about that. The chain was hacked from his left wrist and the Saxons formed a circle about the two men. Ranulf glanced towards Alice and Hal. He saw that they had turned away, unable to watch and somehow this stiffened his resolve. He had wanted revenge, and if it wasn't *Le Couteau* himself it was at least his instrument of torture, the bastard that had closed his eye and beaten him half to death. He felt a surge of anger course through his veins and, as he had done so many times in the past, he let it feed, let it burn until it was a furnace.

As expected Bonchamp made the first attack, coming at him with great sweeping arcs of his sword, attempting to finish it quickly. But Ranulf had chosen swords because he was familiar with the weapon; had been through more sword fights than most men could remember. And as Bonchamp came at him with crude, clumsy strokes, Ranulf parried carefully, patiently, waiting for the opening. He was careful to keep Bonchamp on his right side, away from his closed eye, and as the fight progressed he could feel Bonchamp becoming ever more anxious. Bonchamp was strong; he was a very large man, but after a few minutes Ranulf had the measure of him, could anticipate the next stroke. Their swords clashed again and again as Bonchamp, desperate now, swung wild, uncultured strokes at the Saxon and the noise rang out across the empty landscape. And then, just as Bonchamp let loose another great swinging blow, this time aimed at his head, Ranulf ducked beneath the flashing blade, felt the rush of wind as it whistled closely overhead. In the same instant he drove the point of *Requitur* hard into Bonchamp's chest, the force of the blow propelling Bonchamp backwards. A crimson fountain erupted from his chest and as Ranulf ripped *Requitur* out and angrily drove it in again he knew that Bonchamp was a dead man.

"You took your time," the blonde man said as Ranulf pulled *Requitur* clear of Bonchamp's chest.
"I was savouring it," he said dryly. "I'm not sure when I shall have the chance to settle with that other bastard." The blonde man looked at him quizzically. "The one that escaped," Ranulf said. "Calls himself *Le Couteau* – the knife. Claims that he was the man that butchered the King on Caldbec Hill. Either way I intend to finish with him. But this one will do for a start." He glanced down at Bonchamp's corpse. Already it had begun to turn grey, his blood feeding the rich, dark fenland. He bent over the corpse and pulled his stiletto from the dead man's belt, tucking it into his own.
"Tell me," Ranulf said, "How did you know I could beat him?"
"I didn't," the blonde man said. "But Bonchamp was right about one thing: I dare not risk the boy. I thought you would want your chance."
"You should have just killed him."
"Perhaps you're right," the blonde man acknowledged. "But answer me this," he said, "Do you love your son?" Ranulf looked around for Hal and saw him, locked in a tearful embrace with Alice.
"Of course." Ranulf gave the obvious reply. The blonde man nodded.
"That is good," he said. "A father should love his son." He paused. "I have no children," he said, "no son to remember me, but if I had I would not trade his life for a Norman...not for a thousand Normans." And as he spoke these words Ranulf saw something in the strange grey eyes that had not been there before. He understood. He understood very well...
"We owe you our lives," he said, "and as yet we do not know your name. I am Ranulf Redbeard, Champion to the late King Harold, who was slain on Caldbec Hill."

"And I am Hereward," the blonde man replied; "Hereward the Wake."

Chapter Seven

Cambridge

The Conqueror lifted a candle to the crude map and jabbed a heavy finger at it. He had put on weight in the three years since Senlac Hill, since he had been crowned King of England, but his appetite for power remained undiminished, unsated. He lifted his gaze from the map and turned towards his seneschal, William Fitz Osbern, recently arrived from York:
"It was here, you say?" He tapped the map again.
"So my man says." Fitz Osbern wore a look of weariness as he gave his reply. He had marched his army well over two hundred miles to rendezvous with the King and the effort had taken its toll. William noted the evasion in Fitz Osbern's answer and allowed a hint of irritation into his voice:
"I am asking you, not your man." Fitz Osbern hesitated.
"I am sure it was there, Sire," he said eventually, "but my informant is outside if you wish to question him directly." There was a look of hurt in Fitz Osbern's eyes and William knew that his barb had found its mark. He liked William Fitz Osbern, and trusted him, as far as he trusted any man, but he had made Fitz Osbern rich and demanded nothing less than his total commitment in return.
"That won't be necessary for the moment." He studied the map again. It was stretched across his campaign table and weighted down at the corners with four golden lions, the symbol of his royal power.

"If you are correct, and the attack took place here," he jabbed again at the map, "it must follow that there is some method of crossing the fen at that point." He looked hard at Fitz Osbern but was uncertain whether he had grasped the significance of what he was saying. "If the renegades can get out of the Isle we can also get in. Is that not so?" Understanding slowly dawned in Fitz Osbern's eyes.
"Your logic is infallible, Sire."
"Yes, quite." He examined the map again. Just north of where the attack had taken place an area of low lying fen was shown, crossed at its mid point by the river Ouse, running east to west. The Aldreth fen, it looked impassable, but he knew from long experience that maps could often be wrong.
"How far is it, from this point, Belsar's Hill, to…here?" His finger tapped the map, indicating the southernmost tip of the Isle.
"About a mile, I believe."
"A mile?"
"I believe so Sire."
"Then how did they cross it?"
In truth Fitz Osbern had no idea how the Saxons' had crossed the fen and neither, he suspected, did *Le Couteau.* But he did not intend to accept the blame for de Bernay's bungling.
"My man will know this," he said. "I suggest we call him in and you can question him directly."
William knew where Fitz Osbern was leading: the abrogation of his own responsibility. He was wriggling, but he did not intend to let him off so easily.
"I had expected you to have done so already," he said acerbically. "Let him wait a while."

He rose from the map and paced the length of the Keep. Perched high on its earth mound the Keep had a panoramic view of the surrounding countryside. Outside it was a coal black night, the moon obscured by heavy cloud cover, a perpetual cloak of misery hanging over the land. Inside the Keep huge torches had been lit to relieve the gloom and now they cast their radiant light on the rich tapestries hanging from every wooden wall, scarlet and silver and yet more golden lions.

It had taken just two years to construct Cambridge Castle, a motte and bailey construction, simple but effective, the base for the forthcoming campaign. Twenty-seven houses had been demolished on the site where it now stood; twenty-seven families dispossessed. Saxons, they hardly counted. He wondered idly where they had gone after their homes had been turned into detritus. Perhaps they were now on Eel Island with the man that claimed to be their Saviour. He shrugged. Everyone knew what had happened to Christ and his followers. *Christ,* who had walked on water. Perhaps, like Christ, the Wake had crossed the Aldreth fen by simply walking over it. He would be a hell of a man if he could do that. Then again it was more than likely that they had crossed by boat. But Fitz Osbern's report had made no mention of boats, and if there had been boats why had they not been seen or heard?

"Your man," he said to Fitz Osbern, "did he make any mention of boats?"

"Boats Sire? Nothing was said of them." No boats then. So how had they crossed? He studied the map again but it offered no help.

"This man of yours," he said. "I will see him now."

Alain de Bernay paced restlessly backwards and forwards outside the Keep and blew on his hands to warm them against the chill night air. Fitz Osbern had warned him that the King would probably wish to speak to him personally and he guessed that the King was now keeping him waiting out of political expedience. Precisely what Fitz Osbern and the King would be discussing he did not know but he was as certain as he could be that it would not be good news for him.

Nine miles he had ridden to Cambridge to report the Saxon's surprise attack, the slaughter of his men, and to avoid difficult questions he had exaggerated the Saxons' numbers. But now, as he awaited his audience with the King he guessed that his half-truths would not stand the Conqueror's cross-examination. And that was what he feared. Fitz Osbern, weary and cold from his own forced march had been annoyed to learn of the deaths of twelve of his best men, but de Bernay had blustered and obfuscated until Fitz Osbern had been satisfied; almost. But satisfying Fitz Osbern was one thing, the King was quite another.

And de Bernay knew that responsibility for the disaster lay with himself. He had been their leader, charged with hunting down and executing the renegades from York. But he had allowed himself to be sidetracked whilst he dreamed of glory, of cutting the Saxon into a hundred pieces instead of posting the sentries that any competent commander would have done. It was his fault, and he sensed, as he continued his pacing under the watchful eye of the castle guard that he would now have to answer for it. Fitz Osbern wanted him here for one purpose and one purpose only: as a scapegoat. And he knew that Fitz Osbern would not hesitate to sacrifice a mere Captain if it meant saving his own neck. His mind was running along these lines, of finding some way of extricating himself from the situation when the door opened, throwing an arc of light into the blackness of the night and he was summoned into the chamber beyond.

"You say there were a hundred Saxons?" The King's eyes bored into those of de Bernay as he fired his question. No formalities, no polite introductions, he stood over his campaign table as he scrutinised de Bernay and began to gather the facts. He held Fitz Osbern's report in his hand but had looked up from it when de Bernay had entered the Keep. He had noted the man's feline grace, the easy way that he carried himself. He noted also the scar running down the cheek; a duelling scar perhaps. His first impression was of a supremely confident man, and a dangerous one. Those qualities were fine when it came to fighting Saxons but not when he employed them in deceiving his own masters' and he suspected that de Bernay had already deceived Fitz Osbern in his account of the ambush.

"About that number Sire." De Bernay's reply, when it came, was equivocal.

"A hundred. Where did they come from?"

"Where Sire?"

"Yes man. The question is simple enough. Where did they come from?"

"Out of the fens, Sire; it was a sudden attack. We were overwhelmed in seconds."

"You posted a watch of course?"

"Yes Sire, of course." The answer came quickly. Too quickly. William sensed that the man was lying. It was intuitive, his ability to get to the heart of a man, what made him tick. He deliberately narrowed his eyes and watched de Bernay's reaction, his glance toward Fitz Osbern. The man was lying; he was certain of it. He pressed his point.

"But they saw nothing, heard nothing?"

"No Sire."

"Were they asleep?"

"No Sire."

"No! Then either they were blind, or deaf, or we are chasing phantoms!"

De Bernay, surprised by the sudden outburst looked again at Fitz Osbern as though expecting his aid. Fitz Osbern studied his feet.
"It was misty, Sire," he said hastily. "The mist obscured the sentries view, and deadened the sound of the Saxon approach. The first thing we knew was a rain of arrows that killed half of the men in the first rush." This much at least was true. "We had no chance," he said, "no chance of escape."
"But *you* escaped. How?" Again he noted the man's glance toward Fitz Osbern before he replied, the slight hesitation in his voice.
"I had wandered off to take a piss, Sire," de Bernay said. "When the attack started I lay hidden, there was nothing I could do. It was a slaughter."
"How fortunate for you, Captain," he said, "that you have a weak bladder." He studied the report for a moment, cross-checking his facts, "or perhaps you have a weak stomach."
"Stomach Sire?"
"Yes man. Stomach for the fight. I think you ran, leaving your comrades to their fate. Is that not so?"
"No Sire!" de Bernay protested his innocence. "It was a slaughter, we were outnumbered! We had no chance!"
"So you lay hidden whilst your men were being slaughtered. Very noble Captain," he said. "Tell me, did you see, from the safety of your bolt-hole, what the leader of this band of phantoms looked like?" This, at least, was one question that de Bernay could answer truthfully.
"Blonde, Sire," he said. "Tall, broad, blonde hair, grey eyes."
The King grunted, turning now to Fitz Osbern, who had maintained a studied silence during his interrogation of de Bernay.
"That's our man," he said.
"Yes Sire, no doubt of it."
"The question is how do we get to him?"

The Conqueror had tried for weeks to find some way into the Isle of Ely but his scouts had all reported back with the same answer: there was no way in. And yet these Saxons had appeared from nowhere to commit a murderous attack on his men. There had to be a way in and he simply needed to find it. And he was convinced that this attack from the direction of Aldreth held the key to the puzzle. He turned his attention back to de Bernay.

"You estimate there were a hundred men in this attack?

"Yes, Sire; more or less." He could hardly admit there had been only nine, and the housecarl.

"A hundred men cross the fen and no one notices."

"It was misty, Sire, as I have said."

"So you have said." William left the campaign table and paced the floor. He did not believe de Bernay's account of the Saxon's numbers; was certain that he was exaggerating their strength in order to excuse his own failings. The difficulty was that he could not disprove what de Bernay was alleging.

"These men," he said, "did they use boats? If they had used boats you would surely have heard them?"

De Bernay thought long and hard. He had certainly not seen any boats but the question of how they had arrived at Belsar's Hill had not been uppermost in his mind until now. Perhaps they had used boats, but if they had he had not mentioned them in his report.

"No Sire," he said. "I am certain there were no boats." The King nodded.

"Very well," he said, "we shall take a look for ourselves, and *you*," he glared at de Bernay, "shall come with us. You may go." De Bernay turned on his heels and left, relieved the interrogation was over. William watched him leave.

"I dislike that man," he said to Fitz Osbern. "And I will not tolerate liars. Reduce him to the ranks. First thing tomorrow."

Chapter Eight

The work party were up to their waists in mud, struggling to finish the task. All day long they had been cutting timber, fitting it to shape before carefully handling it into place, one log on top of another until the dam had begun to take form. But as day turned to dusk and the shadows lengthened, the effort was beginning to tell. The dam was almost complete; three feet more and the water that had been their constant enemy would become a reluctant ally, sealing off the Isle between Coveney and Witham, making an assault from the west impossible.

The sun, barely seen all day, sank beneath an invisible horizon and now, as a pale moon filled the sky the men hefted the penultimate log chest high, the muscles in their arms and back screaming with the effort. Slowly the log was manoeuvred into position, the men gasping with the strain, their feet slipping and sliding in the mud as they fought for purchase, their chests heaving as they attempted to fill their lungs with oxygen.

Water poured through the still incomplete seal, a torrent that soaked the men, adding to their difficulties. A man cried as he fell, the timber slipping from his grasp. Wynter and Lightfoot tried to grab it, to take the weight before it was swept away but they were too late. Caught by the torrent the log was hurled forty feet before its impetus was spent, coming to a halt in a swirling eddy of water. The work party, released temporarily from their efforts, collapsed on the banks either side of the dam, fighting for breath like fish out of water.

The Wake gave a small sigh. He needed fresh legs and fresh lungs. That, or leave the completion of the dam until morning. He looked to the heavens; the moon was full and bright, despite the cloud cover. Enough light for another half hour.

"Have a rest lads," he said, "I'll get you some help." He turned away from the still incomplete dam, the men gasping and choking on the bank, and made his way back to the camp. Once the dam was sealed the camp would be secure and the Conqueror could do his worst.

It had been three days since the bloody encounter at Belsar's Hill and his scouts had reported that the Conqueror himself had now visited the site; that the Norman King was probing for a crossing. The Normans would never find it. And if they did they would never make it across a mile of swamp in single file, under fire from his archers, unless the water dropped. And that was his one fear, his only concern. He dismissed it from his mind. The immediate task was to finish the dam.

On the outskirts of the camp was the small rush hut that he had found for his new ally, the housecarl and his family. Ranulf was recovering well; three days of rest had eased the pain although swelling was still apparent around the jaw and eyes. He walked over to the hut and saw the boy playing in the mud by the entrance.

"Is your father inside?" The boy nodded without looking up, engrossed in the piles of mud that he had moulded into crude warriors. He ducked under the flap of cloth that covered the doorway. It was dark inside; darker than the moonlit evening and it took a few seconds for his eyes to adjust. At first he thought the child had been wrong, that the hut was empty, but as his eyes adjusted to the light he saw what he had at first missed: two bodies moving together in the far corner, oblivious to all else save each other. They were naked, he saw, the girl's slim thighs wrapped around those of her lover, her back arched, her thighs and breasts covered with sweat as she moved rhythmically against him. She sighed as the housecarl thrust against her, her eyes closed, unaware of the stranger in their midst, the violation of their sanctuary. The girl lowered her face to that of her lover, covering it, bruised and swollen as it was, with her kisses. The man held his hand to her face, then to her raven hair. She shuddered, and he gave a cry, their bodies moving against each other harder now; the final throes of their pleasure.

He ducked out of the doorway as silently as he had arrived, drawing a deep breath, his head raised to the night sky. After a few moments he hurried back to the work party still laid on the bank, awaiting his return. His mind swam with the vision of what he had seen, so unexpected, so intense, that he had almost forgotten himself. He slipped off his jerkin and breeches and leapt into the icy water, welcoming the cold that washed over him. He waded out towards the log, floating idly where it had come to rest, and hefted it onto his shoulders. He carried it back to the dam and even as the work party, seeing his intention, rose wearily to help him, he rammed it home with every ounce of his strength, fighting the torrent of water that swept over him, the sudden emotions that had consumed him….

The Saxons lay hidden in the reeds on the north bank of the Ouse watching the activity a half-mile distant. A watery sun cast a pale glow over the land, heralding the start of summer, the start of the Conqueror's campaign. At last, it seemed, the King was ready to make his move.

In the distance, just south of Belsar's Hill, the Norman army was busy at work. Like a great army of ants hundreds of men were stripped to the waist, toiling in the late May sunshine, doing the Conqueror's bidding. Some men were carrying trees cut down from the nearby forests, whilst others were stripping the cut timber of its branches, leaving only the upright trunk. And other men, dozens of them, were waist deep in the treacherous mud, driving the timber piles deep into the swamp bed until only three or four feet protruded above the level of the fens.

Reed beds too, were being cut down, the reeds and rushes piled in the sun to dry. The air, usually so silent, was full of noise: the scrape of saw against timber, the crash of the trees as one by one they were felled to the ground, the shouted orders of the Captains, the hammering of the piles into the swamp and high above, dispossessed of their long time homes, the cry of cranes and waders and warblers and geese, angrily crying their outrage.

For over twenty minutes the Saxons' studied this activity in silence, each of them engrossed in watching the Norman army at work.

"Busy little bastards, they are," Wynter muttered beneath his breath as yet another pile was lifted into position and hammered into the soft mud, one man, presumably an officer, directing operations with angry, shouted orders.

"Aye, but to what end?" Lightfoot posed the question that was on Hereward's mind. The Wake inclined his head towards Ranulf, sprawled beside him on the riverbank. Had Ranulf seen him, in the gloom of his hut two evenings ago? If so he had given no sign, at least outwardly, of having done so. On the contrary, now that his wounds were healing and his strength returning the housecarl was throwing himself into the defenders' preparations for the forthcoming campaign with enthusiasm. He would be a good man to have at his side when the chips were down and the Wake was as certain as he could be that that day would not be long postponed.

The Norman army had at last swung into action, but to what end he could not be sure.
"Seen anything like this before?" he muttered as he turned his grey eyes once more to the front.
"No," Ranulf said, his eyes also locked on the events half-mile distant. "But the bastards have never had to cross a swamp before. Perhaps they are constructing a jetty."
"A jetty?"
"Perhaps," Ranulf said uncertainly. "A jetty for their boats. But if so where are they? They would need a fleet to carry that lot across."

The Wake mentally counted the numbers of men toiling away in the midday sunshine. There must be a thousand, if not more. He watched them for a few moments longer; the men stacking the rough timber, others carrying it out to the fen, the piles being driven deep into the black mud; row upon row of them, pale in the sunshine, reaching out to him across the marshy void. And as he watched this activity, the remorseless driving of the piles into the soft miasma, an understanding dawned and a frown furrowed his brow.
"Not a jetty, Ranulf," he said. "They're building a bridge."

Chapter Nine

They sat around the campfire staring vacantly into the flames. Beyond the circle of light, hidden in darkness, children played happily together, laughing and shouting as children do, unmindful of the menace that daily grew nearer. A dog barked somewhere, disturbed from its slumbers by the childrens' game, and once more their laughter could be heard ringing through the night, accompanied now by the barking of the dog.

Hereward watched Ranulf pluck a small piece of eel from the flames and blow on it before carefully placing it in his mouth. The chewy meat was too hot and he spat it into his hand, allowing it to cool before placing it in his mouth again. Hereward laughed and slapped him on the back, almost causing him to choke and this brought yet more laughter from the men gathered about the fire. It was light relief; welcome, but fleeting. The Conqueror was coming and in the three days since the bridge had been started the Norman army had barely stopped to draw breath. Day by day, foot by foot and then yard by yard the bridge had slowly taken shape, reaching out over the treacherous swamp of the Aldreth fen. And as yet the Saxons, secure for the moment on their island stronghold, had failed to come up with an answer to it.

The Norman army's activity had given added impetus to the defenders' own preparations. Around the perimeter of the camp an earth wall was being thrown up, a physical barrier twelve feet high with a solid oak gate. It was not impregnable, but it was better than nothing; would buy them precious minutes when all else had failed. Time perhaps for escape, or more likely the opportunity to take their own lives rather than face the uncertain justice of the Conqueror. For ultimately the Wake knew, as he stared into the flames, there was only one way this rebellion could end. And recognising this he had begun to excavate a tunnel under the southern ramparts. It was hard going for the men, labouring underground in the mud and the water, but it was necessary and kept them busy.

For months he had hoped that Morcar and Edwin would appear with their men, or that other parts of the Country would rise up against their Norman oppressors, but now it seemed that both hopes lay in ashes. After York, after the Norman army of Fitz Osbern had butchered every man, woman and child for twenty miles around, there was simply no-one left, or prepared, to fly the Saxon Standard. No one save himself; fool that he was. And now the Conqueror was coming to crush him just as he had crushed all the other attempts to wrest the Crown from his head. If only Godwineson had left an heir of adult age; an heir, or a brother; anyone that could lead a Saxon army, a field army, against the Conqueror. But there was no one. Godwineson's only son was still only fourteen, was believed to be in Ireland, and his brothers, Gyrth and Leofwine, had both perished with him on *Senlac* Hill. What a butchers' yard it must have been. He glanced at Ranulf, staring into the flames, lost in thoughts of his own. He had been there, on *Senlac* Hill, almost to the end, but he never spoke of it. Perhaps the memories were still too painful, too vivid to speak of. But he was curious nevertheless.

"Harold Godwineson; what kind of man was he?"

Ranulf turned towards him. Hereward saw that his face, still slightly swollen, had taken on a faraway look, a mask that he wore like a protective suit of mail.

"He was a man like any other," Ranulf said, "ambitious, proud, flawed in many ways, but he was also generous when it suited him. He was my friend, and I failed him."
"Failed him? How?"
"At the end, when the Normans were pressing in, he knew the battle was lost. He could have escaped, but he chose to stay. He ordered me to save the Queen but I was too late. The Normans captured her. Later they made her identify his body."
"What happened to her?"
"She killed herself. It was my fault." Ranulf turned towards the flames. "My fault," he repeated, and Hereward noted the catch in his voice.
"You should not blame yourself. In the heat of battle things happen that we later regret. The King could have escaped; you said so yourself." Ranulf listened, poked the fire with a stick, but said nothing in reply. The silence hung between them like a shroud.
"No," he said eventually. "He could not leave any more than you could leave here. It would have been a betrayal; of himself, of his friends." The Wake nodded his understanding. The housecarl was right; he could not leave either.
"What was it like; on Caldbec Hill?" he eventually asked. "I need to know."

Ranulf studied the men gathered about the fire. Wynter, Lightfoot, the Heron; he felt as though he had known them forever. But he was not certain that they were ready to hear what he was about to say. Not certain either, that he was ready to say it.
"Come walk with me a while," he said.

The two men rose from the fire and walked together around the camp. There was less mud than even a few days ago. The sun was at last showing itself, warming the land, drying the land. They wandered from hut to hut, small islands of light in the blackness of

the night. From the far side of the camp came the soft voice of a mother singing to her baby. A lullaby, it could have been a lament.
"You asked me what it was like," Ranulf said at last. "For an answer I can only say this: imagine your worst nightmare and then multiply it a hundredfold. That is the only way I know how to describe it. Even that does not come close." His voice had thickened with emotion and the Wake thought that Ranulf had finished but there was more to come.
"The ground where we stood was covered in blood. Bodies were piled so high that the Normans had to climb over them to get to us. The slope of the hill was the same, a sea of blood, littered with dying men and horses. Time and again we repulsed them, hammering them until our arms were numb and red with their blood, until our backs were breaking, until we thought they had had enough. But still they came on, squadron after squadron of their damned cavalry. They just never gave up. I can see them now, hurling their mounts up that cursed hill until at dusk we broke. It was like a flood when it came, a flood…"
Hereward saw that he was close to tears.
"I'm sorry," he said. "I shouldn't have raised it."
"It's alright; you needed to know."
"Yes."
The two men walked back to the fire, needing its warmth against the chill of the night, the shadow cast over them by Ranulf's tale. On the far side of the camp the lullaby was ending, the last notes of the mother's song dying in the cold night air.
"Can we beat him, Ranulf?" The Wake asked the question that had been uppermost in his mind ever since he had seen the bridge begin to take shape.

Ranulf looked at the earth ramparts surrounding the camp, brooding and silent in the near darkness. Harold Godwineson had asked the same question of him four years ago, before the slaughter on Caldbec Hill. They had deluded themselves then. There was no room for delusion now.

"Not like this," he said. "We are like rats in a trap if we stay here."

"What do you suggest then?"

"We should take the fight to him."

"I agree, but we haven't the men to test him on the field of battle."

Ranulf looked at the faces gathered around the fire: Wynter and Lightfoot deep in conversation, the Heron staring silently into the flames; they were hardly aware of his presence.

"These men know the fens like no Norman ever can," he said. "We cannot hope to defeat the Bastard by sitting here but we can take the fight to him. Your archers are second to none...I have seen them for myself. Hit and run, that is the only way. If we can frustrate him for long enough he may tire of the campaign and sue for peace. That, I think, is our one hope; that, and pray for winter."

The Wake noted Ranulf's use of the Conqueror's old title: *The Bastard.* It suited him better, he decided. Bastard by name and bastard by nature. He would use it in future. And he agreed with Ranulf about something else: his men did know the fens like the backs of their hands, and his archers were good; they were bloody good. Better than any Norman with their cumbersome crossbows. His men could loose six arrows by the time a Norman had rewound the clumsy ratchet mechanism that primed their crossbows. He had been thinking along these lines for the last three days and now, it seemed, the housecarl had read his mind.

"I agree," he said. " I have been contemplating precisely that myself. We shall make a start in the morning; hopefully surprise the bastards again."

He suddenly felt weary. His bed awaited and he was about to rise from the fire when a slim figure appeared from out of the gloom, walking slowly toward them. It was the housecarl's woman, Alice. In the few days since their arrival the strain had gradually

lifted from her face and now, washed and wearing a fresh shift, she seemed to be somehow changed. In the glow of the flames she appeared to him almost radiant, as though touched by a divine spirit. He made room for her by the fire and she cuddled up to the housecarl, draping her shawl around them both. Her eyes sparkled in the firelight, adding to the impression she had already made and he realised, after a few moments, that he had been staring at her.
"Have some food," he said quickly, and offered her a piece of eel, plucking it from the flames with his scaramax. She smiled and thanked him, picking it from the point of his knife with long, tapered fingers. He noticed her small, perfect white teeth as she carefully chewed on the meat. His gaze passed from her to the housecarl who, like himself, was staring into her face. For a moment he felt like an outsider and to break the silence he spoke across the flames to Wynter and the others.
"We make an early start in the morning," he said. "I have a plan that may cause our Norman friends a few difficulties. I want every quiver full and every bow tested before we depart." He clapped Ranulf on the shoulders and rose from the fire.
"My bed beckons," he said. "Sleep well."
"Sleep well yourself."

He wandered back to his hut. The children were quiet now, asleep perhaps. The dog too, no longer barked. The camp was settling down for the night. His hut, when he reached it, was silent and cocooned in darkness. He lifted the flap and went inside. He saw that Torfrida was already asleep, her familiar frame curled up in the far corner, a rough blanket thrown loosely over her. He quickly undressed in the darkness and lay naked on his cot. After some time spent listening to the sounds of the night he fell into a shallow, fitful, sleep. Eventually he dreamed…

Chapter Ten

Alain De Bernay cursed under his breath. The sun beat down from a late May sky and as he hammered yet another pile into the bottomless marsh sweat poured from his naked torso. His hands were blistered and his back screamed with pain, and as the Captain who had replaced him bellowed his orders from the relative comfort of the causeway he silently cursed those responsible for his present predicament. And above all he cursed William Fitz Osbern. Fitz Osbern, who had made him Captain, who had given him the task of rounding up the renegades, and who, at the last, had deserted him. He would not forget Fitz Osbern, or any of the other bastards that had brought him to the position in which he now found himself; chest deep in thick, glutinous mud, building a causeway for the pittance that was the regular soldiers pay.

"Put your backs into it!" Captain de Guise, his immediate replacement, bellowed dissatisfaction with the work party's progress. De Bernay ignored him. He would work as hard as any man when it was for his own benefit but he was damned if he was going to allow de Guise the satisfaction of claiming the credit for building the causeway when the fat bastard hadn't yet lifted a finger to help. He shot a glance upward, from his lowly position in the mud, and envied de Guise his elevation to Captain. There he stood, hands on hips like some bloody overseer glaring down at the poor wretches labouring in the mud. *Le Couteau* fingered the knife at his belt. Like the rest of him it was covered in mud. It was his prized possession and he felt something approaching guilt as he thought about the state that it was now in, his beautiful weapon, but he was not about to be parted from it, no matter how dirty it got. But he was angry nevertheless. He glanced upwards again, to where de Guise was bellowing down his orders and imagined sliding the blade into the fat bastards belly and then twisting it, so that it drew out his entrails slowly, painfully, to screams of agony and cries for mercy. If the chance arose...

"Give us a hand." One of his new comrades, if they could be called such, was struggling with yet another pile. De Bernay saw that the man's hands were raw and bleeding from handling the rough-hewn timber as he struggled to manoeuvre it into position. De Bernay reluctantly took the weight and the soldier – he didn't yet know his name – manhandled it upright before plunging it end first into the oozing black mud. De Bernay held it in position while the man hammered it deep into the marsh with his mallet. Deeper and deeper it went until it disappeared completely beneath the quagmire. The mud closed over it as though it no longer existed.

"Not long enough," the man said. He shook his head in wonder and looked at Captain de Guise.

"We need some longer piles Sir," he said. "The mud's too deep at this point. No bottom to it."

"No bottom to it? What do you mean?" De Guise bellowed down at the man.

"He means, *Sir,* that the swamp's too deep. The timber isn't long enough. I should have thought it was obvious." De Bernay could not resist the barb. De Guise switched his glare from the soldier to himself.

"Shut your bloody mouth. When I want your opinion I'll ask for it." De Bernay shrugged, a touch of insouciance, and de Guise ignored him.

"These are the longest we have," he said. "I'll have to go and report."
"Take as long as you want," De Bernay whispered beneath his breath, "our relief is due in an hour." The words were just loud enough for the other men to hear. They laughed, and *Le Couteau* allowed himself a smile. It was a start. He had formed a plan, but he needed the help of others to execute it. Ivo Taillebois, Lord of the Bourne Estates had that morning issued a reward of one hundred silver pennies for the capture of the Wake. His capture; or his head. And *Le Couteau* intended to claim it. For one hundred pieces of silver Taillebois could have both the Wake and the housecarl. He had unfinished business with both of them but even his formidable talents could not deliver their heads without help. He needed these men. Ultimately of course they would be expendable but they need not know that.
"Good to meet you lads," he said. "I am Alain de Bernay, but you may know me as *Le Couteau.*"

Dawn's grey light saw the Saxon war party descend once more into the Aldreth fens, closely following the carefully marked spine of land that they had struggled to locate on their last venture south. As before The Heron had taken the lead, unerringly guiding them through the treacherous meres and shifting reeds until mid-morning saw them reach the north bank of the Great River Ouse.
"This shall be our first line of defence," The Wake whispered to Wynter and Ranulf as they hugged the riverbank, careful to avoid detection. "And, when the time comes, we shall hold them at Aldreth. The advantages are all ours. We must not fail."
"We won't fail." Ranulf narrowed his eyes and peered into the middle distance to where the Norman army were busy at work. They were much closer now, the causeway stretching out across the

treacherous fens to within three hundred yards of where they lay, hidden in the reeds on the banks of the river. Ranulf estimated that the Norman army had already constructed well over five hundred yards of timber to reach the point where they now laboured. It was a phenomenal achievement, even by the Conqueror's standards. They had to stop them, for if they were allowed to continue at their present rate of progress the Norman army would be over the Ouse and reaching out for Aldreth itself within two to three weeks. And it was still early summer.

He narrowed his eyes again and studied them at work. There were so many of them: on the causeway, busy with saw and adze and hammer, constructing the timber planking that rested on the piles. In the far distance men were still cutting down trees for yet more timber and, much closer, labouring in the mud, an army of men were engaged in a task that he could not quite determine. Certainly they were no longer piling, and they seemed to be putting together bundles of something that looked like sticks or faggots, but whatever they were doing the thought did not trouble him. Within a few minutes, if everything went to plan, they would be dead.

He allowed his eyes to roam over the men working on the causeway and not seeing the figure that he was searching for amongst them he switched his gaze to the lesser individuals labouring in the mud. He could not see de Bernay amongst any of the work parties and he felt a tinge of regret. He felt drawn to the man as the moth is drawn to the flame. He knew his feelings for what they were, and recognised the danger inherent in them, but there was an inevitability to it that could not be avoided. They would meet again, but when, and where, he could not be certain. But his feelings persisted, and he determined not to fight them. Destiny would take a hand, and when it did, he would be ready.

Last night he had put *Requitur* to the grindstone, sharpening the edges until the slightest touch would draw blood. The stiletto too, he had sharpened, but he knew that if it came to a knife fight with *Le Couteau* there would only be one winner. In moments of solitude, out of the sight of Alice, he had practised with the stiletto, switching it quickly from hand to hand as experienced knife fighters do to confuse their opponents, but the practice did not come easily and he knew that given the choice he would prefer to face *Le Couteau* with *Requitur* in his hand. He shrugged inwardly. Whatever came to pass he would have to be ready and destiny would decide the outcome. And he was certain that destiny *was* guiding his conflict with de Bernay for if his boast was to be believed, it was de Bernay that had mutilated his King. He had sworn revenge that dreadful night four years ago on *Senlac* Hill, and now, it seemed, destiny had shown him how revenge might be achieved. When the time came he would be ready and *Le Couteau* had better look to his laurels…
"We should be moving off." The Wake's voice cut across his thoughts, bringing him back to the present. No de Bernay, but there was a whole army to fight and the sooner they started the better.

There were twenty men in the war party, the best archers amongst them, and now they brought up the light, basket shaped coracles that would ferry them across the Ouse, two men to each craft. They would divide into two groups of ten, one taking the right flank, the other the left. The Wake would take the right with Wynter, Lightfoot, Hurchillus, Villicus and five others from the volunteer army, chosen for their ability with the bow. The second party, Ranulf, the Heron, Alsinus, Osbernus, Lefwinus and five more, all equally skilled, all equally determined, would take the left. And between them would be the Norman army, caught in their crossfire. They could not possibly kill them all, there were too many, but they could halt their progress. That at least, was the plan, and now they must try to execute it.

They had agreed that Hereward should lead off and now his small party, their oars muffled to prevent any sound, slowly headed out into the river. As they reached the far bank the Wake signalled that Ranulf's party should also cross and Ranulf, sharing one of the flimsy craft with the Heron, carefully paddled across the river. It was a still, calm day and the heavy waters of the Ouse hardly made a ripple. He glanced behind; the rest of his party were following him and within minutes they had all made the far bank.

The Wake now signalled Ranulf's party to break off to the left while his own party moved to the right. The swamp was so deep beyond the banks of the Ouse that they continued to use their coracles. The flimsy craft would not be a firm base from which to loose their storm of arrows but would at least allow them the opportunity to retreat into the reeds should the Normans attempt a counter attack.

The causeway was being patrolled by crossbowmen, lookouts whose task it was to guard against the very attack that the Saxons had in mind. The plan was to kill the crossbowmen first and then to finish the others before any defence could be organised. It would require careful timing and Hereward had agreed a series of birdcalls with the Heron; sounds that they could both make, and recognise, when the time came.

Ranulf's party moved off through the reeds, keeping low, keeping quiet, until they were within arrow shot of the causeway. The distance was barely fifty yards. And now they halted, hearts pounding, paddles stowed, waiting for the Wake to launch his attack. A kingfisher dived into the water beside them and emerged moments later with a fish caught in its beak. Silver scales flashed in the sunlight, the fish struggling for freedom, and for a moment

Ranulf thought the activity must attract the attention of the Normans but a glance showed him that they had seen nothing.

A crane called its raucous cry far to their right and the Heron now touched Ranulf's shoulder.

"That's the signal," he said. "Make ready." Ranulf looked around. The rest of the party were already stringing their bows, Osbernus and Alsinus carefully selecting their arrows for this first, vital, confrontation.

Suddenly the calm of the morning was shattered by the hiss of arrows; the Wake had launched his attack. Ranulf cried to his men to loose their own and now the air was full of arrows, from right and left, as the Saxons began their murderous assault. On the causeway men were running frantically backwards and forwards, unsure of where the attack was coming from, unsure of what to do. Orders were screamed but largely ignored; men were more concerned with saving themselves, of avoiding the arrow storm, than fighting back.

Some men ran back towards the land; others simply leaped into the mud, desperate to escape the driving rain of iron tipped death. Those wearing chain-mail were sucked into the swamp, screaming and shouting for help as the mud pulled them down, struggling for air even as the muddied waters closed over them, silencing their despairing cries. The crossbowmen, taken by surprise, were being slaughtered. Those still on the causeway were hit in the chest, others brought down from behind. There was nowhere to turn, no escape, and their chain-mail was no defence; the iron-tipped arrows pierced the coats of mail as though they did not exist. To the men on the causeway it must have seemed that they were surrounded by phantoms for the arrows seemed to rain down from all directions. From right and left they hissed through the air and now, as the causeway emptied of soldiers, the rain of iron swung onto those wallowing in the mud, directed by an unseen hand. The fens, thick and black, turned crimson with blood.

It had lasted barely five minutes but the carnage caused by the attack was immense. On the causeway and down in the mud the dead and dying lay everywhere. Already carrion crows had begun to gather, anticipating the feast. The cries of the wounded filled the air and the stench of death hung over the fens, sweet, sickly, nauseous.

Eventually quivers began to empty, the storm of arrows to abate and the Normans, organising themselves, began to fight back. A fresh body of crossbowmen were ushered onto the causeway and soon crossbow bolts were banging across the fens and into the reeds. The Saxons were not there. The Wake, realizing that his men were running short of arrows had already signalled the retreat and now, even as crossbow bolts thudded into the empty reed beds, the Saxons were paddling their way across the Ouse and to safety.

From his vantage point on the north bank Hereward looked back at the chaos three hundred yards away. On the causeway, bodies were being cleared away, the dead and the dying alike. And in the bloodstained swamp men still cried for help, their cries of anguish audible even from this distance. At one time, long ago, before the murder of his brother he would have been moved to pity at the deaths of so many men but now he felt nothing. They were the enemy, brutal, uncompromising, determined upon his destruction. Between Saxon and Norman there could be no regrets, or guilt, or pity or mercy.

"A good morning's work I think." He glanced at Wynter, sprawled on the ground beside him, his chest heaving as he fought to get some air into his lungs.

"Eighty men at least, I should say!" Wynter's ruddy complexion was flushed with colour, his deep-set eyes wild with excitement.

"At least that," he heard himself reply. The Wake looked around. Ranulf, The Heron and their party were now clambering up the bank side. Their faces, like Wynter's, were flushed with excitement, the success of the attack. He mentally counted them. *Ten.* Like his party they had all returned safely. It *was* a good morning's work. But it was not the end, only the beginning. Tomorrow they must do it all again, and the day after that. And on and on, carrying the fight to the enemy until winter. *Or death has called for us.* These thoughts he kept to himself, but as he looked around at the familiar faces lit up in triumph he could not help but wonder how many of them would live to see winter. He needed more men. More men, more weapons, more archers. He looked to the heavens, to the sun blazing down from a clear blue sky and offered up a silent invocation.

And two hundred miles away, in the blackened wasteland of Northumbria, his prayer was being answered.

Chapter Eleven
Northumbria

The shallow grave lay in the shade of an ancient willow tree. Its tendrils hung low, caressing the soil with gentle fingers whilst the wooden cross, planted at its head, remained in the glare of the midday sun for all to see. A rough carving into its surface announced, almost as an apology, the name of the man that now occupied his allotted six feet of earth.

Edwin, former Earl of Mercia, was dead. Before the Conquest one of the most powerful men in England, his vast Earldom stretched across the heart of the Country from Wales to East Anglia. But now, at just twenty-seven his mutilated corpse occupied a mere six feet of soil under a willow tree, a hastily dug grave the final resting place for a man betrayed.

Earl Morcar stood impassively over his brother's grave, his head bowed in a respectful silence observed by the men of his hearth-troop. For five minutes he had stood like this, stock-still in the heat of the sun, head bowed in prayer as he remembered his brother as he would have wished to be remembered; proud, full of the strength and impulsiveness of youth, immortal. They had fought together at Fulford Gate and survived. A miracle perhaps when so many had died and perhaps it would have been better if they had also died. Too late to play any part in the slaughter on *Senlac* Hill, they had sworn a reluctant oath of allegiance to the Norman King. Little good it had done them. Dispossessed of their Earldoms they had bowed to one inequity, one insult, after another until they could take no more. The rebellion in the fens had been the catalyst that had decided them. They would make one last stand with their uncle Hereward, a desperate gamble perhaps, but they were desperate men with little to lose, save their lives, and now Edwin had lost his.

Morcar picked up a handful of soil and threw it onto his brothers' grave. Outwardly calm, his heart was full of hurt and burning anger. His brother should not have died like this, on a lonely road, hacked down by his own men, frightened men that had been reluctant from the first to follow him. The Conqueror cast a long shadow in this land, longer perhaps than either of them had realised, and Edwin's men had been in fear of it. Fear had turned to plotting and plotting to murder and so his brother had died, his body left to rot, and his men returned to their homes.

And to what? They would be safe enough for the moment, perhaps forever, but their lives would be ruled by fear and poverty, a miserable existence under the heel of their Norman overlords until the day that they died. In this land, he reflected, death was the only victor. And so he would offer himself to her. Like his brother, like Harold, the last true King, like his comrades at Fulford Gate and Stamford Bridge and *Senlac* Hill. He would be like them, die like them, for what was the measure of a man save the life that he led? His brother was dead but *he* still lived, and if his brother was watching he knew that he would approve.

He took a last look at Edwin's grave, whispered a prayer, and turned towards his stallion.

"I go to join my uncle," he said to the men gathered around him, their faces averted out of respect. "Follow me if you wish. If not, go home. I don't care." He gathered up the reins and leaped into the saddle. He had gone twenty yards before he looked back and saw that they were following him, a cloud of dust kicked up behind them as they swung along the road in his wake. A lump rose in his throat. Not one man had gone home, not one. He sawed on the reins and the stallion slowed. He waited for them to reach him.

Chapter Twelve
The Fens

The Normans had stopped piling. As the causeway took shape, reaching to within fifty yards of the Ouse they found the swamp too deep, the piles not long enough to hold in the bottomless mire. Now they were having to build a floating causeway, the timbers resting upon faggots of sticks and twigs, countless bundles of them, tied one to the other, the whole floating mass held together with mile upon mile of rope.

The men building the causeway were protected from the Saxons' attacks by wicker fascines, twelve feet high, erected around the head of the causeway and behind which the army toiled day after day to complete their task.

Even these precautions had not prevented the Saxons from taking a toll. For two weeks, as May turned to June and the causeway grew ever longer, the Wake's attacks stained the fens red with Norman blood. But these attacks only served to increase the Conqueror's determination. For every Norman killed two more appeared to take his place. Where before a thousand men laboured on the causeway now there were three thousand. Three thousand men, cursing and sweating and dying in the English fens, their one aim the defeat of the Wake. And then, one hot afternoon in the middle of June they reached the Ouse.

On the north bank the Wake mustered every man that could draw a bowstring and for three hours until their quivers began to empty and their arms and fingers screamed with pain they poured a withering fire upon the Norman army as they attempted to force the crossing. Boats were launched, each boat carrying a dozen men, their kite shaped shields held before them for protection against the arrow storm but the Saxons fired their arrows high into the clear blue sky to rain down on the men in the boats like hail. There was no escape. Most of the boats capsized as panic stricken soldiers dived over the sides to drown in the Ouse, their coats of mail dragging them beneath its muddy waters, their cries for help drowned out by the screams of agony from those still trapped in the boats. In some cases the boats managed to turn back to the south bank, laden with their cargoes of dead and wounded. The Conqueror, beside himself with anger, berated them for cowards and ordered them back again.

And so it went on. Assault after assault was launched across the Ouse, only to be repelled by the Saxon archers, determined to hold their ground. Afternoon turned to dusk and the waters of the Ouse ran red with blood. The Conqueror called more men forward, hundreds of them, to join in the assault and eventually, after hours of endeavour, he succeeded. A tenuous foothold was established on the far bank. The threat could not be ignored and the Wake was forced to withdraw. As he retired into the reed beds beyond the north bank his men came under fire from the Norman crossbowmen, able, at last, to retaliate. Seventeen Saxons fell in that retreat and Hereward was forced to leave them to their fate, the dead and the wounded alike. They could expect little mercy from the Conqueror.

And now, as the end of June beckoned and the sun continued to shine in a bright blue sky the Conqueror spanned the Ouse with a bridge and his engineers began to negotiate the last half-mile between the river and the tiny village of Aldreth, the Saxons' last line of defence.

Alain de Bernay picked his way amongst the rows of wounded men. Belsar's Hill had been set up as a temporary dressing station for the care of the injured and the ancient Iron Age fort stank of blood and faeces. The stench filled his nostrils but he ignored it, just as he ignored the moans of pain and pleas for help as he studied each face in turn before moving on to the next man. A medic turned away from dressing a wound to look at him, his harassed expression the prelude to a question that had been asked twenty times that morning:
"Who are you looking for?"
"Captain de Guise."
"Over there, under the tree." The medic pointed to the oak tree that the mare had once been tethered to; the mare upon which de Bernay had made his escape and left Bonchamp to his fate. It was not Bonchamp, but a different Captain that had brought him back to this place of death and now he made his way to where de Guise lay injured in the shade of the tree, his head and left leg roughly bandaged, his right arm strapped to his chest. Dried blood, dark and crusted, showed through the bandages on arm and leg; arrow wounds taken in the assault over the Ouse. De Guise was asleep, or unconscious, his chest rising and falling with every shallow breath. Beads of sweat covered his face beneath the bandage even though the sun could not reach him in the position in which he had been laid out, his head shaded by the trunk, his torso stretched out at its foot.

De Bernay reached out and shook him, not roughly, but enough to wake him, if he were sleeping. De Guise made no response, the only tangible sign of change being a hesitation in the pattern of breathing before it resumed its regular flow. The ebb and flow of life; how fragile it was. Every man clung to life while he could but willpower was no defence against an iron-tipped arrow ripping through flesh and de Guise had taken two, leading an attack on the north bank. He had been knocked backwards, smashing his head against the prow of the assault craft before someone had hauled him back on board and to safety.

De Bernay studied the bandages, the impregnations of blood. Neither of the wounds appeared to be fatal, but de Guise had lost a lot of blood and it would surprise no one if he were to die of them. It happened all the time in this charnel house called the fens.

He looked around; at the men either side of de Guise; sleeping, or dying. At the medic, engrossed in cares of his own, his arms bloodied to the elbow as he fought to save another life, another poor bastard on the conveyor belt of death.

He reached inside his doublet and pulled out his knife. The Toledo steel shone like silver. De Bernay had spent all night polishing it, honing the edge. Once again it was a thing of beauty, his passage to immortality. He had a plan for the capture of the Wake, or preferably his death, and with it the collection of Taillebois' reward. But de Guise stood in the way; while he lived.

De Bernay looked around again, casually so as not to attract attention. No one was watching him. Why should they? A friend come to visit a comrade. He took hold of the bandage around the leg and gently tried to work it loose. It was not easy. The bandage had adhered to the congealed blood and de Bernay was worried that if he pulled too hard de Guise would regain consciousness. He abandoned the attempt to massage the bandage free and now resorted to his knife. *Le Couteau* deftly cut the bandage over the site of the wound, the knife slicing through the congealed linen as though it were not there. With his left hand he gently probed for the entry wound until he found it with his forefinger. De Guise stirred, his lips moving as if in protest and *Le Couteau* withdrew the finger, leaving the wound exposed. His heart, usually so calm, beat like a hammer until he was sure that de Guise had slipped back into unconsciousness. He looked around again. He knew that he must be careful, that if anyone suspected what he was doing it would mean the rope and an eight-foot drop. And de Guise was not worth that, the fat bastard.

He inserted the knife into the wound. His study of anatomy told him that the arrow had just missed the femoral artery. But who could say whether or not it had been punctured, a tiny nick that no one had noticed until de Guise had bled his life away? It happened all the time. Medicine was an uncertain art.

He probed the wound, gently until he found what he was looking for. The slightest turn of the wrist, almost a caress, and it was done. He withdrew the knife and saw that the tip was reddened with fresh blood. He looked at the lesion. It was beginning to fill, but it would be several minutes before anyone realised what was wrong and by then it would be too late. He rearranged the bandages to disguise their disturbance and rose to his feet. It struck him that the way de Guise had been laid out, his head to the tree, that he could have been a corpse, laid out to rest. He laughed under his breath. Soon the fat bastard would rest for eternity. And *Le Couteau* would achieve immortality.

Chapter Thirteen

The Heron narrowed his grey eyes against a setting sun as it sunk beneath the horizon. It had been a glorious day and he had spent it doing what he loved best: scouting his beloved fens for allies and for some sign of the enemy. He was alone, save for the housecarl, their latest and most welcome recruit.

The two men had set off together at dawn and he had headed west, leading Ranulf through the villages of Wentworth and Sutton with their fishermen's nets drying in the early morning sunshine, the coracles pulled onto the mud ready for the start of the new day. The Heron had once been a fisherman himself but all that had changed when he had rescued four men from a hanging at Wroxham Bridge. Then he had become an outlaw, seeking refuge with the Wake, his knowledge of the fens of incalculable value. Who else could cross the Aldreth swamp without a boat or a causeway? He smiled to himself as he thought about the thousands of Normans labouring on the Causeway this very minute. If only the Conqueror knew. He would have a fit.

He turned his angular face to the housecarl, who, like himself was laid flat to the ground, searching the empty horizon for some sign of life.

"See anything?"

"No." The housecarl shook his head, confirming the Heron's own impression. The watery landscape, bathed in an orange glow, slid away from where they lay towards a river, sparkling in the late evening sunshine, a half-mile distant. The Heron scanned the horizon again, shading his eyes against the glow of the sun that had all but disappeared. The fens were empty, save for a V of geese, silhouetted against an amber sky.

He didn't really expect to see anyone; access to the Isle of Ely from the west was nigh but impossible, unless it was by boat. But they had to maintain a permanent watch, just in case. He inclined his face towards the housecarl, who, like himself was bare headed. It would not do for the sun to catch a helmet or weapon and betray their position…

The Heron noted with satisfaction that Ranulf wore his sword in a full-length scabbard rather than a simple loop on his belt, which would have exposed the steel of the blade to the sun. And he had discarded his useless chain-mail, preferring instead to wear a simple padded jerkin. He was learning fast. The fens were not an easy place for an outsider to adjust to but the housecarl seemed to have found an inner peace in the few weeks that he had been with them. And with it had come a thirst for knowledge of the fens that had persuaded the Heron to allow Ranulf accompany him today. He did not know him well as yet, but he found himself instinctively liking him, his straightforward manner, his willingness to learn. And he trusted him, trusted his judgement. After all the housecarl had seen things that the rest of them could only guess at. What had brought him to the fens for yet more butchery he could not imagine. He had his reasons, no doubt.

"We should be getting back. It will be soon be dusk," he said. He studied the horizon for the hundredth time. The sun had now sunk below the land and the sky was tinged with magenta. A cock pheasant, seeking shelter for the night suddenly rose into the sky, followed by six more, the beat of their wings making the two men turn toward the sound. The pheasants were heading west, towards a stand of trees on the banks of the distant river. It was nothing unusual and the men were about to leave when a second sound stopped them in their tracks. It was not the beat of wings, the call of the wild, that caused them to halt, but a sound that was entirely man made. It was an arrow, launched from a bow. And it was well aimed. The arrow, fired from the west, took the pheasant through the chest and the two men instinctively threw themselves to the ground as they watched the bird plummet to the ground like a stone not twenty yards from where they had been standing.

"We were wrong my friend!" the Heron hissed through pursed lips. "There is someone here after all! Stay down, he may not have spotted us."

"Whoever it is he can bloody well shoot."

"Aye," the Heron nodded his agreement. "Hurchillus would have been proud of that."

"Look!" Ranulf exclaimed beneath his breath. A coracle had cleared a bed of reeds and two men were paddling hard to where the pheasant had fallen, a bow slung over the shoulder of the man in the rear of the tiny craft. They looked like Saxons but who they were Ranulf could not tell.

"I am going to take a closer look," he said. "Coming?" He raised an eyebrow and the Heron smiled.

"After you, my friend."

The two men crept forward in single file, clinging to the cover of the reeds. Ranulf saw that the men in the coracle had temporarily lost sight of the pheasant for they were circling the area but without success. He crept forward again, his jerkin and breeches soaked to the skin, but he was oblivious to this. It was a common occurrence in the wetland of the fens.

And then he saw the pheasant, impaled by the arrow, nestling against a stand of bulrushes. And as he crawled closer a smile slowly creased his face. For what he saw was something he had seen before but never expected to see again. The goose feathers on

the arrow protruding from the bird's breast had a familiar marking, a marking that told him they had finally found what they had been searching for.
"What is it?" The Heron whispered, his voice tight with anticipation.
"It's Morcar," Ranulf said quietly. "By God, it's Morcar."

Morcar was much changed since Ranulf had first seen him four years ago. That had been at York, in the Great Council Chamber reserved for matters of State. King Harold had used it as a feasting hall to celebrate his victory over Hardraada at Stamford Bridge, oblivious of the titanic events that would shake his Kingdom until it crumbled. He had celebrated in style, placing Morcar on his right hand side, a mark of honour and approval for the young Earl of Northumbria. Ranulf could still recall the young man, almost a boy, that he had seen on that first occasion. He could not have been more than twenty years old then, an innocent youth with his life before him. So he had thought. So they had all thought. But that was before William the Bastard had landed at Pevensey and changed things forever.

At twenty-four Morcar had put on weight and his face was flaccid and pale, the result, Ranulf suspected, of heavy drinking. But the changes were not just physical. Now, in place of innocence he carried an aura of world-weary cynicism around his shoulders, the result of four years subservience to William the Bastard. But for all that Ranulf could sense that a fire still burned in his belly. What fuelled it he did not know; it could have been one of a number of reasons, or perhaps the sum of them. It did not matter. Each man had his reasons for being here, himself no less than Morcar. It was enough that Morcar had come to fight; for his uncle, for his freedom.

They sat around a hastily built fire on the west bank of the river: Ranulf, the Heron, Morcar, and three of his men. The smell of roasting pheasant was strong in their nostrils and a full moon shone brightly in a star-filled sky. It was a beautiful night but the men were silent as they chewed the meat and pondered their problem, a problem to which, as yet, they had no solution: How to get an army onto Eel island? Easily put, but a solution was hard to find.

Ranulf studied Morcar from across the fire, his cloak wrapped tightly around his shoulders, his dark eyes dancing in the orange glow of the flames. He seemed unaware of Ranulf's scrutiny, unaware of anything as he stared into the flames, lost in thoughts of his own, of the problem at hand perhaps, or of his late brother, whose death must have been a shock to him.

"How many men do you have?" he asked, shaking Morcar from his reverie. Morcar raised his face, reddened by the heat of the fire, to answer him and Ranulf noted again the weariness about the eyes, as though he had not slept for weeks.

"Two hundred, more or less. Why?"

"I was thinking," Ranulf said, "of those fishing villages we passed through this morning." He turned to the Heron seated beside him. "What were they called? Sutton and…what was that other one?" The Heron provided the answer.

"Wentworth. What of it?"

"They had coracles, pulled onto the mud. Dozens of them." A smile creased the Heron's face as understanding dawned.

"And you're thinking we could use them?"

"Why not? It may take some time, but if we run a line across with the first one, we could use that as a type of pulley; haul on the rope instead of using paddles. It will be much quicker, much less effort." The Heron laughed and slapped Ranulf on the back.

"I should have thought of that," he said. "I really should." Ranulf smiled at the compliment and turned back to Morcar.

"It will take an hour or more to fetch the coracles – hopefully the men of the villages will help. But we shall need you to be ready. Those Norman bastards can't be far away." He looked around, as though the Norman army were lurking beyond the arc of light cast by the fire but of course there was nothing. They had posted a guard.

"We shall be ready," Morcar said. "But there's one thing more."

"Yes?"

"My stallion. I can't leave him."

"Your stallion?"

"Over there." Morcar pointed to where an unblemished white stallion was grazing the tough marsh grass. Two men had it on a halter, but the stallion appeared not to mind this. Ranulf noted the way that it would occasionally lift its head from the grass to cast a glance in their direction as though checking on its master before returning to the grazing with a small whinny of disapproval.

"He's magnificent. What's his name?"

"Galahad. I have had him for three years now. I reared him from a foal. I can't leave him. He's all I have." Once, Ranulf knew, Morcar had a quarter of all England but this thought he kept to himself.

"Galahad?" he asked.

"Yes, after Sir Galahad – the knight that sought the Holy Grail, the Cup from which our Saviour drank at the Last Supper. Only the purest knight in Christendom could search for the Grail and Sir Galahad was that knight. My stallion is just like him. Pure blood. Pure Arab."

"Then he must come with you." Ranulf turned to the Heron. "Perhaps we can rig some kind of harness for him?"

"For the purest stallion in Christendom I have no doubt we can arrange something," the Heron said, a twinkle in his eye.

“Although I fear those fishermen’s nets will stink worse than Galahad himself!” The three men laughed.
“We had better be making a move. This will take all night and I would like to be finished by dawn.” Ranulf reluctantly rose from the fire accompanied by the Heron. They had an enormous amount to do before the sun appeared over the eastern horizon. It occurred to him that in the past few hours he had grown in stature: in the esteem of the Heron and in his dealings with Morcar. *Morcar.* Ranulf could sense something of himself in Morcar, his world-weariness, his deep cynicism. But to name his stallion *Galahad?* It spoke of a desire, subconsciously expressed, to reach out for something better, to an age before the world had been ripped apart by William the Bastard and his butchers. Perhaps they were not so different after all. He looked down at Morcar, his eyes lost in the flames, in a private world of his own again. They were both lost spirits, he reflected, both searching for something that perhaps would never be found. He shrugged inwardly. It was pointless to speculate. They were here and he had a job to do. He gave Morcar a final glance before heading into the shadows.
Galahad indeed.

In the event it took all night, and part of the following morning, for Morcar’s men to be brought over to the Isle. The fishermen from the village worked with a will, anxious to help, carrying the coracles on their backs and then paddling them over to the mainland, to where Morcar and his men patiently waited. They had, as Ranulf suggested, been able to sling a line over the mere. Three ropes were tied together, each end secured to a tree, and by this means the weary fishermen were able to haul themselves backwards and forwards, hand over hand with their human cargoes until exhaustion set in. Then Ranulf, the Heron, and some of the others took over, ferrying the men, one by one, until by mid-morning all two hundred had crossed. All, save for Morcar and Galahad. Morcar would not leave him.

They roped three coracles together for stability. They hobbled Galahad's front and rear fetlocks to prevent him smashing the flimsy craft to pieces. They slung a harness, a fishermen's net, under him and secured it to the line. They placed a blindfold over his eyes to prevent him from panicking. Morcar spoke soothing words to him, nuzzled his nose, fed him an apple, almost rotten, but all that he had. And then they set off on the perilous journey across the mere. Morcar never left Galahad's side, never once stopped whispering soft words to him as he stroked his nose, his ears, until they were across. They could have been lovers in a gentle caress. Galahad, finding himself on *terra firma* again, ran wild for five minutes, bucking and kicking, galloping round and round as though to celebrate his freedom before returning, like an obedient dog, to his master. They were just like lovers, Ranulf decided, Morcar and Galahad, and he was suddenly glad for them both. And glad for every man that had come here to fight. For now they had an army. And the Conqueror was coming.

Chapter Fourteen
Aldreth

The air was still and heavy, promising thunder. To the south, dark clouds were building on the horizon, thunderheads that foretold the coming of a storm. There was no birdsong, no noise whatsoever, save the stifled breathing of his men as they made a final check of their weapons, adjusted their bowstrings, smoothed the goose feathers of their flights and offered up a prayer to their maker to watch over them. They stood behind a turf rampart, hurriedly thrown up on the island shore and they gazed south into the distance, searching the horizon for some sign of the human storm that was soon to break over them. The rampart that sheltered them was ten feet high with a hoarding of timber that they would employ to shower the Norman army with arrows and stones when the time came. And that time, Hereward guessed, was just minutes away.

He narrowed his eyes against the glare of the midday sun and looked south again. The causeway was silent and empty. It lay before him, stretching out over the black marsh of the Aldreth fen into the distance, its pale, rough-cut timbers shimmering in the heat of the sun as though it were a sleeping serpent. For days it had been the centre of the Conqueror's attention but for the moment it was devoid of men, devoid of life.

He cast his eyes down to where a floating sow, stitched together from the skins of twenty cattle lay just below the turf ramparts.

Yesterday the engineers working on the causeway had risked life and limb from his archers to manoeuvre the sow, covered with timber and moss for protection, to the head of the causeway and now that floating sow bridged the gap between the Causeway and the island.

The Wake had thought of destroying it, if he could, but had judged it too risky. He dare not venture off his island stronghold for that or for any other reason. The island was his citadel and he needed it, now more than ever. And he could not set fire to the sow for the moss, well watered, was immune to flame. So the floating sow would stay where it was, anchored to the causeway, the last piece in the Conqueror's jigsaw, the final link in the chain between the island and the mainland.

Soon the Conqueror would launch his army along that causeway, half a mile of floating timber, stretching from the Great Ouse to Aldreth itself. What a sight that would be. He narrowed his eyes, straining them, willing them, to see what he wanted to see but his eyes were no longer young and there was nothing, save for the causeway, brooding and silent in the midday sun, and the endless black marsh of the Aldreth fens. This waiting was the worst. His head was sweating beneath his steel helmet, his hair matted to his scalp and his mouth felt as parched as he could ever recall. He reached down to his belt and took a swig of water from the skin carried there. He offered the skin to Wynter, and then to Lightfoot. Like him they were sweating beneath their steel helmets, rivulets of sweat running unchecked down their foreheads as they gazed into the distance and he knew that it was not just from the heat of the sun. The skin, when finally it was returned to him, was almost empty and he gave it to an aide to refill. His checked his dispositions again.

He held the centre of the line, the place where the fighting would be fiercest, with his own men. Wynter, Lightfoot, the Heron, and with them the finest archers in England: Hurchillus, Villicus, Alsinus, Osbernus, Lefwinus and the rest. The Normans would have a bloody fight to overcome them, protected as they were by their earth rampart. On the wings, to right and left, were Morcar's men. God, but he was glad to have them. Two hundred archers, it was a gift from heaven. His nephew was calmly picking his way up and down the lines on his white Arab, offering words of encouragement and advice to his men. When he had last seen him Morcar had been a young man, almost a child, but now, watching him ride calmly backwards and forwards he saw a child no longer but a man…

He heard voices behind him, Ranulf, in conversation with the Heron, pointing to something far to the south. Both men were gazing in the same direction, following Ranulf's outstretched arm, their eyes shaded against the sun. Thunderheads were building rapidly now and the sky was beginning to darken overhead. But it was not this that they were looking at, he felt sure of it.

"Do you think they'll come? I don't think they'll come. Not today." Lightfoot's voice cut across the silence and for the first time in his life Hereward thought that his old friend sounded nervous. He had every right to be.

"They'll come," he said quietly. "The bastards will want to get this over with. They think we're here for the taking." But they didn't know about Morcar and his two hundred men. And that, he reasoned, as he followed the housecarl's outstretched arm, was where the battle could be won.

Sunlight flashed on something far to the south. He strained his eyes to see what it was but could not make it out. Ranulf was pointing again.

"What do you see?" he called across to him.

"Not sure," came the reply, "but there's definitely something. Some movement to the south-west." He heard a noise and when he turned around he saw that Lightfoot had pulled his short-handled axe with its terrible spike out of his belt and that Wynter, too, was drawing his sword from the scabbard strung down his spine. Both men looked to the south, their faces serious, concerned. *So they felt it too*. Strangely the knowledge served to steady his nerves.

"Not long now lads," he said, and somehow he forced a smile. He looked around again. They had done all that they could, were prepared as well as they could ever be. Yet even so it was an uneven fight. He had three hundred men, give or take a few. The Conqueror had three thousand. He felt his palms break out in sweat and he wiped them on his breeches. He pulled his own sword from its scabbard and the metal, cold in his hand, comforted him. It would not be long now. Not long. Bring on the bastards.

A crash of thunder caused him to look up. The sky had suddenly darkened, was full of menacing clouds. They would be fighting in a storm. It would, he thought, be like Armageddon itself, the final conflict between good and evil. *Then let me prevail Lord.* He offered up a prayer.

"Look!" He turned at the cry and saw Ranulf standing stock-still, staring fixedly to the south. The Heron was beside him and both men seemed rooted to the spot, frozen in time as they gazed wide-eyed at the southern horizon.

"Christ preserve us," someone said softly. He looked south again. And this time he saw the movement of men on the distant horizon, countless numbers of them, tiny figures like an army of ants, filling the horizon from east to west. He watched in silence, unable to move as brigade after brigade of infantry swung into view, marching down to the Ouse, kicking up clouds of dust as they did so. Most of them were footmen in padded jackets, the rank and file of the Conqueror's army, but behind them came the knights, the Norman nobility, their chain-mail and helmets dull grey beneath the ever darkening sky. They stretched into the distance as far as he could see, a mass of men and shields and spear points raised to the heavens and pennants and banners growing ever larger, ever closer, this vast army of men hurrying forward as though directed by some unseen hand. He tried to count the different regiments but there were so many. *Perhaps too many.* He felt a lump rise in his throat and he swallowed hard.

"Make ready," he said as calmly as he could. He raised his hand. Behind him came the sound of bows being strung, arrows plucked from quivers, notched to bowstrings. He did not look around. Instead, like Ranulf, he stood stock-still, hand raised, as the Norman army poured down to the Great River Ouse, the banners of each regiment clearly visible now: blue and white and scarlet and gold, and so many other colours and fantastic designs that he could not count them all. He thought of Ranulf, and of how he must have felt before *Senlac* Hill. It must have been something like this. And today he would face it again. God help him then. God help us all. *Amen.*

Thunder crashed across the sky and now he felt the first drops of rain on his face. He looked up and moments later the heavens opened, the rain lashing down to soak his face, his beard, with a cold, driving malevolence. Somehow it seemed to clear his head, to wash away his fear.

He looked again to the front. The Normans were hurrying over the bridge now, a great mass of them, almost a crush so eager were they, so confident of victory. He heard Lightfoot cough, attempting to clear his throat, and turned to him.

"Have courage my friend," he said. "The Lord of Hosts is with us...he must be for I'm damned sure he's not with those bastards." Wynter laughed and Lightfoot rewarded him with a smile. *Better.*

And now the Normans had reached the causeway, hundreds of them, waiting for the signal to advance. The rain was beating down now, sweeping across the fens, hammering off the timbers of the causeway, the floating sow. He smiled a grim smile. The Conqueror would not have wanted this. The slick timbers would make the attackers footing uncertain, would even up the odds. He searched for some sign of the Conqueror himself but could not see him amongst the thousands of men. It did not matter. He guessed he would be there somewhere. *William the Bastard,* as Ranulf called him.

A blast of trumpets rent the air, audible even above the din of the thunder, the hammering rain. The Normans were moving forward again, along the causeway now. Five hundred yards, he estimated.

"Steady lads."

They were advancing in columns of ten, row after row, a solid wall of men behind their kite-shaped shields. He counted back ten rows. *One hundred.* He repeated the exercise three times and then gave up.

Four hundred yards. "Wait." His hand still raised.

He forced himself to look beyond them. There were more men on the causeway now, reaching back to the bridge, and beyond that even more, a great mass of them, waiting their turn. His eyes flicked back to the front rank, to the immediate threat.

Three hundred yards. They had broken into a run; he could hear their boots pounding on the wooden boards. They looked determined beneath their steel helmets, their spear points levelled behind their shields. Determined, but so was he. The rain lashed down, almost blinding him.

Two hundred yards; within bowshot, but still too far. Wynter gave him an anxious glance. He shook his head.

"Not yet." He turned back to his front. They were charging now, desperate to reach the floating sow, their gateway to his island fortress before the arrow storm broke over them. Some, he saw, carried grappling irons to help them scale the ramparts.

One hundred yards. He could see their faces, dark beneath their nasals, flushed with excitement and fear, stung by the driving rain. "For Christ's sake give the Order!" Lightfoot was screaming at him, his nerves shredded, his eyes wild with excitement. He looked to his front, to the wall of infantry tearing towards him, their spear points levelled, their eyes and mouths opened wide, braced for the shock.

Fifty yards. *Wait.*

Forty yards. He counted to five.

He dropped his hand.

"Loose!"

The chapel's altar candles guttered as distant thunder rolled across the sky. The woman kneeling at the altar rail ignored the sound, the flickering candles, as she studied the figure of the crucified Christ. Hanging on the wall, nailed to his Cross high above the altar, he gazed down at her from beneath his circlet of thorns. She noted the bloodstained forehead, the way in which the circlet had been forced onto his head by those determined to humiliate him. The anguish in the eyes was evident too. What he must have been thinking as he hung dying she could not imagine. *Father, why hast thou forsaken me?* Towards the end even his unshakeable faith had been tested. Her mind flew back to Belsar's Hill, to the thoughts that she had harboured moments before seeing the face, blonde and bearded, amongst the parting reeds. She had denied her maker then, before he had liberated her, set her life on a new course. But today it could all end, for three miles to the south the Norman army were approaching, determined upon their destruction, and in her fear, her uncertainty, she had turned to the one person she could think of.

She studied the face again; the pain, the fear, written there. For a moment she imagined that it was Ranulf gazing down at her from the Cross; another tortured soul, but like her he had found a certain peace, a sense of belonging in the wilderness that was the fens. Her eyes travelled along the body to the outstretched arms, to the hands, nailed through the palms to the Cross. What fear, what pain, had he known as the nails were hammered in?

She looked at his torso, painfully thin, the ribs visible beneath the pale flesh. The wound on his left side wept blood; a spear thrust, designed to hasten the end…

Thunder crashed across the sky, louder now, and she crossed herself. A door opened behind her and quickly closed, a gust of wind sweeping the chapel, causing the candles to gutter and smoke. She turned at the sound and saw a priest in the doorway, his thinning hair a silver fringe below the tonsure, his habit wrapped tightly against the elements. He seemed as surprised as herself to find anyone there.

"I am sorry Father, I did not know where else to go. I hoped that I might stay here for a while."

"You are welcome child," the priest said softly, and as he spoke she noticed the left side of his face that was strangely frozen, unmoving, giving his mouth a lop-sided smile. But he had kind eyes, she noticed; kind eyes set in a half-dead face.

"The House of God is open to everyone. It is the battle that brings you here?"

"Yes Father, the battle..."

Hugo Brittanious had been the priest for the Parish of Ely for forty years. It was not much of a Parish, a few hamlets, a few hundred souls. He had seen many things in his lifetime but he had never seen anything to compare with the last four years. His world too, had been torn apart by the Normans. The church had not been immune either.

"Will you take Communion, child?" he asked her suddenly, "Renew your faith in the Lord?"
"Yes Father, I would like that." Somehow he had divined her need. The blare of trumpets, distant but shrill, sounded away to the south and she felt a shiver run down her spine. It would not be long now…The priest too, had heard it, had seen the shadow cross her face.
"I will not be a moment child," he said. He hurried away to prepare himself and Alice returned to studying the figure of Christ. Outside, to the south, the earth would shake to the sound of battle but her world had suddenly been reduced to this; four walls, an altar, her crucified Lord. Her faith.

"The body of Christ." Hugo Brittanious placed the bread on the woman's tongue.
"Amen." She offered the response and swallowed. The priest returned to the altar and picked up the chalice. This too, he offered to the woman, a stranger to him, until today.
"The blood of Christ," he intoned. The candles suddenly flickered again as thunder crashed across the sky, directly overhead now. Outside, rain hammered against the chapel door as though demanding admission.
"Amen." The woman drank from the cup. Hugo Brittanious replaced the chalice on the altar.
"Thank you Father," the woman said quietly. He turned to study her as she knelt at the altar, her face very pale beneath her hood. He could imagine why she was here: The battle; her lover or husband swept up in the terrible events that threatened them all. These were awful times, he reflected, and perhaps it would have been better if the sickness had carried him off. As it was he had been left with feeling in only half of his face and at night, alone in his bed, his

mouth dribbled...He was old and his time was near. He did not care to spend it as he had spent the last four years. But if the Lord still had work for him, who was he to question it?
"I must leave Father," the woman said suddenly, rising from the altar, crossing herself.
"Where are you going, my child?" Rain hammered noisily off the roof of the chapel. The woman wore only a woollen mantle; within moments it would become a rag. He saw the uncertainty in her face before answering.
"My man fights with the Wake...and I have a young child at the camp. I should be with them." He watched as she walked to the door, opening it. Outside the rain swept across the fens, obscuring the land, turning the ground to mud. He saw her hesitate, noted the uncertainty in her footsteps. He moved towards her, placed a hand on her shoulder.
"Your child is being cared for?" he asked. The woman turned at his touch, his voice, nodding her affirmation.
"Then come inside," he said. "If your man fights with the Wake there is little you can do now. I find that there is no comfort, at such times, as the power of prayer. Let us pray together." The woman paused for a moment. Outside the rain beat down with no sign of abating. She closed the door again.

The air hissed with noise, arrows thudded home, fired from close range, and the first ranks went down, felled like corn before the scythe. The sound of battle filled the air; the hiss and thump of the arrows, the crash of thunder across the sky, the hammering of the rain on the timbers, and above it all, rising into the air like the wailing of a banshee, the cries of those cut down.

But they were coming again and the Wake watched this fresh brigade surge forward beneath their lion banners, driven remorselessly on by their Captains, praying to succeed where the first wave had failed. His hand swept down, the air hissed, and they too were met with a withering volley of iron, the storm of arrows smashing them backwards onto the timbers. Down they went, felled by the hailstorm, their tangled and bloodied bodies joining those of their comrades on the Causeway. One Captain, pierced through chest and leg, tried to raise himself to his knees, to urge his comrades forward, but an arrow took him through the neck silencing him forever. The second wave faltered, just like the first, and the pile of bodies grew.

Hereward allowed himself a thin smile as the second wave went down but with no time to pause, to think, he raised his hand again and heard arrows being notched to bowstrings. The third wave was coming, a densely packed mass of men, spear points levelled over their shields, their helmeted heads bent low as though into the wind. He forced himself to wait until they reached the fallen bodies of their comrades and when they slowed, as he knew they would have to, he gave the order again.

"Loose!" His hand sliced down and the air hissed again. Fired low, the arrows thudded into the densely packed mass of men. There was no hiding, no escape. To screams of pain and cries for help the third wave faltered just as the first and second waves had done, unable to make any progress against the storm of arrows sweeping over them.

He cast a quick glance to his left. Already Hurchillus, Villicus and their comrades were notching their bows, and he knew that if they could maintain this rate of fire they would win. No army in the world, not even an army of William the Bastard could march into an arrow storm such as this and survive. But still the Normans were coming on and again he raised his hand to the heavens. He stared into the distance, to the head of the causeway. The Norman army now filled it from end to end, a great unruly mass of men and arms pressing forward, choking it with bodies. He smiled again. They were committing suicide, packing the causeway with so many men, so desperate were they to force the crossing. He checked his line again. They were ready. Arrows had been notched to bowstrings, his archers ready to draw and loose. The Conqueror had forced this battle, had created it by building this causeway, and now he would reap his reward. Ten arrows a minute, an arrow loosed every six seconds; no man could stand against that. Let them come then. Their deaths would be a lasting memorial to his greed, to his folly.

He looked to the heavens. The rain continued to lash down, soaking the corpses of the fallen, spilling their blood over the timbers and into the mud. *Washing away their sins.*

He let the rain soak his own face, reviving him, steeling him for the slaughter still to come. He turned back to the causeway. They were hurrying forward again, an endless stream of footmen and knights, their faces grim, some showing fear: they had seen their comrades' fate. But *he* felt no fear for he knew that his prayers had been heard. Let them come. He was ready, and God was with him. His hand raised, he looked along the line: Ranulf and Wynter, shoulder to shoulder, steely faced, determined; Lightfoot, calmer now that the tide had been halted; and Morcar, still riding his stallion, still speaking calmly to his men. He swung back to the causeway, to the packed ranks pressing forward. He waited, judging the moment. His hand sliced down…

Alain de Bernay watched with dispassionate interest as the first assault was launched across the causeway. At first he thought that they might make it onto the floating sow but as they broke into a charge, storming to within thirty yards of the island, the air suddenly filled with arrows, thick and black, almost as black as the sky above them, and the first wave went down, blown away like chaff in the wind.

And now the second waves were going in, ordered forward by Fitz Osbern, given command of the battle by the Conqueror. From the banks of the Ouse de Bernay had an unobstructed view of the awful scenario as it began to unfold. The Norman army were determined, of that he had no doubt, and they were lead by brave men. Brave men and fools, for only fools would willingly charge into the teeth of that storm. But he could see from where he stood that unless the arrow storm abated they had no chance of breaching the Wake's position. To attack on such a narrow front, barely fifteen feet wide, was suicide. And this thunderstorm was not helping, dampening their spirits, making a difficult task even harder.

He saw the second wave break into a charge, their lion banners fluttering above their heads, spear points levelled over their shields. He watched, fascinated, as the Saxons allowed them to approach within what he guessed was fifty yards and then, just when they thought that they might charge home, the air hissed with noise, turned as black as night and the second wave went down, cut to ribbons like the first.

The King had called the Wake a phantom, but the arrows slaughtering the first and now the second waves of men were real enough. So too the blood that poured from their wounds. And the corpses of those who had already died would testify to that; laid out in rows for the burial parties each morning, those that had not already gone to their graves beneath the stinking black waters of the fens.

The Wake was no phantom; he was the Devil himself. And this land was his domain, his personal Kingdom. For the Norman army it was fast becoming a Hell. On that, at least, he and Fitz Osbern were agreed. *The arsehole of England,* Fitz Osbern had called it, anxious to finish the campaign before the onset of winter. And now his anxiety was slaughtering the army, making him reckless, for even as he watched he saw the third and fourth waves preparing to attack along the causeway. *More meat for the grinder.* And he was buggered if he was going into it.

De Guise had died of his wounds two days ago. He had been told that the surgeons had expressed surprise, but with so many other wounded to care for no one had bothered to investigate. These things happened in a war. So now he was left without a Captain, was answerable to no one; for the moment. And that was precisely what he had intended.

He turned to the men at his shoulder, his new comrades, as they thought of themselves. Rive, Sanglier, Feroux: Three men from the ranks, common footmen. But they could swing a sword, and stop an arrow meant for him. He had earned their trust by ridding them of de Guise, although no one knew how he had done it, and now he was providing them with a means of escaping the butchery a quarter of a mile away. And then there was the reward that he had offered to share with them…

"Lets go," he said, slipping from the bank side into the rain-lashed reeds. The cold hit him like a knife but he ignored it; he was already soaked to the skin.

He waded through the reeds until he found what he was searching for: a canoe, abandoned by the Saxons, that he had discovered whilst labouring on the causeway and had discreetly hidden until the opportunity to use it arose.

The four men lowered themselves into the canoe, de Bernay at the front, and using two paddles that had conveniently been left for their use, they negotiated their way through the windswept reeds, heading east, away from the battle, the slaughter on the causeway. After ten minutes of hard paddling the noise of the battle began to recede and they changed direction, heading north, towards the island…

The third wave faltered, stopped in their tracks by the wall of iron-tipped death, just as the earlier ones had been. But now a handful of men, desperate men driven beyond reason by the madness of the battle somehow raised themselves from the slick timbers and carrying their shields before them succeeded in reaching the sow. Arrows peppered them from right and left as the Saxon archers attempted to dislodge them but they managed to cling on to their twenty feet of floating hide, a foothold at last.

Seeing their comrades success the fourth wave came on even more strongly, tearing in towards the ramparts, ignoring the rain, their heads lowered, their spears couched, shields held high against the arrow storm that they knew would be coming. A yell of triumph erupted from their lips for at last they sensed a glimmer of hope, that the tide of battle was turning, the arrow storm abating.

Fitz Osbern heard the yell and rode forward over the river to see what was happening. Something had occurred, of that he was certain; some change in the tide of the battle to give his men new heart. He looked along the causeway. It was packed with men, all of them pressing forward beneath their banners with new determination.

"What is it!" he called to Captain D'Evreville. He had to shout to make himself heard above the din.

"Some men have reached the sow!" D'Evreville called back. "The Saxons are breaking!"

"Breaking? Are you sure?"

"Yes Lord, I am certain of it. See how our men press forward!"

Fitz Osbern stared along the causeway. The army were pressing forward with new vigour but from this distance it was impossible to tell with certainty what was happening. He hesitated. Battles were uncertain things. The difference between winning and losing could often be as simple as the toss of the dice. Sometimes it was those that made the least mistakes that won. The Conqueror was a brilliant battle commander as he had demonstrated time after time since *Senlac* Hill, but he had handed command of this battle to him. A revolt had erupted in Flanders and the King seemed more concerned with that than finishing off the Wake. So it was up to him; success or failure rested upon his shoulders. *But if he got it wrong?* He stared along the causeway again. If only he knew what was happening. Should he commit the reserves? Or not? The men were still pressing forward, but the cry of battle could plainly be heard in the distance; the Saxons had clearly not yet broken, despite D'Evreville's optimism. He shook his head uncertainly. He was damned if he did and damned if he didn't. But better, perhaps, to be condemned for courage than for cowardice. He called across to D'Evreville:

"You're right, I believe. Send in the reserves. Now."

He hoped to God he was right. He watched the reserves move forward, the knights in their chain-mail, confident, proud. If anyone could finish the Wake they could. He turned his stallion around and trotted back over the bridge.

The Wake knew that the crisis of the battle had arrived. There was always one moment, one event, that would dictate the outcome of the day and as he watched the Normans fight their way onto the floating sow he knew that this was it. He had to dislodge them, for if he failed to do that they would gain a foothold from which to launch their final, and perhaps, fatal, attack upon his position.

Already he could see them preparing their grappling irons, unravelling the long coils of rope ready to swing the barbed hooks up onto the ramparts, the assault upon which all would depend. Behind them, on the causeway, the fourth wave were coming on like madmen, scenting victory, their eyes wild behind their *nasals*.

His hand swept down and as before a hail of arrows thudded into the ranks of the enemy, some taken upon their shields, others finding the gaps, piercing flesh, but even as the arrows hissed overhead he could tell that his archers were tiring; that, or they were running out of arrows. The fourth wave went down like the others had done, but within seconds many of the men in its ranks were rising from the timbers to charge in again, leaping onto the sow to join their comrades. He tried to count them. There were at least twenty he reckoned, hidden behind their kite-shaped shields whilst they prepared for the assault. The sow could not hold many more. But twenty men storming the ramparts would take some holding, especially when there was always one more to take their place. And there were plenty of those. The causeway was packed with men from end to end, a great crush of men pressing forward, his defeat their only object.

He looked along the causeway again, wondering what to do when he saw something that he had not seen before. The causeway was lower in the water now; definitely lower; the weight of the thousands of men pressing upon it was causing it to sink. Already some of the Normans were ankle deep in water but so determined were they to press forward that they had not noticed. Only the sow, anchored to the causeway, prevented it from sinking entirely. He studied the sow, the enemy preparing themselves for the assault, and in that instant knew what he must do.

He turned to the men at his side: Wynter, Ranulf, eyes blazing with hatred beneath his steel helmet, Lightfoot, the Heron, as animated as he had ever seen him.

"We must clear the bastards off there," he said as calmly as he could, "and then we must cut loose the sow. It will be desperate

work but I think we have no choice." He glanced at their faces, gauging their reaction. "Who is with me?"
"Count me in," Wynter growled. "I speak for us all." He looked around. There was no demur from the others.
"Well then, that's settled." Hereward looked at the twins: Hurchillus, Villicus, the rest of his archers.
"Cover us," he said. Hurchillus nodded.
He turned to the men gathered about him:
"I may not have a chance to say this later and so I shall say it now: never has a man had such friends as you." He studied their faces, one by one. "Thank you," he said. "Thank you, my friends."
"Thank us afterwards." Ranulf spoke now, his eyes locked balefully upon the sow, upon the Normans busily preparing for the assault. "Lets get to work."

The Wake watched him pull *Requitur* from its scabbard and casually leap over the rampart as though it were nothing. He landed heavily, ten feet below, his feet sliding on the wet surface. Moments earlier he had been standing with them. It was astonishing, the housecarls' courage, his *anger*. He was paralysed for an instant, unable to move, and then, as if in a dream, he was climbing onto the rampart and flinging himself over the side, following Ranulf onto the sow, his sword gripped tightly in his fist. "A Wake! A Wake!" he cried, stomach in mouth, his legs whirling in mid-air, his arms flailing wildly until he was landing on the sow, the breath forced from his lungs by the impact. He struggled to his feet, saw Ranulf turn at the sound and smile a rare smile before his attention was dragged back to the enemy. *Like brothers*, he thought. *We are just like brothers*. The thought flashed through his mind and then it was gone as three Normans came to meet him, their spears levelled, eyes wild with excitement. He heard a noise beside him and from the corner of his eye saw that Wynter and Lightfoot were here now, and the Heron, just landing. He smiled a grim smile even as the first of the Normans came at him, his dark eyes flashing as he manoeuvred for an opening. Hereward smashed him backwards with a scything blow that sent him tumbling from the sow into the swamp. *My little band of brothers.* The odds were not good, but if these men of his could not succeed no one could. Arrows whistled down, Hurchillus giving him the promised cover. He saw the remaining two Normans hit in the chest, thrown backwards in a spray of blood. But others were coming to take their place, eager to claim his death. He hurried forward to meet them…

"In Nomine Patris, et Filii, et Spiritus Sancti...Amen." The priest blessed her, closing his psalter, and Alice, head still bowed, made the sign of the Cross.

"Thank you Father," she said, rising from the altar. She lowered her hood and listened for the sound of the rain drumming on the roof but all she could hear now was silence. At some point during their prayers the thunderstorm had moved on, passing overhead towards the sea. She felt a glow on her cheeks and saw that through the western window a thin sun was showing its face, illuminating the land, the figure of Christ carrying the child on his back. *Bearing the sins of the world.* It was almost as if he had heard their prayers and answered them. She turned to the priest, studying his face, the half frozen mask that hid a generous heart.

"You have been kind," she said, "so kind." She paused, wanting to say more, but not knowing what to say. "If there is anything that I can do…any way to repay your kindness…" She hesitated again, not knowing how to finish.

"The Lord does not expect favours, child," Hugo Brittanious said softly, "and neither do I." He smiled at her, the same strange half-smile that she had first noticed when he had surprised her at the altar.

"And yet," she said quietly, "I have heard it rumoured that the King has promised to build God a great Cathedral on the island if he defeats us." She looked at him again, seeing the wrinkles crease his forehead as he considered the point she had made.
"Yes, child," he admitted. "What you have heard is true. But the compact is with our father the Pope, not our Lord in heaven."
"But are they not the same?"
"The Pope is the Lord's servant, like myself."
"Then I do not understand, Father," she said. "You – the English Church – are said to support the Wake, his fight for freedom, and yet the Pope would seem to oppose you."

Hugo Brittanious studied the young girl, her pale face turned enquiringly towards his. She had surprised him with the perceptive nature of her question, precisely identifying the conflict within the English Church. The Pope supported the King; had indeed, sponsored his conquest of England; provided him with a Papal banner, the relics of St. Peter, and in return the Conqueror had built the Pope Cathedrals, great Cathedrals that reached to the heavens, that were a symbol of God's everlasting glory, his limitless Majesty. They were a symbol too, of the power, barely imagined before the Conquest, of the Norman dynasty. And yet, for the most part, the Saxon Church stubbornly refused to conform. And amongst the non-conformists the fens were foremost in their opposition. These things he did not mention to the pale young girl but instead gave the only answer that was his to give:
"The Pope serves the Lord in his way, and I serve him in my own, much smaller way, child."
"Yes Father," she said, "I understand." She moved away from the window, towards the door, and the sun's glow left her face. She went to the door and opened it. Outside the sun was shining brightly again; it was a glorious summer day. But three miles away a battle was raging and remembering the priest's last words, kindly

meant, she felt a shadow cross her soul. She stepped outside, this time closing the door behind her.

The Wake's sword clashed once, twice, jarring his arm to the elbow, then felt it meet flesh as he beat the Norman's parry and plunged the point into his chest. The man cried, dropping his sword, his eyes wide with shock, but there was no time to pause for another of the enemy was coming for him, spear levelled at his belly, hoping to take him through the gut. He ripped his sword from the dead man's chest, felt the familiar sucking motion as he tore it out just in time to parry the spear thrust. He turned the point aside then chopped down with edge of his sword, cleaving it into the man's skull, his steel helmet no protection against the force of the blow. But still more of them were coming, intent on victory, their numbers seemingly endless. He felt the presence of Ranulf to his right, large and reassuring, and, to his left, the solid bulk of both Wynter and Lightfoot. Of the Heron he could sense nothing.

From the corner of his eye he saw Ranulf hack down a Norman with *Requitur* and then step forward a pace. He moved forward also, restricting the area within which the enemy could manoeuvre for their attacks. The Saxons were fighting shoulder to shoulder, presenting a wall of steel to the enemy, and he was suddenly reminded of a tale his father had once told him as a child: of a Roman legionnaire, Horatius, and his two companions, who had once held a bridge against the whole Etruscan army. The bridge was so narrow that the Etruscans could only come at them in two's and three's and Horatius had been able to hold the army at bay whilst his friends had cut loose the bridge, saving the City.

Now he needed to cut loose this sow. But first there was more fighting to be done and even as the thought came to him he saw several Normans leaping onto the sow to help out their comrades, adding their weight to the attack. He prepared to take their charge but even as he did so he heard the hiss of arrows overhead and saw three of them go down, smashed down by the rain of iron from his archers. They were doing a good job, buying him precious seconds, some breathing space, and he instinctively moved forward again.

To his left Wynter was heavily engaged with two Normans coming at him simultaneously. He felt the rush of air past his head as Wynter's two-handed sword hacked down one then saw Lightfoot's axe crash down onto the helmet of the other. The massive spike bit deep through the metal into the man's skull and as Lightfoot ripped it out he saw brains and blood leap from the spike as the man crumpled to the ground already dead. He smashed down with own sword as yet another Norman came for him, sword raised to strike. His blow was parried and he struck again, harder still. The man backed away and he took the opportunity to fill his lungs before taking another step forward. It was hard to believe but they were succeeding, slowly forcing the enemy backwards onto the last remaining feet of the sow. But then they must cut it loose, and he knew that that would be the hardest task of all. He dismissed it from his mind; they had to get there first, and that meant there was more killing to be done. He smashed his sword down yet again and this time the Norman slipped as he parried the blow. Without hesitation he drove it down through the Norman's chest and ripped it out, blood and gore flying from the blade just as it had flown from Lightfoot's axe. He stepped forward again to within six feet of where the sow was anchored to the causeway by great coils of rope, each as thick as his arm, binding the sow to the corridor of death…

Alain de Bernay leaped out of the canoe and onto the island. "Tie it up," he said to Sanglier, a bull of a man with arms like tree trunks. Sanglier secured the canoe to a sapling near to the water's edge and the four men gathered up their weapons and the rope that would be needed when the time came. De Bernay looked up and studied the sky. Bright blue now, no sign of the thunderstorm, it reminded him of Normandy, and just for a moment he was transported to the golden meadows outside the town of Bernay where he had grown up and first learned his art. Learned too, the secret desires, the dark nature of his soul…If his plan succeeded he would soon be returning to Normandy, perhaps to a chateau and land of his own. The King might even be prepared to grant him a knighthood, his earlier transgressions forgiven. The Wake's head was a prize worth far more than the one hundred silver pennies offered by Ivo Taillebois but even that was not a negligible sum. There was a great deal that a man could do with that kind of money…

He cocked an ear and listened for the sounds carried on the summer air: the hum of bees and dragonflies flitting from one wildflower to another; the chatter of birds, active again now that the storm had passed. To the south, far in the distance, he imagined he could hear the sound of battle raging, men killing and being killed, whilst to the north, not far away now, came the unmistakable sound of Saxon voices: women, men too old to fight, the shrill tones of young children. His mouth twisted in a smile but there was no humour in it.

He saw that a rough path had been hacked through the meadow and he had no doubt that it led to the camp. Fitz Osbern could hammer away at the Wake all day if he wished, but he had a subtler plan. Still, he would have to be careful; the Wake might have left some archers to cover the camp. Even now they could be hiding in the undergrowth, biding their time. He turned to Rive, the coil of rope slung over his shoulder, his sword held easily in his calloused hand.

"Lead the way," he said. "I will cover your back." No point taking chances. Rive nodded and headed off along the uncertain path, de Bernay and the others close behind.

Hereward's arm was beginning to tire but there was no respite from the need to keep fighting, to keep killing. Nor would there be until he had severed the sow from the Causeway. He hammered down with his sword and felt it turn in his hand as his Norman adversary brought up his shield to deflect the blow. His hand was sweating and blistered but there was no time to adjust for the Norman launched a counter thrust of his own and it was only with luck that he managed to parry it in the nick of time, his arm taking the shock of the blow, sending arrows of fire lancing up to his elbow. He was about to strike again when Ranulf's sword suddenly arced through the air from his right, cleaving the surprised Norman's skull with the force of the blow. The Norman dropped like a stone and Hereward glanced sideways, muttered a quick word of thanks, adjusted his grip and prepared to meet his next opponent.

For how long they had been fighting like this he could not say. Time had ceased to have any meaning, each minute measured only by the number of blows taken and received, the bodies that littered the sow from end to end.

To his left Wynter and Lightfoot were fighting together; shoulder to shoulder, hacking their way through the enemy and to his right, in a blood-soaked world of his own was the housecarl. Ranulf, he saw, was almost within striking distance of the ropes that bound the sow to the Causeway and even as the next Norman came at him, eyes narrowed, focused upon the fight, he knew that he needed to support Ranulf, to somehow buy him time to hack through the ropes. He parried a cut to his head and swung hard and low, hoping to catch the Norman unawares but this time his own blow was parried, sparks flying from the blades as they clashed and parted and clashed again. This Norman was good, better than some of the others he had hacked down. Or perhaps *he* was tiring, slowing.... he dismissed the thought; such thoughts were dangerous. He needed to support Ranulf. The Norman hacked at him again; a great scything blow that he managed to parry but once more he felt the muscles in his arm scream with pain from the shock of the blow. The Norman struck at him again, and once more he parried, aware that his arm was not responding as it should. For the first time he began to feel desperate, and a bead of sweat ran down his cheek. The Norman, sensing that his opponent was weakening came at him again, harder still, swinging his sword right and then left in the hope of finding an opening. The Wake blocked and parried as best he could but found himself stepping backwards. He cast about anxiously, seeking help, but his comrades were all committed. He parried again, the pain in his arm unbearable now. He grimaced and stepped backwards once more, slipping on the slick timbers so that his feet shot from under him. He felt the sow rising up to meet him. His head cracked against the timber flooring, causing him to see stars. In a daze he realised that the Norman was moving in for the kill, arm raised, ready to strike. He involuntarily closed his eyes. He heard a scream, not his own but another's: *French.* He opened his eyes and saw the Heron standing protectively over him; he had hammered the end of his staff into the Norman's face, breaking his nose beneath the *nasal.* The Norman staggered backwards, bloodied hands held to his ruined face, and now he saw the Heron hammer the Norman again, using the end of the pole like a lance, this time hurling the Norman off the sow and into the swamp. The Norman screamed and then he was gone, his mail coat dragging him down beneath the black mud.

He rose to his feet quickly; there was little time to rest.

"Where have you been?" he shouted to the Heron above the din.

"My ankle!" the Heron called back. "Turned it when I landed!" He shook his head. "But it's alright now!"

"Thank God for that!" he cried, the pain in his arm forgotten. He picked up his sword and even as he did so saw that the crisis was not yet over, that Ranulf was trying to hold three adversaries, their faces flushed beneath their helmets as they manoeuvred for an opening. He saw Ranulf cut and parry wildly, sparks flying from the steel of *Requitur,* his sword a blur of continual motion. But even he could not hold three men forever.

"A Wake! A Wake!" he cried as he rushed to the housecarl's aid, the Heron beside him as he launched himself into the fray. The Normans, taken by surprise, turned to face their attackers. Ranulf, seizing his opportunity, hacked down one before he could react. The two remaining Normans fought hard, fought for their lives, and one of them managed to snap the Heron's staff, the momentum of the blow carrying the sword edge through to the Heron's chest. Hereward heard him cry, saw him fall, and drove the point of his own sword through the Norman's chest, hurling him backwards. He ripped the point out and looked down at his friend. The Heron grimaced through his pain, forced a smile, and only then did he notice the crimson stain. He looked into the Heron's pale face, paler than ever now and made himself smile back. He turned back to the fight and at last saw the chance that he had been praying for:

"Cut the ropes!" he cried to Ranulf. "Cut the ropes! We shall cover you!" The housecarl did not hesitate but now brought his sword down onto the great knot of ropes that tied the sow to the causeway. Once, twice, three times he hacked down, the ropes fraying and whipping like writhing serpents under his blade, and still he hacked down, *Requitur* rising and falling like an executioners' axe as the ropes parted beneath his fury.

On the causeway the Norman soldiers realised for the first time the peril that they were in. The mud was above their ankles now and seeing what the Saxons' intended several rushed forward to try to prevent the sow from being cut loose. Hereward was ready for them. He looked behind, to where Hurchillus and his archers were lining the ramparts and as he brought down his arm he heard the hiss of arrows overhead and saw the packed ranks of the enemy go down. The archers could not miss from this range. More men pressed forward, men desperate to save themselves, and a few managed to leap onto the sow, hoping to avoid the arrow storm. Barely had they landed before Wynter or Lightfoot hacked them down with sword or axe. The tide was turning; it was becoming a slaughter.

He heard a noise over to his right and saw that some of Morcar's men were launching coracles onto the water with the intention of enfilading the causeway, adding to the panic that was now evident in the enemy ranks. A dozen coracles were fanning out, each craft carrying two men, their bows slung over their backs as they paddled madly toward the enemy. From behind the ramparts Morcar was exhorting them to greater efforts, his face flushed and animated by the madness of it all, Galahad snorting and tossing his head as Morcar sawed on the reins in his excitement. And then the first wave of arrows was fired from the coracles, hissing and spitting into the mass of men on the causeway, causing yet further panic amongst the enemy. He saw half a dozen Normans go down, several falling headlong into the swamp to disappear from view. He smiled a grim smile and turned back to the sow, to where Ranulf was doggedly going about his business.

The last few strands of the ropes were parting beneath *Requitur's* blade, the massive weight on the causeway hastening the end. Ranulf chopped down again, one final time, and now the ropes parted completely, snapping and whipping this way and that. The sow, freed at last of its burden floated loose, and as it did so the causeway swayed first one way and then the other, lurching sickeningly. The men trapped upon it tried to stabilise it, screaming and shouting instructions to each other but finally, inevitably, like a dying animal, it rolled…

The Wake watched the causeway roll and knew then that the fighting was over. He removed his helmet and dropped his sword arm, unaware that he was doing so. He stared at the spectacle before him and once again it was like a dream: the slow roll of the causeway, the spilling of the men from its timbers into the mud. He saw their despairing attempts to cling on; heard their cries as they were thrown into the mud, watched the causeway slowly disappear beneath the swamp…

And finally he witnessed the end; the wild thrashing of arms and heads, the mud boiling with bodies, hundreds of bodies, like a great shoal of fish as the doomed men discarded clothing, tore off helmets, chain-mail, anything in an attempt to stay afloat. He watched them clutch at each other, clinging on for dear life, climbing onto each other, tearing at hair, eyes, anything that could prevent them sinking beneath the mud. But still the mud pulled them down, clawing at them with grasping fingers, dragging them under, one by one. And then came the screams, the terrible screams, the cries for help, the mad struggle to keep heads, mouths, noses, above the mud. And at the end, as seconds turned into minutes and the heads disappeared and the waters slowly calmed, he heard the silence, the terrible, deafening silence.

He looked at his comrades; at Ranulf, his features impassive in the face of this disaster, no sign of elation or despair; at Wynter and Lightfoot, both of them sweat-streaked and silent, exhaustion etched into every line; at the Heron, his broken body sprawled on the blood-stained timbers. He bent and closed the eyes, barely aware that he was doing so. The smile was still on the Herons' face, as though frozen there forever. He rose and looked around. His men were speaking to him and to each other but somehow he could not hear them. The massive silence was deafening him, dulling his mind, but slowly, slowly it began to sink in: They had won. These few men, the only ones still standing, had beaten the cream of the Conqueror's army. These men and, of course, his archers.

He looked back, towards the island, to the men still lining the ramparts: Hurchillus and his twin, Villicus; Alsinus, Osbernus with his pale, moon-shaped face; Lefwinus his simple conical helmet rammed onto his head, all of them silent now, moved beyond words by what they had witnessed. He saw his nephew, Morcar, still astride Galahad, his face flushed with excitement but his head now bowed, as though in prayer, perhaps for the enemy but more likely, he thought, in memory of his brother Edwin, who would never know what a glorious victory they had won this day.

He turned towards the south and gazed into the distance. The bridge still stood, spanning the Ouse half a mile away, and on it he could just make out a few solitary figures standing, like himself, in a respectful silence. Or perhaps, he thought, they were in shock. It would hardly be surprising. Where the causeway had been there was now only mud; half a mile of thick, black mud with no sign of the great army that had laboured on it, fought on it, died on it. *Three thousand men;* three thousand, buried beneath the black peat of the Aldreth fens. He could hardly credit his senses. He closed his eyes and for a moment he could see again the moment when the causeway rolled, the terror on the faces of the enemy as they were spilled into the mud, their awful, terror-stricken struggle to survive and then the despair as the mud closed over them, silencing their screams. God forbid that he should see the like again. The memory would stay with him forever and he suddenly felt humbled, somehow ashamed.

He heard a noise and saw Ranulf stirring from his own reverie, scabbarding his remarkable sword. He noted the look on the housecarl's face, the change written there from just a few moments earlier.

"What have we done?" he said, catching Ranulf's eye. "What have we done here today?" He had never expected to feel like this. The words came out as a plea and he saw the surprise register on the housecarl's face.

"No need for guilt," Ranulf said, as though he had read his mind. "They would have done the same to us. I have fought the bastards before."

No expression of sorrow or regret; he should not have expected it. He nodded in acknowledgement of Ranulf's simple truth. He was right. It might have been them. Had it not been for The Herons' timely intervention it would have been. He suddenly felt bone weary, sickened to the core by it all. He gazed across the fens, peaceful in the late afternoon sunshine, no sign of the violence that had marked the past few hours. But the bloodstained corpses littering the sow told a different tale. They were piled high in places, two or three deep where they had tried to grab a foothold before being hacked down by himself, his comrades. And then there was the Heron, still lying where he fell. He might have been asleep but for the crimson stain across his chest. He would remain here forever, in his beloved fens. Where he belonged.

"You are right," he said. "No guilt then." He picked up his helmet and sword and saw that it was bloodied to the hilt.

"You know what you are, don't you?" It was the housecarl's voice again.

"What's that?" he said carelessly.

"A miracle worker," the housecarl said. "A bloody miracle worker."

And perhaps he was. But he didn't feel like one. And somehow he knew that after what he had done today he would never know any peace. Not until he rested in the earth would that pleasure be afforded to him. He felt different, now that it was over. He searched for the word, trying to identify his feelings. And then it came to him:

He felt dirty. He just felt dirty.

Chapter Fifteen
The Camp Of Refuge

Torfrida lifted the flap to her hut and looked around the camp. It had stopped raining and the sun was shining brightly once more. Only the wet ground betrayed the fact that there had been a thunderstorm. Puddles of water still dotted the camp, lapped at by dogs and cats, jumped over by the children playing an impromptu game. She stared idly at the children, some playing games, skipping, jumping through home made hoops or over the puddles, others in animated conversation. But for all that she could sense the tension, the excitement, in the air, knew that they had detected with their children's intuition that all was not as it should be.

Her mind was not upon the childrens' activities but upon the battle raging to the south. She had wanted to be there, to give her support to her husband but Hereward had refused. It was too dangerous he had said; he would be worrying about her when his mind should be on the battle. She had accepted his refusal with good grace. She understood his reasoning for not wanting her there. But all the same it was hard to accept. At times she wondered whether he thought about her at all; what he wanted her for, if he still did…

The children were playing with a rope and one of the girl's from the camp was skipping over it whilst two other children gyrated it round and round, over her head, faster and faster, making her skip ever harder to keep pace with the rotation of the rope.

She noticed the small boy turning one end of the rope and recognised him as the son of the housecarl and his woman. Hal, they called him. A strange child for one so young, somehow remote from the other children, reclusive almost, as if in a world of his own. Even now, engaged in the childrens' game he seemed to be somehow apart from it, as though his thoughts were somewhere else.

The sight of the small child reminded her suddenly of her past, of her failings as a mother, and as a wife. She had been just seventeen when they had married, a golden couple with their futures before them. One day her husband would be Lord of Bourne Manor and she would be his Lady. They would have servants to wait upon them, fine silk sheets on their bed and children by the score to love and to fill their world with laughter.

But that was long ago, when they were still young. They had settled into a wing of Bourne Manor and each night her husband would come to her bed. Their nights had been filled with passion and wonder then, the discovery of new pleasures, the discovery of themselves. But the months had turned into a year and then into two, and still no sign of their first offspring had appeared.

She sought advice from the locals in the village, each with a different remedy, a miracle cure that would see her belly swell with child. But none of them had worked.

And so she had journeyed further afield, unknown to her husband, seeking advice, returning with one herbal cure or another, but again to no avail.

And then finally, blessedly, her monthly flux had failed. She could remember her excitement, the anticipation even now, after all these years. One month, then two slowly passed, and still no sign of the flux. She was with child; she was sure of it.

Two months became three and her excitement grew further. People in the village began to talk of a new heir at Bourne Manor.

Baby clothes would be left on their doorstep, deposited there by anonymous well-wishers. She was happy then, ecstatic almost, for their first child was on the way. She could recall how Hereward would place his head on her belly to listen for some sound of the child, the first pulsating signs of a tiny life, and although he had said that he could hear something she was never quite so certain. But it did not matter, not then.

The months passed; three months became four, and then five, and in the fifth month she noticed something odd. The bellies of the other women in the village had begun to swell at about this time, but hers remained flat; as flat indeed as when she had first married. She raised her fears with her husband but he had dismissed them, perhaps not wanting to distress her. "You have always been slim," he had said. "The baby will not show for some time." And she had believed him, just. But as the sixth and then the seventh months arrived and went with no swollen belly the awful truth hit her. She was not pregnant, not with child, and never would be because she was barren. *Barren.*

Hereward had cried like a child when she had told him, a grown man, crying like a child and it had broken her heart to see it. She had tried to comfort him, and, in so doing, comfort herself, but it was no good. Something between them had been lost and would never be regained.

Hereward took to sleeping on his own. She tried to be a wife to him, to tell him it did not matter but she knew she was deluding herself, deluding him, for it did matter; it mattered a great deal. And after a while she stopped trying, resolved to carry on with her life as though nothing was wrong. And she might have succeeded, but for the Normans. Life, even a barren life such as hers, would have been endurable if they had been allowed to continue to live at Bourne Manor. But the Conqueror had changed all that; the Conqueror and Ivo Taillebois, who had been granted their home, their lands, in return for his butchery on *Senlac* Hill. It was the one thing she still shared with her husband, their hatred of the Normans. That, and their desire to return to Bourne Manor. But even as the thought came to her she knew that it would be impossible. Impossible, for their time had been and gone. And now she faced years of squalor and deprivation and she was not sure she wanted it, could live like it, any longer.

She cocked an ear and listened carefully for some sound of the battle and imagined that she could hear the clash of steel ringing out across the empty landscape. Perhaps she could, but she could not be certain. Nothing was certain any longer. Only death. And sometimes, in her darkest moments, her loneliness, she considered embracing it…

She turned to watch the girl skipping over the rope and it seemed to her at that moment that each revolution was like the passing of the years, turning faster and faster until it was over: one moment the full blossom of youth, the next an uncertain old age. Her youth had gone long ago, had disappeared the day she had learned the awful truth about herself.

She saw the little girl fall as the rope caught her ankle, spilling her into the mud. The girl was crying as she rose to her feet, her face and hair muddied, her knees grazed from the fall. She could not see Agnolda, the girl's mother, and was about to go to her, to offer what comfort she could, when she heard a commotion coming from the east end of the camp. For a moment she hesitated, wondering what it could be when she saw Rahenaldus, their steward from Bourne Manor, hurrying towards her. Too old to fight, he had remained at the camp with the women and children. Almost seventy now, his hollow chest was rising and falling as he gasped for air, his face locked in a fearful expression as he forced aged legs to greater efforts. She went to meet him, sensing that every second could be vital.

"The Normans!" he cried, "the Normans are here!" He barely paused for breath before pointing to the east, the direction from which he had run. "They will be here any moment. You must save yourself my lady!"

She looked across to the children, the little girl being comforted by the housecarl's boy. There was so little time. She turned back to Rahenaldus, unsure of herself, unsure of what she should do. She seemed to be incapable of thought, her mind frozen with fear.

"You know where to go!" Rahenaldus was shouting at her, his eyes fixed upon hers. "The place we prepared. You remember! I will try to delay them. I will find you later."

She hesitated again, wondering whether she should collect up the children, take them with her. But there was no time for that, no time for anything, and there may not be room for them where she was going... Her mind rebelled against the thought of that place, the horror she must shortly endure, but in that instant she made the decision; there was no alternative.

"Take care, dear friend," she said. She glanced over his shoulder, towards the east. They had entered the camp, four of them, swords drawn, eager for blood...

She started to run.

As he burst into the camp through the perimeter gate Alain de Bernay knew that his plan could succeed. No archers, no lookouts, just old men and women and their brats. His heart raced with excitement as he quickly scanned the camp for some sign of the woman that held the key to the Wake but for the moment he could not see her.

"Spread out!" he shouted to his comrades, and Rive and Sanglier cut off to the right. Feroux headed left. They had their orders, knew what was expected of them; he wanted her alive.

He ran through the outer circle of huts into the centre of the camp. There were some children in a tight little group: a small girl crying, two small boys. The younger of the two had his arm around her, was trying to comfort her, but he ignored them. He was searching for the Wake's wife for he knew that when he had her he just as surely had the Wake himself.

An old man, balding and thin, confronted him, his eyes wide, showing his fear, his hands clasped together in an entreaty.

"Where is she!" de Bernay snarled, his voice harsh, demanding. The man shook his head, looked anxiously behind, perhaps expecting help, or more likely, he thought, looking to see that the bitch had made good her escape.

"Who?" the old man said, "Who are you looking for?"

"His whore!" de Bernay snapped. "The Wake's whore! Where is she?"

The man shook his head, a vacant look on his face.

"Not here," he said. "I do not know - " Rahenaldus did not finish for de Bernay's impatient knife had whipped across his throat, slitting it from ear to ear. De Bernay did not bother to check the result; the old fool would be dead before he hit the ground. He plunged further into the camp; men and women were running backwards and forwards, children flung up into their arms, snatched from the ground, terrified that they might be next. He quickly scanned the camp. To his right, Rive and Sanglier were checking the huts, first one then the other, but as yet there was no sign of her. He cursed beneath his breath and felt his scar suffuse with blood. He had to be quick. Someone would surely raise the alarm. Find her quickly then.

He saw the largest hut in the centre of the camp, a little way from the others, and ran over to it. Without hesitation he ducked beneath the flap. The interior was dark and cool compared to the brightness, the warmth, of the late afternoon. Scattered about were some rudimentary pieces of furniture: two rough cots, a fire lit long ago, now a pile of ashes, a woman's shawl, some pewter dishes of good quality; too good for a fen dweller. He guessed that this was the Wake's hut and looked for some sign that might tell him where she was. But there was nothing. He cursed again, and simply for spite took out his cock and urinated on the cots. The bastards could lie in it tonight if they were not already dead.

He ducked outside again, into the bright sunlight, and saw that Sanglier had a young girl on the ground, was holding her by the throat. She was clearly terrified, her legs and arms thrashing as he slapped first one side of her face and then the other, firing questions at her as he did so.

"Where is the whore? Where is she?" The girl was not responding. De Bernay saw that her eyes were closed, her face streaked with tears and swollen with dark welts from Sanglier's fist. He ran over to them.

"Let her up!" he snapped.

"Little bitch! Sanglier hit her again, ignoring the command, snapping her head to the side. De Bernay grabbed his hair, yanked him off the girl. Sanglier was heavier than him, but de Bernay hurled him backwards with an ease that belied his physique.

"Let her up, I said."

Sanglier glared at him with barely controlled fury as he picked himself from the ground.

"If we are to succeed, to survive, we must work together," de Bernay said. "And that means you must obey me. Do you understand?" Sanglier nodded slowly but his anger was still apparent.

"Now," he said, turning back to the girl, speaking to her in rudimentary Saxon. "It is very simple. Co-operate with me, and you shall live. Defy me and you shall die. Do you understand? Nod if you understand."

The girl looked at him, no hint of having understood what he had said. Perhaps she had not understood. Or perhaps she was simply feigning ignorance. She was, after all, a Saxon, and could surely understand her mother tongue. There was one way to test her. He turned back to Sanglier.

"You were right," he said, still speaking in Saxon. "A stupid bitch. Find me another." He raised his knife to her throat, the blade still red with the old man's blood.

"No!" the girl screamed and de Bernay smiled.

"Ah," he said, "so she does understand." He stroked her cheek with the flat of the blade, leaving a trace of the old mans' blood upon it. The girl swallowed hard, and he could see her breasts rising and falling beneath her shift. For a moment he thought about pleasuring her. But they were wasting time. At any moment those damned archers could arrive and that was a risk he dare not face.

"Where is the Wake's woman?" The knife was at the girl's throat now, the point applying pressure. "Tell me girl." He twisted the point and the girl winced, her eyes closing again, as though to shut out the possibility of what might happen. She opened her mouth, closed it, but the point was twisted again and now she told him all he needed to know:

"There is a tunnel against the south perimeter ramparts, covered by reeds. They are laid out as though to dry but they simply hide the entrance. It leads beyond the camp." De Bernay smiled, but just as quickly it was gone.

"Which way?" he snapped, his eyes cold, humourless.

"Over there." The girl pointed to a section of the southern rampart, bathed in late afternoon sunshine. It was to be her last view of the world. De Bernay sliced his knife across her throat and her head sunk onto her chest, blood pouring from the gaping wound to stain the woollen fabric of her shift. She dropped to the ground like a stone.

"You told her she would live," Sanglier said, his voice registering surprise at de Bernay's summary execution.

"I lied." De Bernay bent to wipe the blade on a clean part of the dead girl's dress. "Now," he said, "we must find that other bitch."

He was about to set off when his gaze fell upon the three small children. They had not moved since the drama began, were rooted to the spot, and as his eyes swept over the smaller boy he realised that his face was somehow familiar. He had overlooked him earlier, in the first flush of excitement, but now, he realised, the boy was known to him. He tried to place him but for a moment could not do so. And then, like the lifting of a veil, the recollection suddenly came to him: *The housecarl's brat.* A thin smile crossed his face. He looked for Rive and Feroux and called them over.

"The Wake's whore has gone to ground, but we shall flush her out."

"Where is she?" Rive asked.

"Trapped like a rat in a tunnel." He paused. "But I have another task for you." He indicated the coil of rope that Rive still carried, slung over his shoulder.

"You will need that," he said.

Torfrida inched her way forward, one hand in front of the other, groping blindly in the darkness. It was as black as night in the tunnel, and wet, and the cold water of the fens lapped around her wrists, her knees, her ankles, soaking her gown, chilling her mind, already reeling from the horror of her predicament.

At first the tunnel had sloped downwards, burrowing beneath the earthern walls that her husband had constructed to keep out the enemy, but now she sensed that it was levelling out, had reached a plateau, and here, in the bowels of the earth there was no light at all. It was like a coffin, like being buried alive. She could scream forever and no one would hear her. She felt a tide of panic wash over her and she closed her eyes, pushing these thoughts to the back of her mind. There would be light at the other end, on the outside, and she made herself concentrate upon that, upon reaching the point where the tunnel erupted into the bright sunlight. *Keep going then, keep going.*

Her head bumped against the roof dislodging a few small lumps of earth and she realised to her horror that the tunnel was narrowing even further. There was no room to turn, even if she wanted to, no chance to go back and if she did she would only be prey to the Normans. She moved forward again, her hands groping in the black wetness for the way ahead, her mind fighting the panic that threatened to engulf her at any moment.

She heard a noise behind her. She stopped and listened, every fibre of her body tensed to prevent any sound, any betrayal of her presence. She heard it again: a scuffling sound, growing louder, closer, in the inky blackness. Too loud for a rat, she somehow knew that the sound had been caused by a human. Perhaps it was Rahenaldus, come to find her, but immediately she rejected the idea. He was too old for this, and in any event she knew that he would be waiting for her at the other end of the tunnel, if he still lived…

She started moving again, scrambling along on hands and knees, the noise behind her adding a fresh urgency to her efforts. She scrabbled forward for what seemed like an eternity and now discovered the tunnel narrowing even further, closing around her like a fist, constricting the space above her so that she could no longer kneel. She went down onto her belly, the cold water knifing through her, causing her to gasp from the shock. She tried to ignore the fact that above her was tons of earth that could collapse at any moment. Hereward had said something about not having had time to prop the shaft but she had barely been listening to him. They were as bad as each other, she realised, both engrossed in their own private worlds, but if she escaped from this nightmare she resolved to do something about it, to make up for lost time.

She wriggled forward on her belly, like a worm, twisting right and left, her feet propelling her forward. The water was just below her chin now, cold and foul smelling and it was only with an effort that she managed to prevent herself from swallowing any.

The thought occurred that if the tunnel narrowed any further it would fill with water entirely. God help her then, for no one else would. She closed her mind to that possibility. She heard, from somewhere behind her, the sound of voices echoing in the blackness but they were not voices that she recognised. These voices were foreign, excited. French. *God, they were pursuing her.* Her stomach lurched, her mind reeled, and now she scrabbled forward as fast as she could, ignoring the pain in her knees, her hands, her torn fingernails, as she fought to escape this hell-hole that might yet become her grave. She should never have come down here. Never. She felt tears sting her eyes at the thought and once more a tide of panic washed over her. Just a few minutes earlier, before this nightmare had begun, she had harboured thoughts of taking her own life, but now all she wanted to do was to live. To live to see the daylight, the water filled landscape that she had always taken for granted, resented even. Oh God, how she wanted to live! Tears rolled down her cheeks as she plunged into the blackness, her hands and feet clawing at anything that would give her purchase against the suffocating walls, her mind filled with the overpowering fear of claustrophobia and death at the hands of an unseen enemy…

Sanglier could hear the bitch somewhere ahead of him, crying and scrabbling her way in the blackness. She could not be too far distant now; he could sense that he was gaining ground, closing the gap between them. Soon he would have her and then the fun would begin. He had had to discard his weapons before descending into the mouth of the tunnel, handing them to de Bernay before leading Feroux into the black maw, and he had felt uneasy about it, almost like being naked, but he knew that they would only be an incumbrance in the confined space of the tunnel. And, after all, she was only a woman.

He stopped and listened. Ahead of him, perhaps only a few yards now, he could hear the frantic sounds of scrambling and crying. She could cry all she liked. No one could hear her. Only himself and Feroux.

"I'll have you, bitch!" he cried into the blackness and he was rewarded by the sound of screams and renewed sobbing and scrabbling from somewhere ahead of him. Feroux bumped into him, unaware that he had momentarily stopped.

"Keep going!" Feroux snapped from behind him, "I want to get out of this shit hole even if you don't."

"Hold your nerve!" Sanglier snapped back. "We shall have the bitch soon enough."

He wriggled forward again, like the woman, compelled now to move on his belly. He was a big man and despite his words to Feroux he was uncomfortably aware of how the tunnel had narrowed over the last few yards, as if the Saxons' had not had time to finish it properly. He forced himself forward, urging his body to greater efforts and then he felt something ahead of him. It was just a fleeting touch but he knew it was her foot, slipping and sliding as she strove for purchase in the mud. He lunged forward, reaching out a hand, catching her by the ankle.

Torfrida felt the hand grasp her ankle and for a moment her heart stopped. It was as if the devil himself had her and was pulling her down to his subterranean kingdom. In her panic she lashed out with her free foot, smashing it wildly backwards, using her heel, hammering it over and over into the face of whoever had her. She felt a crunch of bone, heard a scream, a cry of anger, and suddenly her foot was free. She scrambled forward again, hand over hand, ignoring the pain, the water, the inky blackness, everything but the need to escape her pursuers. She could hear them behind her, unseen in the blackness doggedly pursuing her like the demons of hell. Her heart beat like a hammer; she could feel it thumping wildly in her chest as if it too was desperate to escape the walls that contained it. Her breath came in quick, short, bursts that never gave her the oxygen she needed. Her legs ached beyond belief but she dare not stop, she simply dare not. She pressed on doggedly, her eyes closed, her mind focused upon the need to escape, to feel the sweet, sweet air in her lungs, the sun on her face…

And then, at last, she sensed the tunnel sloping upwards, reaching up to the light. It was still as black as night down here but if she could just keep going she might make it. They were still there, in the tunnel; she could hear their unholy scrabbling somewhere behind her. The noise drove her on. Taking a deep breath she summoned the last of her reserves and began her climb towards the light…

Rive held the boy under his arm, his legs and hands bound by the rope. He had fought like a wildcat at first, until they had bound him, and then he had screamed until he was fit to burst. The boy would have been screaming now but for the rag stuffed into his mouth, silencing him at last.

De Bernay looked around the camp and spotted an aged woman with lank grey hair staring fearfully at him from the opening to her hut. She hurriedly ducked inside when she realised that she had been seen but he ran over to the hut and dragged her out, ignoring

her screams of pain, her pathetic pleas for mercy. Her hair, held in his fist, was coming out in handfuls as though she was moulting, like a cat.
"Don't worry old hag," he spat at her as she cowered before him, "I shall not kill you; not today. Hell awaits you soon enough, I think." He laughed at his joke. "But before you go I have a use for you." He saw the puzzlement in her tear-stained eyes slowly replacing the fear.
"Yes," he said, "you can be useful to me. Are you not curious woman; do you not wonder what use you could possibly be?"
The hag just stared at him with no sign of comprehension on her wrinkled features. These Saxons were so stupid. He felt a deep well of anger rising within him, unexpected, ungovernable. It had always been so and he knew from long experience that there was only way to indulge it.
"Answer me woman!" He slapped her face, once, twice, snapping her head first one way and then the other.
"Yes," the hag muttered through bloodied lips, and he felt the anger evaporating like a summer mist.
"Now," he said, "you know the housecarl, the father of this boy?" He pointed to Hal, bound and gagged in the arms of Rive.
"The hag nodded without looking at the boy. He saw that her lips had thickened and swollen, that blood was running from her lips, dripping onto the ground.
"Good," he said. "Good. Now listen. I have a message for him, and you will convey it for me. Do you understand?"
"Yes."
"Then tell him I have his brat. Tell him that the boy still lives but that if he wishes to see him again he will come to me and we shall dance the dance of death. Tell him that; he will understand. Tell him to come under a flag of truce. It will protect him…until the dance begins."

"How will he know where to find you?" The woman spoke in a sullen monotone, her senses dulled by the beating.
"He will know. We met there before, when I was cheated of his death. Tell him that the ground is still stained with the blood of my men; that their ghosts cry out for vengeance." He liked that touch, the feeling it gave of a moral ascendancy, something that happened only rarely in his life. He paused again, relishing the control he held over her.
"One final thing," he snapped. "Tell the Wake that we have his whore." The hag looked up sharply and he smiled to himself because he knew that she had not expected this.
"Oh yes, we have her too," he said. "And in three days time she shall burn as a witch." He smiled again, a cold smile that never reached his eyes. "The stench of her burning shall carry across the fens. Tell him that."
The old woman nodded, her lips still dripping blood, her eyes registering an emotion that he recognised as hatred. They could certainly hate, these Saxons, but so could he…

He looked around the camp, deserted now, but at any moment the Wake might appear with those damned archers of his. It was time to go. He beckoned Rive and they hurried away, the boy carried over Rive's shoulders like a sack of corn. It had partly been a bluff; he did not yet have the Wake's whore. But that was only a matter of time. And if he were any judge his threat would have the Wake leaping to her rescue before the day was out. And then he would have them both, the housecarl and the Wake…
And *Le Couteau's* name would live forever.

Chapter Sixteen
The Camp Of Refuge

Alice returned to the camp. She had been undecided, after leaving the chapel, whether to go to the battle, to find Ranulf, or to return to the camp. She decided upon the camp. Her son was there; she should be with him. Her mind was racing, pondering the priest's last words, what precisely he had meant by them. She was worried too, about events to the south, about Ranulf, and the Wake. She knew the odds that they faced. She had seen the Norman army before; its cold brutality, and wished that she could be in both places at once. If only she knew what was happening… She entered the camp through the open gates deep in thought, deeply concerned, despite the priest's attempts at reassurance. She was not aware of her surroundings, only the comforting familiarity of them: the circle of huts, drying in the sunshine, the barking dogs. She did not hear the silence of the people, did not sense their despair.

What did he mean, the priest, when he spoke those last words? The implied criticism was plain enough, even to her. The Pope supporting the Conqueror, the English Church the Wake. They could not both be right, both be loyal to God, subservient to His will, for they supported opposite sides in this conflict. And if the Pope had a greater voice than the English Church, did it not follow that the Pope's wishes would prevail? This was a disturbing revelation, for if God was with the Normans how could the Wake ever hope to succeed? Her mind ran down alleyways of thought but always she returned to the beginning, to the inevitable conflict that could not be unravelled, reconciled.

She reached the centre of the camp and for the first time saw the crowd gathered around an old woman. She recognised her as Elfrida, the widow. She immediately sensed that something was wrong. She looked around and now saw other groups of people huddled together, silent people, *people afraid. S*he could almost smell their fear. And then she saw the bodies stretched out on the ground: An old man: Rahenaldus, and a young girl. She did not know the girl but she instinctively knew that they were dead. She saw the blood and glimpsed the awful and identical wounds to the throat that had killed them, their bodies covered by makeshift shrouds. What has happened here? She began to panic. She pushed through the crowd, her visit to the chapel forgotten. Elfrida saw her and beckoned her over. The crowd parted to let her through, unable to look her in the eyes. Despite her tears, her swollen lips, Elfrida began to talk. *He* has been here, she learns, the monster that had once held them captive. He has murdered and moved on, gone before the Wake returns. He has Torfrida...and her son. *Her son....*

She fled the camp and ran south, to Ranulf, if he still lived, her only hope, her son's only hope of salvation. Tears stung her eyes. She tripped and stumbled like a blind woman, her heart beating wildly as her conscience screamed at her: *You should have been there; you should have been with him...*

Torfrida burst from the tunnel into the light, into the world. The sunlight, brilliant and white, blinded her and for several moments she could not see. She blinked rapidly and gradually, like the lifting of a veil, her vision returned. She glanced quickly around, knowing that she had little time. They were still pursuing her, still inside the tunnel. She thought of using a rock, or something heavy, to block the tunnel but she could not see anything that would suit. In any event she would not have the strength to lift a rock and if she could lift it so could the Normans. She dismissed the idea. She must flee, must find a place of safety, somewhere to hide until the danger was over.

She looked around again. The camp was not an option. She reasoned that these Normans must simply be the advance party. And if they had forced the camp did it not follow that her husband was defeated? She knew that she could not go back there. She did not know where to go. She cast about for somewhere to hide. She was in the wilderness here, nothing but meres and swamp, the land running away to the horizon, to the bottomless black peat of the Haddenham and Smithy Fens and beyond those the shining, endless stretches of water of the Holy White Lake.

To the right was a stand of reeds, a hundred yards away. It was better than nothing and there was nowhere else. She began to run, her legs stiff and cramped from the confines of the tunnel. She glanced back and was relieved to see that there was still no sign of her pursuers. She crashed into the reeds and lay low in the mud, heedless of the cold, just glad to be alive after the suffocating nightmare of the tunnel. She looked back again, her eyes riveted upon the point where she had erupted from the ground. The first man now appeared, his face red and swollen from her kicks, a ribbon of blood streaming from his nose. She saw him struggle from the hole, pulling himself out on muscular arms. He was much bigger than her she saw; she could imagine the struggle he would have had to squeeze his bulk through the tunnel. She found herself wishing that he had died down there, choking to death in the blackness.

Another man was emerging from the tunnel now, a smaller man, leaner, but just as menacing. Thank God this second man had not been behind her; he would have caught her, she felt sure of it.

Unless she had kicked his face in too. She rebuked herself for the thought, but then a smile lit her eyes. She did well with those kicks, she thought, her desperation adding to her desire for freedom. She smiled again and realised with a shock that these were the first smiles for months, perhaps for years. She looked into the sky; it was bright blue, a brilliant blue, but in the west tinged with magenta. Dusk was approaching. It was a huge sky, she realised, when she studied it, a sky that dominated the empty landscape. It was as if she was seeing it, really seeing it, for the first time. Perhaps she was. The realisation slowly dawned that something had changed. *Something inside her...* as though the journey through the tunnel had somehow been a journey of a different kind; a metamorphosis from darkness into light. A tingle went through her, running down her spine. Her life was about to change. She did not know how, or why, but she knew it just as surely as she knew that the sun, lowering now towards the western horizon, would soon be setting.

And then she would begin again.

Alice met the Saxon army returning to the camp. Her eyes hurried over the faces of the warriors, some familiar, others strangers to her. But she was concerned with only one and when she saw it, bearded and sweat-stained, etched with the weariness of battle she ran to him, flinging herself into his arms, kissing him, hugging him, the tears streaming unchecked down her cheeks. They had won a great victory, she learned, the Normans sent to the bottom of the peat-black fen. But now she had her own terrible news to impart and instinctively she pulled away from him as she forced herself to speak. She saw the hurt in Ranulf's face turn to anger as her words came out, tumbling into each other in her haste to get it over with. She told him of de Bernay, of Hal and Torfrida.

She was sobbing uncontrollably and Ranulf folded her in his arms, held her tight to his chest as she finished her tale. She could smell his sweat, the blood from the battle upon him, could feel the anger coursing through him as he gradually gave vent to his feelings. He was crushing her as though he was crushing de Bernay himself and she gave a small cry of pain. It was enough for Ranulf to remember himself and he pulled away from her. His face was unrecognisable now, contorted and reddened with anger. He was almost beside himself. *I will go to de Bernay now,* he cried. *I will tear out his heart!* He seemed barely aware of what he was saying and Alice, for once, had no answers. She turned to the Wake, seeking his intervention. Already Ranulf was preparing to leave; *Requitur* had been ripped from his scabbard, was held in his fist, his knuckles white with rage.

"You cannot go alone, my friend." The Wake's calm voice cut across the silence. "That is what *Le Couteau* wants…and, no doubt, myself."

Ranulf stopped in his tracks, wheeled around angrily.

"What do you suggest then!" His eyes were wild, his anger raging unchecked and Alice thought, just for a moment, that he would turn upon the Wake as though he were *Le Couteau* himself but once more the Wake answered in the same calm voice:

"I do not know…yet. But I shall come up with something. *Le Couteau* thinks he has outwitted us but we shall have him, I promise you that." She saw the hatred, the doubt, written across Ranulf's face as he weighed the words and rejected them.

"Promises! What good are promises?"

The Wake nodded, considering the response, and moved towards him.

"As good as the man that gives them," he said. She saw him fix Ranulf's eyes with his own and the men were suddenly eye to eye.

"I promise you," he said again, his words barely a whisper. Alice looked from one to the other, the emotions running backwards and forwards between them, the blue eyes of her husband locked upon the grey of the Wake. She noted, absently, that in height the two men were the equal of the other and what the outcome would be if it ever came to a fight she could not begin to guess. Pray God that it never came to that… For long seconds the two men stood toe to toe and then she saw the anger ebb from Ranulf's eyes and knew that it was over.

"Sheath your sword," the Wake said softly and Ranulf, a look of surrender written in every line of his features, did so. She felt herself sigh with relief and then she remembered Hal and the crushing weight of her own pain, her own guilt, revisited her like a hammer. Her eyes welled with tears. It did not go unnoticed for the Wake shifted his gaze towards her, fixing her with the same pale grey eyes that he had locked upon her husband. Now however it was a look of a different kind, for where before they had been full of steely determination, they now seemed to be infinitely kind, infinitely sad, so that she could not help but stare into them and wonder. She realised that she was colouring under his scrutiny and she hurriedly turned away, breaking the contact to wipe at her tears.

"You shall have your revenge," the Wake said softly, his voice like silk, as though they were the only two people present. "This I swear to you. Upon the blood of my father I do swear it." His words, so obviously meant for her, dragged her eyes back to his own and once again she could feel herself being drawn into them, deeper and deeper, as though he were allowing her a glimpse of his soul.

"We should get back to the camp, my friend." Ranulf's voice broke the spell, bringing her back to the world. "There is much to do, to plan, if we are to turn the tables on this Norman." His words were reasonable enough but there was an edge to them that was unmistakable. The Wake glanced at him, nodded and without another word headed towards the camp.

She went to Ranulf and put her arms around him. He hugged her to him, kissing her on her still-wet cheeks. She kissed him in return, on the lips and could taste blood from a cut to his mouth. She turned to watch the Wake, disappearing rapidly into the distance, followed by his men. Something had passed between them that she had been quite unprepared for: the pale grey eyes that had beckoned her forward, the look on his face when Ranulf's voice had cut across the silence, breaking the spell. Strange, she thought, that she had not realised before...

Chapter Seventeen
Cambridge Castle

William Fitz Osbern stood silently before the dais whilst the King read the report, held in one massive fist. He had been standing for fully five minutes and the King's eyes had not met his once since he had been summoned into the royal presence. Fitz Osbern knew this to be a bad sign. Not just bad, he reflected. The worst.

The Conqueror was wearing his favourite suit of chain-mail and over it his scarlet and gold surcoat with the two golden lions that proclaimed him to be King of England. He had not yet spoken and Fitz Osbern knew this to be another bad sign. He had prepared himself for this audience, rehearsing the arguments that might yet save his neck, but he was not optimistic.

The King looked up from the report and now fixed him with the cold, dark, eyes set in the granite face that he had come to know so well. There was no compassion there, barely a hint of recognition despite his long years of loyal service. Fitz Osbern was a hard man himself, forged in the furnace of the Conquest, steeped in the blood of *Senlac* Hill and Exeter and York. Even so he felt a shiver run down his spine.

"Three thousand men. Three thousand, lost in an hour, most of them in less than a minute." The King's voice was quiet, calm even, but Fitz Osbern was not fooled. He had seen it, heard it, many times before: The calm before the storm.

"I have been good to you, William," the King said, still in the same calm voice. "Would you agree that I have been good; generous, even?"
"Yes, Sire," Fitz Osbern heard himself reply. There was nothing else he could say. It was the truth; the Conqueror had made him a wealthy man. The Earldom of Hereford, the Lordship of the Isle of Wight, the great Manor House at Hanley in Worcestershire and finally the Governorship of the magnificent new castle of Winchester. All of these had been given to him for his services to the Conqueror; and today he faced losing them.
"I lost three thousand men on *Senlac* Hill," the King said suddenly. "You remember that day, William?"
"Indeed, Sire," he said. "It is burnt into my memory." Again it was the truth. He would never forget that butchers' yard, not as long as he lived. He could close his eyes and see it again as clearly as if it were here before him: the Saxon army lining the ridge, row upon row of them, their shield-wall running the length of the hill like serpents' scales, the hedge of spears, dulled with Norman blood, the red and gold banners of the false King Godwineson. And then the carnage, the slaughter that went on all day and seemed to have no end…
"Charge after charge I lead up that cursed hill," the King said, as though he had read his thoughts. "Three horses I had killed under me until at dusk, when all seemed lost, I broke the Saxons."
"Yes, Sire," he said, "you were magnificent that day. An inspiration to us all."
"And I had no choice!" The explosion came, catching him off guard, and Fitz Osbern knew that he was lost.
"I had no choice because it was them or us! No second chance, no chance to take stock, to regroup, to retire, for the bastards would have done for us!" The King's eyes blazed into his now, and Fitz Osbern could only stand and listen.

"But *you* had a chance!" the Conqueror stormed, warming to his theme. "You had a chance that I never had! And you failed to take it! Three thousand men in less than an hour! What were you doing? Three thousand men for God's sake! What the hell happened?" Fitz Osbern had no answer.

"I am sorry, Sire," he said, "I truly am." And he meant it. Tortured by visions of them drowning, haunted by his failure to secure the victory the Conqueror had demanded, he had awaited this moment with terrible foreboding.

"Where shall I find another three thousand?" The King was speaking again, questioning, probing. "The northern army no longer exists, thanks to you. My army of the south is being despatched to Flanders, the rest spend their days patrolling the borders, putting down insurgents."

He rose from his chair and crossed to his campaign table. Stretched across it was a map of England dotted with figures, red, blue and gold. He bent and swept his hand over the map, north to south, then east to west, as he carefully studied his dispositions, his face a mask of concentration. Eventually, after what seemed an eternity, he raised himself from the map and confronted Fitz Osbern.

"There are no more men, William," he said. "See for yourself." The King waved his hand at the map but it was not necessary. Fitz Osbern knew full well the scale of the disaster, the strain on resources, without looking at a map.

The Conqueror returned to the table and picked up a list of names. He scanned it thoughtfully, began to read from it. His voice was quiet at first, speaking almost, Fitz Osbern thought, with reverence. But as the list of names grew so did the voice, rising to a crescendo, ringing around the rafters. It was a list of the dead, Fitz Osbern realised. And to his dismay it went on and on until it seemed that there was not a single nobleman, a single Earl or Baron or Knight that was not mentioned on it. And it was his fault.

"Why did it happen, William?" The King put down the list, his cheeks suffused with blood but at least he was speaking calmly again now, in control. *Perhaps.*
"It is difficult to say, Sire," Fitz Osbern said equivocally. "We heard that the Saxons were breaking, and decided to commit the reserves."
"Reserves? You mean the chivalry?"
"Yes, Sire. You used the same tactic at Val-es-Dunes you might recall." Immediately he said it Fitz Osbern knew it was a mistake.
"At Val-es-Dunes my centre was about to break! What reserves had I left? Nothing but my chivalry! I had to throw them in or lose the battle!" The Conqueror's face was dark with anger, his eyes bulging from their sockets. "And I could *see* the enemy's dispositions! What could you see William! Tell me! What the hell could *you* see?"
"Nothing Sire," he said. He had no choice but to admit to it. "The Causeway was packed with men. It was hard to see anything. But Captain D'Evreville reported that the enemy were breaking -"
"D'Evreville! That fool! And you believed him?"
"Yes, Sire," he said. "He seemed to be so certain, so confident of victory." He paused. "It seemed to be the right thing, the only thing, to do."
"It was *not* the only thing to do!" The King circled around behind him, round and round, like a cat circling its prey. "You could have withdrawn, waited even, before committing the chivalry."
Fitz Osbern recognised the truth of this. He had been too impatient, had wanted to please his sovereign a little too much and it had led him into error.
"I am disappointed in you William," the King said softly, sadly, almost. "You have been my most constant ally, my ablest commander. I had expected better than this; much better."

"Yes, Sire," he said. "If there is any way to redeem myself..." He could not finish. The silence hung in the air between them, the victors of *Senlac* Hill, their friendship severed by the disaster ten miles to the north. The Conqueror moved to face him, stood just two feet away. Fitz Osbern inclined his head, awaiting the declamation that he knew would, eventually, be coming.

"You know of the crisis in Flanders?" the King asked suddenly, surprising him with the question.

"Yes, Sire," he said. "Everyone knows." Everyone did. The King's brother in law, Count Baldwin, had recently died, had barely been laid in his coffin before the regency was claimed by his kinsman, Robert of Frison. The Count's widow was struggling to hold his forces, her knowledge of warfare little more than she had read in a book.

"Then you know what I want of you," the King said firmly. "Take command of the army. Support the Countess. She will be awaiting you. I sent a despatch on the last tide."

So his fate had already been decided. From the moment he had entered the chamber he had been doomed... but the King was speaking again and he had no choice but to listen.

"I give you this chance, William, because you were once my friend. I expect you to acquit yourself with honour. You will leave England today. You shall forthwith surrender your titles, your estates in England, which I give to your son."

Fitz Osbern swallowed hard. *Banishment.* He was to be banished from the realm.

"Farewell William," the King said. "We shall not meet again." It was over. He turned on his heels, walked swiftly to the door, opening it.

"William!" The Conqueror's voice pulled him up.

"Yes, Sire?"

“I have heard that the Countess is still a handsome woman. And that she pledges marriage to the man that aids her. You could do worse for a man in your position…no wife, no titles no estates. Think on it William…when you are in Flanders.”
He opened his mouth to respond but the words would not come.
Like his titles and estates he had been stripped of those too.
So it was Flanders then.
Oblivion.

Chapter Eighteen
Cambridge

Alain de Bernay rose from the bed and padded toward the low casement window. He was naked, and in the dim light of the single tallow candle his lean torso glistened with the sweat of his lovemaking. The whore that had shared his bed, his passion, for the last hour lazily ran her eyes over his tanned, muscular spine before switching her gaze to the whites of his buttocks as he obligingly stooped to peer through the window into the street below.

The army, what remained of it, were pulling out to lick its wounds and to regroup for the next assault upon the Isle, whenever that would be. A torch lit procession of carts carrying the wounded and disabled trundled past the window, illuminating the room in the tavern that de Bernay had rented to while away the hours and to contemplate what the army's defeat would mean for his own plans which were now, as a result of that defeat, in tatters.

The Conqueror had abandoned the fortified hospital station at Belsar's Hill, judging it to be too dangerous to remain there any longer and so de Bernay had had to leave too, his *rendezvous* with the housecarl, his plan to capture the Wake, frustrated. And now the army were returning to their tented village on the southern perimeter of the City, to await the Conqueror's next move, and to contemplate what had gone wrong.

De Bernay knew full well what had gone wrong. They had attacked on too narrow a front. The causeway had signalled, as clearly as if a message had been sent to the Saxons, where the army intended its assault and the Wake had been ready for them. And Fitz Osbern, fool that he was, had sent them to their doom by packing the causeway with men, causing it to collapse. De Bernay had anticipated the disaster when he had made the decision to strike out on his own. And had it not been for the wholesale destruction of the army he might well have succeeded. But now, with the remnants of the army moving south, he must go with them; that, or desert and face a hanging if he was caught. But first he had needs to fulfil, a deep anger to assuage, and he had sought out Odette, a willing partner from the past. And she had been happy to oblige.

The last of the carts, laden with their cargoes, were moving past the window now, the noise and the smell of human and animal detritus passing into the night. As the glow from the torches receded and darkness descended into the street de Bernay turned away from the window and studied the girl sprawled naked on the covers. In the soft light of the candle her obvious imperfections were rather less obvious. She was pretty, in her own way, her dark hair and eyes being her best features, but her nose was too long and her mouth too narrow for her to be called beautiful. But for all that she was a willing partner, vastly experienced in her calling, and, de Bernay knew, she was in love with him.

He moved to the bed and lowered himself onto it. He turned toward Odette, pulling her face towards his, kissing the narrow mouth before settling back onto the covers.

"You will marry me one day?" she said softly. "You did promise."

"One day," he said, his mind not on his marital station but upon other, far weightier problems.

"And we shall have children, yes, lots of them." She appeared not to have noticed the equivocation in his answer, or if she had she had pretended not to notice.

"As many as you like my love," he said. It was a wonder that she did not already have a brood of them running amok but as far as he was aware she was still childless. Perhaps she used a sharp stick or something. It was all one to him whatever she did. She did not feature in his plans, save for what was left of the night. He returned to contemplating his own plans, what he might do to salvage the situation.

Across the street, in the stable, his three recruits were minding the brat. They had wanted to free him from his bonds but de Bernay had refused. He did not want another blunder. They had already failed in their attempt to capture the Wake's whore and Sanglier had a broken nose to prove it. The last thing he wanted was the boy to escape. Then again, now that the army were retreating he could not see much profit in holding onto the boy. He knew that he should kill him, a swift turn of the knife and it would over, but somehow he sensed that the boy could yet be useful to him. He was a link with the past, a link to the housecarl, and despite this temporary setback he still harboured dreams of slicing up the housecarl whilst the army looked on, admiring each slice of the blade, each finesse, as he brought the housecarl to his knees. Let the boy live then, for the moment…

Odette's hand had moved down to his thigh, stroking it gently, backwards and forwards and he knew that she wanted to make love again. She had an insatiable appetite for a whore but then so did he. He took a nipple between his thumb and forefinger and slowly massaged it so that it was soon hard and inviting. His hand slipped down to her groin, between the dark curls, and she gave a soft sigh. "You will make such a good father, *Cheri,*" she said, "when we are married." He did not reply initially; this was dangerous ground, and best avoided.
"But first we have a war to win," he said, removing his hand from her groin. "We could not contemplate marriage whilst I am still in

the army. Soldiers tend to make widows and that would not be fair, on you or the children."

His reference to children was mistake.

"Oh *Cheri*!" she exclaimed, "you are so kind, so considerate to your Odette! I would be proud to have you for my husband, war or no war. We should marry as soon as possible. Say you will marry me soon, say it my love!"

She grasped his member, massaging it up and down. He felt himself swell under her ministrations and before he knew it he was agreeing to her demands.

"Very well, my love," he said. "If that is your wish I shall see a priest as soon as I can."

"Oh thank you *Cheri,*" she said. "You will not regret your decision. And Odette will prove it to you." She lowered her head and her mouth closed over his swollen *glans.* He cursed himself for his weakness but moments later as the sweet, sharp, spasms wracked through him he thought that perhaps it had not been such a bad idea after all. Promises were made to be broken. He had broken them all his life. And if she wanted a child so badly he knew just where to find one…

Ranulf wandered around the hospital station at Belsar's Hill. Deserted now, the only evidence that it had once been inhabited were the discarded bandages, the pails of faeces and vomit, the tubs filled with amputated hands and arms, sometimes a leg; the legacies of war. The ground, still soft from the thunderstorm, was deeply rutted from the wheel tracks carved into it by the mule carts that had carried away the sick and the dying. Strange to think that it had begun here, all those weeks ago when he and his family had been captured by *Le Couteau.* And now *Le Couteau* had his son again. At the height of the battle, when they were slaughtering the

Norman army, *Le Couteau* had crept into the camp like a thief in the night and stolen away his son.

He pulled off the Norman helmet and jerkin and angrily hurled them into the mud. It had been a good idea of the Wake's, to strip the bodies on the sow, to disguise themselves as Normans, but with the Norman army gone, retreated to Cambridge, their disguise was of little use. What he would do now he was not entirely certain. The Wake had failed him, had failed them both, despite his promises and Ranulf knew that it was now up to him. He should have followed his instincts the day of the battle, when the trail was still fresh. At least then *Le Couteau* would only have gained a few hours. Now he could be anywhere. Ranulf cursed and swore under his breath, angry with himself for his weakness, angry with the Wake for persuading him against his will. He had to find Hal, dead or alive, because there would be no rest for himself or Alice until he did. *Alice.* He knew that she blamed herself for Hal's capture, for being at the chapel, at prayer, when she should have been with her son. He had tried to reason with her, to deflect the blame away from her onto himself. They should have taken precautions, he had said, left some men at the camp, but they had failed to do so. It was their failure if it was anyone's, but Alice was not to be persuaded. And now she sat alone in the gloom of their hut, not speaking, not eating, engrossed in her thoughts, her private world of misery and guilt.

It was almost unbearable, this not knowing; not knowing whether Hal was alive or dead, or where he was, or whether he was in torment and he knew, as certainly as he had known anything his life, that unless he found the answers he would never live again. The world was dead to him now, dead to them both, for how could they live their lives with this burden hanging over them? It was worse than being dead; it was a living hell, a daily reminder of their failure and he was not sure how much longer he could bear it.

He was suddenly reminded of Cnut, the enigmatic youngster that had joined the King's housecarl regiment before the butchery on Caldbec Hill. He knew now something of the cancer that had eaten away at him, hour by hour, day by day, until at the end he had sought his own death to find redemption and a release from his torment.

He heard footsteps behind him and turned to see the Wake, who, like himself until moments before, was clad in the uniform of the enemy. Also like himself the Wake had scraped his face in the Norman fashion, had trimmed his hair, and although Ranulf guessed it should have made him look younger it somehow exposed the inner man, making him seem naked and vulnerable. Perhaps he was grieving for his wife who had not been seen since entering the tunnel. Or perhaps the Normans now had her, as *Le Couteau* had boasted, or God forbid, that she was now dead.

It was strange, he realised, when he came to reflect upon it, that the Wake had barely mentioned Torfrida when Alice had broken the terrible news on the march back from Aldreth. He had shown little emotion then and Ranulf had attributed it to the exhaustion of the battle, the dulling of his senses, but the Wake had had a full day now to reflect and yet amongst all the talk of rescuing Hal he had barely mentioned his wife. He had his reasons, no doubt.

"Run like those damned rabbits of theirs, back to their burrows," he said as the Wake came alongside him.

"Yes, but they will be back; perhaps next month, maybe next year. Whenever it is we must be ready for them." The Wake gave a shrug of his massive shoulders. "We can expect little mercy now."

"Mercy is a word the Bastard does not recognise," Ranulf said. "I have seen them before, remember."

The Wake clapped him on the shoulders in the familiar way that he had of acknowledging a point but for once there was an absence of warmth in the gesture, as though it were somehow contrived.

"Of course, my friend. I was forgetting. Forgive me," he said.
Ranulf looked around the deserted camp. His eye strayed to the tree that *Le Couteau* had manacled him to and then beaten him senseless and he felt a well of anger rise from deep within, extinguishing the uncertainty, the fear, surrounding Hal. He consciously let it burn, let it feed itself upon him, for he knew that this was where his strength came from.
"I must leave soon," he said. "There is something I must do."
"I know." The Wake's reply was sanguine, as though he had expected this.
"You know then?"
The Wake shrugged. "What else is there for you to do? I wish you luck. You will need it. I am only sorry that my plan has failed you." He paused to reflect upon what he had just said and when he spoke again his voice was full of remorse. "You must hate me," he said, "for bringing you to this." Ranulf turned to him in surprise.
"Hate? No. Hatred I reserve for my enemies; for the Bastard, for *Le Couteau* and his kind." He forced a grim smile. "In any event I once failed a man and he was a King. I know what it is like. Do not punish yourself for what you cannot change."
The Wake nodded and for a few moments there was silence between the two men.
"I will not fail you again," he said. "Whatever happens I shall be there at the end." He picked up the helmet and jerkin that Ranulf had thrown to the ground and studied them in silence. "*Parlez-vous francais?*" he said. Ranulf stared at him blankly.
"I thought not," the Wake said. "Be careful then, my friend. Perhaps you would do better to remain a Saxon, re-grow your beard, blend into the background until you find what you are looking for."
"My plan exactly," Ranulf said. "My only plan, in fact." He shrugged. "And you? What will you do about Torfrida? If *Le*

Couteau is as good as his word she may already…" he did not know how to finish but already the Wake was shaking his head.
"Torfrida has learned to be resourceful," he said. "I do not think that *Le Couteau* has her. If he had he would not have bothered with your son."
"Then where is she? If she is not at the camp and not in *Le Couteau's* hands where can she be?"
The Wake rubbed his chin, red and sore from the blade that had scraped it clean and Ranulf saw again the look on his face that he had first noticed the day they had met.
"Torfrida and I have not been…intimate… for many years," the Wake said softly. "It is a private matter that I care not to discuss. But I think she is alive, and if she is, I believe I know where she will have gone. She will be safe there, and happy; something that she has not been for many years, and for the moment I intend to leave her where she is."
Ranulf stared at him, lost for words.
"She is your wife," he said after what seemed an eternity. "You know best I suppose."
The Wake regarded him with pale grey eyes that seemed to stare right through him.
"It is sometimes better to bow to the inevitable," he said.

Ranulf looked south, towards Cambridge, to where he must go to kill *Le Couteau* and to find his son. Cambridge; where yet another army would soon be gathering to hurl itself against the Isle. And as he watched wisps of smoke from the distant City spiral into the air he wondered whether the Wake had been referring to Torfrida or to something else entirely…

Chapter Nineteen
Crowland Abbey

Abbott Thurstan closed his eyes and allowed himself a smile as the last notes of the *Te Deum* soared up to the vaulted ceiling of the Abbey. As fresh and green as the day they were penned the notes echoed through the air, ephemeral and haunting, and the Abbott knew that if God were listening he would surely approve. *You God we praise;* the opening words set the tone for the remainder of the hymn, a celebration of the Glory, the Majesty of the Creator. The *Te Deum* was a work of genius, he thought, as though the composer had somehow glimpsed heaven itself and had captured it in his music.

As the final notes died away he rose stiffly from his seat to deliver his sermon. He was getting old, and the arthritis in his hips and knees was sometimes more than he could bear. Only the tincture of laudanum that he carried in a phial around his neck gave him any relief from the pain and sometimes he relied upon it a little too much. He studied the gathered assembly packed inside the Abbey. Mainly novices, young and still keen, his chosen theme for the evening was the Temptation of Christ. He knew the lesson by heart; it was a favourite of his, and especially relevant in these troubled times. *Thou shall not tempt the Lord thy God.* And yet King William was attempting to do just that, promising to build God a great Cathedral at Ely when the Wake had been crushed. The Conqueror was a hard man, he reflected, sunk in greed. And greed was at the heart of the Country's, the Church's, problems. And so it was his responsibility, and the responsibility of men like him, to spread the true gospel, to fiercely oppose the Norman King whenever he should stray from the straight and narrow, and tonight was an opportunity to do just that.

He cleared his throat and began to recite from Matthew 4. He needed no scripture to help him; he was word perfect, and he could see from the rapt attention of his audience, the young novice monks with their freshly shaven tonsures illuminated by the light of dozens of candles, their upturned faces fixed upon his, that he had their undivided attention. And God had already shown the King the error of his ways, he said, illustrating his sermon with what he considered to be a perfect example of it. The disaster on the causeway at Aldreth was as much the will of God as the work of the Wake, and was a clear signal that God would not be tempted. He did not mention the role of the Pope in the King's plans; it was not politic to do so in public and privately he did not agree with the Pope's aiding and abetting the King's offer. For was it not also written: *Thou shalt worship the Lord thy God and only him shall ye serve?* And who was the Pope serving in all of this? The Almighty? Himself? Or perhaps, he decided, his counterpart in the form of the King. He was uncomfortably aware of how the Pope had strayed from the word of God over the last four years, allowing himself to be bribed with promises of land and Cathedrals in England in return for his support to the Conqueror.

But these last thoughts he must keep to himself, for the moment. Tomorrow he would visit the chapel on the Isle of Ely, a small seccursal cell, the last within the See. He would arrange to be rowed across by boat, his preferred method of travel about the fens in his latter years. If he had been younger, and fitter, he would have used the secret path running from Soham to Ely itself, a path known only to himself and one or two others. But those others were dead now, gone to their maker, and as far as he was aware he was the only one still aware of it. Even the Wake did not know of its existence. He debated briefly whether he ought, perhaps, to tell the Wake, but then decided against it. A secret was no longer a secret once it was shared. And if the Wake discovered it what was there to stop others discovering it too? He decided to keep it to himself. He may have use of it one day…

Tomorrow he would visit Hugo Brittanious, the parish priest, and he would look forward to the visit for despite his age and the paralysing sickness that had struck Hugo down, he also knew that he would be assured of a warm welcome. There was a humility about Hugo that he liked and they could talk frankly without fear of reprisal.

He returned to his sermon, reminding his audience of the need for constant vigilance, to be wary of the sins of pride and envy and avarice, for it was well known that the Devil was ever present, ever ready to seize upon the slightest weakness, to tempt them, as he had tempted Christ, with offers of power and wealth and the pleasures of the flesh if they would only forsake the true God and follow him.

As he moved toward the end of the sermon he was gratified to see that the eyes of the novices, reflected in the guttering candlelight, were still fixed upon him, still hanging upon his every word. The future of the English Church rested upon their young shoulders, upon his ability to inculcate the Church's true values and beliefs. He enjoyed the chance to spread the Creed whenever he could, to be a force for good, and now, in the twilight of his years he spent most of his time doing so, secure in the knowledge that whatever else occurred in these turbulent times, he would never be found wanting.

The lights of the distant Abbey glowed like coals in the blackness of the night, warming and welcoming. Torfrida stumbled towards them with renewed urgency now that her goal was in sight. Her feet were bleeding and sore and her gown was stiff with mud. She was bitterly cold, for a northerly wind had sprung up from nowhere and was whipping across the open fenland, chilling her to the bone. She was tired and miserable, but it was a superficial misery for the deep conviction that she had felt since escaping the tunnel had never left her. Not once had she regretted her decision; not when she had had to hide in the reeds to evade detection by her pursuers, nor later, when a blanket of cloud had covered the sky, cloaking the brightest star in the heavens, the one that she knew pointed the way north. Nor even when, time after time, she had stumbled across an impassable stretch of water and been forced to retrace her steps. All night she had slowly headed north, constantly alert for some sign of danger, some sign that her pursuers were on her heels. But save for the wildlife that inhabited the fens, and the wind that whistled about her ears she had seen, had heard nothing. She had headed north, driven onwards by an inner voice that told her to keep going, keep going...

And so she had, until in the pale grey light of early dawn she had spotted a lone fisherman out on the mere with his eel nets and bait. She had called to him, and after hearing her tale he had agreed to ferry her over to the mainland. She had nothing to offer him, save her thanks, but he had shared his food with her and wished her well before returning to his nets and the daily struggle for survival.

And now, after almost a day of journeying north she had reached her final destination. At first, when she had left the tunnel and hidden in the reeds she had no idea where she would go, what she would do; only that something inside her had changed. But as dusk had turned to nightfall and the stars had appeared in the northern sky, she had seen the star shining brightly and it seemed to her, at that moment, that it was shining just for her. She was instantly reminded of her childhood, of the magical story of the three Kings that had followed the star all the way to Bethlehem to see for themselves the Christ-child that would give his life to save the world and offer life eternal. And as she gazed at the star she had heard a whisper, carried on the north wind, speaking only to her and she had known then what she must do.

As she approached the Abbey she heard voices raised in song, coming from within. She stopped and listened, and it was as if the voices were welcoming her home. It was the *Te Deum,* not heard since she had been forced to leave Bourne Manor. The beauty of the music, the strong melodious voices rising and falling with each cadence brought sudden memories flooding back, and with the memories came tears, surprising her, and she wiped them away with the sleeve of her gown. She had not realised how deeply the wounds had penetrated, how scarred she had become. But today all that would change for she would begin a new life; start again.

She took several deep breaths to calm herself and summoning her resolve she grasped the ring of the knocker and hammered loudly on the solid oak of the door. She stepped back a pace, smoothed her dress, her hair from her face, and waited for a response. After a few moments a small panel in the door slid open and the face of a young monk appeared.

"Who is it?" he asked, peering into the darkness, and Torfrida realised that the monk could not see her as she was still in shadow. She stepped forward so that she was only inches from the panel and as she did so the monk raised a candle, illuminating her face. She was acutely aware of how bedraggled she must look after her journey but the monk appeared not to notice.

"The Lady Torfrida!" he exclaimed, obviously recognising her, and surprised, no doubt that she should be venturing out alone on a cold, windswept night.

"A Lady once," she smiled wearily, "but as you can see, I am a Lady no longer."

The monk looked her up and down and then quickly unbolted the door.

"Come in! Come in!" he said, "and warm yourself by the fire." The door led into a small antechamber with a stone bench and a brazier that was piled high with spitting, cracking, logs. She went to it and let the heat slowly thaw her out.

Beyond another solid door, from somewhere in the Abbey, she could hear a voice that she recognised as that of Abbott Thurstan, delivering a sermon, no doubt. Abbott Thurstan was old now, but she could still recall the sermons that he used to deliver during his visits to their tiny chapel at Bourne Manor when she *was* a Lady and the world was a different place. His messages were simple then, full of fire and brimstone and the threat of eternal damnation for those foolish enough to ignore the word of God. She smiled at the thought.

"What can I do for you, Lady?" The young monk's question brought her back to the present and the reason for her journey.

"I would like to speak to the Abbott," she said, "when it is convenient. We are old friends."

"Can I tell him the purpose of your visit?" The young monk was polite but insistent.

"Yes," she said, making up her mind in the instant. "Tell him that I wish to take Holy Orders, to devote my life to God." Surprise registered on the young monk's face but he quickly remembered himself.

"I will tell the Abbott you are waiting," he said. "Please take a seat." He indicated the stone bench and disappeared through the heavy door.

She settled herself before the brazier, staring into the flames, emptying her mind of the past, preparing herself for God.

Chapter Twenty
August 1070

The sun blazed down from a clear blue sky and as the Conqueror trotted his stallion over the bridge that he had constructed to span the Ouse he wiped the sweat from his brow and peered into the middle distance. Half a mile to the north the Isle of Ely was clearly visible through the heat haze, its green spine running south towards him before ending abruptly at the hamlet of Aldreth. He put his spurs to his stallions' flank urging it forward and the stallion splashed through the wet marshland where once a causeway had been. The stallion's forelegs suddenly plunged into a deep, black, pool that he had not seen and he was almost thrown from the saddle. Only his reactions saved him. Were he not an excellent horseman he might have been thrown. As it was his breeches were soaked to the waist and he cursed under his breath as he put his heels to its flanks and prompted it forward with a click of his tongue. The stallion fought its way onto firmer ground and the Conqueror reined to a halt.

He had come to see for himself the difficulties that his new army would face and the events of the morning had done nothing to dispel his doubts. Behind him his entourage were cursing and exhorting their own mounts through the mud, clear evidence that they were having the same difficulties as himself. He studied the sky, a deep azure blue, not a cloud to be seen. It had not rained for weeks and elsewhere, inland, the country was scorched and brown.

Here though, in the wetlands, the ground was soft and yielding beneath the hard, sun-baked crust and even as he watched the rest of his party rein to a halt he knew that an infantry assault across this terrain could be just as disastrous as the last.

"Stinks worse than a Saxon's arsehole." The Conqueror's son-in-law, Count Alan Fergant of Brittany and Earl of Mercia reined to a halt beside him and eyed the bleak landscape with undisguised contempt. "The bastards are welcome to it, I say."

Alan Fergant, called Alan the Red by those closest to him, had fiery red hair and a temper to match. It was said that he had never been seen to smile. Certainly the Conqueror had never been so favoured, despite his generosity after *Senlac* Hill. Fergant had commanded the Breton division that day, had been to hell and back with his men, and had been there at the end, his chain-mail bloodied and torn, when finally the Saxon shield wall had disintegrated and the butchery had begun. He had played a full part in it, putting to the sword any Saxons found alive. Not that there had been many of those. The King had rewarded him with the Earldom of Mercia, one of the richest prizes in the land, and now the King was relying on him and his men to finish this campaign.

"An arsehole, yes, but also a running sore, and I want it removed." The Conqueror was in no mood for his son-in-law's bleak humour. His men, his youthful vigour and his leadership qualities were what he wanted, and within the next few weeks a fresh army, made up of the remnants of his own men and Fergant's Bretons would be ready to launch a further assault against the Wake. And this time, there could be no mistake.

He looked north again, to where the tiny hamlet of Aldreth lay hidden from view, nestling against the green spine of the Isle. *Aldreth;* the mere thought of it brought his blood to the boil. The worst defeat of his career. His *only* defeat. And he wanted revenge. He wanted it so badly that it consumed his every waking thought.

Even the rebellion in Flanders had paled beside this. He wanted it ending. *Now*. He turned to Fergant:
"In two months the rains will start again. Your task will be doubly difficult then. The ground is still soft," he indicated Fergant's muddy boot, "and it will be tough going but there will never be a better time to force the Isle. How long do you need to prepare?" He studied Fergant with equanimity, awaiting Fergant's reply. In truth he was testing him, his resolve, his assessment of the situation. Alan Fergant rubbed his chin, covered with three days' stubble before shading his eyes, studying the land, peering north just as the King had done. He rubbed his chin again before giving his answer.
"As you say, the ground is still soft. Ideally another month, six weeks; even then we shall have to build a causeway. Armed infantry can never cross it unaided."
"I built a causeway before and what happened to it?" The Conqueror waved his hand at the empty stretch of marshland. "Sunk without a trace. Three thousand men drowned. This place is a graveyard," he said, "and like to be one again if we do not mind our business. I do not favour this idea of a causeway," he said. "I do not favour it at all."
Fergant shrugged.
"What other way is there? The Saxons have chosen the perfect place to defend. No way in, save by boat, but boats could never cross this shit. Not under fire from their archers at any rate. It would be a blood bath."

The King looked around at the rest of his party, at their mounts. Most of them were knee deep in mud. Ivo Taillebois, a heavy man, like himself was almost drowning in it, his small mare struggling to carry his weight over the soft ground. His mood was sour but he almost laughed at the sight. He did not like Taillebois, had invited him along because this was his land, given to him for his efforts on *Senlac* Hill. A common adventurer, but he had to be paid along with the rest of them, in land. *The arsehole of England* as Fitz Osbern used to call it. And Tailbois was drowning in it. Fergant was right. It would, he knew, be a blood bath if they tried to cross by boat. The men would be exhausted after just a few hundred yards. In any event they did not have enough craft. So what alternatives were there? A causeway then, but he did not like it.

"This causeway of yours, where would you build it?" he snapped, putting an edge in his voice. Fergant looked right and left, contemplating the question. He hesitated, apparently uncertain of himself for once.

"Well?" The Conqueror snapped again. The heat was making him irritable.

"You chose well last time," Fergant said eventually. "But if it were me, I would build it two or three hundred yards to the left."

The King looked over to the left. Marshland again, soft and treacherous, but here the ground was covered with reed beds, thick and tall.

"Why there?" he barked.

"Two reasons," Fergant said. "First, the reeds will give our men cover from the Saxon attacks."

"And the second?"

"Because this," Fergant said, pointing to the open ground in front of him, "is a bloody graveyard. You said so yourself." He raised a beetling red eyebrow. "We don't want our men digging here do we Sire? Never know what they might dig up."

For once, the Conqueror was lost for words.

Chapter Twenty-One
Cambridge

The Norman cavalry were pressing in hard on their flanks, sensing victory, determined this time to force the breakthrough. On the right his shield-wall was buckling under the strain, his housecarls, those that still stood, barely able to hold the incessant attacks. The stench of blood, of death, was everywhere. Arrows were raining down from a blood red sky and beside him two men were hammered to the ground by the iron-tipped shafts, their cries lost in the din of the battle. He raised his shield above his head and felt the jolt as an arrow thumped through it, the point narrowly missing his cheek. He heard another cry, from close behind, and instinctively turned toward the sound. The King was down, his eye removed by an arrow. Blood was everywhere. He ran to him and held him tight, clutching him to his chest as the King bucked and writhed in his arms, his face unrecognisable beneath the red mask. The King was screaming something but he could not make out the words. He looked at his hands, his breeches, soaked in the King's blood. He heard another cry, loud and shrill, and he tore his eyes from the King only to see that the Normans' had broken through. A tide of fear washed over him as they charged towards him, the King still clutched to his chest, their lances couched for the kill. Men were streaming for the woods, their resistance broken, their weapons discarded. Cnut's face was suddenly before him, inches away, screaming at him to run, to run...

Ranulf woke with a jolt. For a few moments he felt disorientated, wondering where he was before his senses recovered and the familiarity of the tiny room gradually calmed him. His face beneath his re-grown beard was soaked with sweat but his chest was ice cold. He rose from the straw, a makeshift bed, and padded over to the pitcher of rancid water that served for both drinking and washing and splashed some onto his face. He closed his eyes for a moment, consigning his dream to the farthest reaches of his consciousness. Outside, in the street below, he could hear raised voices; it was those that had woken him.

He returned to the straw and felt under it for *Requitur* and the stiletto; both still there, close to hand, should they be needed.

He moved to the window and quickly glanced out. It was barely dawn, but the Breton soldiers of Fitzalan Fergant were already patrolling the streets, questioning anyone looking suspicious. An altercation was taking place between six Bretons and three bedraggled Saxons. The Saxons were all in their middle years, looked hardly a threat to anyone, but the Bretons had drawn their swords and were threatening the Saxons with them, shouting and swearing in French, their faces only inches apart. One of the Saxons' tried to run but he was not quick enough and a sword was thrust brutally into his back. The man gave a cry and collapsed to the ground, his spinal column shattered. The Breton ripped his sword from the dead man's back without so much as a glance at him. The remaining Saxons looked on in horror, their protestations silenced by the death of their comrade. The Bretons now bound their hands and to the prompt of a sword point the two Saxons accompanied them up the street and out of sight. The dead man was left where he had fallen, his blood pooling around him.

Ranulf sighed and collapsed onto the straw, knowing there was nothing he could do. He knew what was happening: Fergants' Bretons were rounding up all the fit Saxons and pressing them into service upon the construction of the new causeway. Some were being made to cut timber, others to carry, or ferry, it out to the construction site, and the rest, the youngest and fittest, made to labour upon it. This way, Fergant reasoned, his own men would be spared for the assault itself and the Wakes' attempts at sabotage frustrated. He would hardly kill his own kind.

Ranulf had gradually sunk, like Alice, into a pit of depression. It was easy to lie on the straw all day but that would not find his son. Or *Le Couteau*. The thought of *Le Couteau* and the burning hatred that he felt for the man eventually roused him from his lethargy. He held the thought, the hatred, whilst he dressed, forced down a mouthful of dry oatmeal, took a few sips of the rancid water, and slipped the stiletto under his jerkin. He made his way out into the streets.

For a week he had been combing the City, searching for some sign of *Le Couteau,* or his son, but so far without the slightest hint of success. He guessed that if he could find the Norman he would also find Hal, or at least learn what had happened to him, and he figured that it would be easier to find his distinctive adversary than it would be to find a young boy. So he had concentrated on tracking down *Le Couteau*.

At first he had been optimistic. There could not be that many Normans' with the distinctive scar that *Le Couteau* bore and a few Saxons had seen men with scars such as he had described. And one by one he had tracked them down. But none of them had been the man that he was seeking and he had come to realise, after a few days of fruitless searching, that the task would be more difficult than he had first thought. Many Normans bore the scars of battle; he had scarred many himself.

He reached the end of the street and cautiously looked around. He had to be careful; his appearance marked him out as a warrior and the last thing he wanted was to draw attention to himself. He had feigned a limp, and a stoop, to make himself appear older than he was. Even so he knew that he could not relax his guard for one mistake could find him pressed into service for the enemy. Or worse. Normans and Bretons guarded every gate into the City and their patrols were on many street corners. The streets themselves were rank with stench: of unwashed bodies and of open sewers, of putrefaction, of disease, and above it all, pervading the very air that he breathed, the unmistakable stench of fear. Cambridge was a City in the grip of fear. The Conqueror, and now Alan Fergant, had stamped their heel on the citizens, and they went about their lives in a cowed, sullen silence, terrified of attracting the attention of their oppressors. Even the ebullient landlord that had rented him the tiny space beneath the eaves that he laughingly called a room had been in fear of them.

"Every man entering the City must report his business to the procurator," he had said with a tremble in his voice, but of course Ranulf had no intention of doing that.

He paused to consider his next move. The Breton patrol that he had seen earlier had disappeared for the moment, gone to hand over their latest recruits no doubt. The street was empty but soon, he knew, there would be other patrols, just as eager. One day he would make a mistake and that would be that. He felt for the stiletto tucked beneath his jerkin and fingered it softly, running his hand over the razor sharp edges that tapered down to the point. The feel of the weapon in his hand suddenly reminded him of why he was here, and with the knowledge came the sickening certainty of what he must do. Perhaps he had never had any choice; from the moment Hal had fallen into *Le Couteau's* hands. Destiny was guiding him; let destiny decide it then. He looked up and saw that the sun was already climbing above the rooftops. It would be another hot day; too hot to spend rotting in the City, searching for someone who was not there.

Clinging to the sides of the buildings, keeping to the shadows, he headed into the southern quarter of the City then out into the fresh air of the fields beyond, to where the Conqueror's army, swollen with Fergants' Bretons, were encamped in line after line of gleaming white tents and colourful pennants. It was a daunting sight; one to unsettle even the steadiest of nerves and Ranulf stopped to rest and to think. If he approached the camp under a white flag of truce there was no guarantee that it would be honoured for there was no such thing as honour between Saxon and Norman. On the other hand he could think of no other way of getting into the camp without being noticed. It would have to be a white flag then, and hope for the best. It carried a risk but that, he decided, was a risk he must take. For somewhere amongst the rows of shimmering white tents he knew he would find *Le Couteau.*

And then he would kill him.

Chapter Twenty-Two
The Isle

Under a sweltering sun the Conqueror was building a new causeway. In the harsh glare of noon the raw timbers shone like bleached bones against the anonymity of the fens. Three times as wide as the previous causeway, the Bretons of Fitzalan Fergant and their unwitting Saxon allies were making remarkable progress.

The Wake turned his back on the sight. He had seen it all before; had hoped never to see it again, but the activity to the south had destroyed that hope. The Conqueror's capacity, his eagerness, to wage war, seemed limitless. One army destroyed but already another had been found to take its place. It could go on forever; except, of course, that *he* could not go on much longer. Sooner or later they would run out of food, or fresh water, or simply lose the will to fight and then the Conqueror would force the Isle and that would be the end. For all he knew that end was now in sight with the construction of this latest causeway. Sometimes, in the quiet moments, when the world was asleep and he lay awake on his cot, he almost wished for it. He was tired of fighting, tired of killing. He wanted peace and the chance to live an ordinary life, but what peace could there be between Saxon and Norman? So he must fight, to the death if needs be; at least then he would have peace, the same peace that Torfrida had evidently found; at last.

He reached inside his jerkin and pulled out her letter, brought to him by Abbott Thurstan. It was written in her neat, careful hand;

adult, sophisticated, a far cry from the life she had led as the wife of a renegade:

Husband, it read,

May I call you that? For you are still my husband in the eyes of the Lord our father. Forgive me. I hope that you will find it in your heart to do so for despite everything I still love you. But love itself is not enough. I sense that you understand this and in many ways I believe that you will welcome my decision. God has called for me and I have gone to him. There is a peace here, a contentment that I have longed for. I hope that you will understand.

Torfrida.

He folded the note and slipped it back into his jerkin. *I hope that you will understand.* Two lives, twenty years, disposed of in seven lines of neat handwriting. He should have been angry but he wasn't. For years their marriage had been a marriage in name only. Torfrida had made the right decision, for her, and, perhaps, for him. He shut her out, like the closing of a door, and forced himself to concentrate upon the problem at hand.

The Bretons of Alan Fergant were going about their business with an alarming efficiency. Working from dawn until long into the night, the causeway was almost half built. It was difficult to believe that the Conqueror had chosen the same method of assaulting the Isle as the one that had failed so disastrously, but this time there were differences. The location was slightly different; some three hundred yards to the left of where the original causeway had spanned the swamp, this one was cutting its way through high reed beds whereas the first had been arrow straight across the open flood plain of the Ouse.

There were other differences too. Many of the men labouring on the causeway were Saxons; poor, wretched souls whose backs had been stripped bare under the overseers' lash. For three days he had sat and watched the slow, inexorable progress of the causeway, the sinking of the piles into the mud; great long piles, much longer than the piles used on the first causeway, the ends spliced together, then lashed together with ropes, before being driven deep into the thick back mud. The Conqueror obviously did not intend this one to float, or to sink, as the first had sunk.

So for three days he had sat and watched, fascinated, and with a growing sense of alarm, as the Norman and Breton army - and their Saxon work parties - had slowly erected the causeway, piece by painful piece, and he had racked his brains to find some way of destroying it.

This causeway was being built to last. It was evident from the painstaking way that it was being put together; the width of its span across the mud, the girth of the timbers used in its construction, the thickness of the ropes that bound it together. Three times as wide as the former causeway, the Conqueror could attack on a much wider front, commit far more men to the point of attack. It would be harder to stop them next time; perhaps impossible. And when it was over, and the Isle had been subjugated, the causeway would stand as a memorial, a reminder to those that followed of the futility of rebellion, of the Conqueror's endless will to prevail.

Wynter and Lightfoot approached from the west, their reconnaissance apparently complete. Both were sweating profusely beneath their heavy beards.

"Any ideas?" He asked more in hope than expectation.

"No," Lightfoot murmured, shaking his head. "I am still working on it."

"Keep working, old friend," he said, "keep working."
"We could always ask him to surrender," Wynter joked; a tired joke, touched with desperation, and Hereward forced a laugh.
"I don't think he will do that somehow. He's a cold hearted bastard that one."
"Aye, that he is," Wynter acknowledged and returned to studying the causeway; the endless activity of lifting and carrying and hammering and splicing and lashes cracking in the noonday sun and Saxon backs running red with blood.
"What do you think?" he said. "They will soon be on top us." He wiped his brow with the sleeve of his doublet and when he pulled his arm away the soft leather was stained dark with his sweat. "It's bloody hot," he muttered. "Poor bastards, having to work in this." He stared into the distance at the Saxon work parties hefting and carrying the huge raw timbers. He pulled a water skin from his belt and drank deeply from it.

Hereward glanced at the sun. The harsh glare burned his eyes and he quickly averted them. Wynter was right; it was bloody hot and the fens were drying up. Every day his forage parties were returning to the camp with less and less food. Children were going hungry, the adults were starving, and fresh water was becoming hard to find. The water that they had stored at the camp was brackish and stale. And still the sun beat down. It was the last thing he wanted. Soon the Isle would be an Isle no longer and although the Conqueror could not simply walk across, it did make his task easier; the pace at which the new causeway was taking shape was evidence of that.

He wiped a rivulet of sweat from his own brow. The movement, the wiping of the sweat suddenly triggered a distant thought; a spark only, like a long forgotten memory. It was something to do with the sun, the heat, but he could not capture it, not yet. It would come. Wynter handed him the water skin and he put it to his lips. It

was almost empty, just a few drops left to slake his thirst. "Thanks," he said, a touch of irony, handing it back.
"Must have leaked," Wynter said. "The seal's gone. Perished in the heat. Damned sun."

Whether it was the sun or Wynter's thirst that had caused the skin to empty he was not certain but even as the thought came to him so did another: *Icarus. Icarus,* from his childhood; another story told to him by his father. He turned excitedly to his comrades.
"Ever heard the story of *Icarus?"* he asked. Wynter and Lightfoot shook their heads.
"Icarus, uncle? The fellow from Greek legend, you mean?" Morcar rode up on Galahad, the stallion looking more magnificent than ever in the bright noonday sun, his white coat, like the raw timbers of the distant causeway, in stark contrast to the black peat of the soil.
"The very same," he said. "Tell my friends what you know of him."
Morcar paused to consider and his tanned, handsome face, leaner than when he had first arrived, and somehow harder, wore a slight frown. He leaned down from the saddle to address them, almost, Hereward thought, like a teacher lecturing a child:
"Icarus was the son of Daedalus; architect, engineer, and a great inventor. Daedalus had incurred the wrath of King Minos of Crete and the King had imprisoned both him and Icarus on his island.
"What had he done wrong?" Lightfoot interjected, but Hereward silenced him by raising his hand.
"It doesn't matter," he said. "Just listen." Morcar continued his tale. "To escape, Daedalus built himself a giant pair of wings, stitching the feathers together over a timber frame. He tested them and they worked. But there was his son, Icarus. He couldn't leave him on the island and so he had to build a second pair of wings for him, smaller and lighter. The problem was that Daedalus had run out of

thread. So he glued the wings together with wax. He cautioned Icarus not to fly too high for the sun would melt the wax and Icarus promised to heed his warning. But when the time came and they made their escape Icarus could not help himself. Like a bird he soared, into the sky, higher and higher, ever nearer the sun until the wax melted, the wings fell apart, and Icarus drowned."

Wynter looked at Hereward. "How does that help us?" he said. "Unless you're planning to fly of course."

"Fly? No. I would that I could." He smiled. "But the tale is worth telling is it not?"

"Is it?" Wynter cast a glance at Lightfoot who clearly shared his doubts.

"I would have thought that yon causeway was worth more than some Greek legend," Lightfoot said. "If we can't stop that there will be no more fairytales; Greek or Saxon."

"True enough," the Wake acknowledged but there was a lightness in his voice that had previously been absent, as though a burden had been lifted from his shoulders.

"Well?" Wynter pressed him. "What are we going to do?" He studied the causeway, cutting its way through the reeds like a scar. A quarter of a mile yet, he estimated. Another week.

"Nothing," he said. "Absolutely nothing."

The Wake watched the housecarl's woman cross the camp toward the water butts, her slim frame wrapped in a tight woollen shawl drawn protectively about her. The evening was cooling the air and the camp was stirring into life after the torpid inactivity of the afternoon. He saw her draw a ladle of water, the daily ration, from one of the two water butts and carefully pour the contents into a bowl before heading back towards her hut. Her face was very pale; the result, he guessed, of spending too much time inside, and her eyes were ringed with dark circles; evidence of lack of sleep. It was hardly surprising; her son and now her husband, both of them gone, perhaps forever.

He knew that he had failed her. On the road back to the camp he had promised to avenge her but in that, as in many things in his life, he had failed to deliver. *Le Couteau* had disappeared and Ranulf had gone after him. Whether Ranulf would succeed where he had failed he could only guess. The odds were not good. Why had he allowed him to go? Should he have offered to accompany him? He had subconsciously avoided the questions until now, afraid, perhaps of the answer.

His mind fled back to the time he had seen her alone with the housecarl, inside their darkened hut, their bodies moving together as one. It had sparked the beginnings of something that he did not fully understand, something that he had thought beyond him. They were two sides of the same coin, he reflected, jealousy and desire, and he had kept his distance, fearful perhaps, of where it might lead. He had almost crossed the line the day of the battle, the chance meeting on the road to the camp. He had caught her with his eyes and given her a glimpse of his soul. He knew that people were hypnotised by his eyes, the strange contrast from light to dark grey, and he was usually able to hide it. But that day the veil had slipped and he had shown her something of himself that he had not intended. And he had seen her reaction.

He watched her returning to her hut, carefully holding the bowl so as not to spill any of the precious water. He followed the lines of movement beneath her shift, the careful footsteps, small and neat, like her figure. He was reminded of the night she had appeared at the camp fire, her face aglow with her new found freedom, the long tapering fingers that plucked the eel from his knife, the small white teeth that chewed the meat…

She had almost reached her hut when she tripped, spilling the water. Afterwards Hereward would wonder whether providence had caused that trip, the tiniest of errors, but now, as the water seeped into the parched earth and Alice hurriedly bent to scoop it up he hurried forward to help her.

At first she seemed to be unaware of him, her attention riveted upon the fast disappearing water. Her tiny hands with the slender fingers clawed frantically at the earth in her attempt to salvage something but already he could see that the water was gone. There were tears in her eyes, her skin stretched tight over her cheekbones. She was, he could see, at the end of her tether.

"It doesn't matter," he said softly, "we shall get some more." She looked at him then, as though seeing him for the first time and nodded silently. A tear rolled down her cheek and he pretended to ignore it. He took the bowl from her hands and offering her his free hand helped her up. It was the first contact between them. She had said nothing yet, but as they made their way over to the water butts she said in a voice that trembled with emotion:

"We shall be taking another's ration. It isn't fair."

"You can have mine," he said. "I have already drunk my fill." A lie, but he didn't care.

He glanced around the camp and was aware that several pairs of eyes were fixed upon them: Wynter and Lightfoot, some of Morcar's men, some women from the camp. *Let them look.*

When they reached the water butts he took the ladle from Lefwinus, assigned the task of ensuring that there was no foul play, and dipped it into the butt.

"Almost empty," Lefwinus, said. "We could do with some rain."

He was right, Hereward reflected, but in many ways he was also wrong. He needed the sun to shine, for a week at least. He dipped the ladle into the butt and scooped up the water. He had to reach almost to the bottom and when he withdrew the ladle he saw that the water was opaque, discoloured. He poured the contents into the bowl and handed it to her.

"Thank you," she whispered, her words barely audible. She turned towards her hut. There was no reason for him to accompany her further but something made him fall into step alongside and they walked back to the hut together. He was conscious of the eyes still upon them, judging them, ready, perhaps, to pass sentence.

They reached the hut and seeing that Alice would struggle to open the flap with the bowl in her hands he moved past her and threw it open. He stood there for a few moments, holding the flap, longing for her to invite him inside.

"You must go," Alice said quietly. "Now, before people talk of this." She ducked inside the flap, disappearing into the blackness beyond.

He turned on his heels and walked back to his hut, the loneliest walk of his life.

Chapter Twenty-Three
The Norman Camp

It was late afternoon before Ranulf made his approach toward the camp. Having decided that a flag of truce was the only way of getting into the camp alive, he then had to find one. He retraced his steps into the City to search for something suitable and eventually found a piece of old sacking, which, if not exactly white, was close enough for his purposes. He tied it to a piece of stout ash and now, with the flag held tightly in his fist and heart pounding in his chest he walked toward the picket lines ringing the camp.

The camp was bathed in a golden glow, giving it an altogether gentler appearance than it had appeared at noon, the harsh white lines of the tents fading to amber, dappled with sunlight and shadow. The camp could have been asleep but he knew that appearances were deceptive. The Conqueror, it was rumoured, never slept. As he approached the pickets walking slowly up and down, as yet unaware of his presence, a bead of sweat trickled into his eyes and he flicked it away with a shake of his head. He was nervous, he realized, despite the deep well of anger directed at *Le Couteau*. He decided that a bold approach would be the best, perhaps the only, way of achieving his objective and he consciously lengthened his stride. Somehow it helped to ease his nerves.

At thirty yards he saw the pickets start at his approach, aware of him for the first time. For a few moments they regarded him quizzically, as though unable to believe their eyes, but then he saw them reach for their scabbards, heard the rasp of steel as swords were drawn and pointed menacingly towards him. It was no more than he had expected but it was still difficult to keep going. Anything could happen. If one of the guards panicked he could be dead…

He raised his makeshift flag even higher and hoped that they noticed the movement. His free hand, too, he raised, as in surrender, although he did not intend to surrender. He intended to kill *Le Couteau* and to find his son. He made himself think of *Le Couteau,* of what he might have done to Hal and as his anger rose, the fear subsided.

At ten yards he fixed the nearest guard, a young man still in his teens, with an icy stare. The guard looked away, to his right, to where other men were hurrying over, their swords also drawn, concerned or merely curious at this strange development. Before he knew it he was surrounded in a ring of steel but as yet no one had made a move to touch him. He stood still, the sacking flag held high and waited for them to make the next move.

"Quel est cet homme?" An older man, perhaps in his mid-thirties, was questioning the young guard in a sharp voice. From the chevrons on his shoulder and authoritative manner of speaking Ranulf guessed that he was a Captain or similar rank. The young guard shrugged, looked over towards him, and muttered something in response.

The older man now approached him, parting the ring of swords with a sweep of his hands. His dark eyes scrutinised Ranulf from beneath his steel helm, settling for a few moments on the sacking flag before flicking back to his face.

"I am Sir Roger de Cany, son of the Comte de Cany," he said, in almost perfect English. "I am responsible for this excuse of a guard. I apologise for your reception. My men are tired and hungry

and it makes them nervous." He waved at the ring of swords and instantly they were gone, returned to their scabbards with the same harsh rasp that had greeted his arrival.
"They should know how to honour a flag of truce," de Cany said apologetically. "I fear that honour is a scarce commodity these days. But both sides are guilty of that, yes?"
Ranulf simply nodded; the Norman spoke the truth.
"You are a Saxon of course?" His eyes, darkly shadowed beneath his helmet with its broad nasal, never left Ranulf's face.
"Yes," Ranulf nodded again.
"And I gather from your, er, flag, that you are not armed?
"I have a stiletto," Ranulf replied evenly and he fished it out of his tunic with his free hand. "But I was invited to bring it by the scum that I have come to kill."
"Indeed?" De Cany's eyebrows, dark like his eyes, leaped in surprise. "Then you must keep it." He motioned to Ranulf to return it to his jerkin and Ranulf slid it back.
"And who is this...*scum*, as you so eloquently put it?" de Cany asked. There was, Ranulf thought, genuine curiosity in his voice.
"He calls himself *Le Couteau*," he said. "Do you know him?"
De Cany smiled a wry smile, showing his strong white teeth.
"I know the man you seek," he said. "What has he done that you should risk your life coming...how shall we say...like a sheep into the wolf's lair, to search for him?"
"He has my son." Ranulf spat the words, forcing himself to sound angry.
"Your son? What does he want with him?" De Cany's eyes narrowed.
"To get at me," Ranulf said. "We have some unfinished business."
"It seems that he has succeeded." De Cany made the obvious point and Ranulf, aware that the guard still encircled him, fell silent, unsure how to respond.

De Cany went for a walk, also needing to think. He knew *Le Couteau* well enough. Knew him for a dangerous, backsliding, insubordinate bastard. He also knew never to turn his back when *Le Couteau* was around for if he did he might find it full of Toledo steel. He knew that *Le Couteau* was determined to regain his Captaincy, and more, and he suspected that this giant Saxon was part of his plan. He scrutinised him again, noting the heavily muscled shoulders and arms, the calloused hands that spoke of a warrior, the proud way that he carried himself. It would be no great loss to the army if *Le Couteau* were killed and perhaps this Saxon was the man to do it. Perhaps… but he also knew that *Le Couteau* was a genius with the knife.

He recalled an incident two years earlier between one of his men, Dupois, and *Le Couteau* and *Le Couteau* had called him out. Dupois had agreed to use knives, a mistake. *Le Couteau* had played with him like a cat with a mouse. Blinded first in one eye, and then the other, so that he could not see where the next cut would come, he had flung himself around and around, lashing out wildly, trying to anticipate *Le Couteau's* lethal finesses but of course it was hopeless. Eventually Dupois had begged to die but de Bernay had taken a sadistic pleasure in prolonging the fight, dragging it out, cut by cut, until the man's flesh had been flensed from his bones. The crowd that had gathered to watch had begun to drift away, sickened by the spectacle, and he had stepped in to slit Dupois' throat, ending his torment. He should have done it earlier. Even so he had seen the look on de Bernay's face, denied his ultimate triumph, and he had watched his back ever since. Yes, he would be glad to be rid of de Bernay but was this Saxon man enough? He could not be sure but he deserved his chance. At least it would a Saxon's life if he failed…

He wandered back to the Saxon, noting how he stood head and shoulders above the tallest of his own men. He was a warrior all

right; no doubt of that. He wondered idly what stories he would have to tell, what had happened to cause this argument with de Bernay, how much Norman blood he had already spilled. It crossed his mind that the safest course would be to kill him and have done with it. Then again the prospect of setting him against *Le Couteau* was irresistible. He raised his face to look into that of the Saxon's. It was calm; almost, he thought, resigned.
"Come with me," he said.

De Cany led Ranulf through the lines of tents, row upon row that made up the Norman and Breton camp. Ranulf was disconcerted to see the sheer size of the camp, the hundreds of soldiers settling down at their fires to enjoy an evening meal, or sharpening their blades on the whetstone in preparation for the battle ahead, or wrestling each other, bare chested, much as the Saxon warriors of Hereward did in trials of strength. Of *Le Couteau* he could see no sign.

Eventually they reached a tent, slightly larger than the others but in design no different from the rest. De Cany threw open the flap, inviting him to enter.
"These are my quarters," he said. "You must wait here. I may be gone some time." Ranulf ducked inside and looked around. It smelled of sweat and flies buzzed around the remains of a simple meal, forgotten, no doubt, in the excitement of his arrival.
"I am placing a guard on the entrance," de Cany said. "It is as much for your protection as to prevent your escape. There are those here who would not hesitate to slit your throat." He smiled again, the same wry smile that he had shown earlier. "You may use my bunk. Get some sleep, if you can."

The flap was flung down, shutting out the last of the evening light. Through the canvas the soft glow of the campfires could be seen, illuminating the gathering gloom, relieving the dark interior of the tent.

He found de Cany's bunk in the corner and laid down on it, placing the stiletto by his right hand. Outside he could hear the laughter and argument of the men, the neighing of horses, the barking of dogs, the occasional shouted order of the Captains: the sounds of an army in the field. He was reminded of that other army, the army in which he had served four long years ago, the night they had camped by their fires along the ridge of Caldbec Hill. Like the men themselves that army no longer existed. It was a ghost army, its time gone forever, destined to live only in his mind, to haunt him for the remainder of his days...

The smell of roasting beef and mutton brought him back to the present, reminding him of his hunger. He had eaten nothing since the handful of oatmeal at dawn, a lifetime ago.

He rose from the bunk and scooped the remains of de Cany's leftovers into his mouth, ignoring the flies that had settled upon it. He chewed the meat slowly, savouring the taste of the fatty beef and settled back onto the bunk. Through the canvas walls he could see the silhouetted figures of the guards, placed there for his protection, and the thought that he was in the wolf's lair, as de Cany had put it, caused him to feel for the presence of the stiletto. His hand closed about the hilt and he felt momentarily reassured. Even so he found himself wishing that it were *Requitur.* But *Requitur* was back at the Tavern, hidden from prying eyes beneath the timbers of a loose floorboard. So it would be his stiletto against *Le Couteau's* Toledo steel, just as the Norman had planned. Then God help him, for no one else would.

He closed his eyes, contemplating what tomorrow might bring. The bunk was comfortable and well worn and before he knew it he was drifting into oblivion, the noise of the camp, the myriad fires, fading with nightfall.

He awoke in the small hours, whilst it was still dark, the time when the senses are at their dullest. At first he was uncertain what had caused him to wake, save, perhaps his own troubled dreams but after a few moments he became aware of noises outside the tent. It could have been the sentries on their patrol of the perimeter but somehow he knew that it was not the sentries that had woken him but other sounds, less regular. He groped in the dark for the stiletto and snatched it up, holding it before him, rising quickly from the bunk as he did so.

He could hear voices now, lowered to match the quiet of the camp. A pitch torch was lit somewhere beyond the entrance; he could smell the rank odour of the pitch and could see the soft light that it gave off as it moved steadily towards the opening. He darted toward the farthest corner of the tent; it would take a few seconds longer for the intruders to find him in its arc of light; a few seconds that could make the difference between life and death. He could feel his heart pounding in his chest like a hammer and he wished again that he had *Requitur* with him. The flap opened noisily. Whoever it was they had not worried about disturbing him.

He did not recognise the men that first entered the tent, the torch held before them. One was large and muscular, his nose recently broken, the bruising still apparent about the eyes. The other man was much smaller, wiry, with quick, sharp, features. At first they did not see him, the light from the torch illuminating the empty bed before it swung around the tent to reveal him standing in the corner, the stiletto held before him. They smiled to one another and instinctively looked behind them as a third man entered. He slid into the tent like a cat, silently, easily, and followed the direction of his comrades' gaze. He smiled a mocking smile that never touched his face, save for the livid scar that marred his features, puckering around the edges, pulling down the corner of his left eye.

Ranulf forced himself to look into the face, lit by the smoking torch. He was somehow drawn towards the eyes, black pools dancing in the flickering light, and despite himself he gave a shudder for the eyes spoke to him of a time soon to come.

And the words that they spoke were of death.

Chapter Twenty-Four

Dawn arrived slowly, imperceptibly, and Ranulf paced the tent like a condemned man in a cell, unable to sleep, reliving the brief encounter with the enemy that he had come to kill. At times he wondered whether he had simply been dreaming, simply imagining that *Le Couteau* had appeared like a vision from hell in the dead of night but the words that he had uttered still rang in his head, a death sentence waiting to be executed: *In the morning then.* And as silently as he had arrived *Le Couteau* had disappeared, his henchmen following him through the flap, throwing the tent into inky blackness once more.

He shook himself from his reverie and tried to concentrate upon the fight, imagining the moves he would make, the mistakes he would have to avoid. It was growing lighter and he pulled back the flap of the tent to reveal dawn's cold light hanging over the camp. The sun had not yet risen and beyond the tent the grass, trampled and flattened underfoot, was damp with dew. A low mist hung over the trees but he knew that the sun would soon burn it off. *Watch the sun.* The thought came to him instinctively. He knew that *Le Couteau* would use any advantage he could, and manoeuvring his opponent into the sun was one of them.

He took a few paces into the morning air and the night sentries, hearing his footsteps, turned and nodded a surly greeting. He pointed to the latrine and again they nodded as he walked over to relieve himself. He could feel their eyes on him, knew that they were watching him closely, and he could not help but wonder what had transpired in the dead of night that had allowed *Le Couteau* to enter the tent unopposed. Anything could have happened, a bribe perhaps; he was, after all, the enemy, and no one would lose any sleep if he had been murdered where he lay. On the other hand he knew that *Le Couteau* was a sadist, vainglorious and arrogant. Murdering his victims in their beds was not his style, not when he could cut them up in front of the whole army. He left the latrine and wandered back to the tent.

Other soldiers were stirring now, some stretching and yawning as they greeted the new day, some idly watching him with genuine interest, others with undisguised hatred. A man cursed him under his breath, just loud enough for him to hear, and he studiedly ignored it. For the hundredth time he reminded himself why he had come and the thought helped to sustain him. Even so he was relieved to reach the sanctuary of de Cany's tent and he pulled down the flap. The sentries resumed their positions outside. He sat on the cot, trying to calm himself, to put his thoughts into some sort of order. He closed his eyes.

"It is time." De Cany's voice cut across the silence and he realised that he must have fallen asleep. He cursed himself as he rose, and slipping the stiletto into his belt followed the Captain outside. The sun was much higher in the sky; he must have slept for an hour or more. The day was brighter too; the mist had burned away and overhead was a clear blue sky. *It was a good day to die,* he thought, *a good day.* And then he remembered his son. His anger rose, familiar and strangely comforting, and he decided after all, that he would live.

He fell into step beside de Cany and although both men had been silent thus far, the Norman now began to speak in quiet, accented tones:

"There are two things to remember when fighting *Le Couteau.*"

Ranulf turned sharply towards him but de Cany ignored the movement.
"Don't look at me. Keep looking, walking, straight ahead."
They were passing a crowd of soldiers, angry and vocal, and he did as he was instructed. Shouts of derision came from his right, from some of the younger men, and once more he tried to ignore them, to avoid eye contact. Someone spat at him but missed.
"Two things, remember." De Cany was speaking again. "First, *Le Couteau* will not wish to kill you quickly. He is jealous of his reputation, of his skill with the knife, and will wish to demonstrate it by prolonging the fight. You can use this to your advantage."
"And the second?"
"He likes to go for the eyes. He has a favourite move, a feint. He aims for the heart with the knife in his right hand but at the last second switches the blade to his left and flicks upwards towards the eyes. Be careful. Without your sight you are lost. And remember, he is very, very, quick."
"Thanks," Ranulf said. "Why are you telling me this?" De Cany gave another of his wry smiles.
"It is a long story," he said, "as long as my family's lineage, which can trace its roots to Charlemagne, and perhaps, if you live, I will tell you. But now you must forget me and prepare yourself for the greatest test of your life. I wish you luck."

De Cany led him towards a clearing, an open area of compacted ground beyond the confines of the camp. Ranulf saw that around this clearing a crowd of soldiers had already begun to gather, anticipating the fight, ringing it two or three ranks deep. He could sense the men's hostility as they approached and when de Cany pushed through them, opening a path for him, he was jostled and someone struck him a blow to the back of his head causing him to see stars. He managed to avoid stumbling, shook his head to clear it, ignoring the laughter aimed at him and then he was through

them. He took a deep breath to calm his nerves then stopped to look around, giving the men that had jostled him an icy glare.
He looked around the clearing; it was large enough for his purposes, plenty of room to move, to avoid his enemy's deadly thrusts. He saw that a number of men with crossbows had been stationed at strategic points around the perimeter.
"What are they doing?" he asked de Cany. "I thought this was to be a knife fight not an archery contest." De Cany's voice, when he replied, was devoid of humour.
"They are here to see that neither man runs," he said. "If either attempts to quit the field the archers will be given orders to shoot."
"And who will give the order?" Ranulf asked, looking for a marshal but seeing no one.
"I will," de Cany shrugged. "So do not run."

Over to his right, beyond the clearing, a crowd of soldiers were surrounding, mobbing, another man stood on a makeshift bench. This man was shouting and writing furiously, gesticulating at figures scrawled on parchment, pegged to a board.
"What's going on there?" he asked de Cany.
"They are placing bets on the outcome. The man on the bench is offering the odds." He shrugged again. "De Bernay's reputation is well known. Your visit to the camp has caused quite a stir. A knife fight is something out of the ordinary and when it is a grudge fight it is inevitable that men will wager on result. You are a celebrity, my friend...let us hope that you live to enjoy your new found status."

On the far side of the clearing there was a sudden frenzy of activity as *Le Couteau* entered the circle, striding confidently through the crowd of soldiers that opened respectfully before him. His appearance was the cause of shouting and cheering and, from his closest supporters, the waving of knives.

"What are the odds?" Ranulf asked de Cany as he was manoeuvred by the Norman Captain onto the far side of the clearing so that the two men faced each other across the open ground.
"Ten odds to one that you will not survive twenty cuts; fifty to one that you will be blinded first – remember what I told you – and a hundred to one that you will last one hundred cuts."
"And the odds on my winning?"
De Cany turned to him, his face expressionless.
"You cannot get those odds," he said. "*Le Couteau* has never been beaten."
"There's always a first time," he replied. De Cany ignored the comment.

On the far side of the clearing *Le Couteau* was preparing for the fight, stripping off his jersey to reveal his naked torso. Ranulf saw that he was tanned and lean with not an ounce of fat on his body. His lightly muscled arms and chest glistened in the sunshine. One of his aides – Ranulf recognised him as the smaller of the two men that had accompanied him into the tent last night – was rubbing oil onto his limbs. Every so often *Le Couteau* would glance across at him but for the main part seemed content to concentrate upon his own preparations. Ranulf stripped off his tunic so that, like *Le Couteau*, he too would be fighting bare-chested. He was, he realised, much bigger than *Le Couteau,* but in a knife fight size was no advantage. Speed and agility were the key and *Le Couteau* had these in abundance.
"Why is he oiling himself?" he asked de Cany, who had now moved a few yards away, anxious perhaps, to distance himself from the foreigner. He could not complain. De Cany had given him this chance; had even, for reasons best known to himself revealed some of *Le Couteau's* tricks. It was understandable that as the man responsible for arranging the fight he would wish to be seen as impartial.

"He does not wish you to gain a purchase on him - and the oil will cause any glancing blow to slide off rather than cut the skin."

Ranulf watched his adversary quietly preparing himself: the oiling of his body, the testing of the edge of his knife with his finger, the methodical flexing and unflexing of his limbs. It dawned upon him that *Le Couteau* was being very careful. Perhaps, after all, he was afraid. No, *afraid* was too strong a word for what he was witnessing. *Concern* then. *Le Couteau* was concerned that for once he might be bested. He sensed it just as acutely as he had sensed disaster the night he had first seen the long-tailed star; the night he had met Alice. *Le Couteau* was concerned about this fight; that was why he had visited him in the dead of night in an attempt to unnerve him. That was why he was now oiling his torso and testing his knife and barely acknowledging him. He felt a surge of confidence course through his veins and without realising it he found that his nerves had vanished, replaced instead by a calm assurance.

Whether de Cany had sensed the change Ranulf could not be sure but now he beckoned the two men toward the centre of the clearing. The crowd stirred, and cheering erupted from the end at which *Le Couteau* had been standing. Ranulf saw that the crowd had thickened even further and was now four or five ranks deep. The two men met in the centre and the crowd suddenly fell quiet again so that a hush descended upon the proceedings.

"You both know why you are here," de Cany said quietly but his words carried clearly through the summer air.

"The rules are simple; a fight to the death with knives. If any man runs I will give the order for the men-at arms to shoot."

Ranulf glanced at the crossbowmen, their weapons levelled at the horizontal. He would not run; he had come too far to meet his end like that.

"Any questions?" De Cany looked from one man to the other. His earlier conversational tone had gone and he now seemed remote, impartial. *Le Couteau* shook his head, saying nothing, but Ranulf felt compelled to speak, to ask the one question that still mattered: "Where is my son, you bastard?"

The words were spoken, not to de Cany, but to *Le Couteau,* and now he saw the dark face of his adversary crease into a smile.

"Not here, Saxon," he said. "And if you kill me you will never know. It is something of a dilemma, *n'est pas?* If you kill me you will never find your son and if you don't kill me I will assuredly kill you. What will you do Saxon? Fight? Or run?" His dark eyes danced with amusement.

"Enough!" De Cany interceded. "Enough of this! When I drop my arm you may settle your differences as you wish. And may God smile on one of you!"

He stormed away, his arm raised, poised to drop.

Ranulf pulled the stiletto from his belt and felt the weight of the steel, cold in his hand. He went into the crouch, his weight balanced, arms extended, his senses singing with anticipation.

The soldiers ringing the clearing began to bay…

Chapter Twenty-Five

Alice clambered onto the timber ramparts, reaching up with her slender hands to pull herself onto the platform that ran the length of the hoarding. From her elevated position she stared south, unmoving, across the fenland. The sun was high and she shaded her eyes against its glare. She had, she knew, been too long hidden away in the confines of her hut, too long absent from the world and this morning she had determined to do something about it. It had not been easy; the hut was her sanctuary, somewhere to hide, to pretend that all was well beyond its walls of mud and wattle. But she could not hide forever and this morning she had risen early, donned her favourite cloak and walked down to the shoreline, to where the isle narrowed down to a finger then sank abruptly beneath the black mud of the fens.

She was surprised to see how the waters had dropped since she had last been here. For miles around the terrain was now unbroken mud, thick and black, stinking of decay, of dead fish starved of oxygen, of stunted trees, high reeds beds, dry and parched by the sun, and the Conqueror's latest causeway, cutting through it with the precision of a knife.

Her eye swept over the causeway, ignoring the men working upon it as she switched her gaze to the far horizon, to a distant forest that, like the isle, ended abruptly at what was once the waters edge. The basin of the Ouse was a sea of mud. Everywhere she looked was mud, cracked and dry and pitiless. How the fen dwellers made their homes here she could not imagine. The isle that she had once thought her home had become a prison. She longed to be gone, but to where? And there could be no leaving, not without Ranulf. Not without her son.

They were out there somewhere, beyond the sea of mud. For days she had refused to believe it, had given them up for dead, but last night in the seclusion of her hut she had found a new resolve and now she stood staring at the empty horizon searching for some sign of them. It was foolish, she knew. The odds were infinitesimal. But Ranulf was out there, she felt sure of it, and if he were alive he would find her son. She had doubted him once before; she would not doubt him again.

She was about to turn away, to return to the camp, when her eyes, now accustomed to the brightness, fastened upon some distant activity that she had not first noticed. She focused intently upon the activity and as she watched she knew that the Conqueror had moved to the second stage of his plan and that whatever hopes Hereward and his comrades had had of defeating him again they were nothing more than dreams.

For in the distance there were more men on the causeway, hundreds of them, hauling for their lives on a dozen ropes, their faces contorted and covered in sweat, the muscles in their arms and legs knotting like cord as they dragged their ballistas' forward foot by foot. *Ballistas.* She knew these weapons well, and feared them with good cause. She had witnessed them at work the day the Norman army had taken York; had hoped never to see them again.

She closed her eyes and recalled that day; the fear on the faces of the rebels, the panic stricken citizens, their impotence to resist as the huge siege weapons were rolled forward towards the City walls under the cover of fascines and then the massive power unleashed as they had hurled rocks, huge rocks as large as five men, into and over the curtain wall. Those that had hit the wall had caused the ground to reverberate with the shock, stonework and masonry crumbling like dust upon impact. Those that had carried the wall had landed on top of buildings, houses, barns, stables, animals, people. The chaos and devastation had been overwhelming, demoralising. These were terrifying instruments of war, utterly detached from any notion of chivalry, killing and maiming with a remote anonymity that she would have not have believed possible had she not seen them with her own eyes.

Now, it seemed, they were to be used again; this time to smash the ramparts that Hereward had erected along the shoreline to protect his archers; the same ramparts that she was presently standing upon. A direct hit would smash the timbers like matchwood and go on to kill or maim anyone unlucky enough to be in the vicinity when they struck. And sometimes, she knew from bitter experience, it was better for the victim to be killed than to suffer the awful injuries that these weapons could inflict. She recalled the plight of some of the injured at York, the mangled bodies, the cries for help barely recognisable as human. There had been nothing that they could do to help people with injuries like that, save to give them a quick death. And it took little imagination to guess what would happen to these timbers when the ballistas were put to use, the hundreds of splinters, large and small, that would fly in all directions to lodge in the victims' flesh, wounding and maiming and blinding with impunity.

She turned quickly away, a little too quickly and caught her hand on a splinter of wood, a tiny but graphic example of the destruction that the ballistas could cause when eventually put to use. She examined the wound; it was already filling with blood. It was deeper than she had at first thought. She tore a piece of cloth from her mantle and quickly bandaged it. Gingerly she climbed down from the ramparts. Someone must be warned of these developments. She looked along the shoreline, right and left, and saw that the Wake had posted a few archers, but of Hereward and his comrades she could see no sign. He must be told. He would know what to do, if anything could be done about such terrible weapons. She had subconsciously avoided him since the incident with the water, sensing some deep emotion within him that was both unexpected and disturbing. She knew that he had only wanted to help, had indeed shown her kindness, but as he had held the flap to her hut, his eyes riveted upon her as though unable to tear them away, she could feel his need reaching out for her.

She had been unprepared for it. The memory of Ranulf, his recent absence, was too raw, and then there was Hal. *Hal.* The thought of him suddenly caused tears to well and for her chest to heave with the familiar racking sobs that had punctuated her days and filled her nights since he had gone. She had thought that she was beginning to come to terms with it but she had been wrong. She wiped her eyes and took several deep breaths in an attempt to calm her shredded nerves and after a while she felt a little better. She examined her hand again. The blood had stained the cloth dark red. But this was not the time to think of herself. Hereward must be told. She must find him, quickly.

She lifted her skirts and began to run.

De Cany dropped his arm. *Le Couteau* sprang to his right and Ranulf adjusted to face him. Even as he did so he realised that he had made his first mistake for now he faced into the sun, which shone into his eyes from beyond *Le Couteau's* right shoulder, almost blinding him. He immediately adjusted again, but in less time than it took to register the movement *Le Couteau* had made his first attack, his knife arcing through the air, beyond Ranulf's outstretched arm, the blade aimed at his left flank. He tried to avoid it, moving on instinct, and for a moment thought that he had succeeded but then he heard the cry from the crowd and immediately felt the pain, like a sharp sting. He risked a glance at his arm and saw that it had been opened to the bone. Blood, warm and wet, was trickling down to his elbow.

"Un!" The crowd erupted and *Le Couteau* smiled a thin smile. Ranulf backed up a pace, steadying himself for the next attack, his eyes riveted upon his adversary. The smile left *Le Couteau's* face as he went back to his business, circling Ranulf like a cat, stalking him as though he were some prey, whilst Ranulf turned and wheeled to face him, attempting to anticipate the next move.

He came in quickly again, the knife in his right hand but then switched, by some sleight of hand to his left. The Toledo steel flashed in the sun and once more Ranulf felt the sharp, sweet sting of its edge on his skin, this time along his right forearm. God, but he was quick, so quick... De Cany had been right about that.

"Deux!" The crowd cheered again and once more *Le Couteau* smiled, a cold, humourless smile that chilled the soul.

"My blade will be soaked with your blood."

Ranulf made no reply. Stung by the suddenness of the attacks he could only wonder where the next one would come from and how on earth he could counter it. His earlier confidence had already evaporated, replaced by the pain in his arms.

Le Couteau circled him again, waiting for an opening, totally in control. He feinted with an attack to the right and when Ranulf wheeled to face it, a clumsy, desperate movement by comparison, *Le Couteau* pulled out at the last moment to leave Ranulf floundering for balance. As he attempted to steady himself *Le Couteau* launched another attack, his knife whipping through the air, carving a semi-circle through his leggings and into his thigh. The wound filled with blood, staining the leggings, and he grimaced as he forced himself to take his weight on it.

"Trois!" The soldiers ringing the clearing roared again, a primitive roar, tribal, unbridled in its lust for more. And as the roar went up it flashed through Ranulf's mind that this was how the gladiators of ancient Rome must have lived and died, bleeding their lives away in the great Colosseum, fodder for the insatiable masses. He risked a glance in the direction of de Cany; his face was impassive, giving nothing away. He tried to remember the advice that de Cany had offered but the noise from the crowd was deafening and the pain in his arms and thigh made it difficult to think. He shook his head, tried to concentrate. *Le Couteau* was coming at him again, his dark eyes cold and soulless. He prepared to meet him…

Alice ran into the camp, her chest heaving with her exertions. She instinctively headed for the Wake's hut, passing by groups of men engaged in various activities. There was a buzz about the place that had been absent for the past few days and she realised that the Wake had finally stirred himself, had put in hand his preparations for the Conqueror's next assault. Even more reason then to make him aware of the awesome capabilities of the ballistas' that she had just witnessed.

She ran past a group of men busily engaged making arrows for their bows, testing the straightness of the shaft by rolling it in their hands or examining the point or carefully fitting the goose flights that would cause the arrow to fly true. The bow, she knew, was their one chance of keeping the Conqueror at bay – it had demonstrated its value in the previous assault and she knew there could never be enough of them.

She saw other men gathered around campfires, boiling great, blackened, cauldrons of what appeared to be pitch or tar. The stench filled her nostrils and caused her eyes to water and she did not stop to enquire what they were about.

Outside the Wake's hut Lefwinus was keeping a watchful guard, his hand resting upon his sword hilt. She told him, between breathless gasps, of what she had seen. He nodded gravely and ducked into the gloom of the hut. After a few moments he reappeared and motioned for her to enter.

Inside, several men were gathered about a dimly lit table; the Wake's war-council: Morcar, Wynter, Lightfoot, Hurchillus. They were in animated conversation but fell quiet the moment she entered, a mark of respect, she assumed, for the appearance of a lady. Men often showed the same respect to widows…

Hereward was seated at the head of the table, facing her, and for a few moments he regarded her in silence, his eyes, shadowed by the gloom, betraying no sign of his emotions.

"Leave us," he said. She saw Wynter and Lightfoot exchange uneasy glances. Morcar rubbed his chin, heavy with several days' growth. She could feel the sudden tension around the table and was uncomfortably aware that she was the cause of it. Hurchillus' voice cut through it, fracturing the silence:

"If the lady has some information we should all hear it." This was the first time, she was to realise later, that she had heard the Wake's authority questioned by one of his men.

"Later." He spoke firmly, forbidding further argument. Hurchillus shrugged, the tiniest sign of dissent, and rose from the table, heading for the flap. After a few moments Morcar Wynter and Lightfoot followed him out, Wynter closing the flap with what she thought to be an excess of vigour.

The light in the hut was poor after the brightness of the day and only a single tallow candle, placed upon the table, illuminated the interior. Hereward lifted it to light another and this too he placed on the table before him. Now, lit by the two candles, she could see his eyes, the strange contrast from dark to light grey. He motioned to a chair:

"Sit," he said, "please." She sat, transfixed by the eyes, locked upon hers.
"Some wine?" He indicated a skin by his elbow.
"No, thank you." Shaking her head. He pushed the skin away.
"You have some information for me?" His eyes had dropped to her chest, still rising and falling from her exertions. She looked away, to the corner of the hut, to where a cot and a tangle of bedding were unmade from the previous night.
"Ballistas…" she said, conscious of his eyes still upon her. "The Normans have them…I have seen these weapons before…" He nodded.
"And?"
She swallowed. "At York, at the end, the Normans used them to breach the walls…they were terrible… frightening things. We had no answer to them…" She found it hard to continue, to say all that she had meant to say but again she saw him nod his understanding. And then he frowned, quite suddenly, the lines creasing his forehead. He leaned toward her and now she could see the concern in his eyes.
"Your hand," he said. "You are hurt." She glanced at the injury, forgotten in her excitement. The scrap of cloth was crusted dark with blood.
"It is nothing," she said. The Wake shook his head.
"Let me look." He rose from his seat and moved towards her, taking her hand in his. She could feel the calluses on his palms. Ranulf had those too…He removed the cloth, parting it from her skin with obvious care, his grey eyes focused entirely upon the task. He had blonde eyelashes, she noticed, just like an angel's…

The congealed blood was making the task difficult, despite his obvious care, and when she winced as the cloth caught in the wound he pulled his hands away as quickly as though he had been burned.

"I'm sorry," he said. She shook her head.
"It didn't hurt."

He took her hand again, holding it between his own and this time there was a different quality to his touch. She swallowed again, barely able to breathe. She sensed that he had departed from his role of physician and was now taking the part of another in this intimate, private play.

As though he had read her mind his hands suddenly enfolded hers, the scrap of cloth hanging forgotten from her injured hand as he looked into her eyes.

"I love you," he said. "God forgive me but I love you. From the depths of my soul I do swear -"

"No!" She pulled away from him, her chair tumbling across the floor as she rose but he hardly seemed to notice. He moved towards her and took her in his arms, pulling her to him, crushing her against his chest.

"I love you," he said. "I love you." His mouth moved to her cheek, smothering her with his kisses, his hands running wildly through her hair.

"No! Please!" She managed to pull a hand free and struck him on the chest, pain lancing through it as she struck again and again, leaving the marks of her blows written in blood.

"No!" she cried again. "This cannot be! Please stop before we are all brought to ruin!"

Her words seemed to have an effect for at last he pulled away, still holding her, but at arms length, like a small child. She looked into his eyes and saw the wildness, the hurt, the whirlpool of emotions written there.

"Ruin?" he said. "You speak of ruin? Are we not ruined already?" He glanced at his jerkin, at the bloodstains from where she had struck him with her injured hand. "That we should come to this." His hand swept around the hut: the mud and wattle, the tangled cot, the grey embers of a fire, the stinking floor rushes, the skin of wine, almost finished. "We are already ruined; all of us. What hope can there be?"

She stared back at him, saying nothing, seeing him for the first time in a different light. She had thought him immune to pain, to adversity. From the moment she had glimpsed his face through the parting reeds...But now she saw him as he really was; alone, afraid, a simple man brought to his end, like so many Saxons, by the changing wind that had carried the Conqueror's butchers across the Channel...and she had not been immune either. Ranulf and Hal would never come back. She had been wrong, simply fooling herself to think otherwise. They would never come back because they were dead. She saw it written in the Wake's eyes as clearly as though she had seen their deaths for herself. He had been hiding the truth from her, afraid, until now, to hurt her. He was right; they were already ruined, without hope, beyond redemption...

She moved towards him and buried her head against his breast, ignoring the bloodstains, the wounds she had earlier inflicted. She felt a tear fall from his eye onto her cheek as he folded his arms around her and held her as though he would hold her forever...

Le Couteau came in again, feinting to the right before launching his attack on Ranulf's left flank, the blade slipping from hand to hand in a dazzling display of magic. Before this onslaught all Ranulf could do was to retreat, but he could not retreat far and he could not run lest de Cany gave the order for the crossbowmen to fire. He was losing this fight, slowly, slowly, cut by cut, and even as he faced up to *Le Couteau* again he knew that he would have to do something to change the pattern of the fight. That, or bleed his life away whilst *Le Couteau* strutted and swaggered as he cut him to pieces.

The soldiers ringing the two men were going wild now, the noise deafening so that he could hardly hear himself think. The men that had placed bets on de Bernay were screaming and shouting, their faces twisted and contorted with hatred in their desire to see his death. He was like a cornered animal with nowhere to run, nowhere to hide.

Le Couteau attacked again, his knife flashing in the sun.
"Quatre!" The crowd screamed as the blade opened up a cut over his ribs that quickly filled with blood. He put a hand to the wound and saw that it was stained crimson. He began to feel light headed. This could not last much longer. He went into the crouch, prepared for the next attack but soon, he knew, he would lose control of his movements and then it would all be over; one way or the other.

And then it came to him, in the split second that it takes for the thought to find its voice. He was not an animal, but a *warrior.* And warriors' did not run. Warriors' did not hide. Warriors' *fought,* to their last breath if needs be. And he could bloody well fight. *Le Couteau* might be an artist with his lightning moves and deft finesses, but *he* was a street fighter, from the gutters of London, and he was a winner. He had proved it before; he would prove it again. He was the King's Champion; Harold's bloody Champion. And Harold wanted revenge.

His arms, his chest, were soaked with blood and the pain from his thigh lanced through him every time he moved but he forced himself to keep moving because soon, he knew, *Le Couteau* would make the one attack that would decide this match forever.

He saw the glint in de Bernay's eyes and suddenly knew, as certain as he had known anything, that that moment had arrived. *Le Couteau* was confident of victory now, would want to put on a show for the men. And what better way than to taunt a blind man, unable to defend himself? Ranulf staggered deliberately as his weight went onto the injured leg and he saw a smile cross *Le*

Couteau's lips. But he would wipe that smile away for the voice that had spoken to him was not his own but destiny's. And destiny would not be denied. De Bernay shaped for the next attack and he prepared to meet it. *Come on bastard. Make the move.*

He backed a pace and forced himself to grimace, as though the pain were becoming unbearable. *Le Couteau* switched the blade from right to left and back again, almost too fast for the eye to see. He snarled as he went into the crouch and then he struck, as fast as a cobra, the point aimed for Ranulf's heart. He responded on instinct, aware that it was not his heart but his eyes that were the target and as the blade flashed towards him he leaned backwards and kicked viciously upwards with his injured leg, putting everything he had into the kick.

His booted foot caught de Bernay between his legs, stopping him in his tracks, causing him to double in agony. Arrows of fire lanced up Ranulf's leg but he ignored the pain and punched the stiletto into de Bernay's stomach before he could react, driving it in to the hilt before ripping it out in a fountain of blood. *Le Couteau* staggered backwards, surprise and pain written across his face but Ranulf was not yet finished. He had longed for this moment for months and now he thumped in the stiletto again, twisting it, ripping it upwards and sideways in a fierce exultation before dragging it out in a mass of heaving, blood soaked, intestines. The soldiers that moments before had been keening for his blood had suddenly fallen silent, unable to believe what they were witnessing. "That's for Harold, you bastard."

His words cut through the air, audible to the hushed audience, but *Le Couteau* was not listening. Bent double, his hands clutched uselessly at his bloodied entrails, the life slowly leaving him. Just for an instant the head lifted and the eyes, dark pools in a face as pale as linen, fastened upon him. The mouth opened and closed but no words would come. A trickle of blood emerged from the lips.

The head dropped again, the flame extinguished. *Le Couteau's* body hit the ground and was still.

Ranulf turned away, dropping the stiletto into the dirt.

It was over.

Chapter Twenty-Six
Aldreth

The ballistas' rumbled forward in the blackness like fantastic creatures brought to life from the pages of legend. Only the smoking torches carried by some of the Captains served to illuminate, in small arcs of flickering light, the path that would take them to their final destination. Their huge timbers had been greased where they came into contact with the timbers of the causeway but no amount of grease could hide the noise, like the keening of lost souls, that was made as they were dragged toward their final positions just yards from where the causeway ended.

As before the rank and file were being used, like beasts of burden, to haul the ballistas' forward, their bent backs, heaving chests and contorted faces giving them the appearance, in the dull, flickering light, of creatures somehow less than human.

The Wake turned away to check his lines. It was like witnessing a vision from hell and he cared not to dwell upon it. Time for that soon enough.

To right and left his men were in position, manning the palisade: Wynter, Lightfoot, Hurchillus, carefully stringing his bow. His was an important task today; he would need to be on his mettle; Hurchillus and all his archers. Beyond them, beyond the palisade, Morcar and his two hundred men lined the shore, cloaked in darkness, watching, waiting, their bows as yet unstrung; anxious, no doubt to begin. Abbott Thurstan too, had joined their ranks, was walking up and down the line of archers with his crucifix held high, giving absolution, adding God's voice to their efforts. He had brought news of Torfrida. She was well and happy, content to devote herself to her new life. She wished the same for him…

He briefly studied the night sky. It was clear, bright, with no sign of cloud. Stars were twinkling in the firmament. An hour yet to dawn, he estimated. A gentle breeze ruffled the fur of his collar. Conditions were almost perfect for what he had planned but the Conqueror had made an early start, conscious, no doubt, of the shortening days. He had left it late at *Senlac* and clearly intended to leave no room for error today.

He turned back to the causeway. The ballistas' were a little closer now, but it was slow progress; the soldiers' exertions were telling on them. They would, he thought, be ready for a change soon. A new work-party, fresh, and eager, would double the rate of progress.

A cluster of torches beyond the ballistas' drew his attention to a fresh activity: a procession of carts, laden with rocks. Bullocks were pulling these to the crack of whips and the urging of their masters and the braying of the cattle could be heard above the screeching of the timbers, echoing into the night.

He checked the sky again and looked toward the eastern horizon. There was, he thought, the slightest hint of grey amidst the black. He turned to the west and immediately turned back again, the contrast clearly apparent. Dawn was beginning to break. He turned to Wynter, wrapped, like himself, in a woollen cloak, proof against the cold. Proof too, in his case, against the bloodstains on his jerkin, the blows from her hand…

"Time to begin," he said. "We shall want the men in position before those instruments of the devil begin their work. Tell Morcar to give his men the order."

"Very good." Wynter nodded and turned away, his boots sounding loud on the palisade as though beating out his disapproval. There had been a dilution of their friendship since her visit to his hut and he regretted this. Wynter was his oldest friend, his staunchest ally, but now, it seemed, a barrier had come between them. It could not be helped; he could not help himself. It was destiny, and destiny would not be denied.

His mind fled back to the events of yesterday, to Alice's visit, to the strange surreality of their conversation, his dressing of her wound and the opening of the floodgates of his desire.

What had brought about the change in her he was not certain; only that there *had* been a change, a thaw, that had led her from what she once was to what she had now become…

He watched Wynter descend the companion ladder and walk over to Morcar. The two men exchanged a few words before Morcar, all grim determination today, his jaw set firm, marched smartly over to his men. He was not riding Galahad, not wanting to risk him when the missiles began to fly.

Within moments there was a flurry of activity: coracles, half a dozen of them, were pushed out onto the swamp, two men clambering into each. One man in each pair had his bow slung over his shoulder, his quiver of arrows clutched tightly in one hand, a paddle, muffled against sound, in the other. The second man also carried a paddle and a small bucket of pitch.

The coracles disappeared soundlessly into the blackness but soon, he knew, if his scheme went to plan, they would reappear in a blaze of light that would bring his own kind of hell to the man that had already been his ruin and was now set upon his annihilation.

The Conqueror jabbed his spurs into the flank of his stallion and urged it over the bridge. The stallion responded with the surefooted confidence that he demanded from all of his mounts, halting the instant that he pulled sharply on the rein with his leather-gloved fist.

He peered into the distance, to where his army, his own Normans and the Bretons of Fitzalan Fergant were labouring to seat the ballistas' into position. Behind them the bullock carts were being carefully unloaded, the huge rocks manhandled by no less than six men each. One by one, to shouts and curses and groans of pain they were being stockpiled, ready for use.

The clatter of hooves loud behind him caused him to turn at the sound but it was only Fergant reining to a halt on his chestnut stallion, a little too close for etiquette to be observed. Sometimes, he thought, they should show more respect. He had made them what they were, had been generous beyond all reason; in Fergants' case the Earldom of Mercia with huge tracts of land to go with it. They owed him everything but gave him nothing. He shrugged the thought away. He was the King. He *was* everything, everything that mattered in this land.

"We shall start at first light," he said. "These Saxons shall learn what it means to challenge a King."

"Perhaps they will surrender," Fergant volunteered, "when they know what awaits them."

William shook his head.

"No," he said, "they will not surrender. These people are as immutable as rock." He dropped his eyes to his surcoat, to the two golden lions emblazoned across it. "They believe this land to be theirs, but it is mine. And when this is over I shall prove it to them. I shall prove it to the world."

Fergant saw the look in the eyes, set wide in the granite face, and did not doubt him, not for a moment.

"Better make a start then," he said. He pricked his heels into the flanks of his stallion and cantered off into the distance to where the ballistas, brooding and silent in the slate-grey of dawn, were waiting to serve their masters.

Alice lay on the Wake's cot, the smell of him still strong upon her. A tear rolled down her cheek and she subconsciously wiped it away, unaware that she was doing so. She lay on her side, her feet curled beneath her in the foetal position, her naked body covered only by the coarse blanket that the Wake had hurriedly thrown over her before he had left to do battle as though hiding his guilt…

She half-turned onto her back and stared into the blackness, listening to the silence of the camp. She welcomed the darkness, the cloak of invisibility thrown over her, rendering her anonymous. In the dark she could imagine that the real world, with all its sorrows and anger existed elsewhere, could not touch her with its pitiless hand.

The camp was deserted now, save for the women and children left behind, huddled together inside their walls of mud and wattle. It was, she knew, an illusory form of safety for if the Conqueror forced the camp, mud and wattle would not save them from an inevitable fate. Not that she cared any longer. It would, she thought, almost be a release. A few moments of pain but after that would come the peace that she longed to embrace…

We are already ruined, the Wake had said before she had gone to him and he had enfolded her in his arms but what she had felt for him she now recognised, not as love, but as pity. She had felt pity for him, for what he had been brought to, and, she was only now aware, pity for herself, for her own irreplaceable loss. And in exorcising that loss, at the very moment it had vanished in the familiar, sweet paroxysms of fulfilment, she had betrayed the man that she cared for more than anyone else in the world. She was

Ranulf's woman no longer, but the Wake's. She had become the Wake's whore.

Hereward, she knew, was unaware of these feelings; was aware only of his own abiding passion and the censure, keenly felt, of those closest to him. She had seen it in Wynter's eyes when he had come for him afterwards, and in the averted gaze of Morcar, his respect for his uncle too strong for anything more. No, Hereward would be unaware of how she felt, would be devastated to learn the truth. She recalled how, at the end, he had cried her name, repeating it over and over, the word like a chant on his lips as though to weave a spell around them whilst with each thrust he had dissolved into her, oblivious of everything save the moment of his release...

She felt fresh tears start in her eyes but this time she let them form, let them roll down her cheeks like tiny raindrops until they fell onto the blanket and were lost. She raised her head and hoped that somehow Ranulf could see her tear-streaked face, could bear witness to her guilt. She called his name in a cracked, broken voice but there was no reply, nor, she knew, would there ever be.

She flung herself onto the cot, burying her face into the blanket, silencing the sound of her sobs, the cries of rage that accompanied them...

It took six men to lift the first rock onto its spoon-like cradle, their faces and eyes bulging with the effort, the veins in their temples and arms standing out like cord as they hefted it into position. The rock rolled backwards and forwards in its cradle and then it was still. The lifting party gasped their relief and dragged some air into their lungs.

"Stand clear!" Alan Fergant gave the order himself. When it came to taking the credit for the Wakes' defeat he intended to be first in line. His father-in-law had already been generous but he knew there would be more to come if he could give the King the Wake's head: the Wake's and all the rest. Earl Morcar too…a traitorous dog if ever there was one. But the King wanted him alive; had other plans for him. He had not enquired what those plans might be but he could guess that they would be somehow appropriate to the crime…

"Release!" Fergant dropped his arm and as the ratchet pin was pulled he felt the causeway shudder and in the same instant the rush of air past his head as the rock was slung with incredible power towards the Saxons' ramparts. In the grey light he could just about follow its trajectory and heard it land with a dull thud somewhere up ahead. He scrutinised the ramparts for damage but after a few moments realised that they were untouched; the missile had overshot them altogether. Some minor adjustments were required but this did not surprise him; it often took several shots to find the range.

"A few more of those and the bastards will sue for peace." He turned to see Ivo Tailbois at his shoulder, still riding his ridiculously small mare, his feet almost touching the causeway. Like the King he instinctively distrusted Taillebois and could not help thinking that if he had handled things differently they might not have a rebellion on their hands at all. He shrugged inwardly. That was in the past and was therefore irrelevant. He was a pragmatist and, whatever the cause, he had a task to perform.

"The King doesn't think so," he said pointedly, replying to Taillebois' jibe. "He thinks they will fight. I am not sure about that. But if it were me I would not be standing where those Saxons are stood." He pointed towards the ramparts, to the Saxon archers lining the timber hoarding, watching the proceedings with an interest that he found surprising. He had expected them to be running for cover by now. They were so unpredictable, the Saxons, stubborn and unyielding, especially these fen-dwellers. *As immutable as rock,* the King had said. His assessment was probably right. He shrugged again.

"Once we have the range they will be so much offal," he said and Taillebois, always keen to ingratiate himself with his superiors, laughed at the remark. Fergant ignored it, nosing his stallion around in order that he could watch the second ballista being fired.

The causeway shuddered again as the ballista launched its granite rock, flinging it, like a meteor, into the air. Fergant watched it arc, just as the first had done, over the ramparts and disappear from view. Both ballistas needed adjustment.

"Reload! Adjust five degrees!" He watched the men-at-arms make the necessary adjustments and noted the sun at last showing its face above the horizon, silvering the early morning mist that was rising, like tendrils of smoke, from the black earth of the fens. *Smoke.* His mind had formed the word without conscious thought but now, as the faint but distinct smell of burning reached his nostrils he wheeled his stallion around, its hooves clattering loudly on the rough timbers as he tried to locate the source of the smell. The stallion whinnied nervously as though sensing its masters' unease and he instinctively tightened his grip on the reins. He looked ahead and to either side, but could see nothing untoward save the black fenland, the reed beds swaying gently in the breeze, the Saxons lining their ramparts.

"Fire!" The word was ripped from Taillebois' mouth and now, as Fergant turned his stallion to see what Taillebois had seen moments earlier, he felt a tide of panic wash over him. The reed beds behind them were shrouded in smoke and flames were licking into the air. The bastards had fired the reeds. He glanced quickly to his front although he already knew it was futile; there would be no escape there, the causeway ending abruptly just a few yards away. Beyond that was fifty yards of thick, black, mud. In his chain mail he would stand no chance. As if to emphasise this the Saxon archers now began to pour down a volley of iron and fire, their fire-arrows, coated with pitch, thumping into the timber all around him, choking him, blinding him, adding to the panic. His stallion whinnied and reared onto its hind legs almost throwing him, its eyes wide and round with fear, and only with difficulty did he bring it under control. He looked around for some sight of Taillebois but he had already gone, disappearing into the smoke that now cloaked the causeway from end to end. His men too, were running away, scurrying back to the mainland as quickly as their legs would allow, some carrying their shields before them, protection against the flames, others trying to rip off their hauberks as they ran, anxious to get back to *terra firma* before the fire consumed the timbers beneath their very feet. The ballistas' stood deserted, forgotten in the scramble for safety.

A final glance at the enemy told him what he must do. That, or perish in the flames. The Saxons on the ramparts were leaping up and down in their excitement, others aiming their bows high into the air to bring the rain of fire down onto his head, engulfing the causeway in flame. He noticed a priest amongst them, his crucifix held high on a wooden staff. What the hell he was doing there, supporting the rebels, he was not sure but he made a point of noting it for the future. The priest, he saw, was making the sign of the cross, as if giving him the last rites…

He looked around and saw that he was now alone on the causeway, the rest of his men having already fled. He looked back and tried to peer through the smoke but it was very difficult to see anything for the smoke and flames obscured his vision. His eyes began to sting, to fill with water. He rubbed them and looked again. To his dismay he saw that the flames had spread the width of the causeway, were even now devouring the timbers before him, great sheets of flame roaring high into the air, whipped by the breeze into a frenzy. And through the heat haze, in the heart of the inferno, the burning timbers were glowing white-hot. He swallowed nervously. He had created a death trap. The reed beds, the same reed beds, he remembered dully, that he had recommended to the King for their protection had instead been their undoing. Tinder dry from weeks of unbroken sunshine, they had caught fire and fuelled the flames before anyone had realised what was happening. He stared at the wall of flame, the fingers of fire that seemed to be beckoning him towards her like some malevolent spirit, and somehow fought back his fear. He could delay no longer. He rammed his helmet down onto his head, patted the stallions' neck and with a prick of his spurs turned him towards the flames. He paused for a second, contemplating the white-hot furnace and then he was digging in his heels, hurtling towards the flames, head bent low, arms and legs pumping as though the devil were on his heels, all thought lost but the need to keep going, keep going…

The Wake allowed himself a thin smile as the fire took hold and the causeway, shrouded in black, choking smoke, disappeared from view. The Normans had already abandoned their infernal machines to the fire, fleeing like frightened children as the flames licked ever closer. In the distance the cries of those that had failed to escape could be heard rising above the roar and crackle of the flames, their piteous screams signalling the agony that accompanied this most awful of deaths. Even now, in the moment of victory, he felt the familiar sting of sadness mixed with regret, of sorrow that yet more lives should be lost. He had never wanted any of this. Only one man had lingered for any length of time: a strong, vigorous man with striking red hair and a countenance to match. Sitting astride a magnificent chestnut stallion he had glared with undisguised hatred at the Saxons lining the ramparts but once the flames had begun to lick across the causeway even he had disappeared into the smoke, riding hard for the mainland before the chance was gone forever.

The flames now engulfed the causeway in a conflagration that lit the sky, and as he watched the ballistas fall prey to the all-consuming flames, disappearing in a crackle of burning timbers and melting of rope and leather, he wondered if there could possibly be any more to come after this; if the Conqueror had the stomach to chance his arm a third time. Twice now he had done what no man before him had done; had inflicted defeat, first by water and now by fire. *A miracle worker,* the housecarl had called him after the first battle: *a miracle worker.* He wondered idly what epithet Ranulf would have had for him after this day's work...and last nights...but Ranulf was gone, never to return. There was only himself now, himself and Alice...

Wynter and Lightfoot were suddenly beside him, their eyes sparkling in the reflected firelight, their faces flushed and animated, revelling in their victory. Wynter slapped him on the back rather in the way that he himself had a habit of doing, breaking his train of thought.

"You've done it again old friend! They won't be back after this!"

The Wake stared at the causeway, an inferno of burning timbers. Of the Norman army he could see no sign but in the air, lingering above the devastation, was the unmistakable smell of burning flesh...He turned back to Wynter. *Old friend,* he had called him, his earlier disapproval evidently forgotten, subrogated to the thrill of victory. *Old friend.* For an instant he recalled a time when they were at peace, before the Norman army had set foot in the land, before rebellion had flared, before the housecarl and his woman had trodden a blood-soaked path to his door... It was an illusion, he knew, just as their hopes for a peaceful end were illusory. There could only be one end, and the Conqueror would write it...His

mood, he recognised, was at odds with that of his comrades, his knowledge serving to temper his own euphoria.
"We have Icarus to thank for this," he said softly. "Poor Icarus."
"Icarus be buggered!" Wynter slapped him again. "You thought of it when no one else could!" Wynter seemed transfixed by the sight, the ribbon of flame scorching its way through sun-dried reeds and along the causeway, his eyes wide with wonder.
"Look at it burn!" he exclaimed. "Just look at it. Have you ever seen a more beautiful sight? If only Ranulf were here to see it!"

The Wake turned sharply at this but Wynter's eyes betrayed no evidence of his having grasped the significance of these last words, the heady drug of victory apparently closing his mind to all other considerations.

He nodded his acknowledgement saying nothing in reply, uncertain, for the moment, what to say. He glanced at Lightfoot to see whether the remark had registered but he too, it seemed, had noticed nothing, was now engrossed in animated conversation with Hurchillus and Villicus, the three of them revelling only in the moment.

Ranulf, indeed, he thought. *But Ranulf was dead, leaving behind the legacy of his love, a legacy that he had inherited, somehow vicariously, as though it were only borrowed for a time...*

Wynter's words had sounded a discordant note that sat uneasily with his hopes, his dreams for the future. Without being conscious of it he found himself staring beyond the devastation to where the mainland began, remote and somehow alien after his prolonged absence. He stood in silence, ignoring the revelry all around him, the voices raised in victory, barely acknowledging the one voice that mattered, a tiny voice, no more than a whisper, the voice of a troubled conscience...

Alan Fergant hurtled through the smoke, his head down, eyes narrowed, lungs fit to burst as he tried to hold his breath in the oxygen-starved atmosphere of the inferno. His stallion's iron-shod hooves pounded angrily on the timbers, the insistent, rhythmic, clatter bringing him ever closer to the wall of fire that waited to greet him like the gateway to hell. If he failed it would be. He had not led a good life, a Christian life, by the Church's standards, but by Christ he had enjoyed it. He felt a tinge of regret that it might soon be over and then he remembered the Saxons' lining the ramparts whilst he had been directing the ballistas' and realised now what they had been waiting for. That damned priest too, strangely at odds alongside his war-like comrades, wearing the vestments of his calling, piously giving him the last rites as though it was already up for him...He felt adrenalin coursing through his veins, fuelled first by fear but now driven by anger and he determined, in that moment, that he would live. He would live, and he would extract revenge...

Almost upon him now, the heat from the flames burned his face, singeing his eyebrows, and he was about to bury it in his stallions' mane when he saw Taillebois sprawled on the timbers just ahead, his face contorted in terror and pain, his helmet-less head blistering from the heat, his once lustrous hair curling and shrivelling to nothing. Flames were licking around him, only feet away, and from the way that he was laid Fergant could see that his leg was broken. He had obviously been thrown in the dash for safety. He looked up imploringly as Fergant headed towards him, his eyes crazed with fear, an arm outstretched in an entreaty.

"For God's sake help me!" The wild eyes stared out of a face that was like a grotesque mask, peeling and red, running with sores. Fergant cursed. This diversion was the last thing he needed. He risked a glance at the wall of fire just ahead and even that glance was enough to sear his face. In an instant he made the decision, reaching down and catching Taillebois' arm in his leather-gloved fist. He was a strong man, young and fit; he needed to be. With a grunt he swung Taillebois up and across the saddle, ignoring Taillebois' scream of agony as his broken leg was wrenched into the air. He noticed, dully, that Taillebois had fainted and for a moment envied him his escape from the inferno. With no time to lose he was off again, head down, eyes closed, galloping for his life. He felt, rather than saw the flames envelop him, heard the stallion whinny as the searing heat, unbearable now, closed about them and he kicked with his heels again, kicked for his life. The stallion responded immediately, anxious, like himself, to be free of this nightmare world of smoke and flame. For several seconds he could feel nothing, sense nothing but the blistering heat, the desperate need to fill his lungs with clear air. His head began to swim and he forced himself to kick again, to keep the stallion going. And then suddenly, blessedly, the air began to cool and even though the smoke still enveloped him, he opened his eyes and realised with an elation that he had never before experienced that he was through it. He drew a breath of air into his lungs and even though it was filled with smoke it was the sweetest breath he had ever drawn. He looked at Taillebois, still slumped across the saddle, still unconscious, his face unrecognisable as the man he had seen just moments before the fens had burst into flame.

All around him men were lying about, gasping for breath like landed fish, some of them with terrible burns to face and hands, tended by hard-pressed medics.

He handed Taillebois down to two of them and Taillebois groaned as the pain penetrated deep into his subconscious. He would have to take his chance, along with the rest of the wounded. He suddenly felt bone-weary, as if he had not slept for days. He guessed that it was because the adrenalin had finally stopped coursing through his veins, the madness of those last moments on the causeway giving way to relief. He had it in mind to return to the camp, to grab some rest when he saw the King, motionless in the drifting smoke, staring at the ruin of yet another army, his indifferent eyes giving nothing away, betraying no sign of his feelings.

He galloped over to make his report although he knew the King would be well aware of the scale of the disaster. He would have had to be blind not to know. He was about to speak when the Conqueror pre-empted him, regarding him from beneath his *nasal* with those calm, indifferent eyes:

"Your face," he said, "it is badly burned. You should get some treatment."

"Yes," he said absently. No mention of his failure, no sign of anger; no outward sign of anything save a King's concern for one of his subjects. It was so uncharacteristic of the Conqueror whose volatile temper was legendary. It was almost as if the King had expected this disaster; was somehow reconciled to it.

"I am sorry," he said. "If I had known that the Saxons would fire the reeds…" He was about to say more but the Conqueror waved away his remarks as though they were nothing.

" Taillebois – will he live?"

"I believe so," he said. "His leg is badly broken and the burns to his face…" The Conqueror nodded gravely.

"He must rest," he said decisively. "We must all rest before we try again. This Saxon, this Wake, is the very devil. The devil incarnate."

Fergant nodded his agreement.

"He is that, Sire," he said, "and yet, when I was with the ballistas I saw a priest amongst the Saxon ranks. He appeared to be giving me the last rites."

"A priest? Are you certain?" The Conqueror's eyed narrowed, as if something, at last, had his interest.

"I am certain of it," he said. "He carried a crucifix held high on a wooden staff. It was almost as if he were leading the army of Christ against the infidels, against us." He fell silent, thinking that perhaps he had angered his Master now, but when he gazed into the face of the Conqueror he saw no sign of it, merely something, some spark, that had not been present before.
"Would you recognise him? This priest?" The question was put with urgency, arousing his interest, but the purport of the question, the reason for the King's sudden interest eluded him.
"I do not think so," he said. "His cowl largely covered his face and then the smoke and flames made it difficult to pick out individual features." The King nodded.
"But it can only have been one of two or three," he said. "Two or three that would dare defy me in my own land."
"I suppose so," Fergant said uncertainly. "It should not be difficult to discover which of them it was."
"Quite," the King said. "Quite." There was a period of silence and Fergant felt that he should say something more; offer to make amends. His earlier ebullience had been badly shaken by his narrow escape, the fire-trap that had almost ensnared him.
"We could always build a new causeway," he ventured, "further to the east, where the land slopes - "
"What?" The King interrupted him. "What were you saying?" His eyes had a distant look to them as though he had not been listening.
"I was saying that we could build a new causeway further to the east."
"No. No more causeways," the Conqueror snapped, his first show of temper since the two men had met. "No more causeways," he repeated. "No more disasters like today. We must find another way to skin this cat."

He was staring at the causeway, Fergant noted, at the smoke billowing skywards, thick and black, obscuring the sun, darkening the sky. It seemed like dusk but was still early morning. The King gestured to the wounded with a sweep of his hand. They lay everywhere: blinded and burned, gasping for air, coughing up their lungs.

"See that they get the care they need," he said. "And get some treatment yourself. You look more like a bloody leper than my son-in-law." The King looked around again, at the devastation greeting him from every side. He shook his head as though unable to believe his eyes.

"The very devil," he said. "But I shall find a way to draw his horns. That or I shall see the bastard in hell." Without more he dug his heels into his stallion's flank kicking it towards the mainland, disappearing into the smoke.

Fitzalan Fergant turned back to the causeway, what was left of it. Most of it had now disappeared, collapsing into the fens as the fire had raged along it, consuming it with a voracious appetite. The causeway, the bridge, had both gone, swept away by the inferno unleashed upon them. In the distance however, at the point nearest the isle, the blackened timbers of the ballistas still showed through the drifting smoke, rising above the fens like the skeleton of some long-dead creature, a stark reminder of what had happened here today.

He put his heels to the stallion's flanks and trotted through the drifting smoke until he reached the stretcher parties and medics, busy with dressings and liniment of one kind or another. A man screamed as a surgeon took a saw to his leg, too badly burned to be saved. The man passed out after the first bite of the blade, the pain itself proving to be the anaesthetic…

He rode past scores of men patiently waiting their turn, lying in rows on stretchers or just in the mud. Some had burns so terrible that they would never fight, never walk, again. He sighed under his breath. The King was right. The army needed to rest, himself included. He felt a weariness that he not felt since *Senlac* Hill and that had been four long years ago.

He rode beyond the lines of the wounded, rode as far forward as he could, until the land gave way to the soft miasma, the thick, black peat that was proving so difficult to overcome. He reined to a halt and stared north. In the distance the Isle of Ely stood grey and impassive in the drifting smoke, quiet now, like a sleeping dragon waiting to be roused. He shook his head in wonder, just as the Conqueror had done, and with the memory the words came back to him again: *As immutable as rock.* He sat for a long time, staring and thinking before turning his scorched and weary stallion toward the mainland and what he hoped would be a few weeks of rest. Every so often he would turn in the saddle and look over his shoulder. What he expected to see he was not sure, but the image was always the same: the grey Isle covered by drifting smoke, the remains of the ballistas standing as a memorial to his failure…

Chapter Twenty-Seven

Ranulf opened his eyes and stared, heavy lidded, at the sunlight playing upon the canvas of the tent, the shadows falling across it and moving on in what seemed to be an endless cycle of sunshine and shadow, light and dark. He thought about turning onto his side but the moment he moved a sharp pain lanced through his chest and thigh reminding him of his wounds and he was forced to abandon the idea. He lay back, contemplating the shadows on the tent, the immense silence surrounding him, wondering how long he had been asleep.

His arms had been bandaged and traces of blood, dark and crusted, showed through the linen. So too, he realised, after a few moments, had his chest and thigh. Who had done this, and when, he could not recall, and he supposed that it must have been done after he had been brought back to de Cany's tent. Perhaps de Cany himself had attended to him, a small gesture of humanity in the midst of the madness, but he could not remember it. He could remember little save for the last moments of the fight: the plunging of the stiletto, the ripping and twisting of the blade, the horror on *Le Couteau's* face, the exultation of victory and then the exhaustion, the mind numbing exhaustion that instantly followed, as though he had given every last part of himself in that final act of savagery.

He tried to raise himself onto his elbows but the effort was too great and he collapsed back onto the cot. He felt terribly weak and guessed that it was from loss of blood. He closed his eyes again, too weary to think, and for a while longer he slept.

When he awoke it was to an awareness that the tent was no longer lit with sunlight but with the stub of a candle that allowed just enough light for him to make out the few items of furniture within the tent: the cot, a campaign stool, a small table upon which the candle had been placed; a quill and ink, a bowl containing a blood-soaked rag. The rag showed a deep ochre colour in the dim light and he realised dully, that the blood was his own. His eyes felt so heavy lidded that he wondered whether he had been drugged. Perhaps some sort of draught had been administered to help him sleep.

His eyes strayed to the roof of the tent, now in darkness, with no sign of either sunshine or shadow. The day had passed, he realised, in a state of fitful sleep. The air too, was cooler with the onset of night, and he shivered involuntarily beneath the rough blanket that covered him.

Outside the camp was hushed but the low murmuring of voices, like a distant hum, penetrated the canvas of the tent. There was a quality to the sound that disturbed him but he could not immediately identify what it was. For some moments longer he lay still, listening to the sounds; an owl hooting somewhere in the distance, the barking of a dog, the drone of the same hushed voices, charged somehow, with an unexplained menace.

Another voice now captured his attention, louder and closer, the voice of Captain de Cany, his distinctive consonants and vowels recognisable even to Ranulf's untrained ear. The voice was raised in anger – de Cany was shouting, but he was not giving orders; there was an absence of authority about the voice that indicated that he was struggling with himself, struggling to control those opposing him.

Instinctively he raised himself from the cot, fighting down the pain lancing through thigh and chest and arms. His head swam with the effort and for a moment he felt light headed. He paused to let it pass, then pulled himself off the cot and seated himself onto its edge.

The flap of the tent swung open and de Cany entered, sword in hand, his face flushed and angry. Surprise registered when he saw Ranulf sitting up but his features quickly resumed their former expression.

"Lie down," he said brusquely. "Quickly, there is little time."

Ranulf clambered back onto the cot and de Cany threw the blanket over him in one swift movement.

"Close your eyes. Pretend to be asleep."

"What's going on?" he muttered through pursed lips.

"Be quiet!" De Cany hissed. "Not a word! Your life depends upon it!"

Ranulf lay motionless, his mind racing, wondering what was happening.

For a few moments longer there was only silence and then he became aware of other people entering the tent. It was difficult to be sure because he dare not open his eyes, but he thought that he could detect three or four distinct voices, all of them raised, all of them attempting to make themselves heard in the din of the argument.

De Cany seemed to be nearest him, sounded as though he were standing over the cot, holding the others at bay with a tongue-lashing. *"Il va mal,"* he was saying, *"il va mal."* He heard angry replies, the scrape of swords leaving scabbards and felt his pulse quicken. It was difficult to lay still, to feign sleep in these circumstances, but somehow he forced himself to do it. The voices grew louder and then he heard a sudden movement, quick and precise, heard steel clash on steel, and a sudden cry of pain.

"Allez!" he heard de Cany shout, *"allez!"* Over and over he spat out the word like a challenge. Eventually there was a response, subdued and surly, and then the chill of the air as the flap was thrown open and silence descended once more. He lay still for some moments longer, his heart hammering in his chest.

"They have gone." De Cany's voice, softer, and threaded with relief, broke the silence. Ranulf opened his eyes to see de Cany standing over him like some guardian angel, his faced streaked with sweat despite the chill night, the anger still evident in the eyes.

"What was that about?" he asked.

"Please," de Cany said softly, "keep your voice down." He looked around as though expecting to see them again but there was no one there.

"Your Saxon friends have outwitted us once more. We attacked today but they fired the causeway behind us. Many have died, and many more are badly burned… defeat is not something they are used to and now they are seeking revenge."

"So they came looking for me."

De Cany nodded.

"It is in their nature," he said. "They are soldiers and paid to fight." He shrugged. "But killing a wounded man is something else. Especially one who comes under a flag of truce." Again he looked around, as though afraid to see more of them at any moment.

"You are a brave man," he said after a pause. "It took courage to come here alone. But you cannot stay. The killing of *Le Couteau,* this latest defeat…you are not safe here. I can protect you no longer…"

"How long have I been here?" Ranulf asked, aware for the first time that he may have been asleep for longer than he thought.

"Three days," de Cany said. "You collapsed after the fight. I helped you here myself."

"And the dressings?" De Cany shrugged again.

"I did what I could. You have lost a lot of blood."

He nodded his understanding. Everything was clear now. De Cany himself had shown courage: courage of a different kind; saving the life of an enemy and facing down his own men. Laying his life on the line for a *Saxon*. Without de Cany, he realised, he would be just one more corpse, one more statistic, but why he had done it he would never understand. Perhaps some things were beyond understanding…

He studied de Cany's face in the guttering light, calmer now that the immediate crisis was over; the sweat-stained forehead, the dark, implacable eyes regarding the blood-soaked dressings, his concern still apparent despite all that he had already done. He noticed some smoke-burns upon de Cany's cheeks and realised that he must have been on the causeway along with his men, facing the nightmare beside them. And still he had saved his life, the life of an enemy, some code of conduct, of honour, dictating the role he should play, prevailing over the brutal excesses of war. It was beyond his comprehension and he found himself wondering whether he would have acted as de Cany had done had their roles been reversed and in his heart he knew that he would not…

He struggled to his feet, the familiar shooting pains returning to plague him with each movement that ran contrary to the healing process. He grimaced as he pulled on his jerkin and noting this the Norman came forward to help him, holding the jerkin by the shoulders so that he could shrug himself into it.

"You are not well," de Cany said. "There is a risk that the wounds will become infected. This land does not help; the swamp, the flies, the lack of fresh water…" He paused and said, as though on impulse:

"I do not envy you this land. There is little to commend it to the spirit."

"But your King seems to want it badly enough." He could not help the retort; the scars ran too deep.
De Cany shook his head.
"The King wants only peace," he said. "Peace in his realm. It is not so much to ask."
"It is when the realm belongs to others."
De Cany spread his arms, his hands outstretched.
"And that, my friend, is where we must differ."
"Aye," Ranulf acknowledged, "we have our differences."
"It will be so for many years," de Cany said. He paused, regarding Ranulf with dark, implacable eyes. "But one day, perhaps, we will be one people, one nation, Saxon and Norman together. It is my hope, my belief, that one day this will come to pass."
De Cany's words hung in the air, the silence giving them emphasis. Ranulf noted the Norman's dark eyes, his alien features, a fact of birth that would forever set them apart. De Cany was wrong, he thought. There could never be anything more than this moment of friendship between them for they both wanted the same thing: the land, the country, for their own. The gulf between them was as wide as the Poison Sea; could never be crossed; not, at least, in their lifetime. It was a miracle they had come as close as they had, only their sense of honour, the way of the warrior, bridging for a time the chasm between them.

It was time to go. He sensed this as sharply as he sensed the brooding menace beyond the confines of the canvas. The course of their friendship had run to its end and now his presence was endangering them both. He should go, but one final matter impelled him to linger, and as he regarded de Cany in the dull, almost absent light, he knew that unless he said it now he never would.
"The night he came to the tent *Le Couteau* had some men with him, three of them; accomplices."
De Cany regarded him in silence.

"I know these men. What of it?"
"They could lead me to my son."
"Perhaps," de Cany shrugged. "But I think you should rest. Let your wounds heal first."
"No time for that," he said. "I must find my son."
"And what will you do when you find them? Kill them also?"
"If that is what it takes," he said. "Although as God is my judge I am tired of killing."
De Cany appeared to consider this, weighing the matter in his mind.
"The men you seek may already be dead," he said. "Many perished yesterday. And if they were alive I would not know where to find them. The army will soon be pulling out, withdrawing to Brandon for the winter. I suggest you try there."
"And yourself?"
"The King goes to Warwick, to hold his Christmas court. I go with him." De Cany looked around the tent, at his meagre possessions. "I will be glad to be gone from this place. Even if it does mean playing the courtier for a while."
Ranulf nodded. He would be glad to be gone also and now he headed for the flap. De Cany's voice pulled him up.
"One thing more." he said. "You had better have this." De Cany drew a knife from his belt and handed it to him, hilt first. Even in the poor light he recognised it as *Le Couteau's*. He saw that although it had been cleaned there were still tiny specks of black on the blade. Not rust but blood; his own.
"You have earned it, my friend."
He tucked it into his belt.
"Thanks," he said. He peered through the flap and studied the sky. Still pitch black, no sign of a moon. Dark enough to slip away unnoticed. On an impulse he turned to grip de Cany's wrists as he

had once gripped Guthrum's before Caldbec Hill, a warrior's farewell. De Cany returned it, studying him thoughtfully.
"You know your son is dead," he said resignedly. "You do know that don't you?" The words were spoken with sadness, an assuredness that took him aback and for a moment he struggled to find the words to reply.
"That is a chance I shall have to take," he said eventually, but even so he found it hard to meet de Cany's gaze, to accept the truth of his words. He ducked through the flap into the enveloping blackness and was gone.

De Cany closed the flap and walked over to the cot, still warm from the Saxon's frame. He eased himself onto it, his mind recalling the events of the past few days. Somehow he could still feel the Saxon's presence as though he were here, casting a giant shadow over him. He closed his eyes, seeking sleep, but knowing that sleep would not come easily. He thought of the Saxon, alone in the darkness, and the task he had set for himself.
"*Bon chance,*" he murmured as tentacles of sleep eventually drew him down. "You will be needing it, I think."

Chapter Twenty-Eight

In autumn the rains came again sweeping horizontally across the fens, driven by a biting northerly wind. The rain soaked the land, filling the creeks and meres, rendering them impassable save by boat. The basin of the Ouse became a water-filled landscape, with only the tops of the reed beds visible to the naked eye. Snipe and spotted crake were again in evidence, and the great wild swan, majestic in its dazzling white plumage. The skies too, were filled with birds: with buzzards and hawks, the great marsh-harrier with its incredible wingspan and above all the sound of the curlew, its wild whistle piercing the air like a banshee.

The causeways had long since disappeared beneath the watery veil, but still the top six inches of the ballistas showed above the waterline when the inundation was low, black and covered with slime, and at these times they became a resting place for reed-sparrows in search of food.

A grey heron began to frequent these lone promontories, standing motionless on its long legs for hours at a time whilst it eyed the waters for a catch. Wynter and Lightfoot had it that the bird was the ghost of their dead comrade, come to watch over them. One morning they took a coracle out to where he stood, like a sentinel on watch, and paddled to within six feet of him. The heron regarded them quizzically for two long minutes, its sharp eye turning this way and that, peering at them down the long barrel of its beak before spreading its huge wings and taking flight impossibly slowly over their heads, just a few flaps sufficient to see it airborne and away. After that Lightfoot was not so certain that it was the ghost of their friend but Wynter would always say that there was significance in the way that it took flight, over their heads, as though saluting them. The heron continued to frequent the ballistas but neither man thought to take the coracle out to him again.

Hereward and Morcar set about strengthening the camp's defences, rebuilding the earth walls that encircled the camp, tamping them with fresh mud and shoring them with timber. Their warriors cut new wood, just beginning to harden, for their arrows, and they re-provisioned the camp with the abundance of food that was once again available. Fish was smoked and dried over hickory fires, bread was baked, flat and unleavened; cattle were slaughtered, hens past laying were killed for their meat, and parties were despatched to hunt the wildfowl, the dunlins, the ruffs, redshanks and plovers that had returned, with the coming of the rains, to the swollen waters of the fens.

Alice took to visiting the chapel at Ely. She would rise early with the dawn and, her cloak wrapped tight against the autumn weather, would walk the half-mile or so to the chapel on the edge of the village. She had become firm friends with Hugo Brittanious and looked forward to their discussions upon theology and religion. She spent hours listening to him, her attention riveted upon that half-dead face as she struggled to understand the finer points of his teachings. She found that these visits, soon on a daily basis, had a cathartic-like effect, enabling her to bury her own problems whilst she immersed herself in Hugo's lessons.

She took comfort too, from the figure of Christ, still on his Cross, still bearing the marks of his passion. Sometimes, when she raised her face to consider a point that the priest had made she would catch the eye of her Saviour peering down at her from beneath his crown of thorns. It was almost as if he was saying, *Are you listening Alice? Are you ready to accept me?* On one occasion she found herself actually nodding, as though his voice could be heard as loud and clear as a bell. She never mentioned this to Hugo but she had seen the look of puzzlement cross his face before he had resumed his lesson.

For his part the priest never seemed to tire of talking to her, a strange, half-smile creasing his features as he expounded upon one subject after another until the light faded with the approach of dusk and it was time for her to return to the camp.

She spent most evenings sitting around the great fire in the middle of the circle of huts. Sometimes she would engage the children in conversation, repeating to them the bible stories she had learned. On other occasions she would talk to the women of the camp although in truth she found their line of conversation, dominated as it usually was with stories of their children or men folk somewhat unsettling, an unnecessary reminder of what they had and what she had lost.

And then there were the nights when she sat with the Wake, allowing him to wrap an arm around her whilst they gazed wordlessly into the crackling fire, lost in thoughts of their own. Images, memories, would come and go with the leaping flames like ghosts of their past, and although neither acknowledged it Alice knew that the Wake's hopes were running along a separate path to hers, never converging but always moving in parallel lines, like footsteps in the snow, until they came to a fork and parted.

She had not been to his hut since the battle. What had happened between them had, she knew, been a mistake, something that had belonged to that moment only. Time had moved on, *she* had moved on; she was stronger now, mentally, spiritually, and she sensed that Hereward was aware of it also. He was unhappy and distracted; that much she knew. It was evident in his demeanour, in the way that he conducted himself with others in the camp and she guessed that most of his comrades knew it too but still he refused to recognise it, stubbornly clinging to hope when all reason must have told him there could be none.

And so as autumn turned to winter and the first frosts scored the ground she lay on her cot before the dying embers of a fire thinking of her son, thinking of Ranulf, wondering whether he was out there somewhere, and if so, whether his thoughts ever turned towards her…

Ranulf woke early, frozen to the marrow. He had spent the night in a fold in the ground, wrapped in a blanket of coarse goatskin. Overhead the sky was grey and heavy with the threat of snow. His goatskin was already coated in a light dusting of it and he realised that if a stranger had happened across him in the night he might easily have been mistaken for a corpse, stiff and frozen, laid out to rest.

He eased himself to his feet and felt his muscles cramp through lack of use. He cursed and worked them until the circulation returned. His wounds plagued him like the devil and on occasion, when he breathed too deeply the wound in his chest cut like a knife, causing him to break off from whatever he was doing until the pain subsided. At least there was no infection. The wounds were wrapped around with bandages against the cold but when he had last examined them he had seen that the edges were knitting together as neat as Alice's handiwork.

He walked the few steps to the top of the rise and hunkered down against the line of the ridge, making himself as small as possible. Below him, a quarter mile distant, was the Norman camp: lines of dull white tents, carts for the sick and wounded, the covered wagons of their wives, or their whores, burned out campfires, half built wooden cabins, and, in the distance, to the north, the start of yet another castle. The Normans had not yet roused themselves; it was still early and frost sheeted the ground. No sign of the sun.

A forest of beech and oak and hazel stood to the back of the camp, dark, but dusted with white, affording protection against the biting northerly wind that whipped across the empty landscape. It formed a bleak scene, this small press of humanity huddled together in the lee of the forest, but still he found himself envying the soldiers and camp followers the comforts that were denied him.

He walked back to where he had lain; the long grass flattened in the shape of his body. He picked up his water skin and put it to his mouth. Nothing came out and after shaking it he realised that the contents were frozen. He spat, as much to clean out his mouth as to vent his annoyance and then he realised that he was hungry. He could not remember when he had last eaten a hot meal and all he carried was a piece of frozen bread. He tried to bite into it but it was too hard and so he pulled *Le Couteau's* knife from his belt and cut it into small pieces. One by one he wolfed them down.

He returned the knife to his belt and just for the satisfaction of doing so he unwrapped *Requitur* and ran his eyes over it from the hilt to the point, noting how the steel glinted dully in the grey morning light as he turned it in his hand. Like the knife it was spotted black along the blade where he had failed to remove every trace of blood.

He had collected the sword from his lodgings in Cambridge and could hardly believe the relief that washed over him when he found it where he had last placed it, beneath the loose floorboard wrapped in its woollen rag. After that he had laid down and slept for days, allowing the wounds to knit, staying as motionless as he could although the nights had been restless ones, punctuated with fever and bad dreams.

Eventually, when he had felt fit enough, he had risen from his bed, paid the landlord his dues and collecting up what necessities he could, had set out to follow the army to their winter base, the camp that lay just beyond the ridge.

It was only twenty-five miles or so from Cambridge by his reckoning, but still it had taken five days to make the short journey. The army had been strung out for over a mile as it headed north and then east, passing through an open, featureless landscape that seemed to go on forever before reaching a river almost as wide as the Ouse itself. A bridge had recently been constructed to span it, but even so it had taken the army almost a day to cross.

He had followed at a discreet distance, taking whatever opportunities he could to identify the men that he was seeking, but thus far he had not been successful. Perhaps, as de Cany had said, they were already dead, in which case he was wasting his time but he knew that these men were the only chance left and so he would pursue it to the bitter end, whatever that was.

He picked up the goatskin and returned to the top of the rise. He lowered his frame onto it and from this position of relative comfort settled down to watch the camp come slowly to life. It was a scene that he had witnessed many times during his service with Harold: men lighting fires, others emptying their bladders of the sour beer consumed the night before, men sharpening weapons on the whetstone, breakfast being cooked over open fires.

During the morning it began to snow, lightly at first, but soon flakes were falling heavily from a sullen grey sky that indicated no sign of a let up. The snow settled on the ground, on the tents of the soldiers, on the half-built cabins, on the branches of the trees. He huddled down into his goatskin, but because he was so cold and the vigil held so little promise, he thought about seeking cover elsewhere, if he could find it. He took another look at the scene below him, almost obscured by the whiteout. He did it more in hope than expectation because it was difficult to see anything at all but nevertheless he went through the process of working his way through the parties of men, trying to identify the faces of the well-wrapped figures labouring on the wooden cabins. These were intended to be their winter quarters no doubt, somewhere to rest, to recover their strength until spring came around and the campaign would begin again. He searched the faces of the workers as best he could but could see no one resembling the men he was seeking. The snow fell heavier, whipped by the wind, cloaking the land, obscuring their faces.

He was about to turn away, tired and miserable, to find the cover he had long promised himself when a flap opened on one of the covered wagons over to his right. A small figure emerged, blurred by the snow, clad in a dark hooded cloak that was in stark contrast to the whiteout. The cloak rendered the form beneath it shapeless and he could not tell whether the figure was a boy or a girl. Whatever it was the appearance of this child prevented any further thought of his seeking shelter. The cloak was obviously too large for it, but the child stepped out into the blizzard, clambering down from the tailboard with an assured purpose that seemed strangely familiar. He watched, rooted to the spot, as the figure now went around to the side of the wagon, holding the hood over its head with tiny pink hands. Already it was beginning to blend into the background as snowflakes gathered on the tunic, turning the cloak to white.

He watched, spell bound, as the child bunched the cloth around its waist and urinated, standing, into the snow.

"Hal?" he said. "Hal?"

The boy lowered the cloak and walked back to the wagon with quick, short, steps, anxious to get out of the blizzard. As he did so the wind momentarily lifted the hood, showing his face in profile: pale skin, dark hair.

"Hal!" he said again, louder this time, but his words were whipped away by the wind.

He scrambled down the slope as fast as his frozen legs would allow, but even as he did so the boy, oblivious to his presence, leaped onto the tailboard and ducked inside the canvas shelter. For what seemed an eternity Ranulf stood stock-still, staring at the tracks in the snow where the child had been until a blast of snow covered them over as though they had never existed.

Chapter Twenty-Nine
Crowland Abbey
December 1070

Abbott Thurstan placed the parchment onto the table and after regarding it for a few moments turned to stare out of the window. The sun was low in the sky now, but shining brightly through the distant trees, casting long shadows over the undisturbed snow. It was a beautiful winter day, just three days before Christmas, a day to make the heart rejoice and though he should be rejoicing he felt sick to his stomach. He reached for the phial that he carried around his neck and removing the stopper took a pull at the laudanum. He sat for a few moments, eyes closed, whilst the liquid worked its magic, warming, calming his shredded nerves, and after a few moments he felt a little better. He replaced the stopper and secreted the phial inside his cassock.

He picked up the parchment and read it again. He noted that despite the laudanum his hands were shaking but this had nothing to do with his arthritis. The contents of the note were reason enough for that. He should have foreseen that one day it would come to this, but not yet, not this soon. He was not ready, his work not finished.

He cast his eyes to the bottom of the sheet. There, above the great wax seal were the words that said it all: *William, Rex.* The summons was from the King himself. There could be no argument, no mistake.

His men-at-arms were outside waiting; three of them, burly fellows wearing mail hauberks that reached to their knees and swords that hung from belts, causing them to clatter disrespectfully on the flagstones of the Abbey floor. These were not men amenable to reason, or open to argument. They had a spare horse for him, they said, and food and clothing. There would be no reason for delay. He was required to go with them now, this hour. The King was expecting him.

But Abbott Thurstan did not wish to go and now he gazed out of the window onto the winter landscape, desperately searching for some way out of his predicament. He had bought these few precious minutes by saying that he had to prepare for the journey, needed time to instruct Father Torfael to proceed in his absence. There was much to do, he had said, at this time of year, but Father Torfael could not be found, the minutes were running out, and beyond the solid oak of the door the King's men-at-arms were becoming restless, their voices raised in argument. Soon, he guessed, they would be hammering upon it, demanding that he accompany them without further delay.

He thought for a few moments longer and then reached into the table drawer. He pulled out a knife, single edged, short, but sharp, used for shaping quills; a use far removed from that which he now intended. He pulled the sleeve of his cassock up to his elbow and placed the blade against his skin. He could not look at what he proposed to do and his glance fell upon the carved figure opposite: St. Mary with child, seated upon a throne of wonderful workmanship, completed by Abbott Elsin before his death in 1016. She gazed across at him with eyes infinitely kind, deeply intelligent, as though somehow judging him. What a genius Abbott Elsin had been, to create such a masterpiece, and what a poor successor Abbott Thurstan considered himself to be. That it should come to this…

He applied pressure to the blade, his hand shaking, and waited for the sweet, sharp, sting that would end it all but somehow, impossibly, the blade continued to rest on his skin, the surface of which remained unbroken, inviolate.

"Lord, I beseech thee, give me the strength." His eyes were closed now, screwed tight against the pain that he knew should be coming but still the point failed to pierce his flesh. He looked at his wrist, reddened from where the blade had been, but of his lifeblood there was no sign. Outside they were calling for him, demanding his appearance. He felt tears start in his eyes. He applied the blade again but even as he did so he knew he could not do it. He had not the courage. He removed the point and slid the knife back into the drawer. He wiped his eyes on his sleeve. A thump on the door told him that time, like his courage, had ebbed away.

He rose unsteadily to his feet and walked to the door, unlocking it. Their dark eyes greeted him, cold, unsmiling, censorious. He saw that two of the Normans had drawn their swords, intending perhaps to have used the hilts on the door should it have been necessary. The third man, a Captain, placed a hand on his shoulder, guiding him firmly towards the outer gate. In the yard beyond, four horses were tethered, their coats steaming with sweat despite the crisp, cold air. The King wanted him badly then: they had already been ridden hard.

Some instinct, some feeling of being watched, caused him to glance up to a window and behind the glass he saw pallid faces looking down at him, impassive yet concerned, the flock that he must leave. A hand was raised in farewell and although he could not make out the face, obscured as it was by the misted glass, he somehow knew that it was the Lady Torfrida, her head covered in the habit of her new calling. He would miss her. She had proved

herself an excellent convert, eager to learn, selflessly devoting herself to her new life. He raised his own hand in acknowledgement. Lord alone knew whether they would ever meet again.
"You can ride?" The Captain spoke sharply, bringing him back to the present. He nodded his answer, unable, suddenly, to speak. *He should have killed himself. Better that than this.* A hand hoisted him unceremoniously into the saddle; another slapped the rump of his mare causing it to leap forward into the gallop, almost throwing him. Behind him came the sound of laughter, the escort enjoying a joke at his expense. He thought about looking back, a final glance at the Abbey, at those left behind, but he could not bring himself to do it. Tears of shame pricked his eyes and this time he ignored them, letting them roll down his cheeks into his beard...

Chapter Thirty

Hal shook the snow from his cloak and, as was his habit, curled up quietly in the corner of the wagon, making himself very small. The wind howled through the canvas where he had just entered and he quickly pulled it close, securing it on a hook. The wind receded into the background but the canvas continued to flap and bang, as though shaken by unseen hands. He cast a watchful eye toward the woman opposite him, asleep under a pile of rough blankets but she had not stirred from her slumbers. She slept alone now, but for a long part of the night her bed had been shared by the man Feroux; he was small and dark and ferrety looking, with quick darting eyes, and the noise they had made had gone on almost until dawn. What they had been doing was a mystery to Hal, but it was a regular occurrence, almost nightly, and, save for the fact that he was always glad when the man departed, he did not concern himself with it.

At first, after his capture, he had cried all the time. The men that had abducted him had insisted that he remain tied at the wrist and ankles; but after a while his wrists began to bleed and the ropes were removed. So too, the ankle ties when he complained that he could not feel his feet. The woman had interceded on his behalf and the men had reluctantly agreed. Of the fourth man, the man that had caused all of this, the man with the scar running from eye to jowl, he had seen nothing. He hoped that he never would. He hated him.

But despite his hate he still found room for tears. Day after day he cried until one day he could cry no more; there were no tears left. Instead the tears were replaced by an aching numbness that consumed his every waking hour. He retreated into himself, spending days just sitting and staring blindly before him, oblivious to his surroundings, the cattle and hens that inhabited the barn, filling it with noise, with their smell. Only the chain fastened around his ankle, secured to a great wooden beam, prevented him from escaping but in truth he never gave escape a thought. His thoughts, like his tears, seemed to have fled him entirely.

Occasionally the woman would come with a bowl of oats and offer it to him.

“Eat,” she would say, and he would scoop up the contents and fill his mouth. On other occasions she would bring him a pitcher of water, often stale, sometimes discoloured.

“Drink,” she would utter in her accented voice, and then she would sit and watch while he dutifully drank, all the time jabbering away in a strange foreign tongue that meant nothing to him.

The days passed in this manner, long and empty, devoid of hope.

And then, one day, several weeks into his confinement, he noticed a change in the people around him. The men became tense and irritable, arguing amongst themselves, the woman excitable, clearly nervous about something. What the cause of this was he did not know, but neither did he concern himself. Their feelings meant nothing to him, and in truth he reckoned that if they were arguing about something then it could only be good news. After a while his spirits rose and with it his curiosity.

“What’s happening?” he would ask in his small child’s voice but whether they could understand him he did not know and in any event the only replies he received were sullen glances and silence. The men would not talk and the woman was nowhere to be seen.

And then the men stopped coming and for three days that dragged like three weeks he saw no one at all.

Eventually the woman visited again but even at his youthful age Hal could discern the change in her, knew that something had happened during her absence to cause the transformation that was so clearly apparent.

The woman's eyes were reddened with tears, her face lined and drawn from lack of sleep, evidence of the strain that she was under. Had he known what it was, that she was grieving for her dead lover, slain by his own father's hand, he would have feared for his safety. As it was she merely snapped at him as she handed him a bowl of oats, dry and unappetising, the words as meaningless as the rest of the indistinguishable nonsense that she had uttered over the weeks but now they seemed to have a darker, more sombre tone to them.

The men however, had still not been seen and Hal found himself hoping that he would never see them again. They frightened him, especially the one with the scar. After two more days he began to hope that he had seen the last of them, but then Feroux had made an appearance early one morning, entering the barn whilst he was just waking, and for a moment, in his sleep-induced state he imagined the figure to be an apparition from hell, so strange-looking was his face in the early morning light. It was only when Feroux had placed his face inches from his own and grinned at him in a leering, mocking way through blistered lips, turning his face this way and that for Hal's inspection that he had seen the burns to head and face, the awful scars that were forming above the hairline where the hair had been seared away taking the skin with it. He had closed his eyes and turned away but Feroux had grabbed his chin and yanked his head around, insisting that he keep looking…

And now this Norman, this Feroux, was sharing the woman's bed, coming here, to their wagon each night for reasons that his young mind could not determine.

He was ambivalent about the woman. She was kind to him, in her own way, and insisted that he call her *Maman.* He guessed that it was her word for mama, and although she had protected him, had stood up for him against the others for reasons that he could not determine, she could never replace his own mother. She was, after all, a foreigner. She was the enemy, or so it seemed to his childish mind. So she was his *maman* then, but in name only.

The thought of his own mother, not seen for so long, brought sudden tears to his eyes. He had not cried for weeks but now he found them rolling down his cheeks like a river. He tried to picture her, but somehow the image was beginning to fade, distorted by the passage of time. There were certain features that he had fixed clearly in his mind: her eyes, always soft and kind, her raven hair, the colour of his own, her neat white teeth, showing through her smile, but the whole, the complete picture, was becoming lost. So too, the face of his father, always hidden by a huge red beard, turning lately to grey. What his father truly looked like beneath the mass of red hair he did not know. He doubted whether he would recognise him now...They were becoming lost to him, he realised; lost, perhaps never to be found...The tears flowed again and he wiped them away on the sleeve of his cloak. He cast a glance at the body beneath the blankets, moving rhythmically with each indrawn breath. The woman, his new *maman,* continued to sleep. She would probably sleep until Feroux arrived.

A sudden impulse seized him: perhaps it was the tears, shed for his mother, or maybe it was his fear of Feroux, whose burned face and spiteful manners would soon make an unwelcome appearance. Whatever it was he found himself slipping on his sandles and unfastening the hook on the wagon. Pausing only to pick up a blanket he slid silently through the flap, his cloak wrapped tightly around him as the blizzard roared about his ears. He glanced quickly to right and left and then he was leaping off the tailboard and running for all he was worth, his heart hammering in his chest. Eventually, when he could run no longer, when he thought that his lungs would burst from his chest, he stopped and looked back. Snow drove into his face, blinding him, and he cuffed it away. He screwed his eyes tight and looked again. He had only run a hundred yards but now the wagon, the camp, the hated foreign soldiers, had disappeared into the maw of the blizzard as though they had never been.

He smiled a slight smile, his first smile for weeks, but the knowledge that some soldiers might even now be after him, might be emerging from the blizzard at any moment wiped the smile from his face. He looked around again, trying to identify some familiar landmark, some point to fasten upon, but it was hopeless. The land was obscured by the blizzard just as completely as the camp itself.

For a few moments he felt completely disorientated but then he remembered to look for his footsteps in the snow and after a few seconds of frantic searching found them running back from the direction of the camp. This small certainty seemed to make up his mind, to stiffen his resolve, and head lowered into the blizzard he set off again, maintaining a steady trot that he hoped he could keep up for some time. After ten minutes of steady running he became aware of some tall shapes up ahead which, as he approached them, he found to be trees, stripped bare by winter. He was on the edge of a wood. It was better than nothing. Without hesitation he plunged into the undergrowth and nestled down under a fallen log, pulling the blanket over him.

It was only some time later, when the light began to fade, the blizzard to blow itself out, that the realisation dawned that he was free.

Chapter Thirty- One
Warwick Castle

The Conqueror downed the remains of his tankard and slammed it down in front of him. Barely had his hand left the cup before a serving maid appeared to fill it again, pouring the rich red wine from the skin under her arm into the tankard until it reached the brim and then overflowed, running down the side like so much Saxon blood before pooling on the table before him.

"Bloody lake," he murmured beneath his breath, recalling the soubriquet that his army had given to the butchery on *Senlac* Hill, a day he would never forget. He picked up the replenished tankard and after taking a deep pull slammed it down again, causing the pool of wine to leap from the table and splatter his surcoat, staining the two golden lions a deep scarlet. He looked down and wiped at the wine with greasy fingers, simply spreading the stains, adding to the damage already done.

The King was drunk. He usually drank in moderation, preferring his wine mixed with water, but tonight he was holding his Christmas Court and the wine was a heady brew, heavily spiced and pungent, and the King had drunk too much. His cheeks burned hotter than hell from the wine and from the heavy log fire crackling in the firegrate behind him and beneath the heavy fringe of hair that he sported in true Norman fashion his forehead was running with sweat; he could feel it trickling down his cheek. He raised the same greasy hand and cuffed the sweat away.

He gazed around the Great Hall. Packed with people, it rang with noise: the drunken banter of his Knights and Earls, the songs of his minstrels, struggling to make themselves heard amongst the din of the laughter and argument, the crashing of tankards, the squeals of the serving maids as they were caught or groped by one pair of hands or another.

The Conqueror looked along the table at which he was seated. They were all here, the men that sustained him on the throne of England, nailing down the land with an iron fist: Roger of Montgomery, one of his Marcher Lords, arrived today from his estates in Shropshire with a retinue of a hundred men at arms; his cousin, Odo, Bishop of Bayeux and Earl of Kent, resplendent as ever in his Church regalia, holding forth on the difficulties of managing his vast estates both in England and Normandy. The King felt a sudden flush of anger. He had rewarded his cousin with those English lands, gratitude for Odo's support, his ships and his men, in 1066. If they were so difficult to manage Odo could always hand them back. That would solve his problem at a stroke. Even as the thought came to him he knew that Odo would never do that for his lust for power almost rivalled his own.

His eyes moved steadily along the faces, regarding them with equanimity: his second cousin, Count Robert of Mortain, provider of 120 ships for his conquest of England, the single largest contribution from any of his followers; Roger of Beaumont, one of his Curia, his inner Council, a man that he would trust with his life. He had once thought the same of William Fitz Osbern…

His gaze came to rest upon his son-in-law, Fitzalan Fergant, whose head seemed to be permanently buried in his cup as though by drinking himself to death he could forget the humiliation of his humbling defeat on the Causeway. Unfinished business that; but he had a plan that would settle with the Wake and soon, God willing, he would put it into effect…

His eyes moved further along the table to two of his eldest sons, Robert and Richard, their faces, like his own, heavily flushed with the wine. Even when seated the Conqueror could see that Richard was already outgrowing his elder brother. Robert "Curthose" they were calling his eldest, on account of his diminutive size, his legs like stumps, as though tacked onto his body as an afterthought. Who would have thought that he could have sired such a son? It occurred to him that his wife Matilda was also short, no more than five feet tall herself and he wondered whether it was the case that the woman always dictated the size, the nature, of her offspring. He puzzled at this for some moments for he also knew that Richard was more like himself than his mother, the same heavy set features, the same dark, unfathomable eyes that seemed to pierce to the soul. So too William Rufus, his third son, a moody lad with a fiery temper that would flare up at the slightest cause. Again, much like himself, he realised. His thoughts led him to think of his youngest son, Henry, barely one year old, still in Normandy with his mother. Life could be hard for the youngest child for it was in the nature of things that the eldest usually inherited all. God grant that Henry should have some of his own burning ambition for he would surely need it if he were to make anything of himself…

He took another pull at his tankard and gazed around the hall. His head was swimming and his vision, far from piercing, was becoming blurred. He ought to go outside to get some air, but it was cold outside and here, in the heart of yet another new castle, another motte and bailey construction, it was warm and inviting and filled with laughter. He would stay where he was.

Beside him Fizalan Fergant suddenly rose and vomited onto the floor, a fountain of spew streaming onto the floor rushes, staining them scarlet.

"Oh Christ!" Fergant exclaimed, and then retched again, bringing up more scarlet-black liquid.
"Most of us find Christ in Church," the Conqueror observed, impervious to Fergant's discomfort, "but my son-in-law finds him in his cups." A gale of laughter erupted from those around him, the wine and the heat loosening their tongues, causing them to laugh at even the meanest of his jibes. He knew these men for what they were but tonight it pleased him to have them at hand, to fill the Great Hall with their laughter.

He slapped Fergant on the back as he slowly eased himself into his chair, panting for breath, glazed eyes fixed upon some point in the roof. Fergant looked very pale beneath his shock of thick red hair, and, like the King himself, his face was beaded with sweat although the burns to his face that he had sustained during that desperate flight from the causeway seemed to have disappeared entirely, unlike the scars of his defeat…

He switched his gaze towards Ivo Taillebois, seated amongst the lower nobility at the far end of the hall and managed to pick him out from the crowd of flushed faces. Taillebois walked with a stick now, his leg permanently bent from the fall from his horse. And unlike Fergant, the burns to his head and face still marked him out amongst others, his hair thin and sparse, completely bald in places where the flames had seared his flesh. He had become an object of derision and the Conqueror knew that he should feel pity for him, but even when fit he had been a hard man to like and was therefore a hard man to pity now. He shrugged to himself and took another pull at his tankard, contemplating, in his drunken torpor, what tomorrow might bring.

For tomorrow was Christmas day, the fourth anniversary of his Coronation. Four years. Four years since he had set foot in this land and crushed it beneath his heel. It had been a close run thing though, that day on *Senlac Hill*. Too damn close…He closed his eyes and the memories came flooding back as though it were yesterday: the Saxon *huscarls* lining the ridge, screaming their defiance, beating it out on their burnished shields. The fluttering banners of that devil's spawn Godwineson, the bristling hedge of spears that he had thought would never break; his desperate charges up the hill, and their bloody rout time after time. The panic on the faces of his men when they had thought him killed. Even Fergant for all his bravura, had not been immune, had been ready to give the order to run when he had galloped over to him and screamed into his face:

Look at me! Look at me! See, I am alive!

He glanced across at his son-in-law, still slumped in his chair, still in his cups, that day a distant memory for him now. It could easily have been otherwise…that, he thought, had been his finest moment. For without his calm authority at that point the army would have fled and he, and the rest of them, would be so many corpses now, eaten by maggots and reduced to bones…

And finally there was the end, when it came, in the glow of a blood-red sun, sinking beyond the horizon. One moment he was hacking and lunging and gasping for breath and cursing and exhorting his men to fight, and the next they were through the shield-wall and the butchery began…

He grabbed his tankard and downed the remains of it. A maid came to replenish his cup but this time he waved her away. He had drunk enough.

He had fought under the Holy Rood that day, flying the Papal banner, a golden cross on a gleaming white background. Around his neck he had worn the relics of St Peter, given to him by the Pope himself, God's representative on earth. God had surely been with him and he shuddered to think what might have happened had it been otherwise. His earlier remark about Christ, made in jest, suddenly pricked his conscience, and now he regretted saying it. He had certainly drunk too much…the Church, the Pope, at least, had been good to him, and he had shown his gratitude. The Abbey, still under construction on the site of his great victory, numerous others being built around the country, these were visible signs of his piety, evidence that he ruled with the will of God. But there were others in the Church, misguided individuals, priests that were opposed to him. Some of them even supported the rebels, fought alongside the Wake. His son-in-law had seen one of them with his own eyes. To a man these priests were Saxon, but this was no excuse. They were all subject to the law, spiritual and temporal, and the law must be obeyed. *He* must be obeyed.

He turned to Fergant, seemingly recovered from his earlier *malade,* his head buried in a tankard again.

"That priest; the one from Crowland. Has he arrived yet?"

Fergant raised his head and regarded the King with bloodshot eyes that failed to focus. Wine dripped from his chin onto his surcoat.

"The good Abbott arrived an hour ago," he said, his voice heavy with drink. "Apparently he is shitting himself." He laughed, the first laugh the Conqueror had ever heard pass his lips, and then went back to his cup, downing the contents in one. The Conqueror pondered the matter for barely a moment. He had intended to interrogate the priest this evening but neither he nor his men were in any state to do so. He glanced around the Hall, which reeked of sweat and wine and vomit and rang with the sound of drunken laughter. Not tonight then. Let the good Abbott wait a while. Reflect upon the error of his ways. It was, after all, Christmas Eve, the holiest night of the year…

He glanced at the tallow candle by his elbow, miraculously unscathed despite the night's heavy drinking. Smoking heavily, the candle had burned down to its last ring, the wax melted and congealed in its holder. In an hour it would be midnight; time for

Mass, an event that he always enjoyed. He was about to call for another cup when he thought better of it. Mass was a time for sober reflection he reminded himself, the celebration of Christ's birth. And tomorrow was the anniversary of his Coronation. Four years since he had brought this Godless land back into the fold…

He rose unsteadily to his feet. It was time to retire, to prepare himself for Mass. He was, after all, the King. He must set an example to the others…

Chapter Thirty-Two

Hal woke to the sound of bells pealing out from a distant Church, greeting the dawn with a joyous resonance that rang across the countryside. What the bells signified he could not tell but his instincts told him that it was time to move. He raised himself from his bolt-hole under the fallen log and shook off the blankets that were heavily coated with snow. His hands and feet were freezing and so he blew on his hands and stamped his feet to try to get the circulation going. After a few minutes of this they felt a little better and he stopped to look around. Save for the sound of the distant bells it was eerily quiet, with no sign of man or animal. Only the rhythmic drip of melting snow from the branches of the trees disturbed the peace of the forest and as a thin sun began to show itself between the trees he held his face towards it, letting its mild glow slowly thaw him out. He was cold; as cold, he realised, as he had ever been in his young life. He wrapped the blankets tightly around him and began stamping his feet again, feeling the crisp snow crunch beneath his sandals. It had snowed heavily during the night and the trees, like the ground, were cloaked in it. There was not the slightest breath of wind now, now not even a gentle sigh between the branches. Everywhere was still, everywhere was white; it was a magical world, here in the forest and were it not for his desperate predicament he might, perhaps, have revelled in it. As it was he was cold and hungry. Life with *maman* had had some benefits he thought…

He looked around again, wondering where he might find something to eat. A fire too, would be welcome, but there seemed little likelihood of either. Ahead of him the forest seemed to stretch away forever, dark and forbidding. He looked behind him, but the view was the same as before: nothing but trees and snow all around, stretching away as far as he could see. He tried to remember which way he had run during his flight from the camp but it had been during the blizzard and he had seen very little. He searched for his tracks in the snow, but now there was nothing, no clues whatsoever. Fresh falls had covered them. The forest had closed around him during the night, cold and hostile, and with a sense suddenly of alarm, it came to him that he was lost.

He stood still for a few moments longer, his heart pounding so loud he could almost hear it and then he remembered the bells. They had stopped for the moment, but he guessed they would start again soon. They always did. And where there was a church he knew there would be people. Whether this church lay in the direction he wanted he had no idea; only that he needed to get out of this forest.

He sat on the log in the pale sunshine whilst he waited for the bells to start up again and tried to remember what they called the place where his mother and father would be waiting for him. Something to do with eels, he thought. He didn't much like eels; some of Hereward's men had shown him one once. It had been thin and slimy, wrapping itself around the man's fist before he had prized it loose and with a deft flick of his blade removed its head. Somehow it reminded him of the Norman, Feroux. He was thin and slimy too, full of all sorts of nasty tricks. He laughed to himself at the thought, a child's laughter that dispelled the fears of just a few moments earlier. He would have some tales to tell his parents when he got home and he was sure they would be proud of him.

In the distance the bells started up again, ringing out a new carillon, up and down and up again, over and over. He leaped off the log and with a new found resolve began to thread his way through the trees towards the bells.

At the first hint of morning Ranulf resumed his observation of the wagon. He had debated finding some cover for the night, something better than the shallow undulation in the ground and the goatskin that were his only shelter from the blizzard, but after debating the point he had decided to stay where he was. He felt so close now, so near to finding his son that he dare not leave, he simply dare not.

As the sun began to climb into the sky, a pale yellow globe with little warmth to it, the bells of Brandon church rang out across the countryside, their clamorous peal reminding him that it was Christmas Day. He found little reason to celebrate; it was four years to the day that the Bastard had been crowned in a sullen ceremony at Westminster Cathedral, the prelude to four years of tyranny and bloodshed that had left no Saxon untouched…

The wagon seemed very quiet at first and for a while he wondered whether it was occupied at all. Presently however a man appeared wearing the standard apparel of a Norman soldier, jerkin and breeches, the ubiquitous sword hanging by his side. He leaped down from the tailgate of the wagon and threw back the tarpaulin cover causing a sheet of snow to fall from it, thudding onto the ground in a heap, but Ranulf hardly noticed this for all of his concentration was now focused upon the interior of the wagon, upon the half naked woman, whose pendulous breasts were briefly exposed to the world before she covered herself with a blanket. His eyes moved over the remainder of the wagon and to his surprise saw that the woman was alone, that save for herself and the man there was no one else with them. The boy, glimpsed briefly during the blizzard was nowhere to be seen. Where the hell was he then? The woman must have realised this too, for after a brief conversation with the man, obviously her partner, she leaped down from the wagon and now began to search for him.

Ranulf shook his head in frustration. Sometime, during the blizzard, or perhaps during the night, he must have slipped away. All this time to find him and now he had lost him again. He did not question whether the child was Hal; he had taken that for granted. After all was not destiny guiding his hand?

The woman, whose dark hair hung untidily about her narrow face obviously shared this frustration for now she was busily looking for tracks, inspecting the underside of wagons, calling Hal's name in a cracked, highly pitched voice that both betrayed her emotion and, to Ranulf's utter elation, confirmed his suspicions.

Ranulf wondered idly what might have passed between his son and this foreign woman to cause this outpouring of emotion, what ties might have been formed and now, it seemed, severed...

For several minutes he watched her run from wagon to wagon, checking for Hal's presence, her voice becoming ever more strident, her anxiety increasingly obvious. And then, when the last wagon was checked with still no sign of him, she just seemed to crumple, falling to her knees in the snow, holding her hands to her face. Ranulf guessed she was crying.

The man now walked over towards her, showing an interest for the first time. Thus far he had made little effort to help with the search, merely standing and watching whilst the woman had run backwards and forwards to no avail.

Ranulf took the opportunity to study him. He was slight for a Norman, but he had a hard, lean face, heavily lined about the mouth so that the corners seemed to be forever turned down, giving him a permanently sour expression. For some reason the face seemed familiar, as though he had glimpsed it previously, but for the moment he could not place it. He noted the multiple scars about the face, red and freshly healed, and guessed that he had probably been on the causeway with de Cany when the Wake had fired it. Only fire could have caused marks like that. Nevertheless he had been one of the lucky ones. He had escaped.

This man now spoke to the woman; sharply it seemed to Ranulf, considering her distress and the woman, hurt by it, responded in like manner. They continued like this for some time, shouting and gesticulating, their voices becoming ever more strident and then the woman turned towards the forest, flinging an arm towards it in an angry, or perhaps, despairing attitude. The man shook his head uncertainly and once more there was an angry exchange. The woman began to cry again. The man put an arm around her shoulder as though to comfort her but it was too late and she shrugged him off. She rose to her feet and strode back to the wagon, evidently oblivious to his existence. The man watched her go and kicked the ground in anger. He hesitated, looking around, as if expecting to see the boy at any moment, but then, as if having made up his mind, and with an air of resignation, stomped off into the forest.

Ranulf waited for a while before setting out after him…

Hal ventured deep into the forest and now only the occasional shaft of light pierced the trees, relieving the gloom. Twice already he had tripped over a fallen branch, grazing his knees and cutting his hand and it occurred to him that perhaps he should turn back. The difficulty was that if he turned back he would have nowhere to go, no safe haven other than with his *maman* and he already rejected her. So he must go on.

In the distance the bells continued to ring out and he thought that if anything they sounded a little louder than before, a little closer, but it was becoming increasingly difficult to tell whether they were ahead of him or behind, or off to one side. At times they seemed to be all around him…his lip began to tremble and he felt himself to be on the verge of tears. He stopped and leaned against an old oak tree, its branches twisted and gnarled with age. The bark was rough and cold, but he needed to rest. He felt so cold, so hungry…he caught some movement from the corner of his eye; whatever it was it was moving rapidly in the undergrowth. He tried to follow it but it was moving too quickly and then he saw a flash of red as it left the undergrowth and scurried up a tree. A squirrel; searching for food perhaps. The thought of food reminded him again of his own hunger, the pressing need to escape the forest. He was about to set off again when he heard the unmistakable snap of a branch cutting clear through the air. Only something large could have made that noise. Something large, like a man…

He froze, and cast a glance in the direction from which the sound came, hoping to see what it was but as yet there was nothing. He eased himself round to the other side of the oak, out of sight, he hoped. The bells had stopped. The silence was suddenly immense. He could hear his own breathing, rapid and shallow, could feel his heart pounding in his chest. Tears began to well again and it was only with an effort that he was able to force them back.

He heard them again, footsteps, sounding loud in the snow now, crushing branches, twigs, the detritus of the forest. He closed his eyes. He held his breath. A hand touched his shoulder.

"Hal," a voice said, familiar but at the same time remote, strained, cut through with emotion.

"Thank God I have found you. Thank God."

He opened his eyes and looked into the face of a stranger. The man's eyes were wild with a touch of madness about them; the face too, was blasted and drawn beneath the tangled mat of his beard. At first he thought he must be some sort of outcast, a forest dweller, for the clothes that he wore were little more than rags. And then he saw something in the maddened eyes that sparked a distant memory and the recognition came to him like the opening of a floodgate. Before he knew it he was hugging the man to him and crying and laughing all at once and the man was laughing with him. His father swept him into his arms and kissed him on the cheek and hugged him again and Hal felt tears rolling unchecked down his cheeks.

"Father," he said, "my father." In the distance the bells started up again and hearing them his father stopped and listened then started to laugh again.

"Why are you are laughing, father?" he asked, and his father looked down at him and Hal could see that despite his laughter there were tears in his eyes too.

"Why," he said softly, "it's Christmas Day son. It's your birthday."

Chapter Thirty-Three
Warwick Castle

Rarely in the last four years had the Comte de Cany seen the Conqueror in such a temper. The last time, he reflected, had been on *Senlac* Hill, and then it had been a case of fight or die, and nothing would ever match that, but this, this tirade against the renegade priest had been something to behold.

He studied Abbott Thurstan now, still standing, somehow, before the dais, cowed and broken, an object of the Conqueror's enmity, the light from a dozen torches playing on his ravaged features, exposing the haunted expression, the tremulous lips, the fear in the eyes. He had visibly aged during the course of the ordeal and now de Cany watched him bend almost double as he bowed in yet another apology, another attempt to assuage the King's anger, but the King was having none of it. The Abbott looked to be exactly what he was: a relic from the past, out of touch with the modern world, an old man at the end of his endurance.

For two hours the King had tirelessly conducted this interrogation, this ruthless reduction of the priest to something less than a man, and he had done it brilliantly. Unable to speak much English himself, the King had summoned de Cany to the chamber, enlisting his services as interpreter, using him as the means to destroy all arguments, all excuses that the Abbott had raised. There *were* no excuses, the King had said, for waging war upon him in his own realm. He was the King, the sovereign ruler, the fount of all law, the defender of the Christian faith. The priest, it followed, was a renegade and a traitor. And traitors should hang.

The Abbott had somehow managed to collect himself a little during the last few moments, had gathered together the shreds of his strength and now stood quietly before the dais awaiting his fate. For the moment the Conqueror was silent, deep in thought, but de Cany saw that his face was still flushed from his earlier tirade, that spittle was dribbling unnoticed down his chin… He was certainly making the Abbott wait. De Cany took the opportunity to glance around the hall.

To his right Fitzalan Fergant sat in a studied silence, watching the proceedings with a detached, almost sullen, air, but de Cany knew better. Fergant would be lusting after the priest's blood, just as much as the King, if not more. Fitzalan Fergant, despite all his boasting, had taken a beating on the causeway at Aldreth and he would be wanting revenge. He was not a man to cross, de Cany thought. Burning ambition allied to the means, the connections, to achieve it. A dangerous opponent indeed…

To Fergant's left was Ivo Taillebois, a complete contrast to Fergant; overweight, reduced to a figure of scorn because of his burns, his one ambition the restoration of his lands, the stinking wilderness called the fens, held, despite all their efforts, by the Wake. From what he had seen, the Wake could keep them...

Taillebois sat, like Fergant, in the arc of light cast by a flickering torch, a leg of beef held casually in one fat hand. Since the injury to his leg he had begun to eat even more, was piling on the weight as if tomorrow would never come. Given that he was now a cripple perhaps he was right to live for the day. But much more weight and his leg would collapse under the strain…He despised Taillebois, he realised; despised him for his greed and his gluttony and the bull-headed way he had gone about subjugating the native Saxons, causing the rebellion in the fens and the terrible loss of life that had ensued. The Saxons needed to know their place but tolerance and understanding were also required; qualities that both sides had signally failed to display.

He dismissed Taillebois with a sigh and swung his gaze back onto the King as now he began to speak in a slow, deliberate manner, allowing de Cany time to gather his thoughts and begin to translate. As was his way after any exertion, the Conqueror was slumped in a casual attitude, an elbow resting upon one arm of the chair, his chin in his hand, as though he were discussing some matter of unimportance, of the tiniest moment. But his eyes told a different tale. Like obsidian coals, they seemed fathomless, without the slightest trace of compassion, and they held the priest in a grip of iron as he pronounced sentence upon him:

"Tell the Abbott that my mind is made up. He is an avowed traitor, to the person of the King and to the Church. He must suffer the penalty. Tell him that."

De Cany paused to make the translation into English, to find the right words, and then began to speak. He saw the Abbott swallow nervously as the words emerged from his lips. He was, he thought, merely a conduit at times like this, without form, without character, a simple mouthpiece. The King was speaking again and he had to break off his thoughts to listen.

"He will pay a forfeit of a thousand pounds. Tell him that."

Again he translated, and at this the Abbott seemed to brighten a little, his back to slowly unbend. But the Conqueror was only beginning:

"He will melt down all of the gold and silver maintained at the Abbeys of Crowland and Ely, all Churches within his See. All crosses, altars, shrines, fistulas, goblets, dishes, anything else of value. Nothing is to be exempt. Nothing. Tell him that. All of this will be reduced and brought to me within the month."

De Cany translated again and this time witnessed the surprise, and then the shock, in the Abbott's eyes. He had clearly not been not expecting this. But still the King was not finished:
"The four Virgins, the St Mary with Child, the Madonna, will be brought to me within the month for removal of their stones. If any are missing he will hang. Tell him that."
De Cany paused before translating with care, and now saw the Abbott visibly pale, his lips quivering, his eyes darting here and there as though seeking some refuge from the unrelenting stare of the King but of course there was none. He saw tears welling in the Abbott's eyes, which had now settled upon the floor rushes as though he could seek sanctuary there. This last sentence, it seemed, was the final straw. But still the Conqueror had not finished and again de Cany had to break off his observation to concentrate upon his translation.
"He will make Pilgrimage to Rome, to prostrate himself before the Holy Father for his conduct. This he will do once he has complied with my orders. He will be denied food and shelter this side of the Channel upon penalty of death."
A slight gasp escaped Taillebois' lips at these last words, causing him to break off from his meal of beef. The King rewarded him with a stony glare. De Cany ignored it and began to translate, aware that the torches were burning low now, their flickering shadows crossing the faces of the witnesses to this, the final pronouncement. It was a harsh sentence indeed and as he spoke these words, turning the French into English for the benefit of the Abbott he became aware of the Abbott's expression slowly changing from sorrow to horror, as though the unthinkable had become reality. His eyelids closed and remained closed for what seemed to be an eternity. The Abbott would be well aware of what this last sentence would mean: Excommunication: a fate worse than death, far worse, for his very soul would be damned to everlasting hell. He witnessed the Abbott

fall to his knees, his hands clutched together, oblivious to those surrounding him. Who he could be praying to de Cany could only guess. Even as he knelt there, a pathetic figure, old and frail, de Cany fancied he could see the fires of hell rising up to devour him, licking ever higher, ever faster, consuming him… He was suddenly back on the causeway, the flames licking at the timbers, remembering the panic, the unbearable heat before he had made his escape. God help the Abbott then, if that was to be his fate, for no man could…

And then he saw the King's face, the fleeting smile briefly cross his granite features before it disappeared again and he knew, in that instant, what the King had already known, had known from the very beginning, that the Abbott would never make it to Rome, never even reach the Channel. He was old and arthritic and in poor health. At this time of year, without food and shelter, it was a death sentence. The King had known this all along, and now, as the Abbott finally spoke in a cracked and broken voice, barely audible in the cavernous chamber, he saw that the Abbott had realised it too:

"I cannot survive such a journey. Nothing will be served by that; only my death." He paused to draw breath, summoning, perhaps, the last of his reserves. "And what is my death compared to my mortal soul; it is nothing, less than nothing; a mere pause, a moment of inconvenience on the road to paradise."

De Cany translated and the response from the King came immediately, as though he had been expecting this:

"And your *life?* What worth your miserable *life?"*

The Abbott hesitated, thrown this unexpected lifeline. The King's eyes were riveted upon him, burning with intensity, willing him to answer. The words spilled from his mouth before he could recall them:

"In the spring I will give you the Wake. Spare me and I will deliver him to you."

Chapter Thirty-Four

As night fell it began to snow again, large flakes that settled on trees, on the ground, as soon as they landed. Once the sun had set it had become noticeably colder and Ranulf hugged Hal to him, a dead weight in his arms, asleep now after walking all day. Careworn and weary himself, he cast around for somewhere to rest, to shelter from the fall of snow that was growing heavier by the minute. To either side the forest pressed in on him, the branches of the trees glistening with frost in the moonlight. A few miles longer, he decided, a few miles closer to home, and then he would rest.

He looked down at his son, his face very pale, like a mask, in the moonlight. A few specks of snow had settled on his cheeks and he pulled Hal's hood a little more over his face. He was dead to the world but it was hardly surprising. They had walked all day, a spring in their step at first, talking and reminiscing, sometimes crying, sometimes laughing. Noon had arrived, and went, and still they had walked, but as the afternoon had worn on and the light had faded, Hal's legs had given up on him. Ranulf had picked him up and carried him in his arms.

He studied his son again, unable, somehow, to keep his eyes from the pale mask beneath the hood. It had been so long…As he looked at him now he was suddenly struck by how like his mother he was at this moment; the same pale face, the long, dark lashes and raven hair, the same curve of the lips. She would be overwhelmed to see him again. Just a few days now and they would be reunited. What a day that would be...He heard a movement ahead of him, in the bushes to his right and stopped dead in his tracks. Three men were emerging onto the path. Normans, they carried drawn swords and were advancing towards him in a line. Thirty yards, he reckoned, at most. No chance of outpacing them, not with Hal. He cursed under his breath and forced himself to think. He shook Hal to wake him and even as he was lowering him to the ground with one hand he was reaching for *Requitur* with the other, his eyes fixed upon the closing enemy. One of them, he realised, was the Norman seen earlier in the day, and again he had the feeling that he had seen him somewhere before.

He risked a glance at Hal, saw the confusion, the fear, written in his face. He had only just awoken and was clearly disorientated.

"What is it father?" he said. "Are we home?" Hal's eyes were bleary beneath the hood, not quite focused.

"Not home yet son," he said. "Into the trees with you. I will find you later."

Hal stared at him, frozen to the spot, fear, or perhaps incomprehension preventing him from moving. Ranulf risked a glance at the Normans and saw that they were closing, moving confidently towards him.

"Go!" he screamed the word this time. "Into the trees! Run for your life boy!" A frown, a glance at the foreigners and understanding dawned. Hal bolted from the path into the undergrowth.

Ranulf dismissed him and focused his whole attention upon the Normans. He dragged *Le Couteau's* knife from his belt, holding it in his left hand.

The Normans' were separating now, intending to come at him from three sides, the two larger men moving out to right and left. He backed towards a tree, protection of sorts. The man on the right suddenly made a move towards him, coming in quickly, recklessly almost, as though anticipating an easy kill, his sword blade catching the moonlight as he brandished it above his head. His eyes were wild, eager, as though he had never killed a man before. The blow came from above, intended to crush his skull, but it was clumsily executed and Ranulf instinctively raised *Requitur* to parry the blow. The shock of steel upon steel as the blades met jarred his arm to the shoulder reminding him of his wound, but even as the blades locked together he was thumping the knife into the man's gut with his left hand and wrenching it out and punching it in again. He ripped it clear in a spray of blood as he sensed a movement to his left, felt the rush of air as the second Norman swung at him, a great arcing blow again aimed at his head. He turned just in time to parry it with the knife and now felt irons of fire lancing through his wrist as the blade took the full weight of the blow. He gasped with the pain and prepared for the next blow but now saw that the next blow would not be coming for the Normans' sword had shattered upon impact with the Toledo steel of his knife, leaving him with only the hilt and a few inches of blade in his hand. The Norman hesitated, staring at the shattered sword as though unable to believe his eyes. It was a slight mistake, understandable in other circumstances, but it was enough. Ranulf swung *Requitur* at the point where the neck meets the shoulder and felt the edge bite as it caught the man perfectly. The blow jerked the head back, cleaving through tissue and bone until there was no more resistance and the blade shot free in a shower of blood. The head flew away into the night, spraying crimson into the snow filled air. The headless corpse dropped to the ground, the legs buckling beneath it, the sword falling from lifeless fingers. The man had never moved, had never seen it coming.

Feroux was alone now, his eyes darting from one stiffening corpse to another, unable, it seemed, to believe the savagery of Ranulf's defence.

"I remember you, Saxon!" he screamed. "The night in the tent. You should have died then!"

The words suddenly brought it back to him: the visit by *Le Couteau* in the dead of night, the night before the fight. This man had been one of them, one of *Le Couteau's* scum. He studied the narrow face with its downturned mouth, twisted with hatred and fear, caught in the moonlight, the snow swirling and eddying around him and he felt his gorge rise.

"Perhaps I should," he said. "But *Le Couteau* died instead. Died like a dog at my feet. I have his blade to prove it." He raised the knife as if for inspection and then his hand flickered, too quickly for the eye to see. The point took Feroux in the neck, just beneath the jawline, severing the carotid artery. He reeled backwards, his face writhing, contorting, eyes bulging, hands closing over the hilt. A noise, like the wailing of a hound, erupted from his lips as he ripped out the long blade, hurling it to the ground with bloodied fingers but even as the point exited the wound Ranulf could see that it was over for him. Feroux sank reluctantly to his knees, fighting still, unprepared, it seemed, to accept his death. He swayed backwards and forwards as he fought to stay upright, his hands clutching his throat, blood pumping unchecked through his fingers. The swaying slowed and then ceased, the eyes dimmed, the body toppled sideways into the snow. Ranulf walked over to it and saw that the eyes were open but the corpse was still, save for the twitching of the neck where the blood continued to pump…

Chapter Thirty-Five
The Camp Of Refuge

The Wake caught the movement of her slight figure from the corner of his eye and instinctively swung his head towards her. The distraction was sufficient to allow Wynter to penetrate his guard, stunning his right arm with the flat of his blade, causing him to drop his sword into the mud.

"You're getting careless old friend," Wynter said. "I could have killed you if I had not turned my blade." Hereward nodded in acknowledgement of this simple truth and rubbed his aching arm. After a brief examination of the angry welt he turned to watch the housecarl's woman disappear through the great oak gates of the camp, which now swung shut behind her, obscuring her from view.

He knew where she was going; to see the priest, Hugo Brittanious, to discourse on the scriptures and then, no doubt, to pray. What precisely she prayed for he did not know, but he thought he could guess and even as the thought crystallized, became fact, he felt a tide of emotion that he recognised as jealousy wash over him. It would be the housecarl and her son, both of them forever in her thoughts, casting a shadow even from the grave. He fought down a tide of anger. He had already lost Torfrida to the church; now, it seemed, he had lost Alice also. But there was a difference. Torfrida's loss had given him the opportunity that he had sought. He had not minded her loss; had even been relieved when her letter had arrived. But Alice? Alice was different, her loss something that he had not foreseen, not planned for. She had slipped through his fingers as the days had turned into weeks and the lure of the Church, of Christ, had taken hold, prizing her, day by day from his grasp. He was just an afterthought now; perhaps not even that. Were it not for his status as leader of this rebellion would she think of him at all? Somehow he doubted it. The housecarl, her son, the priest and Christ; those were the people important to her, the ones that truly mattered, and there was a certain irony in the fact that of those four three of them were already dead. And the priest was well on the way. Not that he wished him harm. Hugo was a good man, an honest man, lacking the pride, the ambition, of Abbott Thurstan, who had not been seen since the King's men had arrested him and taken him to Warwick…

He lifted his sword from the mud and wiped the blade and hilt on his knee length coat. He went into the guard position. He needed to vent his anger and Wynter was as good a foil for that as anyone.
"Attack me again," he said. "From the right. Come at me hard. Test my bloody arm." Wynter shook his head.
"No, I do not think so," he said. "Your mind is elsewhere today. Perhaps tomorrow - when your arm is recovered."

There had been a slow but subtle change in his relationship with his comrades since the second battle at Aldreth and now, it seemed, they felt the need to humour him, to *lecture* him at times, like some small child, something that would have been unthinkable before the arrival of the housecarl and his woman. *His woman*. He gazed at the massive gates of oak and imagined that he could somehow see beyond them, could see her slim figure winding its way towards the chapel, her hands clasped together, her head bent low beneath her hood, her eyes downcast, as though she were a penitent. *But it had been his fault, not hers.* And now he hated himself for it. Jealousy and guilt; they made fine bed partners and they both reposed in his breast, gnawing away at him…

He struck hard at Wynter, who, like himself a few moments earlier was unprepared for it. Wynter parried clumsily, caught off balance, and he struck again angrily, deliberately testing his injured arm. Again Wynter parried and this time struck back, causing sparks to fly from the blades, the sound to ring around the camp. A small group gathered to watch the two old friends, protagonists for the moment, trading blows.

"You should bloody well forget her." Wynter's voice punctuated the silence between the clash and parting of the steel, his breath coming in short bursts. He lunged to the right but Hereward skipped away, beyond his reach.

"I can't." The Wake countered with a lunge of his own, catching Wynter on the shoulder, turning his blade at the last moment as Wynter himself had done. Wynter scowled and held his shoulder but it was only play-acting.

"Nothing wrong with your arm," he said. "It's your head that needs fixing. Women. What good are they? You're better off without them."

Wynter could be incredibly perceptive at times, he realised, or perhaps he had become too transparent, his feelings too obvious. Either way the advice was sound.

"You're right," he said, his own breath coming in gasps as he struck again, this time to the left. "They can't fight, they can't drink. What damned use are they?"

"No damned use." Wynter grinned as he parried with ease. "Except for dressing wounds and rearing brats. And who wants them? You should forget her my friend," he repeated obstinately.

"I can't forget her," he said just as stubbornly, aware that once again he was speaking from the heart but unable to prevent himself.

"Though she was never mine I cannot forget her. God help me but I cannot. I will not."

He swung his sword at Wynter as if to underline his feelings, careless of the ache in his arm, heedless of anything but the need to exorcise the hurt, the sense of betrayal that he was feeling and for another twenty minutes the clash of steel shattered the calm of the morning…

Lightfoot strained his eyes to focus upon the coracle as it slowly neared the jetty. Two men and a boy he reckoned; all of them dressed against the harsh winter weather, their faces well covered by the hoods pulled low over their foreheads. It occurred to him that it could be an elaborate plot but even as the thought came to him he dismissed it. It would be suicide to attempt a landing with such a small force, and in any event the man paddling the coracle was skilled in his craft, negotiating it easily through the reeds with an assured hand. He was a fisherman then, a Saxon. His eyes returned to the other two, to the man sat crossed-legged before the fisherman, his arms resting loosely about the child that made up the trio. There was something familiar about the seated man, the hunch of the massive shoulders, the set of his head upon them, but at this distance he could not be certain. He was not getting any younger; this winter was his forty-second as far as he could tell and his eyes were beginning to fail.

The coracle disappeared briefly behind a stand of reeds and as it emerged again he turned to Hurchillus and the half-dozen men beside him.

"Notch your bows," he said, "just in case."

He heard the rustle of clothyard shafts being plucked from quivers as he focused again upon the fisherman, watched him bend into his stroke with a practised ease as he turned the coracle towards the jetty.

"Nothing to fear there." Villicus now spoke, his voice cutting through the silence. "It's Ranulf, and the boy. I would recognise those shoulders anywhere."

"Christ, where has he come from!" cried Alsinus, "I had given him up for dead months ago. Aye, and the boy!"

"Hard to kill that bastard," Hurchillus observed drily. "Glad he's fighting for us and not that other bastard – the French one." There was a ripple of laughter amongst the men and then cheering broke out as the coracle approached the jetty. Fists punched the air in salute, and some of the men began chanting Ranulf's name, a chorus of song that rang around the fens.

Lightfoot stared at the coracle, at the muddy water swirling and eddying around it as it moored up. He saw the occupants rise gingerly to their feet, preparing to disembark. Villicus was right; he would recognise that massive frame anywhere, even though it was considerably thinner than he had remembered it and even though it appeared to be disguised in little better than rags.

As the chanting died away the housecarl looked around the faces on the jetty and recognising him amongst them, raised his hand in greeting. Lightfoot acknowledged it, raising his own. He watched Ranulf leap onto the jetty and then bend to pick up his son. It was like handling a rag doll as he swung the child up onto the slick timbers in one easy movement.

"See," Ranulf called to him across the crowd, "Hal is alive and well. We both are, if perhaps a little thinner." He plucked at his cloak, that seemed to Lightfoot to be in danger of falling apart at any moment. "What will Alice say when she sees us eh? God but I cannot wait to see her again!"

"That will be a reunion to behold," Lightfoot acknowledged evenly, "that's for sure."
"Where will she be?" The housecarl looked around the faces on the jetty again, as though expecting her to be present but of course there was only himself, Hurchillus and the rest of his men. Lightfoot noted the hint of disappointment shadow his face, the realisation that she was absent. In all truth he could hardly have expected it to be otherwise
"At the chapel," he said. "She prays there every day." He could think of another that would also be disappointed by today's events, but disappointment, perhaps, of a different kind. The clash of steel suddenly rang through the air, coming from the camp, reminding him that the third member of the triangle, his boyhood friend, was not far away.
"What's that?" the housecarl said, a frown creasing his brow for the first time. He had aged, Lightfoot realised, in the months that he had been away. He noted again the loss of weight, the beard, long and unkempt, streaked with grey. Up close he could see the lines wrinkling the forehead, the crows' feet and dark circles around the eyes, as though he had not slept for months. He had aged ten years, if not more. God alone knew what he had been through.
"Just Hereward and Wynter crossing steel," he said. "Practicing again. Not that they need it." He shrugged and the housecarl nodded again.
"And Earl Morcar? Where is he? He is well?"
Lightfoot noted the use of the title. Old habits were hard to change. Morcar had not been an Earl for four years, not since the Conqueror had stripped him of the title and given it to his nephew, the Count Fitzalan Fergant.
"Morcar is well," he said. "He is out patrolling with his archers. He will be back by sundown. Seems to prefer his own company these days." Again the housecarl nodded.

"Little has changed then," Ranulf said. He turned to the boy and picked him up, cradling him in the crook of an arm. "Your turn now, my lad," he said. "Time to find your mother. We have a few surprises in store for her eh?" He laughed and somehow the years seemed to drop away. He hauled Hal up onto his shoulders, and marched off in the direction of the chapel.

Lightfoot watched him go. *Surprises in store,* he had said. No doubt there would be. And perhaps, he thought, there would be more than he had bargained for. He could only hope that people kept their mouths shut as he intended to do. They were in enough trouble without the Wake and the housecarl coming to blows. God help them all if it came to that.

He watched the housecarl disappearing into the distance, jogging in his haste to see his woman, his son playfully slapping him around the shoulders, urging him to go faster as he would a horse. It could be any father playing with his son.

Lightfoot sighed and shrugged his shoulders. What would be would be. He was too long in the tooth to worry about such things but as the first snowflakes of the day began to fall from a leaden grey sky and the sound of clashing steel rang out across the fens he could not help but wonder whether it was a portent of things to come.

Hugo Brittanious lay before the altar, his torso half on the altar steps, half on the flagstones. In death he stared upwards with open, sightless eyes, his face contorted into a strange rictus, as though whatever had happened to cause this had come suddenly, like a thief in the night, catching him unawares. Alice bent and closed the eyes and his face was suddenly transformed, looking calmer, at peace with itself once more. His right hand still clutched something, the knuckles white with tension, as though at the last he had been unwilling to relinquish his grip upon whatever it was he was holding. She took the hand in her own; already it was beginning to cool, rigor mortis stiffening the flesh. He had been dead for some time, she realised. One by one she took his fingers and prized them away from their possession and now saw that it was the tiny crucifix that he usually wore on a chain around his neck. The ends of the crosstrees were pressing into his palm, piercing the skin, causing it to bleed, and his palm was still sticky with blood. She closed the hand again, wrapping the fingers around their prize. They had gone together then, he and his beloved Christ and it was not for her to part them …

Her eyes strayed upwards, towards the figure on the wall, the Saviour hanging on his cross above the altar, his face gazing down from beneath his crown of thorns at the lifeless torso sprawled at his feet. She stared at the face and now saw something that had previously escaped her: two tiny streaks of blood, like tears, running down his cheek. She checked herself and looked again thinking that she must be mistaken. But there was no mistake; two vertical splashes of colour ran from each eye, discolouring his cheeks. Had they always been present? If so how had she missed them? Surely, if they had been present before she would have seen them? Curious now, she stepped around the prone figure of the priest and walked the four steps to the altar. She stared at the face beneath its crown of thorns and examined it again. The marks beneath the eyes were fresh and bright, caught in the light from the adjacent window, the colour of the blood in stark contrast to that on his forehead which over the years had turned brown and faded with age. So too the blood on his hands and side. She had no answer to this. She turned back to the priest, his lifeless form indecorously draped across the altar steps. Had he too seen this, or had he been responsible for it? And what had he been doing here, before the altar, when death had struck him down? She puzzled and worried at these matters for some moments before becoming aware that someone was entering the chapel. She turned and saw two figures standing in the doorway, their cloaks spattered with snow, their faces hidden by their hoods, by the shaft of light entering the chapel, briefly illuminating the interior. The brightness partially blinded her but she could see that one was a large man, roughly clad, in a cloak that was frayed and torn. He was tall and thin, but with wide, broad, shoulders, the other much smaller beside him, some kind of dwarf, she thought, or a child. Beggars perhaps. Or murderers. She glanced at Hugo and felt a sickening lurch of her stomach.

"Who is it?" she said as calmly as she could. "What do you want?"

The man stepped forward a few paces and even from this distance she could smell the stench of him.

"Why," he said. "It's me. Do you not recognise me, my love?" He turned to the much smaller figure a few paces behind him. "And your son. He has returned to us." His face was still in shadow, hidden by the hood, but she would know the timbre of his voice anywhere. It was true but surely it was not possible. She took a few hesitant steps towards them, hardly able to believe the evidence of her ears, her eyes.

The man now turned to the boy beside him and she saw them exchange glances. The man nodded and the boy threw back the hood showing his face. He was exactly as she had remembered him: the same dark hair as her own, his fathers' blue eyes. He was a little taller than when she had last seen him, she realised, the day she thought he had been killed…

Her eyes suddenly misted over and a sob caught in her throat and then she was lost in a whirlpool of emotion, drowning in it as she flung herself down the aisle, hurling herself at him, hugging Hal to her, kissing him, whirling him around and around until she felt dizzy.

Eventually, when she felt she had no breath left she pulled away from him and studied the man. He was gaunt, his bearded cheeks hollowed by hunger, his eyes set deep into their sockets, blasted by the weather. He was an old man now, she thought, unrecognisable from the man that had left her. She hugged him to her and the tears came again. She seemed to be unable to stop crying.

"It's alright," he said. "I'm home now. We both are." He smiled, and the wrinkles creased around his eyes made him suddenly younger again. What had happened to him she could not begin to imagine.

"Oh God, thank you," she said, "thank you." She was struggling to find any words. It was all so unexpected, so sudden. She had never imagined it would be like this; at one time she had ceased to imagine it all…

She suddenly remembered the priest. She had neglected Hugo in the last few minutes and now felt somehow unworthy of him, as though she had betrayed a friend as well as a lover.

"He knew you would return," she said to Ranulf, almost a stranger now, so changed was he. Her eyes kept flitting from him to the face of her son, unable to settle on either. It was like a miracle, both of them returned to her, both of them. "Somehow he knew you would return. He had faith enough for both of us you see. I was weak but he gave me strength and somehow I think he knew he had to keep going for me until you returned. His work is finished now." Her eyes strayed upwards from the prone figure of the priest to the figure on the cross. The eyes gazed down as before; filled with compassion, with love, but now, she saw, the tears of blood had gone. Perhaps she had simply imagined them, an overactive mind in a state of agitation. Perhaps…

She turned to Hal and picked him up, relishing the feel of him against her bosom, unwilling to let him go. She wanted to hold him forever. She saw Ranulf watching them, the cares of the past months hanging heavily upon him now that it was finally over. He was exhausted, she saw, physically, emotionally. She reluctantly put Hal down and went to him. She saw that there were tears in his eyes too. The last time had been the day that Hal had been born. She put her arms around him, ignoring the dirt, the stench the unkempt beard.

"It is all over now," she said. "All over." She could feel his ribcage beneath her fingers, beneath the cloth of his cloak. He could not have eaten for weeks. How he had managed to keep going she would never know. She held him in an embrace for what seemed like an eternity, halos of light from guttering candles casting their shadows onto the floor like two ghosts, two spirits that had found one another again. Her eyes moved from the shadows to the priest, still lying where he had fallen, still sprawled in the ugly attitude of death.

"We must tend to Hugo," she said. "It is my turn to care for him now." She pinched Ranulf's wasted flesh beneath her fingers; there was so much less of it than she had remembered.

"And then," she said, "I must care for you." He smiled and wiped an eye; he was as overcome as herself she realised. It was not surprising; they had both been through so much. She gave him a hug and he hugged her back, crushing her to him this time as though he would crush the very life from her.

Chapter Thirty- Six
Spring 1071

The Wake seated himself on a grassy hummock and settled down to watch the shipwrights on the jetty, engrossed in their task of fitting out the last of the three dragon ships that he had ordered to be built. They were busy hammering the mast into the belly of the boat, securing it with wooden pegs. Next they would caulk it with oakum to ensure that the fit was watertight. The final stage would be the rigging of the sails for all three ships and for that he guessed they would need the wind to drop. He lifted his face and felt the breeze blowing from the north, chill and unremitting this morning despite the onset of spring. Winter was reluctantly yielding her hold on the land but it was still bitterly cold and he cursed himself for neglecting his winter mantle as he blew on his hands for warmth. There was a melancholy sigh to the wind as it whistled through the reeds, matching his mood, and he shivered beneath his leather jerkin and folded his arms across his chest for warmth.

These ships, still on their wooden cradles, still unfinished, would be the means of escape for those lucky enough find a berth whenever the time came. Twenty souls each they would hold; sixty in total. He would never get them all out; over five hundred men women and children were now dependant upon him but when the Conqueror finally forced his defences, as surely he would, it would be every man for himself. At least now they had ships, only three of them, but three was better than nothing, an assurance for those seeking it that when the time came they would not be left to the mercy of the Conqueror and his butchers. He had not yet decided who would have a berth and who would be left to their fate. It was difficult to legislate for these things but perhaps it should be women and children only. It was a hard decision to make and for the moment he was content to postpone it.

He heard the distant whinny of a horse and turned to see the familiar figure of Morcar galloping towards the jetty, his braided hair blowing back like ribbons from his face. He also sported a beard now, a light stubble, neatly trimmed, dignifying his cheeks and chin. He was a fine man, he thought, without a trace of the jealousy that coloured his thoughts of the housecarl, whose recent return had so unsettled him. They had barely spoken during the last few weeks, save for the necessity of welcoming him back, and he could not help but wonder whether the housecarl had recognised the betrayal in his eyes as he had greeted him, embracing him like a long lost son. Everyone else knew of it of course but they were all keeping quiet, fearful, perhaps, of the consequences. Alice too, had obviously said nothing yet, but he could imagine the private agonies that she was experiencing, the impulse to unburden herself…He cursed under his breath for the hundredth time. It was *not* his fault, he had now decided, that he had fallen in love with her. And Ranulf had had no business leaving her like that. They had all thought him dead. It was not his fault…

The drumming of Galahad's hooves jerked him from his reverie and he turned to watch his nephew approach. He was a good horseman, man and animal moving together as though joined at the hip. Fit and lean, Morcar had matured beyond his years. This land had something to do with it he reasoned. Harsh and unforgiving, only the strongest flourished here. And Morcar had thrived in it, had somehow cast off the ignominy of losing his earldom, applying himself with a vigour and a willingness that he had found surprising. And he was a good leader to his own band of men, fiercely protective of them when the occasion demanded and loved by them in return. What would become of him when all of this was over? He had heard rumours, as yet unconfirmed, that the Conqueror wanted him alive, wanted to make an example of him. He had already decided that he would never allow that, not if he had to slay him with his own hands to prevent it. His eyes returned to the shipwrights labouring on the last of the dragon ships. The mast had been seated into position now and the men were busy applying the hot, sticky caulk that would cement it into place. *Women and children only?* He should have built more…

Beyond Morcar, far over to the east, the sun was slowly rising above the horizon, turning the silver of the morning sky to pale gold. The Conqueror would probably come that way when the time was ready. His army was still at Brandon but were said to be breaking camp, preparing for the forthcoming campaign. Surely it was no coincidence? Just a short march from Brandon lay the east of the Isle, as yet untried, untested, by the King but there was the Wicken fen to negotiate, a nightmare land, if one could call it land, of shifting sands and cloying mud. The Conqueror would probably chance a number of probing attacks, but he would be ready for him. Wicken fen was his fortress, his only line of defence in the east but for all that it was impregnable. His men knew it like the backs of their hands. The Conqueror would surely regret it if he came that way.

He rubbed his chin and tugged at his whiskers, troubled by a nagging doubt. The south was the more obvious, and shortest, route to launch an assault from the mainland but the Conqueror had already tried the south twice and been bloodily repulsed. Surely he would not try it a third time. Surely not. This time he would try something different. He could sense it as keenly as he could sense trouble in the way that his nephew was hastening towards him, head bent low over Galahad's neck as though persuading him to part with the last ounce of speed.

Morcar reined to a halt, showering both men with mud. The land was still wet and soft, the last of the snows having only recently departed. They had a few weeks yet, he thought, a few weeks more before the storm of war broke over them again.

"The Bastard is on the march, uncle!" Morcar spoke excitedly, using the nom de guerre adopted by the housecarl as though subconsciously allying himself to him. He had seen them talking together last night but had not felt able to join them...

"So soon?" he said, forcing his thoughts back to the present. "I thought perhaps we had longer." Morcar looked grim, shook his head.

"Three thousand heavy foot, including Fergant's Bretons. Fergant is leading them himself. He has sworn to have your head." Hereward smiled a rueful smile.

"Not much of a prize this," he said. Then more seriously: "How do you know?"

"Two of my men found a fisherman to take them across to the mainland. Saw them with their own eyes." Morcar was breathing heavily he noticed; he had obviously ridden hard to tell him this. "They are good men uncle; their word can be trusted." He nodded his acknowledgement. He had never doubted it.

"And Fergant's line of march?" he said, "what did they learn of that?"

"South, towards Cambridge as far as they could tell. They had to be careful not to be seen."

"I see," he said. So it would be the south again. Not east. He scratched his chin for the second time. It made sense, of a sort, even though the Conqueror had already been beaten twice in the south. It was the obvious place. But to try it a third time?

"Take your hundred best men and patrol between Ely and Stretham," he said. "Keep a sharp look-out. I will watch the south. If anything moves send news by war-arrow. I will come as soon as I can. If all else fails fall back on the camp."
Morcar's face creased in concern.
"But if the Bastard comes at you from the south you will be short of men. I do not like this dividing of our forces." The Wake shrugged.
"I like it even less, but something about this does not smell right." He returned his nephew's gaze, mirroring the concern shown there. "The Conqueror has already been beaten twice in the south. Why try a third time? Why not try something different?
"Because, uncle," Morcar said, "there is nothing else to try. No other way in. He has no choice but to come from the south."
He nodded again, saying nothing for the moment, turning the matter in his mind. Morcar was right, he was sure that he was. The east *was* impassable; nothing but swamp and shifting sands. An army could disappear in minutes as though it had never existed. And yet, and yet, what if he were wrong…?
"I am sure you are right," he said eventually with a confidence he did not feel. "But we shall still watch the east, just in case. Take Lefwinus with you and a hundred others. I can manage with the rest."
"As you wish." The inflexion in Morcar's voice betrayed his disappointment. He climbed into the saddle, turning Galahad with a click of his tongue. "I had better round up the men," he said, "just in case."
"The sooner you start the better."
He hated this, the clipped formality of orders when he wanted to say so much more, to say how much he admired his nephew and that he was only doing this because he knew he was right. Morcar's disapproval was evident and that only made it worse. But he *was*

right about this. He *knew* he was. Instinctively he reached up and offered his hand.

"We should not part like this," he said. "Take my hand and let us part as friends. Blood should look to blood at a time like this."

Morcar paused for just an instant before reaching down his hand, accepting the olive branch, taking his own in a firm grip that betrayed no sign of their discord.

"You are right," he said softly. "Goodbye, uncle, until we meet again." A fleeting smile crossed his lips, reaching his eyes, and the cloud that had come between them evaporated.

"Goodbye then," he said. He released the hand and Morcar gathered the reins, pricking Galahad into the gallop.

He watched Morcar disappear into the distance, horse and rider growing smaller and smaller with each hoof beat that carried them away from him. He watched them until they breasted a rise in the ground, until they were hidden from view and only now did he turn to walk back to the jetty. As he did so, at the precise moment of turning, a chill wind cut through him, raising the hairs on the back of his neck. He glanced across at the dragon ships, at the first sail being fitted to the mast. To his surprise he saw that it was hanging limply, with no sign of the breeze that had just troubled him. He thought again of his nephew, of his reluctance to accept the task and wondered whether he should have gone east himself. He shook his head. It was too late now. He cast a final glance at the point where his nephew had disappeared and the memory, the image of him seemed to be imprinted on his mind like that of a ghost.

"Have a care about your work," he muttered softly to himself. "Have a care, my lad."

Chapter Thirty-Seven

Fitzalan Fergant shaded his eyes, weary from lack of sleep, and gazed at the rising sun. Casting a benign glow over the watery wastes it lay directly on his line of march. He smiled a careworn smile, a smile of welcome relief as it rose slowly above the horizon, the quarter becoming a half, and finally a whole as the sky brightened and dawn broke to the chorus of birds and the sound of men clawing their way through mud.

For three days the Norman army had headed south but then, as agreed with the King, he had divided his forces, marching fifteen hundred men north again before turning east. They had marched all night under cover of darkness, at times hardly knowing where they were, but now, as dawn broke and coloured the land in shades of grey he saw that miraculously they had judged it correctly.

Ahead of the column was the Saxon priest, the key to the enterprise. Without him, without his knowledge of these watery wastes, they would be lost. He peered into the sun, still low in the sky, and identified his familiar stooped figure slowly picking its way along an invisible path known only to him, pointing and prodding and sweeping the waters with his staff, the same staff that had once been crowned with a crucifix of silver, now melted down by the King for coin.

Behind the priest were two of his best men, ordered to watch him like a hawk. One of them held a sword, the point of which hovered just inches from his spine, a reminder if any were needed that he was in their hands as much as they were in his. Even so he did not trust the bastard. The sooner they were onto dry land the happier he would be.

Ahead of them, in the far distance, lay their ultimate goal, the Isle of Ely. At present it was shrouded in mist, the breath of the dragon still hanging over it. It struck him that there was something primordial about the place, something that defied man's attempts to subjugate it. Even the Wake only occupied it for the moment, until it tired of him. The dragon had not yet stirred but when it did they would all feel its breath on the backs of their necks. He thought about this as he shivered into his cloak and gazed ahead at its brooding presence. It was almost as if the Isle had taken on a life of its own and that man, far from being the controlling hand, was merely the puppet in the piece, dancing to the Isle's own macabre tune.

He switched his gaze to the Saxon priest, his frame silhouetted against the slowly rising sun. Were it not for the fact that he was needed to lead them onto the Isle he would happily have slit his throat. He glanced nervously from side to side, at the water pressing in all around, lapping halfway up his legs now. One false step and they would be writing his obituary. His men were nervous too, their voices lowered to little more than a whisper, evidence that, like himself they were uncomfortably aware of how precarious their position had become. If the Saxons' attacked now it would mean the end for him, for them all. He thought of the Conqueror, safely ensconced in Cambridge castle, and suddenly envied him his security. He cursed under his breath and rubbed his eyes, willing them to see through the mist that seemed to be thickening as the minutes passed. What an awful place this was. He pulled a booted foot from the oozing mud and planted it in front of the other. Without warning he was up to his knees in mud. He struggled to find his balance and was about to warn those behind when a cry, loud and shrill, erupted just yards ahead of him. His first thought was that the Saxons had launched an assault but then he saw that one of the men had fallen from the path into the bog; that already it was sucking him down.

"Pull him out!" he bellowed. "Quickly! Before the bastard drowns!" All around him men were beginning to panic, their nerves frayed by the long night march, by the uncertainty of their present treacherous surroundings. Someone organised a line, a piece of rope, and now it was tossed out to the drowning man but even as it was thrown he could see that it would fall short of the outstretched hand. The man lunged for it but missed, his fingers clawing the mud in a hopeless attempt to reach it. His mouth wide with terror he screamed for them to cast the line again. Quickly it was hauled in and thrown out to him, the thrower almost losing his balance as he did so and this time his aim was way off. Another man grabbed him around the waist to steady him and he threw it again, reaching forward as far as he dare. The throw was more accurate but still it fell short, and now the man gave a cry of despair as the mud sucked at him again, drawing him down. He screamed and flailed with his arms to keep his head above the water. Mud bubbled up around him, his struggles seemingly making it worse, and some of the men on the path, perhaps comrades of his, were shouting at him to keep still, keep calm. The man was not listening. Panic had gripped him just as it had the rescuers and now he thrashed again, his head tilted backwards as the mud rose up to his chin. Fergant felt rooted to the spot, unable to help, a mere spectator to this awful drama.

The rope was hauled in and tossed again. The mud was almost up to the man's eyes now, which were wild, unfocused. He shouted something and his mouth filled with mud, causing him to choke. Again the rope was tossed, hurriedly, awkwardly, but this time the man was not ready, not looking.

"Try again for Christ's sake!" someone shouted, but already Fergant could see it was too late. The face sank beneath the mud, the eyes shutting as the waters closed over them, leaving only the memory of his last baleful glare, as though accusing him. He instinctively turned away, but some compulsion, some need to witness the end, dragged him back to the drowning man. Only the hands now, were visible, the fists clenching and unclenching as though to grasp an invisible line, until they too disappeared from view as the mud drew him under.

The shouting stopped and a hush descended upon the scene. For long seconds no one moved, all eyes riveted to the spot where their comrade had disappeared, the still bubbling mud marking the place where he had gone down. God alone knew what they were thinking.

"Keep moving or we are all dead men!" Fergant barked, breaking the silence, his voice sounding hoarse and strained in the stillness. The column started to move off again, shuffling forward with reluctant, careful steps. He glanced again at its head, at the priest leading the way, apparently oblivious to what had just happened. Or was he? He was damned if he knew. He stared at him long and hard, at the priest's pale face creased in concentration as he swept the waters in his search for the path. He was tempted to slit his throat now but if he did that he would have to lead the army out of this morass and he had no great confidence that he could. And the priest was a man of God; not much of one in Fergant's estimation, but a holy man nevertheless. He had never had much time for God but he still harboured sufficient unease as to the welfare of his own soul if he sent the bastard where he deserved a little before his time. So, then, the priest must live, God rot him…

He cursed again and tried to comfort himself with the thought of what he would do when eventually they forced the Isle. He risked a glance ahead, to where it lay hidden, somewhere in the distance, rendered invisible by its cloak of mist. The dragon was still sleeping then. But he would rouse the dragon from its slumbers and cut out its evil heart. And then he would make a finish with the Wake: the Wake, his supporters, all of them…

Despite the cold and the damp and the cloying mud that sapped the spirit, Fitzalan Fergant smiled a thin smile. His name was entirely apposite, he thought. *Alan the Red* men called him. The colour of blood.

He would drown the bastards in it.

Chapter Thirty-Eight

Alice sits in the afternoon sunshine watching Ranulf put his warriors through their paces. The morning mist has burned away and it is a lovely spring day, the sort of day she remembers from her childhood. Occasionally she will look down to her lap, to the jerkin that needs darning, but for the most part she is happy just to sit and watch, feeling the sun on her face as Ranulf shows the men how to lock their shields and present their spears to an imagined enemy. Hal is with them also, on the end of the line, his tiny spear presented to his front, copying the others. Ranulf has fashioned it for him from a length of seasoned ash. He will be a great warrior one day, he tells her, just like his father…

She has not told Ranulf yet, of what happened. She knows that she should tell him, that she should unburden herself, but somehow the opportunity has not arisen. There has been time enough since his return but she cannot bring herself to say it, fearing his reaction. Fearing her own.

The camp is half empty now that Morcar has gone east, the Wake to the south. Only Ranulf and Lightfoot remain, and the men that the other two didn't want. Older or infirm, they still make a brave sight with their kite-shaped shields locked together in a single line, their spear-points glinting in the sun. She watches them advancing now, a solid line of forty men with Ranulf at their head, shouting orders, the occasional rebuke, thinking perhaps of his old comrades, his own proud regiment cut to pieces on Caldbec Hill.

She watches him take a spear and shield from one of the men and shows him how to parry with his shield, thrust with his spear. He is looking stronger these days, she thinks, now that he is rested and fed, but the wound in his chest still worries him at times. So too the weakness in his right arm, scarred from shoulder to elbow, a livid pink slash that no amount of rest will cure. But he is scarred all over and thinks nothing of them. She counted them last night, before they made love, tracing their outlines with her finger. There are twelve of them but the scars to shoulder, chest and arms are worst. The enemy always try for those parts first, he said, to kill or to maim. And, of course, the head, the most vulnerable part of all. No helmet yet created will stop a direct blow and the blow is usually fatal. So far he has been lucky. That is what he said. She suspects that he is right although he laughed as he said it, as though it were nothing.

She hates this war. She hates this place too, with its bitter memories of death and betrayal. She longs to leave, but knows that for the moment it is impossible. She senses that one way or the other it will soon be over but how it will end she cannot say. Only that she fears for the worst. And so she continues to sit in the sun, watching the men, watching Ranulf and her son, burying her guilt for their sakes.

Chapter Thirty-Nine

Morcar stared ahead, into the gloom before twisting in the saddle to check the position of the sun. Almost directly behind him now, it was starting its slow downward arc towards the western horizon. In half an hour it would be dark, too dark to make their ultimate destination, the fortified camp at Stuntney, the only high point for miles around. He weighed the matter in his mind, the dangers of pitching camp here, in the open, against the risk of venturing beyond this point in fading light. He peered into the gloom again and shook his head. Before them lay nothing but reed beds and swamp, the land petering out into the Wicken Fen, miles of water crossed only by a narrow path, and even that was submerged when the inundation was high. He rubbed the stubble of his chin, debating the matter for a moment or so longer but subconsciously he had already made the decision. He was exposed out here but at least they were on dry land. He dare not risk the Fen with the light almost gone. He pulled on the reins, bringing Galahad to a halt.

"We shall camp here for the night," he said to the men behind him before dismounting wearily, his legs stiff and sore from a long day in the saddle. The stumbling column came to a halt, fracturing into groups of six or seven as men went in search of wood for their fires.

"You will be posting a guard, Lord?" Lefwinus was suddenly beside him, his hazel eyes narrowed against the gloom, his bow and

quiver strung over his shoulder. Morcar knew why his uncle had wanted Lefwinus with him: to watch over him, to give him counsel when needed, and when it wasn't. He didn't really mind. Lefwinus was one of his uncle's best men and he was glad to have him along.
"Of course," he said, although he doubted that it would be necessary. Only fools would be out here, in the middle of nowhere, with night coming on.
"I will organise the watch if you wish, Lord."
Morcar could see his uncle's hand in this as clearly as if he were here himself. Hereward, concerned for his safety, sending him one of his own men, just in case... He thought of their disagreement when last they had met and now regretted it. He had spoken out of turn, he realised. His uncle knew this land like no one else, save, perhaps, for Lefwinus and The Heron, and the Heron was long dead. He was suddenly thankful that they had made it up before he had left.
"I would be obliged," he said. "But make sure you get some food inside you before too long. It will be a long night I fear."
"Plenty of time for food afterwards, Lord," Lefwinus said, the slightest hint of a rebuke in his voice. "I will get the watch organised." He marched away into the gloom.

Morcar watched him depart; his broad, rounded shoulders heavily muscled from years of drawing a bow. He was a good man, he thought. Solid, dependable; good man.

He fed Galahad some oats from his saddlebag, stroking his head, his mane, talking quietly to him to settle him down for the night. Someone had already started a fire he noticed and, he wandered over to it, seating himself beside the men, engaging them in conversation as they fed the flames with kindling, watching the fire smoke and stutter and then burst into life as the kindling caught.

When he looked up he saw that the sun had sunk below the horizon and beyond the arc of light cast by the fire the sky was in darkness. He was surprised how quickly the daylight had gone once the sun had set. It had been the right decision he thought, to camp here for the night.

Over the fire the men began roasting a chicken and the smell of its burning flesh drifted across to where he was sat. The wind had dropped, he realised, as it often did in these parts once the sun had set, but there was a chill in the air with the coming of night and he drew his cloak a little tighter around his shoulders.

Lefwinus appeared in the arc of light cast by the fire, his hazel eyes darting from side to side into the blackness. What he expected to see Morcar could not guess. Eventually they caught him and now fastened upon him.

"The watch is set, Lord," he said. "Reliefs every two hours." He turned to go the moment he had spoken but Morcar's voice pulled him up.

"Sit with me awhile," he said. "Your work is done for the night." Lefwinus hesitated before seating himself uneasily on the ground, his eyes continuing to dart from side to side, as though he expected to see something in the milky blackness. He was still edgy, Morcar, thought, still nervous about something.

"What is it?" he said. "What can you see?"

"That's the problem," Lefwinus said. "I can't see a bloody thing. But something is out there, all the same."

"Something?"

Lefwinus shrugged.

"Just a feeling I have," he said. "I have had it for the last hour, since we made camp. As though something, or someone, is watching us."

Morcar followed Lefwinus' gaze into the blackness, his unease affecting him also now, but he could see nothing, hear nothing, save the sigh of the wind through the reeds, the occasional hoot of an owl. This was ridiculous, irrational.

"My uncle's anxiety is affecting us all," he said. "There is nothing out there. There cannot be. Not even the Conqueror can march an army through that." He waved a hand towards the Wicken fen, cloaked now in darkness, as if to make his point.

"Perhaps you're right," Lefwinus acknowledged but Morcar saw that he still looked troubled.

"Have some chicken," he said, breaking the silence that had come between them, "and some wine, and tell me more of my uncle. Tell me how he slew a bear with his own two hands."

He smiled as he passed a plateful of meat to Lefwinus and an almost full skin of red wine. And as the skin was passed around the fire, round and round, until it was empty, Lefwinus told Morcar of how, as a young man, his uncle had killed a great bear that had been terrorising their village, slaying it with his own two hands, driving his sword through its head and down into its shoulder blades. And of how, afterwards, he had picked up its massive bulk in his arms and held it out to the frightened villagers as proof that it was dead, and how a beautiful young girl named Torfrida had come forward from the crowd and smeared the blood from the dead bear onto the forehead of his uncle and then onto herself and promised her hand in marriage to him if he would love her forever and father her children and protect her village from that day onwards…

It was pitch black when Morcar awoke, shivering with cold, his head beating like a hammer. For an instant he was disorientated, wondering where he was and then he saw the figures huddled in sleep against the fire, now a pile of grey ashes, and it all came flooding back. He should not have drunk so much. He guessed that it was still early, no more than one or two of the hour, and he half-turned onto his back to check the sky, to search for the moon and stars, but there was no sign of them; a heavy blanket of cloud covered the land, obscuring everything.

He reached for his water bottle, pulling the stopper from the top. He gulped a little of the water into his mouth and sluiced it out, letting the water run over his tongue, his teeth, before spitting it out. The water was brackish and tasted of its leather container, but nevertheless he took another swig, this time gulping it straight down. He replaced the stopper and turned onto his side, pulling his blanket up to his neck.

Across from where he lay, just a few feet away, Lefwinus was sleeping like a baby, his bearded face turned towards him, as though he had fallen asleep still maintaining his vigil. He felt a sudden pang of guilt; Lefwinus it was that had cautioned vigilance, the posting of a guard, and now he was sleeping off the effects of the wine that had been foisted upon him whilst he had told his tale. A good tale it had been too, with an ending, a poignancy that he had not expected.

He closed his eyes, thinking about his uncle, about how he must be feeling now that Torfrida had gone. All those years and what had he to show for it? Nothing. Nothing, save a broken promise, and, perhaps the loyalty of a small band of followers, destined, like his uncle, to end their days in this wilderness, if they were not killed first. He closed his eyes. He was tired, he realised; tired of the bitterness and bloodshed. His thoughts led him to wonder what the future held, whether he had a future. This rebellion could not last forever and was like to have a bloody end. But death was preferable to living the remainder of his life under the heel of William the Bastard. His thoughts fled back to his brother Edwin, to the tiny grave under the willow tree two hundred miles away and for a moment he almost envied him.

He lay thinking about his uncle, about his brother, for some time and tentacles of sleep were just beginning to drag him down when he heard a sound that was so soft, so indistinct that he thought he had imagined it but he knew that he had not for the raised heckles on the back of his neck were evidence enough. Instantly he was wide awake, listening, watching, his breath caught in his chest. For a while there was nothing and then he heard it again, the soft murmur of voices in the far distance, coming from the east. He looked around anxiously. Where were the guard that Lefwinus had posted? Where were they? Had they heard it too? Or had they already been despatched to their maker? He could feel his pulse quicken as he roused himself from his blanket and stretched out a hand to wake Lefwinus.

"What the - "

Morcar clapped a hand over his mouth.

"Listen," he whispered. "Not a word." Lefwinus nodded and he removed his hand. "Out there, to the east. Voices. Do you hear them?"

Lefwinus cocked an ear, listening intently and when he returned his gaze Morcar saw the concern, mirroring his own.

"Normans'" he said softly. "So the Bastard's done it at last. I smell the stink of betrayal." He shook his head as though unable to believe the evidence of his own ears. He looked around, at the men sleeping by their fires.

"Better rouse them," he said. "For one last fight. Take as many of the bastards with us as we can."

Morcar suddenly felt sick. This was not possible. It could not be possible. How could the Bastard have marched an army through that swamp? How? Unless as Lefwinus had said, they had been betrayed. He was reminded again of his last meeting with his uncle. He had been so sure, so certain... He suddenly remembered Fulford Gate, his first battle, the terrible slaughter that had followed when his men had broken and he felt his stomach heave, felt sour wine surging up through his gut, into his throat. And then he retched a heaving retch that doubled him up and the ground was suddenly black with vomit.

"That's right lad," Lefwinus said softly, observing him. "Better now than later." Not a hint of criticism, or of scorn. It could so easily have been otherwise. No wonder his uncle valued him. Morcar gazed back wordlessly.

"Been there myself many atime," Lefwinus said. We're all afraid deep down, all of us." He shrugged. "Rouse the men, eh, while there's still time." He marched off towards the east, towards the enemy, gathering in the darkness.

Morcar watched him go and wiped his mouth on the back of his hand, tasting again the sour wine voided by his gut. *We're all afraid deep down* Lefwinus had said...He bent towards the nearest man, shaking him awake. Even as he did so, even as he saw the man's eyes open he wondered whether it would not have been better to let him continue to sleep, to let them all sleep, for death to come quickly and silently, unseen, unheard...

Morcar listened to the enemy approaching in the darkness, the steady tramp of their feet punctuated by the beat of sword on shield and he swallowed hard. His mouth was dry and still tasted of vomit and remembering his water bottle hanging from his belt he took a swig from it. He replaced the stopper but then it occurred to him that this might be the last drink he would ever have and he took another pull, swallowing the lot.

He looked nervously along his line, one hundred and two men hastily assembled to face this nightmare, staring fixedly, blankly ahead. They all felt the same, he could see, all of them, and his gaze finally settled upon Lefwinus, his great hunting bow strung and notched, ready to be drawn, spare arrows planted in the soft earth at his feet so that he could bend and notch and draw without wasting a second. He had strapped on an old steel helmet, the only protection he had deigned to wear, and a sword and scaramax hung either side of his belt for when the killing came to close quarters, as it surely would, sooner or later…

Behind him he heard the soft snickering of Galahad; he too was nervous, he realised, and when he turned he saw that Galahad's ears were pricked, his hooves pawing the ground, pulling at his tether, sensing the men's unease, smelling their fear.

"It's alright, boy," he said, more to calm himself than anything, and hearing his words Galahad looked towards him, nodding his head.

The beat of sword on shield, louder now, dragged his eyes back to his front. He stared into the blackness and tried to get some glimpse of the enemy but still he could see nothing. There were over a thousand of them, Lefwinus had reckoned, assembling in the darkness, outnumbering them ten to one, if not more. He had known then that it was hopeless. He had seen it in Lefwinus' eyes without having to ask. One last fight then, and die like a man.

He looked along the line again. All eyes were still riveted to the front, all of them, like himself, seeking a first glimpse of the enemy. It was unnerving, this not being able to see them, as though fighting phantoms, but he knew it could not now be long; he could hear the shouted orders of the Captains as they prepared for the first attack. And one attack might do it, he thought, if they brought enough weight to bear upon his line. He tried not to think about it.

"Take out their archers and crossbows," he said, "if you get the chance. Make them come to close quarters." One or two men nodded but most continued to stare fixedly ahead, frozen like statues, gripped with fear. He wondered what they were thinking, whether they were capable of thought. Some, he knew, would be regretting their decision to follow him here, now that death was only minutes away. But it was too late for regrets, too late for anything. Just kill as many as you can.

A crossbow bolt thumped into the line, taking a man in the chest, hurling him backwards. Hardly had he registered the fact before the air was thick with bolts and men were falling all around him.

"Loose!" he screamed, the first word to come into his head, although he could not see a damn thing. Immediately his own men loosed their arrows, the air hissing with noise as they disappeared into the blackness and he was rewarded with several screams of pain.

"Loose!" he cried again, but this time the volley was more ragged. Some men had not had time to notch their arrows before he had given the order. He was impatient, he knew, too damn impatient. He mentally calculated the seconds, counting to ten, took several deep breaths and gave the order again.

"Loose!" The line tensed as arrows were drawn back, left hands straining on the bow, the thumb of the right hand brushing their cheeks and again there was the hiss of noise as arrows were loosed followed by the cry of pain from the enemy ranks.

"That's the way my lads!" he cried. "Show the bastards what we can do!" The madness of battle was on him now, his fear dissolving, replaced by adrenalin, coursing through his veins, rendering him invincible.

"Loose!" he screamed again. "Cut the bastards down! Every one of them!" The line tensed and relaxed as another flight of arrows was hurled into the darkness and for the third time he heard the cries of men hit by the lethal clothyard shafts. No amount of chain mail could resist the power unleashed from these bows and he only wished that he had more men. Another hundred he reckoned, and he could defeat the world.

He mentally calculated the seconds. The Norman crossbowmen had not yet fired a second time. Any Saxon could loose five, or even six arrows before a crossbow could be rewound and fired. Time then for one more volley. He stared into the blackness and now, at last he could see them, Norman footsoldiers, shadowy figures, cast in black and grey, approaching in the gloom, their shields held before them.

"They're coming." Lefwinus growled from beneath his steel helm. "Impatient, it seems."

"Loose!" he cried. "Make every one count!" And now, at last, he had the satisfaction of seeing the enemy fall, his men's arrows finding chinks in the line between the shields, hitting them in the neck, the legs, their arms. They were advancing in three close lines, a thousand of them, three hundred or more to each line, their shields locked together, their spear points and swords levelled towards him. The front rank was barely forty yards away. He glanced to right and left and saw what he had feared most, that the wings of the enemy lines were overlapping his own line, intending to wrap around it and take him in the rear. He just did not have enough men. He hesitated before giving the only order he could.

"Hold your fire!" he shouted. "A final volley and then retire. Wait for it!"

At twenty yards he gave the order. The air hissed with noise, some Normans fell, but not enough and then the Saxons broke, running for their lives. He had meant them to retire in an orderly fashion and then to regroup, to fire further volleys of iron tipped death into the enemy ranks but this was too much for them. It would have been too much for anyone. Morcar ran as well. He grabbed Galahad's reins and leaped into the saddle. Behind him a knot of his men were pulling their swords from their belts, attempting to make a stand, but they simply disappeared from sight, swept away as the Norman tide washed over them. He had made barely five yards before a man, detached from his comrades, pursued by three Normans, grabbed his reins, attempting to wrest them from his hands, but he hit him on the jaw and the man fell away. Barely had he fallen before the Normans were onto him, their sword blades rising and falling, rising and falling before moving on again to find fresh victims. He kicked his heels into Galahad's flank to put some distance between himself and the enemy and soon Galahad was flying, the stallion's hooves eating up the ground, his mane streaming behind him. Morcar risked a glance from side to side as the tide of battle inexorably followed him, moving westwards, spilling over the fens in a wave of blood. Here and there single men were still fighting, sometimes two or three of them, back to back, surrounded by Normans, swinging wildly, fighting like savages until the end. He put his head down and galloped for all he was worth.

Suddenly, to the right of him, he saw Lefwinus, his bow discarded, sword in one hand, scaramax in the other, fighting for his life. His helmet was gone and his head was bleeding profusely above the hairline, blood running down his face as he tried to hold off three Normans. Morcar saw him parry and cut, both hands at once, and then thump his scaramax beneath a man's guard and into his chest and rip it out just in time to parry again. Before he knew what he was doing he was swinging Galahad towards him, dragging his own sword from its scabbard. He crashed into the melee like a thunderbolt, all reason gone, sending men sprawling to the ground. He hacked at a Norman and felt his sword bite deep into the flesh of his neck almost severing the head, felt the blood spatter his face when he jerked the blade free. He saw Lefwinus' eyes flash with recognition from beneath his own red mask but then all his attention was on the fight. Men were coming at him from all sides now, hastening to surround him, to bring him down, spears and swords thrusting, but somehow none of them seemed to catch him. He swung wildly, right and left, his sword striking steel, striking leather, sometimes flesh, and then Galahad was rearing onto his hind legs, his forelegs thrashing, catching one man in the face, hurling him backwards in a spray of blood and teeth. He was vaguely aware of Lefwinus screaming at him, perhaps to run, but then he too was down, a sword blade carving deep into his shoulder, other blades quickly following, and he was lost from view.

He glanced around; the fight was all but over, the ground littered with fallen men. He kicked hard now, anxious to escape, to warn his uncle and Galahad leaped forward but he had to charge through a knot of men barring his way and a spear point took the stallion in the belly, hurling him to the ground. Somehow he managed to throw himself clear, but he landed awkwardly, the wind knocked out of him. When he looked up he saw a dozen or more Normans hurrying towards him and for a moment he contemplated running but even as the thought came to him he knew he could not leave Galahad. The stallion was thrashing and pawing the air, his forelegs horribly broken, his eyes wild with pain, the spear embedded deep in his belly. *The bastards.* Tears welled in his eyes, blinding him and he dashed over to Galahad, all thoughts of himself forgotten. He put an arm around the stallion's neck, holding him close, like a lover, and put his knife to the artery. He drew it quickly across. He felt Galahad stiffen and then relax and he knew that it was over. He heard a noise and turned to see them standing over him, the bastards that had done this, their faces shadowed by their helmets, framed against the night sky. He saw, dully, that their swords were carried easily now that it was over, smeared black with Saxon blood.

He remembered the knife in his hand. They would not have him. Not alive. He put the blade to his wrist. He was about to make the cut, had almost made the first incision when someone grabbed his hand, wrenching the blade from his grasp. He was helmetless he noticed, his red hair matted to his head, his eyes hard as stone.

"No death for this traitor," the red-haired man said. "The King wants this one alive."

Chapter Forty
The Camp Of Refuge

To the east the sky was ablaze in a golden glow as though heralding dawn, but the men lining the ramparts gazed east in a stunned silence, their faces pale and impassive, for it was not dawn that they were witnessing but the burning of Ely and with it the ending of their hopes. Above the glow of the flames black smoke spiralled skywards, choking the air, and in the distance could be heard the crackle and collapse of burning timbers. Ely was in its death throes, put to the torch by a Norman army bent on revenge and soon it would be erased forever.

Ranulf turned away, sickened by the sight and made his way down the companion ladder. He had seen all this at York and knew what would be coming.

It would soon be over, this gallant resistance of the Wake's. Half of his men already dead, he had barely a hundred fit warriors with which to resist over a thousand. And there would be more to follow, once the Conqueror knew the Isle was his. Time perhaps, to leave, to slip away on one of the dragon ships that the Wake had ordered built during the winter. A ship; or, perhaps, escape on foot and chance to luck. One thing was certain: they could not stay here. It was only a matter of time before the Conqueror or his poxed son-in-law marched on them and that time, he guessed, was only hours away; perhaps not that.

He saw the familiar figure of Lightfoot standing anxiously beside the half-opened gates and walked over to him. Lightfoot seemed barely aware of his approach, his eyes peering into the wolf-grey dawn for some sign of the Wake and his men. The moment they had seen smoke spiralling skywards Lightfoot had sent runners south, the youngest and fittest amongst them, to find the Wake, to recall him to the camp. But that had been two hours ago and still there was no sign of him.

"Any news?" he said.

"No." Lightfoot hardly turned his head, his eyes still riveted to the south. Ranulf followed his stare but could see nothing, no sign of the Wake, no sign of anyone. His eyes were dragged back to the east, to the smoke drifting over the devastated village.

"We should leave," he said, "before the Normans arrive."

"You can leave," Lightfoot said testily. "I go nowhere, until I have news of the Wake." Ranulf shrugged.

"We shall be slaughtered then," he said. "And what about the women and children? Are you prepared to risk them? I have seen those bastards at work before. Women raped, kids torn apart; have you thought of them?"

Lightfoot whirled around, quickly, agitatedly, and there was anger in his eyes.

"The Wake will come," he said. "You think he has abandoned us but I tell you he will return." He swung back to the south, to resume his watch on the horizon. Ranulf wandered off. Lightfoot was in no mood to reason. He could hardly blame him. His world torn apart, he was clinging to the only thing he knew: his loyalty to his friend.

Ranulf took a few steps beyond the gate and looked up at the earth and timber walls. Twelve feet high, they would hold the enemy for barely five minutes. And they had nowhere near enough men to man them, and no archers to speak of. They had all gone with Morcar or the Wake. So now it was himself and Lightfoot and forty old men. *God help them then.*

He turned back to the east, from where the enemy must, inevitably, come. The colour of the sky was changing now, the golden glow of the flames giving way to the pale grey of dawn, but a pall of thick, black smoke still hung over the devastated village. For what seemed an eternity he gazed east, watching the smoke billow and swirl above the village like a living thing, pouring ash from the sky to fall like black rain onto the ground. What the hell he would do when all this was over he had no idea. But then he was not important. It was Alice that mattered, Alice and his son. Now he must think of them. Think only of them.

If Lightfoot was determined to stay they must try to organise some defence and an escape plan for the women and children. The dragon ships were the obvious choice but they could only carry sixty souls and who was there to crew them? Every man would be needed when it came to a fight. He turned on his heels, worrying at the problem and walked back through the gates. His legs felt like lead.

Behind him Lightfoot gave the order for the gates to be closed and slowly they were swung shut and barred. They would only now be opened to the Wake. If he returned…

Ranulf felt a hand on his shoulder and turned to see Lightfoot's weather beaten face gazing into his own, his eyes a little calmer now.

"Didn't mean to snap," he said. "But it's not an easy thing, to watch your village burn." Ranulf nodded.

"Forget it," he said. "In your place I would feel the same." For a moment there was silence and then Lightfoot said:

"He will come, you know. You must believe that. The Wake will not abandon us. Not like this. I know him too well; have known him all my life."

"How can you be so certain?" Ranulf said. "To pit a hundred men against a thousand? Any man would balk at that."
"The Wake is not like most men," Lightfoot said. "Not like any man I have known. The numbers will mean nothing to him. Besides this is all he has left. He will return."
Ranulf was about to reply, to trot out some platitude by way of an answer when he heard it in the distance, what he initially thought was thunder or the crash of burning timbers, but when he heard it again and recognised it for what it was the words froze in his mouth. For the noise was the beat of sword against shield, rhythmic, incessant, accompanied by the deeper, percussive beat of Norman drums. The Norman army was on the march again, heading towards them for the final act.
"If the Wake is coming he had better come soon," he said at last. "Or all he will find is ashes."

The last woman, impossibly old and frail, was lifted over the gunwale into the longboat and then, like its two sister ships it was poled away from the jetty into the muddied waters of the Ouse. Some of the women on the tightly packed decks had tears coursing down their cheeks as they waved a final farewell to the men standing on the jetty whilst others sat in a stoic, resigned silence contemplating the journey ahead, wondering perhaps where they were bound, their loved ones left behind.

As the three dragon ships entered midstream the skeleton crews chosen to man them began to pull on the oars, propelling them slowly northwards, up the Ouse towards Wisbech. If they were lucky they would eventually enter the Wash and after that no one could say.

Alice watched them go, occasionally raising her hand, a final farewell to old friends and strangers. It was hard not to feel for them, to share their sense of loss, cast adrift as they were to the mercy of the wind and eventually the tide, if they managed to reach the Wash, that narrow stretch of sea with its treacherous currents and shifting sandbanks. And yet, she guessed, these were the fortunate ones, the sixty women and children that had been chosen to receive a berth on one of the dragon ships built by the Wake. As for the rest of them, the remaining three hundred or so, they would have to take their chance with the men.

She turned away from the river and put an arm around Hal. He had barely left her side since his return. In his hand he still clutched the tiny spear fashioned for him by Ranulf, as though he were her protector… In the distance she could hear the beat of sword on shield, of the drums hammering out their staccato rhythm. The Normans were much closer now, the beat of the drums resonating clearly through the still morning air. It would only be a matter of minutes. She felt her pulse quicken, her heart beat a little faster. She had to do something; for Hal, for the others, and she had to do it soon, before it was too late. She suddenly remembered York and a lump rose in her throat.

She looked for Ranulf but it was Hal that saw him first, on the ramparts with Lightfoot and some of the other men. They were piling stones and rocks either side of the gates and she guessed that these were to hurl down onto the Norman army when they tried to force the camp. They would hardly make an impression. She thought again of York, of the unspeakable things she had witnessed when the Normans had finally entered the City, things she had closed her mind to until now and she realised that she was shaking. Ranulf must have seen this for suddenly he was leaping down the companion ladder, hurrying towards her, holding her in his arms.
"Are you alright lass?" he asked. He looked haggard and careworn, cowed with the strain.

"Just a little faint," she said. It dawned on her that this could be the last time he would hold her, gaze upon her and she instinctively hugged him back. She suddenly wanted to tell him of her betrayal, of how much she regretted it; she could feel tears welling in her eyes, the unspoken words burning her tongue, but somehow she managed to force them back. This was not the time. Perhaps it never would be. Better he did not know. The beat of sword on shield sounded louder than ever.

"I'm fine now," she said. "I'm fine. But what about Hal, the others, the women the children, we must do something for them." Ranulf fell silent, his gaze finally coming to rest on his son and she could tell that he too was remembering York, the babies nailed to doors, the women raped before being cut to pieces…

"The tunnel," he said uncertainly. "It is the only way. At least it has been propped. It should be safe." He did not sound sure.

Alice closed her eyes and imagined herself descending into its black maw, scrabbling in the black earth with her fingernails, not knowing whether she might at any moment be buried alive in the blackness, choking on the soil as it consumed her... And somehow she would have to persuade the others to do it. Her mind recoiled against the prospect but she knew that Ranulf was correct, that the tunnel was their only hope. God alone knew whether they could do it, whether *she* could do it. The beat of the drums, louder than ever now, made up her mind.

"I will organise it," she said. "They will trust me, being a woman. It will give me something to do." She felt Hal's hand suddenly squeeze her own, a sharp, involuntary movement and she lifted her head. "That noise has stopped…"

Ranulf turned to listen and as he did so a shiver ran down his spine for Alice was right. The noise had stopped, the beat of the swords, of drums, had fallen silent. He cursed under his breath and damned Lightfoot for a fool.

For the enemy were here and time had just run out.

The Normans came on confidently, in a single wave, the point of their attack aimed at the main gates. Watching from the ramparts Ranulf saw that they had cut down a large oak tree, a rudimentary battering ram that was now being hefted onto the shoulders of fifty men. In just a few moments they would come at the gates full pelt, hoping to smash the timbers aside. He gave an involuntary shudder and glanced over his shoulder to the far corner of the camp to where Alice was attempting to coax the terrified women and children into the tunnel. Even from this distance he could hear their protests, the wails and sobs of despair and felt a surge of anger course through his veins. Did they not know what the alternative was? Did he have to spell it out, what would happen to them if the Normans caught them? A vision of York sprang into his mind: the woman in the doorway begging to die, her babies cradled in her arms like lifeless dolls dipped in blood…He cursed again and willed them into the tunnel. *Ten minutes Lord,* he thought. *Give me ten minutes.* He turned back to his front, unable to tear his eyes from the danger. Lightfoot was suddenly beside him, his familiar axe with its dreadful spike clutched tightly in his hand, his steel helm with its broad *nasal* jammed firmly onto his head.

"Will the gate hold?" Lightfoot spoke quietly, his voice strained with emotion. Ranulf could guess what was going through his mind: that it was because of him that they were still here; that if they had acted quickly enough they might, perhaps, have made good their escape; that his precious Wake had, at the last, abandoned them, left them to die like cattle…

"Christ knows," he said. "But if it doesn't we're dead men." He paused. "We're probably dead anyway."

He bent to pick up a rock and with an effort hefted it above his head. Some of the others, he saw, were doing the same. He winced as a surge of pain suddenly lanced through his chest; his old wound, still not healed. He did his best to ignore it but the pain cut though him like a knife and he had to drop the rock. It landed with a thud on the ground, kicking up a cloud of dust.

"Are you wounded?" Lightfoot asked, his concern obvious, as though they had been comrades for years. They were strange men, these fen dwellers: stubborn and proud and sometimes, when you least expected it, as loyal as hell. For some unknown reason he thought of Guthrum and those last dreadful hours on Caldbec Hill. How he would have relished this fight, one last chance to settle with the enemy.

"Just my chest," he said, biting back the pain, "nothing to worry about." But his chest was throbbing as though it would burst. He glanced along the ramparts and saw that all eyes were on him, willing him to be strong, as though he and he alone, could save them. Once, no doubt, they had thought the same of the Wake.

"Look to your fronts!" he snapped loudly, annoyed that they had witnessed his vulnerability. "And wait until the buggers are directly beneath us!" One or two men nodded in acknowledgement but he could see the concern still written on their faces; concern, perhaps, for himself, but largely, he guessed for themselves. *Pray God the gate holds.*

A cry went up. The ramming party were finally ready, were coming in as fast as their burden would allow, protected on either side by a solid line of shields. Crossbow bolts suddenly thudded into the timbers, an attempt to keep Saxon heads down while the ramming party did its work. Ten feet away a man was flung backwards as a bolt took him square in the chest, flinging him off the rampart like a rag doll.

At five yards Ranulf gave the order. Rocks and stones were hurled breathlessly, desperately, downwards, bouncing off shields, off helmets, felling one or two, and then the ramparts shook as the tree slammed into the gates with the force of a thunderbolt. He felt the timber planking beneath his feet shudder violently as the gates lurched inwards from the terrible impact but when he glanced down he saw that although the gates were bent and bowed the heavy oak beams that held them close had done their job. There was just room for one man to squeeze through the breach where the two gates had parted in the middle. Without thinking he was leaping off the ramparts, ignoring the pain in his chest and ripping *Requitur* from his belt. He was not a moment too soon. One man was already squeezing an arm through the breach, attempting to dislodge the beams from their cradles. Instinctively Ranulf hammered *Requitur* down, lopping off the arm at the elbow and the man fell back, screaming with pain. Unseen hands dragged him away. For a moment there was silence and the next came the crash of rending timbers as the ram was hammered into the gates once more, causing them to lurch sickeningly inwards. One of the beams was cracking, would give way any second. A few more blows and they would part like the Red Sea. He risked a glance over his shoulder. Alice was getting the women and children into the tunnel, cajoling and pushing them into the blackness but there were still dozens of them crowding around the entrance, almost, it seemed, eager to be gone now that a greater, an obvious, threat had presented itself. *Five minutes Lord,* he thought. *Give me five minutes.*

The gates lurched inwards again, shuddering beneath the hammer blow of the ram and now Ranulf saw that the lower beam had split in two, torn apart by the weight of the blow. Only one beam now held the gates closed and that would go any second. He could hear the roar of triumph from beyond the gates, the knowledge that this one-sided affair would soon be over.

"Get your shoulders to the gates!" Lightfoot's voice cut through the air. His men did as they were bid, hastening down the ramparts towards the gates, throwing their weight against it. Ranulf did the same. It might, if they were lucky, buy them a few more seconds. *And then what?* But he closed his mind to that possibility, unprepared, for the moment, to contemplate it. There was a tremendous crash and once more the gates were hurled inwards, throwing some men backwards with the force of the impact. The tree trunk this time continued on its journey, smashing through the timbers of the gate, splitting them like parchment. One man's head was mashed to pulp, caught by the trunk, showering the defenders with his blood and when Ranulf glanced at his corpse, hurled six feet by the blow, he had to turn away, sickened by the sight.

The ram had become stuck in the shattered timbers of the gate and now the enemy used it as a ramp to scale the gates, scrambling over them like an army of ants. Two Normans leaped down into the camp, landing clumsily and before they had time to recover Ranulf hammered *Requitur* down onto the head of one whilst Lightfoot thumped his spike into the neck of the other. Both men were instantly killed but even as Lightfoot was dragging his spike clear Ranulf could see yet more of them scaling the gates, others pushing their way through the yawning gap opened by the ram, an endless tide of warriors determined to finish them off. It was hopeless. Thirty seconds more and they would be swamped, buried beneath a Norman tide. He cast around desperately, wondering what to do and then it came him, the one thing, the only thing, that would buy them a few moments longer. He was a dead man, they all were, but at least they would die with honour.

"Fall back!" he cried, "and form a shield circle around the women! No chance for us but they might make it!" He saw Lightfoot hesitate, nod, and then give the order, screaming at the top of his voice to make himself heard. The Saxons turned and ran, glancing over their shoulders every few yards. Crossbow bolts whistled past them, fired by the crossbowmen that had scaled the gates.

Ranulf ran for his life, hurrying towards the tunnel, towards Alice. It was only three hundred yards through the circle of huts but it seemed like a mile. His chest felt fit to burst and when he glanced down he saw that the front of his jerkin was stained red where the wound had opened up. He cursed and turned to look back and in his anxiety tripped, falling heavily into the dust, twisting his ankle. When he picked himself up he saw that the gates had finally yielded, bursting open under the pressure, spilling dozens of soldiers into the camp. He tried to run but it was very difficult; his ankle was swelling with each passing second. He cursed again and began to limp towards the hastily forming shield-wall. He could see Lightfoot pushing and pulling men into position, exhorting them to stand, screaming at them from beneath his steel helm. It came to him that this, finally, was the end. He could only hope that when the end came he would die well, die bravely. *Be merciful, Lord, be merciful...*

Alice pushed a woman with steel-grey hair into the tunnel and cast an anxious glance over her shoulder. The Saxon warriors had given up the gate, were hurrying towards her, running for their lives, glancing over their shoulders for signs of pursuit. She swallowed hard and felt a wave of anxiety wash over her.

"On your knees, close your eyes and keep going." The woman nodded, disappeared into the blackness. The next one came forward, a younger woman with a child in her arms, one of Hal's playmates. Erdic, she thought they called him.

"The child will have to go first," she said. "You cannot carry him, there is not the room." The woman hesitated and put him down. The child stared at her with large, round, eyes his hands clutching

onto his mother's skirt. "It's perfectly safe," she said. "Just like a game. Your mother will be right behind you."
"Is Hal coming too?" Erdic asked in a small, plaintive voice. He had been crying, she saw, his face streaked with tears.
"In just a moment," she said. "He will be along in a moment." She forced a smile and Erdic disappeared into the tunnel followed by his mother. She risked another glance over her shoulder. The men were forming a hurried semi-circle around the tunnel, their shields locked together as they had done so often in training and she instinctively looked for Ranulf, expecting him to be organising it, but for the moment she could not see him. Neither could she see Hal. *Where was he?* Her eyes swept the faces gathered around her, the women and children, the agitated, nervous, warriors in the shield-wall. And then she saw him, behind the shield-wall, his tiny spear clutched in his hand as though he intended to fight alongside them. Tears started in her eyes, taking her by surprise; she suddenly felt enormously proud of him, proud of them both. A lump rose in her throat and it was only with difficulty that she was able to cry:
"Hal! Come here!"
Hal turned at the sound of his voice and reluctantly padded towards her, the spear point trailing the ground.
"But I want to fight," he said, "like my father." She hugged him to her, crushing him in her embrace, not wanting to release him.
"One day, Cara," she said, "when you are older, but now you must do as your mother asks and leave here with me." She looked into his eyes and saw the hesitation there.
"Father will be coming with us?" Hal said uncertainly.
"Yes," she said softly, "your father will come too." She looked quickly around. Still she could not see Ranulf.
"You promise?"
"Promise," she said.

Hal smiled, a tiny, crooked smile and Alice thought her heart would break. A final hug and he ducked into the tunnel. Others scrambled in behind him, not waiting to be told, anxious to escape before the shield-wall was blown away like so much chaff. Alice ran her fingers through her hair, searching for Ranulf. She had almost given up on him, had thought him dead, when she caught his familiar figure from the corner of her eye, limping past a row of huts towards the shield-wall, his jerkin, darned with her own two hands, darkly stained with blood. Before she knew what she was doing she was pushing through the warriors, running towards him, calling his name, embracing him, half-carrying him back to the Saxon lines. His foot was badly swollen and his breathing laboured, his face very pale beneath the shock of his red-grey beard.

"You're hurt," she said, her eyes running over his face, the dark stain spreading across his chest. Ranulf glanced down and then quickly away. Perhaps, she thought, a little too quickly…

"It's nothing," he said. "Just the old wound opening up." She sensed with a woman's intuition that he was lying, making light of it for her benefit.

"We must leave," she said. "Now. Before it is too late."

Ranulf was about to reply but some movement behind her arrested his attention before the words came out and she saw him shake his head.

"Already too late," he said in a voice stripped of emotion. She turned to follow his gaze and now she saw what Ranulf had seen and for a moment she was incapable of thought. For beyond the shield-wall, just a hundred yards away, the Normans were moving in quickly for the kill: the footsoldiers and men-at-arms and the knights in their fine mail armour showing dull grey in the morning light. Behind them she could see others putting torches to some of the huts. Thick, acrid smoke was already beginning to spiral into the air, flames licking greedily at the straw and wattle. They were bastards, all of them, just like their bastard King. How she hated them. Hated them…She felt Ranulf pulling away from her, anxious to take his place in the shield-wall and although she could not say how, or why, she did not try to prevent him. For four years he had been waiting for this, for the chance to join his comrades, his King, to expiate his guilt. She knew she must let him go. She watched him push his way into the wall beside Lightfoot, hefting his shield with difficulty onto his arm and once more she felt an overwhelming sense of pride. Tears welled in her eyes and rolled down her cheeks like rain.

"I love you!" she cried, her voice cracked and broken. "I love you my husband!" but whether he had heard her above the din, the roar of the flames and crackle of timbers, she could not say. She moved to the entrance to the tunnel, was on the point of lowering herself into it, unable to watch, when she heard a different sound, a sound that caused her to pause and turn.

Ranulf had heard it too, and from his position in the centre of the shield-wall looked to the right, from where the sound had come. It was clear and unmistakable, familiar and yet terrible, a sound he had heard once before at Belsar's Hill:

"A Wake! A Wake!" followed by the hiss of clothyard shafts launched from hunting bows. He lowered his shield, completely forgetting himself and stood and watched as the front rank of the enemy went down, scythed down like corn by Saxon arrows launched from the earthern walls to his right. He saw, as if in a dream, the Saxon warriors leaping from the walls, hurling themselves like madmen into the left flank of the Norman attack, and even though they were outnumbered, saw that they were cutting it to pieces: Wynter, with his huge double handed sword spattered with blood, Hurchillus and Villicus, the two twins, their arrows spitting like rain from their great hunting bows, their comrades Alsinus and Osbernus and all of the others that he had come to know falling onto the flank of the enemy in a fury, cutting and hacking with a savagery that he had rarely seen before. And above all of this, standing head and shoulders above the rest was the man that had led them here, in the centre of the carnage, swinging his sword right and left, hammering it down with a vengeance that was awful to behold. His torso was covered by a suit of bronze fish scales that seemed to shimmer in the light of the flames and with his blonde hair flying about his head Ranulf thought he had never seen anything so magnificent, so magnificent or so awful, for his face, though recognisable, was twisted into a mask of pure hatred. For a moment longer he was unable to move, unable to do anything but stand and watch and the next he was hurling himself forward, out of the shield-wall, the pain in his chest, his ankle, forgotten, the fatigue fleeing his body, replaced by a desire to kill and to keep on killing until there was no one left. Lightfoot was suddenly beside him, his face lit up in elation, screaming the Wake's battle cry and then turning to him, his face a mask of pure joy, crying: "I told you he would come! I told you!" And then he was gone, racing ahead, launching himself at the enemy as though he were immortal. And just for a second, just before he hammered *Requitur* down, Ranulf felt the tiniest prick of shame. For despite everything, the overwhelming odds, the hopelessness of their position, his own doubts and fears, the Wake had not forgotten them. He had come back just as Lightfoot had said he would.

Ranulf hammered *Requitur* down and sparks flew from the blade as steel met steel. Instinctively he thumped his shield into the face of his opponent, knocking him off balance and before he could recover he slammed *Requitur* forward in a great sweeping arc, felt it meet chain-mail and then flesh as it cut into the man's thigh, severing an artery. The man went down in a welter of blood, his face twisting in agony and Ranulf buried *Requitur* in his chest. He sensed a blade to his right, felt the rush of air and brought up his shield with both hands to meet the blow. The impact jarred to the bone, splintering the hardened linden wood, and realising that *Requitur* was still buried in the dead man's chest he pulled *Le Couteau's* dagger from his belt and thumped it low, into the Norman's groin. The Norman screamed, pulled back, and as he did so Ranulf twisted the blade before ripping it clear so that it brought the man's entrails out with it. He dragged *Requitur* from the chest of the dead man and looked quickly around. Over to his right, almost thirty yards away, he caught a glimpse of the Wake, his bronze fish scales bloodied and torn, his helmetless head running with blood, his grey eyes blazing with fire as he cut down one man, only to be faced with another. Beside him, Wynter and Lightfoot were covering his flanks, fighting like men possessed, cutting and hacking and cursing and swearing as they fought for their lives, for the life of the man beside them.

His attention was dragged away as a man-at-arms came at him and he instinctively thumped *Requitur* down towards the man's head. The blow was parried the first time, and he swung *Requitur* again, lower this time, towards the chest, but again it was parried, the shock of the impact numbing his arm which had still not fully recovered from the fight with *Le Couteau.* Again he hammered *Requitur* down, towards the head once more, and this time succeeded in beating the parry aside. *Requitur* smashed into the steel of the man's helmet and on into his skull. The man went down, felled like a log, his head pouring with blood.

Ranulf glanced to the right again, gulping what air he could get into his lungs. The Wake was twenty yards away, was drawing the enemy like a magnet and still more were hurrying towards him, eager for glory. He sensed that the Wake was becoming isolated, his comrades some yards distant, although Wynter and Lightfoot were still by his side. He noticed, absently, that Wynter's hauberk was heavily stained with blood all down his left side and he guessed that he had taken an injury under his armpit. If so it would only be a matter of time…His eyes cut towards the Wake. The bronze fish scales were now hanging off him, reduced to shreds by the ferocity of the fighting, the cuts he had taken, but he seemed to be oblivious, impervious to it. His face was a mask of blood, a river of blood, twisting and contorting with rage as he poured obscenities upon the enemy. Corpses lay everywhere but still the enemy were coming forward, eager for the kill, desperate to bring him down, almost, he thought, like a pack of wolves with a stag. He felt a sudden rush of anxiety, not for himself but the Wake. Surely he could see the danger? If he became isolated, surrounded, he would be finished…He glanced quickly around, seeking help. He glimpsed Hurchillus and Villicus, indistinguishable now, their jerkins darkly stained with blood, trying to cut their way through to him, but like the Wake they too were fighting for their lives, outnumbered, outmatched. He sensed that the tide of battle was turning, as, perhaps, he had always known it would. He made a decision; he must get to the Wake and lead him out…

He made five yards, saw a knight confronting him, an exquisite suit of chain-mail covering him from head to knees. Beneath his helm, shadowed by the *nasal,* the man's eyes were dark and strangely familiar, but there was no time to think. He swung *Requitur* hard at his left side but the knight anticipated the blow and brought up his sword to parry it. Sparks flew into the air and he felt the shock run up his arm to the shoulder. He grimaced with pain and swung again, but once more the knight anticipated it, parrying easily. He cursed, and hammered *Requitur* forward, anxious to finish this, to get to the Wake before it was too late, but the knight sidestepped the thrust and now swung his sword at his own left side. He instinctively brought up his shield to parry it but the force of the blow split the linden wood like parchment. He felt a searing fire lance through his arm and knew immediately that it was broken. He turned to his right, desperate now, fighting the pain, the desire to sink into oblivion. His head was swimming, his vision becoming blurred. Almost blinded he sensed the knight raising his sword, bringing it down and he brought up *Requitur* to parry, but all he met was air. The blow caught him on the side of his helmet and he felt himself going down. He gazed upwards, saw the knight standing over him, his face in shadow, silhouetted against the sky, sword raised for the kill.

"Stay down if you value your life." The sword swept down, into the corpse of the man beside him. He was aware of the sword being dragged clear, felt bloodstains spatter his face and lapsed into unconsciousness.

When he came to he realised that the battle had passed him by, had ended hours ago. It was late afternoon now, the light slowly departing, giving way to dusk. He lay still for a few moments, remembering, and then tried to get to his feet. His head pounded, his vision swam and his ears rang from the blow he had taken to the side of the head. The knight must have turned his blade at the last fraction of a second…

He managed to get to his knees, nursing his left arm, which was purple and swollen, hanging uselessly at his side. He could not feel his fingers. Somehow he raised himself to his feet. All around were the corpses of the fallen, Saxon and Norman together, and he suddenly felt tears sting his eyes. The air stank of smoke from burned out buildings, stank of blood and death and a wave of nausea swept over him. He retched, and the spasms cut through him like a knife. After what seemed an eternity he somehow managed to collect himself.

Bodies lay everywhere; in every attitude of death. In a daze he wandered through them, looking for some sign of life, barely conscious of what he was doing. Familiar faces now came into view, familiar but changed, distant, impersonal. Osbernus, his pale, rounded face almost perfect until he turned him over and saw that the other half had been hacked away; Hurchillus, his face still anxious, still filled with the desire to reach the Wake, even at the moment of his death. Villicus, his twin, one eye open, the other crusted with blood where a spear-point had entered his skull. He bent and closed the good eye, felt tears running freely down his cheek into his beard, mingling with the blood that had spattered his face, the blood of the corpse that the knight had plunged his sword into rather than himself. He knew, now, that the knight had been de Cany. Only that would explain why he still lived when so many others had died…

He moved on, wandering through the corpses until he reached the place where he had last seen the Wake. He checked the bodies carefully, methodically, one after another and was struck by how many Normans had fallen at this spot. He widened his search, but of the Wake and his closest companions, of Wynter and Lightfoot, he could see no sign. He retraced his steps, and now, in the fading light, saw something glinting in the dust, touched by the last rays of the sun. He bent awkwardly and picked them up, three bronze fish scales, held together with thread. There was blood on one of the scales, perhaps from the Wake himself, or from one of his victims. *I shall be there at the end,* he had once said and at the last he had made good his promise. Ranulf tucked the fish scales into his jerkin.

He heard a sound and turned tearfully towards it, reaching for his knife. For a few moments he could not make out the figure standing by the tunnel and then his vision cleared and he was overwhelmed with emotion. He ran towards her, stumbling his way through the corpses, disturbing the carrion that had settled on some, tears coursing afresh down his face.

He kissed her on the lips, crushing her awkwardly to him. She hugged him back, heedless of the blood, the cry of the carrion that flapped noisily into the air.

Epilogue

Alice watched the land slowly forming, taking shape almost as if it were rising from the sea, a grey-green slash filling the horizon ahead. Overhead a light drizzle began to fall from the lowering grey clouds that had been present since daybreak and she consciously pulled her hood a little further over her face. She put her hand to Hal's raven hair and tousled it affectionately. He was still very pale; the pitch and roll of the tiny vessel on which they had made the night crossing had caused him to void his stomach several times already.

"We shall be there soon," she said, and for a reward Hal lifted his eyes and smiled at her. His eyes were bloodshot, his forehead still beaded with sweat. It was a terrible thing, seasickness, and she wondered how any man could be persuaded to leave the solid comfort of the land to risk the perils of the sea. Thank God their crossing had been short.

Her eyes strayed from the coastline of Flanders to the lean figure leant awkwardly over the stern rail, lost in a world of his own, his left arm strapped across his chest. It would be two moons or more before the strapping could be removed and only then would they know whether the fractures had healed, whether the use and feeling had returned. He still could not feel the fingers of his left hand and she guessed, from what the surgeon, a clever Jewish doctor had said, that he would never get the feeling back. Perhaps it was no bad thing. He had seen enough fighting, enough killing, to last most men a lifetime. It was time now to rest, to find peace and hopefully some happiness, in Flanders.

Her mind strayed back, as it had so often over the past few days, to the last time she had caught sight of the Wake, in the thick of the fighting, his face contorted with rage, spattered with the blood of his enemies as he had hacked them down one after another until, like an avalanche, the Norman and Breton chivalry had fallen upon him and he had been lost from her view. His body and that of his closest friends, of Wynter and Lightfoot, had never been recovered. Some said that the Conqueror had arranged a private burial, others that his corpse and those of his comrades had been hacked to pieces and scattered to the winds. And others said that the Wake had somehow escaped and even now was planning to wrest back his lands. It seemed unlikely. The odds, finally, had been overwhelming and she had turned away, unwilling to witness the end. That Ranulf still lived was a miracle and even now she did not know why. Ranulf had said that the Norman had turned his blade at the last second, unable, it seemed, to kill the man whose life he had once saved. Perhaps there was hope after all…

She rose and crossed to the stern rail and put an arm around his waist. At her touch he folded his right hand over hers and gave it a squeeze. She had still not told him about the Wake and knew now that she never would. Nothing would be served by it save to stir up reminders of the past, currents of emotion that neither of them could contend with. It was enough that they were alive, had their lives before them. Even now she wondered whether the Wake would have returned to the camp to face those terrible odds had it not been for her presence there, the knowledge that she was at the camp when the gates were coming down. In her private moments she prayed that that were not so, that he had been motivated to do what he did by desires, by loyalties, far removed from any feelings he still harboured for her…

Overhead, black-headed gulls cried their raucous cry, wheeling and diving around the stern of the boat in their endless search for food. The sea was slate-grey in colour, sombre and cold, mirroring the day, save for the wake streaming behind like a ribbon. She lent over the stern rail and watched the keel cutting through the water like a knife. Ranulf folded his good arm around her and for a few moments, before turning towards the approaching land, they were lost in thoughts of their own, lost in the wake of the boat as it ploughed headlong through the waves.

Historical Note

Delving into the past is fraught with difficulty; the more so the further back one delves. The events recorded in *The Cold Hand, Cruel Heart* are drawn almost exclusively from *De Gestis Herwardi Saxonis,* ("the exploits of Hereward the Saxon") an account of the life of Hereward the Wake researched and compiled in the 12th Century by monastic scholars. As no contemporary account of his life exists one must question the authenticity of some of the wilder claims made and where such doubt exists I have attempted to corroborate the facts from other sources including the Domesday Book. A Bibliography, for those interested, follows this note. That Hereward the Wake lived at the time of the Conquest and that he gave The Conqueror the toughest and most intractable problems of the early years of his reign there is, however, no doubt.

Born of wealthy parents, said to be Lord Leofric of Bourne and his wife in around 1032, Hereward would have been about thirty-eight years of age at the time of the events recorded in the novel. Intelligent, well over six feet tall, with blonde hair and striking grey eyes, the right slightly darker than the left, he must have cut an imposing figure. *De Gestis* records that as a teenager he was sent abroad by his father to avoid the wrath of the King of England at that time, Edward the Confessor, who could stand his trouble making no longer. Whilst abroad he became skilled in the art of warfare, lending his sword and his followers for mercenary pay to whichever employer could afford him.

Abroad in Flanders during the calamitous events of 1066 he returned to England in 1068 or thereabouts to find that William the Bastard had seized the Throne and that his father's lands and estates had been distributed to his supporters; notably his son-in-law Fitzalan Fergant of Brittany ("Alan the Red") and a lesser noble, Ivo Taillebois, said to have been a base-born soldier from Calvados, subsequently appointed Sheriff of Lincolnshire. His brother, objecting to the loss of the family land had been killed by, or at least at the hand of, Ivo Taillebois and Hereward took his revenge killing, it is said fourteen of Taillebois' men with his own hands. Such a claim must be open to doubt. Whatever the truth of that, his next act, the sacking and plunder of Peterborough Cathedral (known as "Gildenburgh" in those days, meaning, literally, "Golden Borough") ostensibly with the intention of preserving its gold and jewels from the avarice of the newly installed Norman Bishop Turold brought the wrath of the Conqueror down upon him. The enterprise was a disaster. Saxons became caught up in the fighting, some died and Sven Erithson, the King of Denmark enlisted by Hereward to assist him, made off with the plunder, bribed, it is said, by the Conqueror himself.

The Isle of Ely in those days was a formidable fortress, surrounded by swamp and shifting marsh and was almost impassable on foot. Hereward's knowledge of the land gave him a decisive advantage over the Norman oppressors and many were the occasions when he would appear from nowhere to launch sanguinary attacks upon the unsuspecting enemy. Joined by his nephew, Earl Morcar, (Edwin already being dead, killed by his own men) and by a number of leading Saxon Churchmen, the Isle of Ely became the focus for the last and bitterest rebellion against the Norman rule.

De Gestis records that the Conqueror's first attempt to storm the Isle was by way of a causeway built "*at Alrehede,*" the site of the present day village of Aldreth. In recent years ancient timbers, rusted swords and torn chain-mail have been excavated, demonstrating that in this, at least, *De Gestis* is almost certainly correct. Three thousand men are said to have perished when the causeway sank under the weight of men and armour when a floating sow, anchoring the causeway was cut away from the land by Hereward, a fact which, if true, amounted to the greatest disaster of William's reign in England. In *The Wake* blame for the disaster has been placed firmly at the door of the Conqueror's *seneschal* and closest ally, William Fitz Osbern. He was indeed sent by the Conqueror to help subdue the rebellion in Flanders but there is no evidence that this was in any way a punishment for the disaster at Aldreth. Fitz Osbern died in battle on the 22nd February 1071 at Ravenchoven near Cassel doing his master's bidding, loyal to the end. An apology is due.

It is an incredible, but almost certain, fact that the Conqueror chose to build a second causeway just a few hundred yards from the first upon the advice of his closest commanders. Here, the blame must be shared between the King and his son-in-law, Fitzalan Fergant, the Wake (meaning, probably the "wakeful one," or "the watcher") sending hundreds more to their deaths when he fired the tinder-dry reeds through which the causeway had been built.

The rebellion was finally ended in 1071 when the Saxon monks, tiring of the fight and probably seeing the futility of further resistance, showed the Normans a secret path onto the Isle through the Wicken fen that lay to the east. Abbott Thurstan of Crowland is widely credited with the betrayal. He died in 1072, in his own bed, perhaps of a broken heart.

Evidence for what happened to the Wake following the storming of the Isle is anecdotal. Some accounts, *De Gestis* included, maintain that Hereward was pardoned by the King on account of his "noble and determined resistance" to the King's rule and given the return of his estates. Other accounts have it that he was indeed pardoned but that a vengeful Taillebois, stripped of those same lands led him into a trap and had him killed. Yet further accounts say that he escaped with a handful of men and continued to lead a guerrilla campaign from the Bruneswald forest south of Peterborough. This last account has parallels with another, possibly more famous character from fiction, and may have been the inspiration for the story of Robin Hood: There are striking similarities. Both were nobly born and stripped of their lands; the Wake by the Conqueror, Robin Hood by King John. In both cases the hero was Saxon, dealt an injustice by a Norman monarch. Both were known as "The Outlaw". Both used the bow as their main weapon and both conducted a guerrilla campaign from the sanctuary of a forest. Whatever the truth there is little doubt that Hereward was a redoubtable and courageous opponent that tested the Conqueror to the limit.

The evidence for the desertion of Hereward's wife Torfrida to Crowland Abbey (where she is said to have been buried) again comes from *De Gestis* as does his infatuation with a "beautiful dark haired woman" that joined the rebels soon after the siege began. Such pearls are scarce to be overlooked by the writers of fiction.

The names of Hereward's comrades, Wynter, Lightfoot, the Heron et al, are drawn from *De Gestis* but hardly sound Anglo-Saxon. The names ending in *cus* or *us* (Hurchillus, Villicus, Osbernus) have a distinctly Latin flavour – a language that the scholars of the time would have both spoken and written. Nevertheless they have been employed in the novel for authenticity.

Herewards's nephew, Earl Morcar certainly did exist and played a prominent part in the rebellion. His fate was a particularly tragic one. Following his capture he was imprisoned by the Conqueror in one of his castles in Normandy, spending his days there until pardoned by William on his deathbed in 1087. It is said that following his release he was immediately re-arrested by William's successor, William Rufus, dying in captivity in 1092.

Today, almost a thousand years after Hereward's death the fen area still resonates with names from the past. Belsar's Hill can still be found close to the Cambridgeshire village of Willingham, an ancient fort (probably from the Iron Age) even when the events depicted in the novel were taking place. Belsar's Close is just around the corner. Travel to Aldreth and follow Hereward Way to the point where it disappears into a sea of mud, now used for motor bike scrambling and walking dogs. Pause there and stare south towards the Ouse and imagine the struggle that the Conqueror would have had to span that sea of black mud. It is a desolate place even today.

In Peterborough traffic roars around the busy offices of Radio Hereward and the Hereward Centre, but if one heads south, towards Ely, one will find the most eloquent reminder of the past. Dominating the landscape for miles around is the magnificent and imposing Cathedral built by the Conqueror to place his stamp on the Isle forever, to demonstrate once and for all that the land was his. It is a symbol of the power, the enduring quality, of the Norman dynasty that shaped the Country we know today but it is surely also a sign of the tremendous struggle that he had to overcome the man known to history as Hereward the Wake.

Acknowledgments

To my friends and family for their advice and support, to my publisher for his faith in the novel and to my wife for her unending patience, love and inspiration.

Bibliography

De Gestis Herwardi Saxonis. 12th Century. Attrib. Monastic scholars. Revised and re-written by Trevor Bevis

Domesday Book. Text and translation edited by John Morris. Chichester: Phillimore, 1975-92

Anglo-Saxon Chronicles. Translated and collated by Anne Savage

L'Estoire des Engleis. Edited by Alexander Bell. Anglo-Norman Text Society. Oxford: Basil Blackwell, 1960

William Fitz Osbern – The Conqueror and His Companions. J. R. Planche, Somerset Herald. London: Tinsley Brothers, 1874

Hereward the Wake. Edited by Stephen Knight and Thomas H.Ohlgren. Kalamazoo, Michigan: Western Michigan University.